THE
TWELVE DANCING
PRINCESSES ·
and other fairy tales

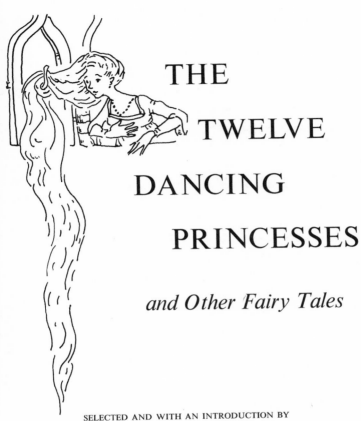

THE

TWELVE

DANCING

PRINCESSES

and Other Fairy Tales

SELECTED AND WITH AN INTRODUCTION BY

ALFRED DAVID AND MARY ELIZABETH MEEK

INDIANA UNIVERSITY PRESS

Bloomington and Indianapolis

This book is a publication of

Indiana University Press
601 North Morton Street
Bloomington, IN 47404-3797 USA

http://iupress.indiana.edu

Telephone orders   800-842-6796
Fax orders   812-855-7931
Orders by e-mail   iuporder@indiana.edu

First Midland Book Edition, 1974
Copyright © 1964 by Alfred and Mary Elizabeth David
All rights reserved

The paper used in this publication meets the minimum requirements of American National Standard for Information Sciences—Permanence of Paper for Printed Library Materials, ANSI Z39.48-1984.

Manufactured in the United States of America

Library of Congress Cataloging-in-Publication Data

David, Alfred, 1929–   comp.
  The twelve dancing princesses.

  CONTENTS: Grimm, J. & W. The twelve dancing princesses. The goosegirl. Rapunzel. The devil's three golden hairs. Briar Rose. Snow White. Our lady's child. The Bremen town musicians.—Asbjörnsen, P. C. and Moe, Jörgen. East of the sun and west of the moon.—Asbjörnsen, P. C. The companion. [etc.]
  1. Fairy tales. [1. Fairy tales] I. Meek, Mary Elizabeth, 1924–   joint comp. II. Title. PZ1.D2673Tw9 [PN6071.F15]   808.83'8 [398.2]
73-16517 ISBN 0-253-36100-1 (cl.)   ISBN 0-253-20173-X (pbk.)

15 16 17 18 19 05 04 03 02 01

Grateful acknowledgment is made to the following:

Pat Shaw Iversen for "The Tinderbox," "The Swineherd," "The Princess on the Pea," "The Ugly Duckling," "The Nightingale," and "The Little Mermaid," by Hans Christian Andersen, and "East of the Sun and West of the Moon," by Peter Christen Asbjörnsen and Jörgen Moe.

Pantheon Books for "Prince Ivan, the Firebird, and the Gray Wolf" and "Vasilisa the Beautiful" by Aleksandr Nikolaevich Afanasiev, from *Russian Fairy Tales,* translated and edited by Norbert Guterman. Copyright 1945 by Pantheon Books, Inc. Reprinted by permission of Pantheon Books, a division of Random House, Inc.

Mrs. James Thurber for "Many Moons" by James Thurber. Copyright © 1943 by James Thurber. Copyright © 1971 by Helen W. Thurber and Rosemary Thurber Sauers. Published by Harcourt Brace Jovanovich.

Dreyers Forlag (Oslo) for "The Companion," by Peter Christen Asbjörnsen and Jörgen Moe, from *Norwegian Folk Tales,* translated by Pat Shaw Iversen and Carl Norman.

CONTENTS

THE
TWELVE DANCING
PRINCESSES
and other fairy tales

INTRODUCTION

There are traces of fairy tales in every conceivable
form of literature, including the very oldest and the very
best. Homer's Odysseus contends against giants and
witches and makes a journey to the underworld. The
story of Joseph in Genesis reads just like a fairy tale.
Joseph is sold into slavery by his jealous brothers, and
through his power of interpreting dreams (much as
heroes in fairy tales solve riddles) he rises to become
ruler of Egypt. The knights in medieval romances are constantly having fairy-tale adventures, and so are the
saints in medieval legends. Saint George the dragon slay-
er is a combination of the two. The choice of the three
caskets in *The Merchant of Venice* is a typical fairy-tale
problem, as is the question King Lear puts to his three
daughters. Goneril and Regan are, of course, the wicked
older sisters; Cordelia, the youngest, is kind and good;
and in the old versions of the tale she lives to wit-
ness the punishment of her sisters.

This is not to say that the *Odyssey,* the story of
Joseph, and *King Lear* are fairy tales or that their
authors were even dimly conscious of using the matter
of which fairy tales are made. It does show the deep
roots traditional stories have in the imagination. Fairy
tales are not, as is commonly believed, a form of chil-

dren's literature; they are, like fables, legends, and ballads, among the many forms of adult literature that children have adopted. Fairy tales have a special appeal for children, but they are not childish. The apparent artlessness of these simple stories is not easily achieved. It is, in fact, the product of an art perhaps older than the art of writing itself.

Fairy tales were at one time told aloud, and there is no sure way of knowing where they come from and through how many generations of storytellers they passed before they were written down. The great collections of folktales * were not made until the nineteenth century, when Jacob and Wilhelm Grimm published their monumental *Kinder- und Hausmärchen* (1812–1815), followed by similar collections by Asbjörnsen and Moe in Norway (1842–44) and Afanasiev in Russia (1855–64). Before that time, a few writers had freely adapted a number of traditional fairy tales so as to turn them, in effect, into original stories. The most important of these was the French author Charles Perrault (1628–1703), whose version of "Cinderella," with the pumpkin-coach and the glass slipper, is much more familiar, except in Germany, than the "Cinderella" of the Brothers Grimm. After the Grimms' collection, a great many writers of the nineteenth century wrote literary imitations of folktales and original fairy tales, and one—Hans Christian Andersen—achieved greatness in that form.

The romantic movement aroused interest in folklore throughout Europe. In the revolt against neoclassicism, romantic writers everywhere turned with enthusiasm to themes of common and rustic life. Spontaneity and simplicity were admired as literary virtues. At the same time, the spirit of nationalism that swept Europe during the Napoleonic era was stimulating a possessive pride in native culture. In this atmosphere, the traditional ballads and stories of the people acquired new value in the

---

* A folktale, as distinguished from a fairy tale, is any story that exists among the "folk" and includes, besides fairy tales, animal stories, jests, fables, and other types of oral narrative. Traditional fairy tales like "Sleeping Beauty," "Snow White," and "Rapunzel" were all originally folktales.

eyes of the intellectual world, and the humble folktale, like Cinderella, was found to have a fresher and
more natural beauty than her literary stepsisters.

The Brothers Grimm, more than anyone else, deserve
the credit for appreciating that the stories told by ordinary peasants, journeymen, and nursemaids were works
of art worthy of preservation in their original form. It
is true that neither the Grimms nor their nineteenth-
century followers transcribed their tales with the scrupu-
lous word-for-word accuracy of the modern folklorist.
Wilhelm Grimm, in particular, could not resist the temp-
tation of "perfecting" his favorite stories from one edition of the tales to the next. As a result many of the
Grimms' fairy tales—including the most popular—are
not in the strictest sense "pure" folktales; they are
rather the stories as Wilhelm Grimm romantically con-
ceived that they might have been told by some naïve
peasant genius. The genius was, in part, Grimm's own,
and in laboring to restore the tales to their archetypal
form, he unwittingly polished his raw material to an artificial brilliance. Nevertheless, the Grimms had a deeply
sympathetic understanding for the traditional style of
the folktale, and this style they succeeded in recapturing
for their readers.

The essence of the traditional oral style is the natural-
ness with which the story tells itself without comment,
explanation, or intrusion on the part of the teller. It is
told in an impersonal, matter-of-fact tone as though it
were a true story. Our pleasure is not caused by its sur-
prises and wonders but by the satisfaction of having our
expectations fulfilled and our knowledge confirmed. We
are in a familiar country where we can predict every
turn of the way. The landscape contains signs of warning
and of hope that we have learned to read long ago. The
characters are all people we have met hundreds of times,
and we do not need to have their histories or their mo-
tives explained to us. Magic objects are household articles like spinning wheels, combs, handkerchiefs, and
keys. Talking animals occasion no astonishment. A poor
cottager answers a knock at his window on a stormy
night and finds a white bear who wishes him good eve-

ning. "Good evening!" replies the man. Such incidents are daily occurrences in the fairy-tale world.

In fact, our response to any one fairy tale depends on its similarity in style and construction to all the other fairy tales we know, and this adherence to a single proven formula undoubtedly accounts for their enduring and universal popularity. It has been suggested that fairy tales satisfy psychological needs for power, wealth, and security. A simpler explanation is that they satisfy an aesthetic need for a good story. They fulfill the universal desire for a clarity, harmony, and order that is possible only in fiction. In place of the bewildering and unpredictable everyday world, fairy tales present us with an imaginary world that is simple, orderly, and just—a fantasy world that obeys its own laws and decorum.

The fairy tale easily dispenses with all the difficulties of time and place. The formula "Once upon a time" projects us into a timeless universe without past or future, a world without historical change, which is as real and present now as it was "once." The entire court in "Briar Rose" (the Grimms' version of "Sleeping Beauty") sleeps for a hundred years, but when the spell is broken, the world is the same and everything resumes its normal course. What matters in fairy tales is the particular time of day or time of year. Night is a time of fear, and winter a season of suffering; dawn and spring bring hope and good fortune.

Just as fairy tales exist outside of time, so they are not confined to any particular place. The points of the compass have no real meaning, and when a girl is told that she must seek her lover in a castle "east of the sun and west of the moon," we understand that this means simply very far away. Rivers, forests, and towns materialize when they are needed. The places in fairy tales also have a symbolic function: the humble cottage or the open road where we first encounter the hero tells us that he is poor and down on his luck; the dark woods, the ogre's cave, and the underground passage are typical places where evil awaits him; the castle is the symbol of the fortune that beckons him on.

The characters who inhabit this world are stock types

who vary little from story to story. Fairy tales, like all great stories, deal with basic human relationships—they are about parents and children, brothers and sisters, masters and servants—but the people in fairy tales are created all of a piece without any of the psychological or moral dimensions of people in real life. Usually the characters do not even have individual names, or if they do, the names often describe some typifying quality or the roles they are destined to play, as, for example, Snow White, Cinderella, Faithful John, or Tom Thumb. For the most part they are called simply the prince, the old woman, the soldier, the youngest. They are entirely good or entirely evil, and each character is made up of one or two basic human virtues or vices. Kindness, courage, and loyalty are opposed to jealousy, pride, and avarice. There is a quality of abstractness even about their physical appearance. The heroine, for example, is always beautiful, but her beauty is almost never described in detail unless, as in the case of Rapunzel's long golden hair, the details have importance for the story.

The sun, the moon and the stars, the winds, and especially the animals take parts in the story. Their role is to help the hero and heroine, for a mysterious bond of sympathy links human virtue and the world of nature. The Grimms' Cinderella plants a hazel twig upon her mother's grave and waters it with her tears. The twig grows into a tree from which a white bird answers Cinderella's wishes and casts down the dress and slippers that she wears to the ball. The more familiar fairy godmother is an invention of Charles Perrault; the story in Grimm, simpler but more profound, suggests that the protecting power of the mother has passed into the tree that springs from her grave.

The plot of fairy tales is always the same success story. The hero starts out deprived, persecuted, or betrayed and triumphs against all odds to make his fortune. He may receive a princess and a kingdom or he may simply go back home. The real significance of the ending is expressed by the familiar words "And they lived happily ever after." To be happy as a king is merely one of the more popular ways of expressing the sense of fulfillment and security that makes the proper ending of a fairy tale.

The satisfying sense of order that comes from the recurrence of familiar places, people, and events is heightened by the repetition of actions and motifs, most often in patterns of three—three wishes, three tasks, three questions. Characters also often appear in groups of three. Such rhythmical use of numbers raises expectations that are never disappointed. The third and last task will be the most difficult; the third wish will be the most (or least) rewarding; the third and youngest brother will succeed where the other two have failed.

The same formalism tends to produce a sharply symmetrical structure. The deeds and fortunes of protagonist and antagonist are balanced like weights in the two pans of a scale, one rising as the other sinks. The substitution of the false serving maid for the true princess in "The Goosegirl" is a fine example of the way meaning is achieved through balance and contrast. The princess stoops down to the river to drink while the servant remains arrogantly upon her horse; the princess waits in the courtyard while the maid mounts the stairs; the princess is paired with the gooseboy while the false bride is married to the prince. The balance is restored when the servant is stripped of her stolen finery and dragged to her death by two white horses.

The kind of poetic justice that overtakes the wicked maid in "The Goosegirl" is very common in traditional fairy tales. There is no attempt here to teach a lesson. It is the aesthetic and not the moral sense that demands that virtue be rewarded and evil punished. Fairy tales do not pose real moral issues any more than they present us with real people. In the conflict between pure good and pure evil, the victory of good must be clear and decisive. If we do not learn the fate of the wicked, we are left with a vague sense that something is missing. The fact that we are never told what becomes of the witch in "Rapunzel" is a flaw in an otherwise perfect story.

The cruelty of the punishments sometimes shocks modern readers, and such endings are often suppressed in children's editions of fairy tales. Few children learn any more that Snow White's stepmother comes to the wedding feast and is forced to dance to her death in red-hot slippers; at best they may be told that her heart burst from jealousy. The story is too good to be spoiled by this kind of amputation or sugarcoating, but a fine touch is lost. The form of the wicked queen's death is not meant to be sadistic or vindictive, but it is genuinely "poetic" retribution. The red-hot slippers are the perfect image for the burning jealousy with which the queen destroys herself.

To translate this kind of image into words is to run the risk of destroying the story. The tales do without explanations and present a surface action that is completely satisfying. Fairy tales have something of the homely quality and also of the marvelous power of the magic objects that occur in them so often. There is more to them than meets the eye. One modern scholar, Max Lüthi, has epitomized them in an image that could be taken from a fairy tale: they are "glass beads in which the world sees a mirror-image of itself."

The first twelve selections in this anthology are all traditional fairy tales. Most of them have undoubtedly been touched up by their collectors, yet all retain the characteristics of stories once told aloud among the people. The rest of the stories are "literary" fairy tales, or, to apply the more exact German name for them, "Kunstmärchen" (art fairy tales). A few, like the stories of Perrault and "Beauty and the Beast," are skillful retellings of old folktales. Others, like Andersen's "The Little Mermaid" or Wilde's "The Selfish Giant," are completely original inventions. These stories differ as much from one another as do the individual personalities and tastes of their authors. They may be light, serious, didactic, satiric, romantic, tragic, religious, whimsical—in short, the fairy tale lends itself to the expression of nearly every variety of mood or theme. Each writer returns to the imaginary world of fairy tales, but each manages to find something new there.

In 1697 Charles Perrault, a distinguished member of

the French Academy, published a little volume of fairy tales under the name of his son since he apparently thought it beneath his dignity to acknowledge himself as the author of such "bagatelles." Perrault simulates the plainness of the oral tradition with considerable success, but he is no folklorist and remains at all times a child of the *grand siècle*. The very different results when a story is told by a scholar, anxious not to depart radically from his source, and when it is handled by a writer who feels free to make whatever changes suit his fancy may be seen by comparing Perrault's "Sleeping Beauty" with "Briar Rose," the Grimms' version of the same story.

The story in Grimm is told with complete seriousness and genuine simplicity. Perrault retells the story in a much lighter vein; it is perfectly obvious that he does not believe a word of it and is simply enjoying himself. In his version the simplicity of the old folktale becomes a feigned simplicity that serves as an ironic screen for a sophisticated and witty commentary on human nature, and more particularly on the age of Louis XIV. Louis XIV was a real monarch, more magnificent than any humble fairy-tale king, and Versailles far outshone any fairy-tale palace. Perrault deftly combines the splendor of the world he knew intimately with the homely fairy-tale world, and the great ladies of France are transformed into the powerful fairies who bestow their gifts upon Sleeping Beauty.

The Grimms' king cannot send the thirteenth fairy an invitation because he has a service of only twelve golden plates. For Perrault such a deficiency in a royal household would be unthinkable; his wicked fairy is left off the invitation list because she has been out of society for so long that society has forgotten her existence. The wisewomen in Grimm (they are never referred to as fairies) endow Briar Rose with virtue, beauty, riches, and "everything in the world one could wish for." Perrault is careful to specify that she also receives every social grace, including the ability to sing, dance, and play various instruments. In Grimm sleep spreads magically through the castle at the instant Briar Rose pricks her finger. In Perrault a futile effort is first made to revive

Sleeping Beauty by unlacing her and sprinkling her with Queen of Hungary water before the good fairy puts everyone to sleep with a wave of her magic wand and flies off in a chariot drawn by dragons. The Grimms' Briar Rose and her prince never exchange a word in the story, but in Perrault the couple converse with the *préciosité* of lovers in a baroque romance. Perrault's fairy-tale world is not timeless. The prince politely refrains from telling Sleeping Beauty that she is dressed like his grandmother, and at the wedding feast the orchestra plays old-fashioned tunes. A delightful sequel is attached, telling of Sleeping Beauty's problems with an ogreish mother-in-law, who wants to devour her and her two children. However, an ogress who wants her victims served up with a *sauce Robert* (invented by the chef of Louis XIV) cannot be taken too seriously. A moral in verse that is also probably only half serious is added at the end of the story: young ladies are admonished by Sleeping Beauty's example not to be impatient to get married.

The fairy tale could serve equally well to teach a serious moral lesson. Madame Leprince de Beaumont, in her version of "Beauty and the Beast," gives delicate expression to the meaning of this old tale of a girl who releases her animal lover from a spell: any beast, if he is kind, may turn into a prince in the eyes of the right girl. "I assure you that I am pleased with your heart," Beauty tells the beast, "and when I think of it, you do not seem so ugly to me." Gradually Beauty's fear gives way to friendship, friendship gives way to affection, and affection ripens into love. Madame Leprince de Beaumont makes excellent use of the French gift for psychological analysis elegantly expressed, and she treats her characters—the good ones, to be sure—with rare tenderness.

The fairy tale is also a natural vehicle for satire. "The First of the Bearskins," by the seventeenth-century German satirist Grimmelshausen, is a tongue-in-cheek version of the story of the man who makes a pact with the Devil to wear a bearskin for seven years. Grimmelshausen writes with an inflated gusto that invites comparison with Rabelais, and he shares Rabelais's love of playing with words and their meanings. In "The First of the Bearskins," he pretends with learned pomposity to be tracing the etymology of the term "bearskin," a colloquial expression for a loafer. Actually he uses the old fairy tale to draw a sharply satiric picture of Germany at the end of the Thirty Years' War. The greediness of fairy-tale villains gives him an opportunity to portray the profiteering postwar generation, and the Devil, who helps the poor soldier to make his fortune, turns out to be the most honorable character in the story.

The appearance of the Grimm collection inspired a flood of literary imitations. One of the writers who caught the fairy-tale fever was the brilliant young German author Wilhelm Hauff. "Dwarf Longnose," his best story, tells what happens to a good little boy who incurs the wrath of a witch who keeps one of the most delightful households in fairy-tale literature. Hauff is a master of the grotesque, but he also has a great deal of humor, and one cannot help suspecting throughout "Dwarf Longnose" that he is satirizing the bourgeois virtues mouthed so complacently by little Jacob, by his parents, and, indeed, by the entire community. The respectability of the good shopkeepers and market women conceals a cruel streak that is unmasked when everyone turns against the dwarf.

But the great name is, of course, Hans Christian Andersen. There is so much variety in his tales that it is difficult to represent him in a few selections. He can retell a folktale, as he does in "The Tinderbox," preserving an outward appearance of simplicity and naïveté but seasoning it with a sharp wit and brilliant invention. Here are the traditional helpful animals of folklore; no one but Andersen, however, would think of a dog with eyes as big as teacups, one with eyes as big as mill wheels, and one with eyes as big as the Round Tower in Copenhagen. His greatest achievements, though, are the original stories in which he succeeds in making the fairy tale a perfect medium for the expression of the spirit of the romantic movement.

The French Revolution had also put an end to the *ancien régime* of the fairy tale, and for Andersen, as for so many of the romantics, the humble cottage instead of the royal palace symbolizes true happiness, and natural beauty is more precious than gold or jewels. Perrault's fairy-tale court reflects the splendor of the actual court at Versailles; Andersen's reflects the snobbery and artificial values of the European upper-middle class. The princess in "The Swineherd" is a poor little rich girl who prefers a music box to a genuine rose. The music master of the Chinese emperor admires the mechanical song of the artificial nightingale because he can analyze it and write books about it. What counts most of all in society, whether at the court of the emperor of China or in the barnyard of the ugly duckling, is to act and think and look like everyone else. The rest of society take their cues from a spoiled child like the princess, experts like the music master, or local dowagers like the old Spanish duck whose high rank is shown by a red rag around her leg. At every turn, Andersen exploits the traditional framework of the fairy tale for social criticism that may be light and gay or deeply sensitive. Often both of these moods occur within the same story, as in "The Ugly Duckling," which begins as a comedy of barnyard manners and turns into a painful study of inferiority feelings. Folktale characters are rarely human enough to enable us to identify with their suffering, but "The Ugly Duckling" lets everyone know what it really feels like to be Cinderella.

Many fairy tales are about characters who long for superhuman powers. In "The Little Mermaid" Andersen reverses this theme and takes the viewpoint of a supernatural creature who longs to be human and to share the pains and the rewards of human suffering and sacrifice. It is as though we were looking at the real world from the fairy-tale world with a longing that is almost unbearable. The little mermaid gives up her beautiful voice for a human form and the chance of winning a prince and an immortal soul. Andersen's own restless and lonely life was not unlike that of his mermaid, and reading him, one occasionally feels in the haunting presence of someone living submerged in a fantasy world, both beautiful and grotesque, who would gladly exchange his voice as an artist for a normal existence above the surface. In contrast to the earthiness of the folktale, a dreamlike and often nightmarish quality pervades many of Andersen's fairy tales. Several of them are masterpieces of the romantic imagination.

John Ruskin's "The King of the Golden River" is another romantic fairy tale. Ruskin has no great gifts as a storyteller, but he creates a true fairy-tale atmosphere in his descriptions of nature. The alpine landscape around Treasure Valley, the cataract, the glacier, and the storm have more interesting personalities than the conventional three brothers. Ruskin also has a genuine feeling for the bond between nature and human nature in fairy tales. The two wicked brothers bring blight upon the valley and are turned into stones. The purity of the youngest, symbolized by a lily with three drops of dew, restores the valley to life.

Oscar Wilde's fairy tales contain, like many of Andersen's, a curious blend of sophisticated humor and sentimentality. In "The Selfish Giant," which is both a fairy tale and a religious allegory, a nostalgia for childish innocence turns bittersweet. In spite of their wit and urbanity, Wilde's fairy tales are among the saddest ever written.

Twentieth-century writers have been more influenced by the nightmarish horrors of fairy tales than by their assurance of a happy ending and a poetic justice. The typical Kafka hero, for example, struggles helplessly in a fantasy world, like Gregor Samsa, who is transformed, not into a raven or a bear, but into a huge insect.

James Thurber is an exception. He has written modern fairy tales that end happily without being sentimental or complacent. "Many Moons" is both a parable of our times and a true fairy tale, which is as much as to say it is a timeless story. It is about a little princess who wants the moon, and as in a true fairy tale, she gets it. The other characters in the story have not been enchanted by a wicked fairy, but they are under a spell of a sort that might be called loss of the imagination. The Lord High Chamberlain, the Royal Wizard, and the Royal Mathematician are well-meaning practical men whose only resource for solving any problem is to use their reason. Given an unreasonable request, they are helpless. The Princess Lenore uses her imagination, and that is why she is wiser than the wise men.

"Many Moons" is not only a fairy tale but also a story about the way fairy tales work. The imagination always demands something better than life, and to provide it is the function of all art, including the art of the fairy tale. Fairy tales may not be true to life, but they are true to what the imagination can make of life. Anyone may have the moon, provided that, like the Princess Lenore, he can use his imagination.

A Note on the Translations

Modern editions of fairy tales very often continue to reprint the standard nineteenth-century translations. Though many of these have deserved their long popularity, they are becoming increasingly dated. They contain occasional bits of editing, as when a Victorian translator turns the little mermaid's fishtail into a pair of "the prettiest white feet" instead of the legs that Andersen unblushingly mentions. More serious is the frequency of deliberately quaint and old-fashioned diction. Often the stories seem outmoded only because of the style into which they have been translated.

The translations in this volume attempt to give an accurate rendering of the stories into modern idiom while preserving, as far as is possible in any translation, the flavor of the original. The plain style of the folktales in Grimm is a very different thing from the consciously elegant French of Perrault and Madame Leprince de Beaumont. Andersen's tales encompass a whole range of styles from racy colloquial dialogue to lyrical passages of description.

Twenty-two translations are printed here for the first time. We wish to express our gratitude to Pat Shaw Iversen for translating "East of the Sun and West of the Moon" for this anthology and for permitting us to use six stories from a new translation of Andersen on which she is presently engaged. Mrs. Iversen with Carl Norman is also the translator of "The Companion." The two Russian tales were translated by Norbert Guterman. All of the French and German stories have been newly translated by the editors.

Jacob and Wilhelm Grimm

IIIIIIIIIIIIIIIIIIIIIIIIIIIIIIIIIIIIIIIIIIIIIIIIIIIIIIIIIIIIIIIIIIIIIIIIIIIIIIIIIII

THE
TWELVE
DANCING PRINCESSES

IIIIIIIIIIIIIIIIIIIIIIIIIIIIIIIIIIIIIIIIIIIIIIIIIIIIIIIIIIIIIIIIIIIIIIIIIIIIIIIIIII

Once upon a time there was a king who had twelve daughters, each one more beautiful than the next. They slept together in a large room with their beds lined up in a row, and at night, after they had gone to bed, the king locked and bolted the door. But when he opened the door in the morning, he saw that their shoes were all worn out from dancing, and nobody could discover how this happened.

The king issued a proclamation that whoever could find out where they went dancing at night could choose one of them for his wife and succeed him as king; but anyone who volunteered and could not find out after three days and nights was to forfeit his life. It wasn't long until a king's son offered to take the risk. He was received with hospitality, and at night he was taken to a room that opened on the bedroom. His bed was made there, and he supposed to see where they went dancing. And in order to keep them from playing any secret tricks or going out by some other way, the door to the bedroom was left open. But the eyes of the king's son suddenly felt like lead and he fell asleep, and

when he woke up the next morning, all twelve had been to the dance, for there were their shoes with the soles worn right through. The second and third nights were just the same, and so his head was chopped off without pity. Many others followed him and offered to undertake the dangerous enterprise, but they all lost their lives.

Now it happened that a poor soldier, who had been wounded and was no longer fit for service, was on his way to the city where the king lived. He met an old woman who asked him where he was going. "I'm not very sure myself," he said, and he added jokingly, "I'd really like to find out where the king's daughters wear out their shoes dancing, and then get to be king."

"That's not so hard," said the old woman. "You mustn't drink the wine they bring you before you go to bed, and you must pretend that you're fast asleep." With that, she gave him a little cloak and said, "If you put that around your shoulders, you'll be invisible and then you can steal after the twelve princesses."

Having been so well advised, the soldier took the matter in good earnest, and so he screwed up his courage, went before the king, and volunteered to be a suitor. He was received with the same hospitality as the others, and they gave him royal garments to wear.

At bedtime he was led to the anteroom, and when he got ready for bed, the oldest daughter brought him a goblet of wine. But he had tied a sponge under his chin and let the wine run into it so that he didn't drink a drop. Then he lay down, and after lying there a little while, he started snoring as if he were fast asleep.

The twelve princesses heard him and laughed. "That one shouldn't have risked his life, either," said the oldest. Then they got up, opened wardrobes, chests, and boxes, and took out magnificent clothes. They primped in front of the mirrors, frolicked around the room, and joyfully looked forward to the dance—except for the youngest. She said, "I don't know, you can be gay if you like, but I have such a strange feeling—I'm sure something terrible is going to happen to us."

"You're a little goose," said the oldest; "you're always afraid. Have you forgotten how many kings' sons have already been here and failed? As for the soldier, I wouldn't have even had to give him the sleeping potion—nothing would have wakened that lout."

When they were all ready, they first had a look at the soldier, but he had his eyes closed and didn't move a muscle, so they thought they were completely safe. The oldest one went to her bed and rapped on it. Immediately it sank through the floor and they climbed through the opening, one after the other, with the oldest in the lead.

The soldier, who had watched everything, lost no time, put on his little cloak, and climbed down after the youngest. Halfway down the stairs he stepped lightly on her gown. She was frightened and called out, "What is it? Who is holding onto my gown?"

"Don't be such a simpleton," said the oldest; "you caught it on a nail."

Then they went all the way down, and when they got to the bottom, they were standing in a magnificent avenue of trees: all the leaves were of silver, and they shimmered and shone. The soldier thought, "You'd better take along some token as proof," and he broke off a branch. The tree gave a prodigious crack.

The youngest cried out again, "Something's the matter —did you hear that cracking?"

But the oldest said, "They're firing a victory salute because soon we shall have redeemed our princes."

Next they came to an avenue of trees with leaves of gold, and finally to a third where the leaves were of bright diamond. Each time he broke a branch, and each time there was a cracking that made the youngest start with alarm. But the oldest insisted they were victory salutes.

They went on and came to a big river. Twelve little boats were floating on the water, and in each boat sat a handsome prince. They had been waiting for the twelve princesses, and each took one in his boat. The soldier, however, went and sat by the youngest.

"I don't know what's wrong," said the prince; "the boat is much heavier tonight, and I've got to row with all my strength to move it along."

"It must be the hot weather," said the youngest. "I'm very warm myself."

On the other side of the river stood a beautiful castle brightly illuminated, from which the gay music of drums and trumpets was sounding. They rowed across and went inside, and each prince danced with his own sweetheart.

The soldier danced along invisibly, and each time a princess took a goblet of wine in her hand, he drank it so that it was empty when she raised it to her lips. The youngest was frightened at this, too, but the oldest always managed to silence her.

They danced until three o'clock the next morning, when all the shoes were worn out and they had to stop. The princes rowed them back across the river, and this time the soldier sat up front with the oldest. On the shore they said good-bye to the princes and promised to come again the next night. But when they reached the stairs, the soldier ran ahead and lay down on his bed, and when the twelve came up wearily dragging their feet, he was already snoring again loud enough for them to hear. "We don't have to worry about *him*," they said. They took off their beautiful clothes, put them away, placed the worn-out shoes under the beds, and lay down.

The next morning the soldier didn't want to tell right away because he wished to see a little more of these wonderful goings-on, and he went along for the second and third nights too. Everything was just the same as the first time, and each night they danced until their shoes fell apart. The third time he took away a goblet for proof.

When the hour had come for him to give his answer, he concealed the three branches and the goblet on his person and went before the king. The twelve princesses were listening behind the door to see what he would say.

When the king asked, "Where did my twelve daughters wear out their shoes dancing in the night?" he answered, "With twelve princes in an underground castle." And he told everything that happened and produced his evidence.

The king had his daughters summoned and asked them if the soldier had told the truth, and since they saw that their secret was out and that lying would do no good, they had to confess everything.

Next the king asked the soldier which one he wanted to marry. "I'm no longer a young man," he answered, "so give me the oldest."

The wedding was celebrated the same day, and he was promised the kingdom after the king's death. But the enchantment of the princes was extended one day for each night they had danced with the princesses.

THE GOOSEGIRL

Once upon a time there lived an old queen whose husband had died many years ago, and she had a beautiful daughter. When she grew up, she was promised in marriage to a king's son far away. Now when the time came for her to be married and the child had to begin her journey to the foreign kingdom, the old queen packed up a great many costly dishes and jewels, gold and silver, goblets and trinkets—everything, in short, that belongs in a royal dowry—for she loved the child with all her heart. She also gave her a maid-in-waiting, who was supposed to ride along with her and to give the bride into the hands of the groom. Each one got a horse for the journey, but the princess' horse was called Falada, and it could talk.

When the hour of parting had come, the old mother went to her bedroom, took a little knife, and cut her fingers to make them bleed. She held a scrap of white cloth up to them and let three drops of blood trickle on it, gave them to her daughter, and said, "Dear child, take good care of them. You will have need of them on your way."

And so they sadly said good-bye to each other. The princess tucked the scrap of cloth into her bosom and got up on her horse, and then she set off to meet her bridegroom.

After they had ridden along for an hour, she became terribly thirsty and said to her maid, "Get down and fill the cup you've brought for me with water from the brook. I would like a drink."

"If you're thirsty," said the maid, "get down yourself and lie down by the water and drink. I don't want to wait on you."

The princess got off her horse because she was so very thirsty, stooped down to the water in the brook, and drank. She wasn't permitted to drink out of the gold cup. She said, "Dear heaven!" and the three drops of blood answered, "If your mother knew this, it would break her heart."

But the bride of the prince was meek. She said nothing and got back on her horse. Thus they rode a few miles further, but it was a warm day, the sun burned down, and soon she was thirsty again. When they came to a stream, she called again to her maid, "Get down and fetch me a drink in my gold cup." For she had long since forgotten all of the unkind words.

But the maid said even more proudly, "If you want to drink, help yourself. I don't want to wait on you."

Then the princess got down because she was so thirsty, and she leaned out over the flowing stream. She wept and said, "Dear heaven!" and again the drops of blood answered, "If your mother knew this, it would break her heart." And as she was drinking and leaning out over the bank as far as she could, the little scrap of cloth with the three drops fell out of her bosom and was carried away by the water, and she was too frightened to notice. But the maid noticed and was glad to get the bride in her power, for by losing the drops of blood she had become weak and helpless.

When she wanted to get back on her horse, Falada, the maid said, "I belong on Falada, and you belong on my nag." And she had to put up with it. Then the maid harshly commanded her to take off her royal garments and to put on her mean ones instead, and last of all she had to swear before the face of heaven that she would tell no one at court about it. And if she had refused to swear this oath, she would have been murdered on the spot. But Falada saw all that went on and paid close attention.

Now the maid mounted on Falada and the true bride got on the common nag, and so they went on until finally they arrived at the royal castle. There was great joy at their coming, and the prince ran to meet them. He lifted the maid down from the horse and thought that she was his bride. She was escorted up the steps, but the true princess had to remain standing below.

The old king looked out of the window and saw her waiting in the courtyard and noticed that she was well bred, gentle, and very beautiful. He went straightaway to the royal apartment and asked the bride about the girl she had brought with her who was standing down there in the courtyard—who might she be?

"She's someone I picked up along the way for company. Give the girl some work so that she won't stand there idle."

But the old king had no work for her and wasn't able to think of anything better than to say, "I've got a small boy who looks after the geese. She can help him."

The boy was called Curdy, and he was the one the true bride had to help tend geese.

Soon thereafter the false bride said to the young prince, "Dearest husband, let me beg you to do me a favor."

He replied, "I'll do it gladly."

"Well then, have the knacker* summoned to cut off the head of the horse on which I rode here because it made me angry on the journey." But the real reason was that she was afraid the horse might tell what she had done to the princess.

Thus it happened, and when the time had come for the faithful Falada to die, the real princess also heard about it, and she secretly promised the knacker a piece of money in return for a small favor. There was a large, dark gateway in the town through which she had to pass with the geese every morning and every eve-

* Someone who buys and slaughters worn-out horses and sells their flesh as dog's meat, etc.

ning. Would he please nail Falada's head up under the dark gateway so that she could see him again more than once? The knacker promised to do it, struck off the head, and nailed it up under the dark gateway.

Early in the morning, when she and Curdy were driving the geese out through the gateway, she said as she passed:

"O Falada, there you hang high."

And the head answered:

"O young princess, there you go by.
If your mother knew this,
Her heart would break."

Then she went still further out of town, and they drove the geese into the fields. When they came to the pasture, she sat down and loosened her hair, which was pure gold. Curdy saw it and was delighted at the way it gleamed, and he wanted to pull out a few hairs. Then she said:

> "Blow, wind, blow,
>   Make Curdy go
>   Chasing after his cap
>   Till I've done up my hair
>   And braided it fair."

And such a strong wind started up that it blew Curdy's cap all over the countryside, and he had to run after it. By the time he got back, she was all finished combing her hair and putting it back up, and he couldn't get any of it. That made Curdy angry, and he refused to speak to her. And so they tended the geese until evening. Then they went home.

The next morning, as they were driving the geese through the dark gateway, the girl said:

> "O Falada, there you hang high."

Falada answered:

> "O young princess, there you go by.
>   If your mother knew this,
>   It would break her heart."

Out in the fields she sat down in the grass again and started to comb out her hair, and Curdy came running up to grab at it. But she said quickly:

> "Blow, wind, blow,
>   Make Curdy go
>   Chasing after his cap
>   Till I've done up my hair
>   And braided it fair."

Then the wind blew, and blew the cap right off his head,

far away so that Curdy had to run after it. And when he came back, she had long since finished putting her hair up, and he couldn't get hold of a single lock. And so they tended geese until evening.

But that night, after they got home, Curdy went to the old king and said, "I don't want to tend geese with that girl any more."

"Why not?" asked the king.

"Oh, she makes me angry all day long."

The old king ordered him to tell what he found to be the matter with her.

Curdy said, "Every morning when we pass under the dark gateway, there's a horse's head on the wall, and she says to it:

'Falada, there you hang high.'

And the head answers:

'O young princess, there you go by.
If your mother knew this,
It would break her heart.' "

And so Curdy told the rest, what happened in the pasture and how he had to run after his cap.

The old king ordered him to drive the geese out again the next day, and in the morning he himself hid behind the dark gate and overheard her talking with Falada's head. And he also followed her into the fields and hid himself behind a bush in the meadow. Soon he saw for himself where the goosegirl and the gooseboy came driving the flock and how, after a while, she sat down and unbraided her hair—it shone forth with a radiant brightness. Right away she repeated:

"Blow, wind, blow,
Make Curdy go
Chasing after his cap
Till I've done up my hair
And braided it fair."

A gust of wind came and carried off Curdy's cap so that he had to run far away, and the girl calmly went on combing and braiding her locks while the old king observed everything.

He went away unnoticed, and when the goosegirl returned home that night, he called her aside and asked her why she did all of these things.

"I cannot tell you, nor can I tell my sorrow to a soul, for that is what I swore before the face of heaven on pain of losing my life."

He urged her and gave her no peace, but he could get nothing out of her. Finally he said, "If you can't confide in me, tell your sorrow to that iron stove," and he went away.

She crawled into the iron stove and wept and complained and poured her heart out and said, "Here I sit forsaken by all the world although I am a king's daughter, and a false maid-in-waiting has forced me to take off my royal garments and has taken my place with my bridegroom, and I have to do menial service as a goosegirl. If my mother knew this, it would break her heart."

But the old king was standing outside by the stovepipe listening, and he heard what she said. Then he went back inside and told her to come out of the stove. He had her dressed in royal garments, and she was so beautiful that it seemed a miracle.

The old king called his son and revealed to him that he had the wrong bride: she was just a maid-in-waiting, but the true one—the former goosegirl—was standing right there. The young prince was as glad as he could be when he saw her beauty and virtue, and a great feast was ordered to which all the good friends and neighbors were invited. At the head of the table sat the bridegroom, with the princess on one side and the maid-in-waiting on the other, but the maid was dazzled by her finery and didn't recognize the princess.

Now, when they had eaten and drunk and spirits ran high, the old king gave a riddle to the maid: What does a woman deserve who betrays her master in such and such a manner, and he went on to tell the whole affair, and asked, "What sentence would such a one deserve?"

The false bride said, "She deserves no better than to be stripped stark naked and put in a barrel studded inside with sharp nails, and two white horses should be hitched to it and should drag her from street to street until she is dead."

"That is you," said the old king. "You have pronounced judgment on yourself, and that is what shall be done to you."

And when the sentence had been carried out, the young prince married the right bride, and they both ruled the land in peace and happiness.

RAPUNZEL

iiiiiiiiiiiiiiiiiiiiiiiiiiiiiiiiiii

Once upon a time there lived a man and his wife who for a long time had wished in vain for a child, and at last the woman had reason to believe that the good Lord would fulfill her wish. The couple had a little window at the back of their house from which they could see a splendid garden full of the loveliest flowers and vegetables, but it was surrounded by a high wall and no one dared to go inside because it belonged to a very powerful witch of whom everyone was afraid.

One day the woman was standing at the window and looking down into the garden. There she caught sight of a bed planted with the most beautiful rapunzels,* and they looked so fresh and green that her mouth began to water, and she felt a very great longing to eat some of them. Her longing increased every day, and because she realized that she could not have any, she pined away and looked pale and miserable. Her husband took fright and asked, "What ails you, dear wife?"

"Oh," she said, "if I don't get some of the rapunzels

---

* A European lettucelike vegetable used in salads. Its English name is "rampion," but since the word is almost as unfamiliar to American readers as the German "Rapunzel," the latter has been retained to show where Rapunzel gets her name.

from the garden behind our house, I shall die." Her husband, who loved her, thought to himself, "Rather than let my wife die, I'll bring her some of those rapunzels, no matter what it may cost." And so at dusk he climbed over the wall into the witch's garden, hastily picked a handful of rapunzels, and brought them to his wife. She immediately made a salad and ate it ravenously. But it tasted so awfully good that the next day her desire was three times as great. If she was to have peace, her husband had to climb into the garden a second time. He went back again at dusk, but as he climbed over the wall, he was terrified to see the witch standing in front of him.

"How dare you," she said with a savage look, "climb into my garden and steal my rapunzels like a thief? This is going to have disagreeable consequences for you."

"Oh," he replied, "temper justice with mercy. I would not have dared if I hadn't had to do it. My wife saw your rapunzels from the window, and she has such a longing to eat some that she will die if she can't have any."

The witch became a little less angry and said to him, "If it is as you say, I will allow you to take as many rapunzels as you want, but on one condition—you must give me the child that your wife is about to bring into the world. It will be well treated, and I will give it a mother's care." The man was so afraid that he agreed to everything, and as soon as the baby was born, the witch appeared, named the child Rapunzel, and took it away with her.

Rapunzel was the most beautiful child under the sun. When she turned twelve, the witch shut her up in a tower in a forest. The tower had neither stairs nor doors; there was only a tiny little window at the very top. Whenever the witch wanted to get in, she stood below and cried:

> "Rapunzel, Rapunzel,
> Let down your hair."

Rapunzel had magnificent long hair, as fine as spun gold. When she heard the witch's voice, she would undo her braids and wind them around a window hook, and then her hair would drop twenty yards down to the ground and the witch would climb up by it.

After several years it happened that the king's son was riding through the forest and passed by the tower. He heard singing that was so lovely that he stood still and listened. It was Rapunzel, who in her loneliness passed the time singing sweetly to herself. The king's son wanted to climb up to her and looked for a door in the tower, but he could not find one. He rode home, but the song had so touched his heart that every day he went out into the forest to listen.

One time, as he stood behind a tree, he saw the witch coming and heard her call up:

> "Rapunzel, Rapunzel,
> Let down your hair."

Then Rapunzel let down her braids and the witch climbed up to her.

"If that's the ladder one climbs up on, I'll try my luck." And the following day as it was getting dark, he went to the tower and called:

> "Rapunzel, Rapunzel,
> Let down your hair."

Right away the hair was let down and the king's son climbed up.

At first Rapunzel was terribly frightened to see a man enter because she had never seen one before. But the king's son began to talk to her kindly and told her that her song had touched his heart so much that he could not rest until he had seen her. Then Rapunzel was no longer afraid, and when he asked her if she would marry him and she saw that he was young and handsome, she thought, "He'll love me better than old Mother Gothel," and she said yes and laid her hand in his hand. She said, "I would gladly go with you, but I don't know how to get down. Each time you come, bring a skein of silk with you and I'll twist it into a ladder, and when it's ready I'll climb down, and you will take me away on your horse."

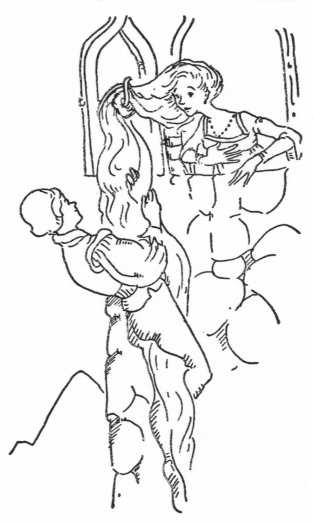

They arranged for him to come every evening because the old woman came in the daytime. The witch suspected nothing until Rapunzel said to her one day, "Do tell me, Mother Gothel, why are you so much heavier to pull up than the young king's son—he's up in a flash."

"Oh, you wicked child," cried the witch, "what are you saying? I thought I had shut you away from all the world, and still you have deceived me." In her rage she seized Rapunzel's beautiful hair, wound it a few times around her left hand, grabbed a pair of scissors with her right, and snip, snap, cut it off. And the beautiful braids were lying on the floor. Moreover, she was so heartless that she took poor Rapunzel to a desert place where she had to live in great sorrow and misery.

On the same day, however, on which she had banished Rapunzel, the witch tied the braids to the window hook, and when the king's son came and cried:

> "Rapunzel, Rapunzel,
> Let down your hair,"

she let the hair down. The king's son climbed up, but instead of finding his beloved Rapunzel, he found the witch, who glared at him spitefully.

"Aha," she cried mockingly, "you've come to take away your lady love, but the beautiful bird is no longer sitting in the nest singing. The cat has got it, and what's more, is going to scratch out your eyes. You've lost Rapunzel, and you'll never see her again."

The king's son was beside himself with grief, and in his despair, he leaped from the tower. He escaped with his life, but the brambles he fell into put out his eyes. He wandered blind through the forest and ate nothing but roots and berries, and he did nothing except to moan and weep over the loss of his beloved wife.

So he wandered for several years in misery and happened at last upon the desert place where Rapunzel lived in sorrow with the twins she had borne—a boy and a girl. He heard her voice, and it seemed very familiar to him. He went toward the voice, and when he approached, Rapunzel recognized him, and she embraced him and wept. Two of her tears fell upon his eyes and moistened them so that they became clear again and he could see as well as before. He took her to his kingdom, where he was received joyfully, and they lived for many more years in happiness and contentment.

THE DEVIL'S
THREE GOLDEN HAIRS

O nce upon a time there was a poor woman who
gave birth to a little son, and because he was
born with a caul, it was prophesied that when he
got to be fourteen he would marry the king's daughter.
It happened that soon after that the king came to the
village, but no one knew that he was the king. When
he asked people for the latest news, they answered, "Not
long ago a child was born with a caul, and whatever such
a person sets out to do will turn out lucky. Indeed, it
has been prophesied that when he gets to be fourteen
he'll marry the king's daughter."

The king, who had an evil heart, was angry at the
prophecy. He went to the parents, made a show of friend-
liness, and said, "You poor people, give me the child to
take care of and I'll provide for it!"

At first they refused, but when the stranger offered
them solid gold, they thought, "It's a good-luck child;
everything is bound to turn out for the best." So they
finally consented and gave him the child.

The king put the child into a box and rode on with it
until he came to a deep stream. There he threw the
box into the water and thought, "I've helped my daughter
get rid of this unexpected suitor."

But instead of sinking, the box floated like a little boat,
and not a drop of water got inside. It floated to a point

two miles above the king's capital where there was a mill, and it caught on the weir. One of the millhands, who was luckily standing there, noticed it and pulled it in with a hook, expecting to find it full of treasure. But when he opened it, there lay a handsome baby boy, lively and gay. He brought him to the miller and his wife, and because they had no children of their own, they were glad and said, "God has given him to us!" They took good care of the foundling, and as he grew up, all the virtues grew in him.

It came to pass one time that during a storm the king took shelter at the mill and asked the miller and his wife if that strapping lad were their son. "No," they answered, "he's a foundling. Fourteen years ago he floated up against the weir inside a box."

Then the king knew that this was none other than the good-luck child he had thrown into the stream, and he said, "Good people, could the boy bear a letter to the queen? I will give him two gold pieces as a reward."

"As your Majesty commands!" they answered and told the boy to get ready.

Then the king wrote a letter to the queen, saying, "As soon as the boy delivers this letter, he is to be killed and buried, and all of this must be done before my return."

The boy started out with this letter, but he lost his way and in the evening came to a large forest. He saw a small light in the darkness, went toward it, and came to a little house. As he entered, an old woman was sitting beside the fire all alone. She was frightened when she saw the boy and said, "Where do you come from and where are you going?"

"I'm coming from the mill," he answered, "and I'm going to the queen, to whom I'm supposed to take a letter. But I'd like to spend the night here because I've lost my way in the forest."

"You poor boy," said the woman. "You've come upon a house that belongs to a gang of robbers, and when they come home, they will kill you."

"Come what may," said the boy, "I'm not afraid. But I'm so tired that I can't go any farther." He stretched out on a bench and fell asleep.

Soon after that the robbers came and asked angrily who was that strange boy lying there. "Oh," said the old woman, "he's an innocent child who lost his way in the forest, and I took him in out of pity. He's supposed to take a letter to the queen."

The robbers opened the letter and read it, and it said that as soon as the boy arrived he was to be put to death. Then the hardhearted robbers took pity, and the captain tore up the letter and wrote another one, which said that as soon as the boy arrived he was to be married to the king's daughter. Then they let him sleep in peace on the bench until the next morning, and when he woke up, they gave him the letter and showed him the right way.

When the queen had received the letter and read it, she followed the instructions, ordered a splendid wedding, and so the king's daughter was married to the good-luck child. And because the young man was handsome and kind, she lived with him in happiness and contentment.

After a time the king returned to his castle and saw that the prophecy had been fulfilled and that the good-luck child had married his daughter. "How did this happen?" he said. "I gave a completely different order in my letter."

The queen handed him the letter and told him to see for himself what it said. The king read the letter and realized that his letter had been exchanged with another one. He asked the young man what had become of the letter that had been entrusted to him and why he had brought another in its place.

"I know nothing at all about it," he answered. "They must have been exchanged at night while I was sleeping in the forest."

"You can't get away with it that easily!" the king said furiously. "Whoever wants to have my daughter will have to go to hell and fetch me three golden hairs from the head of the Devil. If you bring me what I ask for, you can keep my daughter." That way the king hoped to get rid of him for good.

But the good-luck child answered, "I'll manage to bring back the golden hairs—I'm not afraid of the Devil."

With that he took his leave and began his travels.

His journey took him to a large city, where the watchman at the gate asked him what his trade was and what he knew.

"I know everything," said the good-luck child.

"Then you can do us a favor," said the watchman, "if you can tell us why the well in the marketplace, which used to produce wine, has dried up and won't even yield water any more."

"You'll find out," he answered. "Just wait until I come back!" Then he went on and came to another town, where the watchman at the gate again asked him what his trade was and what he knew.

"I know everything," he answered.

"Then you can do us a favor and tell us why the tree in our city, which used to bear golden apples, doesn't even put out leaves any more."

"You'll find out," he answered. "Just wait until I come back!"

Then he went on and came to a great river that he had to cross. The ferryman asked him what his trade was and what he knew.

"I know everything," he answered.

"Then you can do me a favor," said the ferryman, "and tell me why I have to go over and back all the time without any relief."

"You'll find out," he answered. "Just wait until I come back!"

When he had crossed the river, he found the entrance to hell. Everything was black and sooty down there, and the Devil wasn't home, but his grandmother sat there in a large easy chair. "What do you want?" she said to him, but she didn't look so very fierce.

"I'd like very much to have three golden hairs from the head of the Devil," he answered, "or else I won't be able to keep my wife."

"That's asking a lot," she said. "If the Devil finds you when he comes home, that will be the end of you. But I feel sorry for you, and I'll see whether I can help you." She turned him into an ant and said, "Crawl into the folds of my skirt—you'll be safe there."

"All right," he said, "that's fine. But I'd still like to find out three things: why a well, which used to produce wine, has dried up and won't even yield water; why a tree, which used to bear golden apples, now won't even put out leaves; and why a ferryman has to go over and back all the time without any relief."

"Those are hard questions," she answered, "but just keep good and quiet and pay attention to what the Devil says when I pull out the three golden hairs."

As night was falling, the Devil came home. No sooner had he come inside than he noticed something strange in the air. "Sniff, sniff, I smell human flesh," he said. "Something is wrong here." Then he peeked into every corner and searched, but he couldn't find anything.

His grandmother scolded him: "I've just finished sweeping and putting the house in order," she said, "and there you go turning everything upside down again. You're always smelling human flesh! Sit down and eat your supper!"

After he had had enough to eat and drink, he was tired, laid his head in his grandmother's lap, and told her to pick a few lice out of his hair. It wasn't long before he fell asleep and snorted and snored. Then the old woman took hold of a golden hair, pulled it out, and put it down beside her.

"Ouch!" cried the Devil. "What are you trying to do?"

"I was having a bad dream," answered the grandmother, "and happened to grab at your hair."

"What were you dreaming about?" asked the Devil.

"I dreamed that a well in the marketplace, which used to produce wine, has dried up and won't even yield water now. What could be the matter with it?"

"Ha, if they only knew!" answered the Devil. "There's a toad sitting under a stone in the well. If they kill it, the wine will flow again."

The grandmother picked out some more lice until he went to sleep again and snored so that the windows rattled. Then she pulled out the second hair.

"Ow! What are you doing?" the Devil cried furiously.

"Don't be angry!" she answered. "I did it in my dream."

"What were you dreaming about this time?" he asked.

"I dreamed that in a certain kingdom there stands a tree that used to bear golden apples and now won't even put out leaves. What could be the matter?"

"Ha, if they only knew!" answered the Devil. "There's a mouse gnawing at the roots. If they kill it, the tree will bear golden apples again, but if the mouse continues to gnaw much longer, the tree will die. But leave me alone, and if you disturb me one more time with your dreams, I'm going to slap your face!"

The grandmother spoke soothingly to him and picked more lice out of his hair until he went back to sleep and snored. Then she took hold of the third golden hair and pulled it out.

The Devil jumped up, howled, and was going to beat her, but she calmed him down again and said, "One can't help bad dreams!"

"What were you dreaming about?" he asked, for he was still curious.

"I dreamed about a ferryman who complains that he has to go over and back all the time without any relief. What could be the matter?"

"Ha, the idiot," answered the Devil. "When someone comes wanting to be taken across, he must put the pole in his hands. Then the other will have to be ferryman, and he'll be free."

Since the grandmother had pulled out the three golden hairs and he had answered the three questions, she left the old dragon in peace, and he slept until daybreak.

When the Devil was gone again, the old woman took the ant out of the folds of her skirt and restored the good-luck child's human shape. "There are the three golden hairs for you," she said, "and I suppose you heard the Devil's answers to the three questions?"

"Yes," he answered, "I heard, and I'll remember them."

"So now you've been helped," she said, "and you can be on your way."

He thanked the old woman for helping him in his need and left hell pleased that everything had turned out so lucky. When he came to the ferryman, he had to give the promised answer. "First take me across," said the good-luck child, "and I'll tell you how you can get someone to relieve you." When they got to the other side, he gave the ferryman the Devil's advice: "The next time someone wants to be taken across, just put the pole in his hands!"

He went on and came to the city where the barren tree stood, and there the watchman wanted his answer, too. He told him just what he had heard the Devil say: "Kill the mouse gnawing at the roots, and the tree will bear golden apples again." The watchman thanked him and as a reward gave him two donkeys loaded with gold— they had to follow him.

Finally he came to the city whose well had dried up. He told the watchman just what the Devil had said: "There's a toad under a stone in the well. You must find it and kill it, and then plenty of wine will flow again." The watchman thanked him, and he, too, gave him two donkeys loaded with gold.

At last the good-luck child got back home to his wife,

who was heartily glad to see him again and to hear how well everything had turned out. He brought the king what he had demanded—the Devil's three golden hairs. When the king saw the four donkeys with the gold, he was delighted and said, "Now every condition has been fulfilled, and you can keep my daughter. But please tell me, my dear son-in-law, where did you get all that gold? That's an enormous treasure!"

"I crossed a river," he answered, "and that's where I picked it up—the bank on the far shore is covered with gold instead of sand."

"Can I get some too?" asked the king, and he was all eagerness.

"As much as you want," he answered. "There's a ferryman on the river. Let him take you across, and then you can fill your sacks on the other side."

The greedy king set out in great haste, and when he came to the river, he signaled to the ferryman to take him across. The ferryman came and told him to get aboard, and when they reached the other side, he gave the pole to the king and jumped out. And from that time, the king had to run the ferry as punishment for his sins.

"Do you think he is still running it?"

"What do you think? Nobody is going to take the pole away from him."

BRIAR ROSE

||||||||||||||||||||||||||||||||||||||||||||

Once upon a time there were a king and queen who said each day, "Oh, if we only had a child!" but they never got one. Once while the queen was bathing, a frog crawled out of the water to the shore and said to her, "Before a year is up, you will give birth to a daughter."

It happened as the frog had said: the queen had a daughter who was so beautiful that the king was over-joyed and ordered a great feast. He invited not only his kinfolk, his friends, and his acquaintances, but also the wisewomen so they would be gracious and kind to the child. There were thirteen of them in his kingdom, but because he had only twelve golden plates for them to eat from, one of them had to stay home.

The feast was celebrated with all magnificence, and when it was over, the wisewomen presented the child with their magic gifts—one with virtue, the second with beauty, the third with riches, and so on, with everything in the world one could wish for.

After eleven of them had pronounced their blessings, the thirteenth suddenly entered. She wanted to avenge herself for not having been invited, and without a greet-ing or so much as a look for anyone, she cried in a loud voice: "In her fifteenth year, the king's daughter shall prick herself with a spindle and shall fall down dead." Without another word, she turned her back and left the hall.

Everyone was horrified, but the twelfth, who still had her wish, came forward. Since she could not revoke the curse but could only mitigate it, she said, "The king's daughter shall not die but shall fall into a deep sleep that shall last for a hundred years." The king, who wished to guard his beloved child against this misfortune, had orders given that all the spindles in the entire kingdom were to be burned. All the gifts of the wisewomen were fulfilled in the girl. She was so beautiful, virtuous, kind, and intelligent that she won the hearts of all who looked on her.

It happened that on her fifteenth birthday the king and queen were away from home, and the girl stayed behind all alone in the castle. She went about wherever she pleased, looking at the rooms and chambers, and came at last to an old tower. She climbed the narrow spiral staircase and arrived at a little door. A rusty key was in the lock, and when she turned it, the door sprang open. There in a little room sat an old woman with a spindle, busily spinning flax.

"How do you do, Granny," said the king's daughter. "What are you doing?"

"I'm spinning," said the old woman, nodding her head.

"What is that thing that bobs up and down so merrily?" asked the king's daughter and took the spindle because she wanted to spin too. But she had hardly touched the spindle when the magic spell was fulfilled, and she pricked her finger.

The very moment she felt the prick, she fell down on a bed, which was standing there, and lay in a deep sleep.

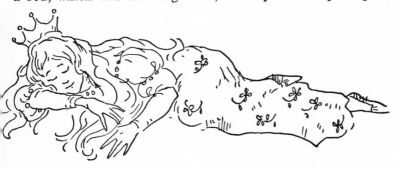

And the sleep spread throughout the castle. The king and queen, who had just come home and entered the hall, fell asleep, and with them the entire court. The horses went to sleep in the stable, the dogs in the courtyard, the pigeons on the roof, the flies on the wall—yes, even the fire flickering on the hearth grew still and slept, and the roast stopped sizzling, and the cook, who was about to pull the scullery boy's hair for some mistake, let him go and slept. The wind dropped, and not a leaf stirred on the trees in front of the castle.

A briar hedge began to grow around the castle. It got bigger each year, until at last it surrounded the castle completely and covered it so that nothing of the castle could be seen any more, not even the flag on the roof. But a legend arose in the land about the beautiful sleeping Briar Rose, for that is what they called the king's daughter, so that from time to time kings' sons came and tried to break through the hedge into the castle. But it was impossible because the briars clung tightly together as though they had hands, and the young men got caught in them and could not get free again so that they perished miserably.

After many long years another king's son came into the land and heard an old man telling about the briar hedge: there was supposed to be a castle behind it in which a wondrously beautiful king's daughter called Briar Rose had been sleeping for a hundred years, and with her slept the king and the queen and the entire court. His grandfather had told him that many kings' sons had already tried to penetrate the briar hedge, but they had got caught in it and died a wretched death. "I am not afraid," said the young man; "I will try to see the beautiful Briar Rose." No matter how much the good old man tried to warn him against it, he did not listen to him.

Now the hundred years was just up, and the day had come on which Briar Rose was to wake up again. When the king's son approached the briar hedge, it had become a mass of large and beautiful flowers that separated of themselves to let him pass unharmed, then closed behind him like a hedge.

In the courtyard he saw the horses and the spotted

hunting dogs lying asleep. On the roof the pigeons perched with their little heads nestled under their wings. And when he came into the house, the flies were asleep on the walls, the cook in the kitchen still held out his hand to grab the boy, and the kitchen maid was sitting before the black hen that she had to pluck. He continued on, and in the hall the entire court were lying asleep, and above them next to the throne lay the king and queen. He went still further on, and everything was so quiet that he could hear the sound of his own breathing.

Finally he came to the tower and opened the door to the little room where Briar Rose was sleeping. There she lay, so beautiful that he could not take his eyes from her, and he bent down and kissed her. At the touch of his kiss, Briar Rose opened her eyes, awoke, and looked at him very tenderly.

Together they went down, and the king and queen and the entire court woke up and looked at each other wide-eyed with astonishment. The horses in the court-yard got up and shook themselves; the hunting dogs jumped and wagged their tails; the pigeons on the roof pulled their heads out from under their wings, looked around, and flew off to the fields. The flies began to crawl along the walls; the fire in the kitchen blazed up and flickered and cooked the dinner; the roast started to sizzle again; the cook slapped the boy so that he cried out; and the kitchen maid finished plucking the hen.

And then the wedding of the king's son and Briar Rose was celebrated with all magnificence, and they lived happily for the rest of their lives.

SNOW WHITE

||||||||||||||||||||||||||||||||||||||||||||

Once upon a time in deep winter, when the snow-flakes were falling like feathers from the sky, a queen was sitting at a window with a black ebony frame, and she was sewing. And as she looked up from her sewing at the snow, she pricked her finger with the needle, and three drops of blood fell upon the snow. And because the red looked so beautiful against the white snow, she thought to herself, "If I might have a child as white as snow, as red as blood, and as black as the wood in the frame." Soon after that, she bore a little daughter who was as white as snow and as red as blood and had hair as black as ebony, and therefore she was called Snow White. And when the child was born, the queen died.

After a year the king took a second wife. She was a beautiful woman, but she was proud and disdainful, and she could not bear that anyone should excel her in beauty. She owned a wonderful mirror, and when she stepped in front of it to look at herself, she said:

> "Mirror, mirror, on the wall,
> Who is the fairest one of all?"

And the mirror replied:

"Lady Queen, you are the fairest one of all."

Then she was content, for she knew that the mirror
told the truth.

Snow White grew up and became ever more beautiful,
and when she was seven, she was as beautiful as the
bright day and more beautiful than the queen herself.
One time when the queen asked her mirror:

> "Mirror, mirror, on the wall,
> Who is the fairest one of all?"

it answered:

> "Lady Queen, you are fairest here, it's true,
> But Snow White is a thousand times more fair than you."

The queen started back, and she was yellow and green
with envy. From that hour, whenever she saw Snow White,
she felt a violent pang in her heart, she hated the
girl so much. And the envy and pride in her heart grew
like weeds, ever higher, so that day and night she had no
peace.

At last she summoned a huntsman and said, "Take the
child out into the forest. I never want to set eyes on her
again. You are to kill her and to bring me her lungs and
her liver as proof."

The huntsman obeyed and led her away, but when he
had drawn his hunting knife and was about to pierce
Snow White's innocent heart, she began to weep and
said, "Oh, dear huntsman, spare my life. I shall run into
the wild forest and never come home again."

And because she was so beautiful, the huntsman
took pity and said, "Run away, then, you poor child." He
was thinking, "The wild beasts will soon devour you," but
nevertheless, it was as if a stone had been rolled from his
heart because he did not have to kill her.

At that moment a young boar came rushing by, and
he killed it, cut out the lungs and the liver, and took them
to the queen as proof. The cook boiled them in salt,
and the wicked woman ate them, thinking that she was
eating Snow White's lungs and liver.

Now the poor child was left all forlorn in the great forest, and she was so frightened that she stared anxiously at all the leaves on the trees, and she didn't know what to do. Then she started running and ran over the sharp stones and through the brambles, and the wild beasts sprang past her but did her no harm. She ran as long as she could still take a step, until night began to fall. At last she saw a tiny little house and went inside to rest herself.

Everything in the little house was small, but neater and cleaner than words can tell. There stood a little table with a white cloth and seven little plates, each with its little spoon, and seven little knives and forks and seven little cups. Against the wall stood seven little beds in a row, covered with snowy-white sheets.

Snow White was so hungry and thirsty that she ate a few greens and a bit of bread from each little plate and drank a drop of wine from each little cup, for she did not want to take everything away from any single one. Next, because she was so tired, she lay down in a bed, but not one of them suited her; one was too long, the other too short, until finally the seventh was just right. There she remained, said her prayers, and fell asleep.

When it had grown quite dark, the owners of the little house returned. They were the seven dwarfs who quarried and mined for ore in the mountains. They lit their seven little candles, and when it became light in the house, they realized that someone had been there, for nothing was in the same order as they had left it.

The first one said, "Who has been sitting on my chair?"

The second, "Who has been eating from my plate?"

The third, "Who has taken some of my bread?"

The fourth, "Who has eaten some of my greens?"

The fifth, "Who has been using my fork?"

The sixth, "Who has been cutting with my knife?"

The seventh, "Who has been drinking out of my cup?"

Then the first turned around and saw a little crease in his bed, and he said, "Who has been lying on my bed?" The others came running and cried, "Someone has been lying on mine too."

But the seventh, when he looked at his bed, saw Snow

White lying there asleep. He called to the others, who ran up with cries of astonishment, fetched their seven little candles, and shone them on Snow White. "Ah, dear God! Ah, dear God!" they exclaimed. "How beautiful the child is!" And they were so overjoyed that they did not wake her but let her go on sleeping in the bed. The seventh dwarf slept one hour with each of his comrades, and then the night was over.

In the morning Snow White awoke, and when she saw the seven dwarfs, she was frightened. But they were friendly and asked, "What is your name?"

She answered, "My name is Snow White."

"How did you get to our house?" continued the dwarfs.

So she told them that her stepmother had wanted her killed but that the huntsman had spared her life and that she had run the whole day until at last she had found their little house.

The dwarfs said, "If you will look after our household, do the cooking, make our beds, do the washing, the sewing, and the knitting, and keep everything neat and clean, you may stay with us, and you shall lack nothing."

"Yes," said Snow White, "with all my heart." And she stayed with them and kept their house in order. In the morning they went into the mountains to look for ore and gold; in the evening they returned, and their supper had to be ready. Because she had to spend the whole day alone, the good little dwarfs warned her and said, "Beware of your stepmother—she will soon find out where you are. Do not let anyone in."

The queen, believing that she had eaten Snow White's lungs and liver, was certain that she was again supreme and that she was the most beautiful of all. She stepped in front of her mirror and said:

> "Mirror, mirror, on the wall,
> Who is the fairest one of all?"

And the mirror answered:

> "Lady Queen, you are fairest here, it's true,
> But over the mountains far away,

Where the seven dwarfs stay,
Snow White is a thousand times more fair than you."

She started back, for she knew that the mirror never lied, and she realized that the huntsman had deceived her and that Snow White was still alive. Then once again she thought and thought how she might kill her, for so long as she was not the most beautiful in the whole land, her envy gave her no peace.

Finally she hit on a plan. She smeared paint on her face and dressed herself like an old peddler woman so that no one could recognize her. In this disguise she went over the seven mountains to the house of the seven dwarfs. She knocked at the door and called out, "Fine wares for sale! Fine wares for sale!"

Snow White looked out of the window and called out, "Good day to you, my good woman; what are you selling?"

"Fine wares, pretty wares," she answered. "Laces of every color." And she got out one woven out of many gaily colored silks.

"I can let in this honest woman," thought Snow White, so she unbarred the door and purchased the pretty lace.

"Child," said the old woman, "just look at you! Come here and let me lace you up properly for once!" Snow White, who suspected nothing, stood in front of her to let herself be laced up with the new lace. But the old woman laced her so quickly and so tight that Snow White could not breathe and fell down as if dead. "Now you *were* the most beautiful," the queen said and hurried away.

Not long after that, toward evening, the seven dwarfs came home, but what a shock they got to see their beloved Snow White lying upon the ground without any motion or sign of life. They lifted her up, and seeing that she had been laced too tight, they cut the lace. Then she began to breathe faintly, and bit by bit she came back to life. When the dwarfs heard what had happened, they said, "The old peddler woman was none other than the evil queen. Beware, and don't let a soul into the house while we are away."

The wicked woman, as soon as she got home, went in front of her mirror and asked:

> "Mirror, mirror, on the wall,
> Who is the fairest one of all?"

And it answered as before:

> "Lady Queen, you are fairest here, it's true,
> But over the mountains far away,
> Where the seven dwarfs stay,
> Snow White is a thousand times more fair than you."

When she heard that, she was so startled that all the blood ran to her heart, for she realized that Snow White had come to life again.

"This time," she said, "I will think of something that will destroy you," and with witch's art, in which she was skilled, she made a poisoned comb. Then she disguised herself as a different old woman. Thus she went over the seven mountains to the house of the seven dwarfs. She knocked at the door and called out, "Fine wares for sale! Fine wares for sale!"

Snow White looked out and said, "You might as well go your way. I'm not allowed to let anyone in."

"Surely you are at least allowed to look," said the old woman, and she took out the poisoned comb and held it up. The child liked it so well that she let herself be taken in, and she opened the door.

When they had agreed on the price, the old woman said, "Now I'm going to comb you properly for once." Poor Snow White, suspecting nothing, let the old woman have her way. But no sooner had she stuck the comb into her hair than the poison began to work and the girl fell down unconscious. "You paragon of beauty," said the wicked woman, "now it's all over with you." And she went away.

Fortunately it was close to evening, when the seven dwarfs always came home. When they saw Snow White lying dead on the ground, they immediately suspected the stepmother, examined her, and found the poisoned comb. Hardly had they taken it out when Snow White came to herself and told what had happened. They warned her once more to be careful and not to open the door to anyone.

At home the queen stepped in front of the mirror and said:

> "Mirror, mirror, on the wall,
> Who is the fairest one of all?"

And it answered as it had before:

> "Lady Queen, you are fairest here, it's true,
> But over the mountains far away,
> Where the seven dwarfs stay,
> Snow White is a thousand times more fair than you."

When she heard what the mirror said, she trembled and quivered with rage. "Snow White must die," she cried, "if it costs me my life!"

With that, she went to a secret and lonely room where no one else ever entered, and there she made a poisoned apple. It was a beautiful sight, white with red cheeks, so that whoever saw it desired it, but whoever took just one little bite had to die. When the apple was finished, she daubed paint on her face and disguised herself as a farm woman. Thus she went over the seven mountains to the house of the seven dwarfs. She knocked, and Snow White put her head out the window and said, "I may not let anyone in. The seven dwarfs have forbidden it."

"Suits me just as well," answered the farm woman. "I'll have no trouble selling my apples. There, let me give you one."

"No," said Snow White, "I dare not accept anything."

"Are you afraid of poison?" said the old woman. "Look, I'll cut the apple in two—you eat the red half, and I'll eat the white half." However, the apple had been so skillfully made that only the red half was poisoned.

Snow White's mouth watered for the beautiful apple, and when she saw the farm woman eating part of it, she could resist no longer. She put out her hand and took the poisoned half. No sooner had she taken the first bite than she fell to the ground dead.

The queen leered at her horribly. She laughed scorn-

fully and said, "White as snow, red as blood, black as ebony! This time the dwarfs can't revive you again."
And at home when she asked the mirror:

> "Mirror, mirror, on the wall,
> Who is the fairest one of all?"

it finally answered:

> "Lady Queen, you are the fairest one of all."

Then at last her jealous heart was at peace, so far as a jealous heart can ever be at peace.
When the dwarfs came home in the evening, they

found Snow White lying on the ground. No breath came from her lips, and she was dead. They lifted her up and searched for a poisoned object, unlaced her, combed her hair, washed her with water and wine, but nothing did any good. The dear child was dead and stayed dead.

They laid her upon a bier and all seven of them sat around it mourning her, and they wept for three days. Then they started to bury her, but she still looked just as if she were alive, and she still had her beautiful red cheeks. They said: "We cannot lower her into the black earth." And they had a transparent coffin made of glass so that she could be seen from all sides. They laid her inside, and on it they inscribed her name in gold letters and that she was the daughter of a king. They placed the coffin on the mountain, and one of them always remained there to keep watch over it. And the birds came, too, and wept over Snow White, first the owl, then the raven, and last the dove.

Snow White lay a long time in the coffin, and her freshness did not fade; rather she looked as if she were asleep, for she remained as white as snow and as red as blood, and her hair was as black as ebony. It came to pass that a king's son wandered into the forest and came to the dwarfs' house to spend the night. On the mountain he saw the coffin and beautiful Snow White within it, and he read the gold-lettered inscription.

He said to the dwarfs, "Let me have the coffin. I will pay you whatever you ask."

But the dwarfs answered, "We would not exchange it for all the gold in the world."

He said, "Then give it to me as a present, for I cannot live without seeing Snow White. I will honor and cherish her as my dearest possession."

When he spoke in such a way, the good little dwarfs took pity on him and gave him the coffin. The king's son had it carried off on his servants' shoulders. Now it happened that they tripped over a shrub, and the jar caused the piece of poisoned apple Snow White had bitten off to fly out of her throat. In a little while, she opened her eyes, raised the lid of the coffin, sat up, and was alive again.

"Dear heaven, where am I?" she exclaimed.

The king's son said with great joy, "You are with me." He told her what had happened and said, "I love you more than anything in the world. Come with me to my father's castle, and you shall be my wife." And Snow White fell in love with him and went with him, and their wedding was celebrated with great pomp and magnificence.

Snow White's wicked stepmother was also asked to the feast. When she had dressed herself gorgeously, she stepped in front of the mirror and said:

> "Mirror, mirror, on the wall,
> Who is the fairest one of all?"

The mirror answered:

> "Lady Queen, you are fairest here, it's true,
> But the young queen is a thousand times more fair than
> you."

Then the wicked woman cursed and became so afraid, so terribly afraid, that she could not control herself. At first, she did not even want to go to the wedding, but she had no peace: she had to go and see the young queen.

When she entered, she recognized Snow White, and she stood there frozen with fear and terror. But already a pair of iron slippers had been placed on a charcoal fire. They were carried in with tongs and set down in front of her. And she had to step into the red-hot shoes and dance until she fell down dead to the ground.

OUR LADY'S CHILD

IIIIIIIIIIIIIIIIIIIIIIIIIIIIIIIIIIIIIIIIIIIIIIIIIIIIIIIIIIIIIIIIIIII

At the edge of a great forest lived a woodcutter and his wife. They had only one child, a little girl three years old. They were so poor, however, that they no longer had enough for their daily bread and didn't know how to find food for the child. One morning the woodcutter went off to work in the forest sorely troubled, and as he was chopping wood, suddenly a beautiful woman with a crown of shining stars on her head stood before him and said to him, "I am the Virgin Mary, the mother of the little Christ Child. You are poor and needy. Bring your child to me. I will take her with me, be her mother, and provide for her."

The woodcutter obeyed, fetched the child, and gave her to the Virgin Mary, who took her up to heaven. There she had a good life: she ate cake and drank sweet milk, she wore clothes made of gold, and the little angels played with her.

When she had reached the age of fourteen, the Virgin Mary summoned her one day and said: "Dear child, I am going away on a long journey. There, take charge of the keys to the thirteen doors in the kingdom of heaven. You may open twelve of them and look at the wonders inside, but the thirteenth, which this little key opens, is forbidden. Beware of opening it, or you will be very un-happy."

The girl promised to obey, and after the Virgin Mary had gone away, she began to look at the rooms in the kingdom of heaven. Each day she opened one, until she had seen the twelve. In each an apostle was sitting in shining glory, and all the majesty and splendor made her happy, and the little angels, who always accompanied her, were happy too.

Now only the forbidden door was left. Then she felt a great desire to know what was hidden behind it, and she said to the angels, "I won't open it all the way and I won't go inside, but I'll open it so that we can catch just a little glimpse through the crack."

"Oh, no," said the little angels. "That would be sinful. The Virgin Mary has forbidden it, and it could easily bring you misfortune." Then she was silent, but her secret longing would not be stilled and chafed and goaded her heart and would not let her rest.

One time, when all the little angels were out, she thought, "Now I am all alone and I could peek in because no one would see me do it." She picked out the key, and when she held it in her hand, she put it in the lock, and when she put it in the lock, she turned it. The door sprang open, and she saw the Trinity seated in fire and glory. She stood there a little while amazed, looking at everything. Then she just barely touched the glory with her finger, and the whole finger turned gold. Immediately she became terribly afraid, slammed the door, and ran away. But do what she might, the fear would not go away, and her heart beat rapidly and would not be quiet. The gold, too, remained on her finger and would not come off, no matter how much she washed and rubbed it.

It wasn't long before the Virgin Mary returned from her journey. She summoned the girl and told her to give back the keys of heaven. As she handed back the bunch of keys, the Virgin Mary looked into her eyes and said, "You did not open the thirteenth door?"

"No," she answered.

Then the Virgin Mary laid her hand on the child's heart and felt how it was beating and beating, and she knew very well that she had disobeyed and opened the door. Then she said once again, "Are you certain you did not do it?"

"No," said the girl for the second time.

Then the Virgin Mary noticed the finger that had turned gold from touching the heavenly fire, saw very well that she had sinned, and said a third time, "You did not do it?"

"No," said the girl for the third time.

Then the Virgin Mary said, "You did not obey me, and you have told a lie besides. You don't deserve to stay in heaven."

Then the girl fell into a deep sleep, and when she awoke she was lying in the middle of a wilderness down on earth. She wanted to cry out, but she could not make a sound. She sprang up and wanted to run away, but wherever she turned she was forced back by a thick hedge of thorns that she could not break through. In the wilderness where she was confined stood an old hollow tree; that is where she had to live. She crept there at night to sleep, and she found shelter there against the storm and the rain. But it was a wretched life, and when she remembered how beautiful it had been in heaven and how the angels had played with her, she wept bitterly. Roots and wild berries were her only nourishment, and she searched for them as far as it was possible for her to go. In the autumn she gathered the fallen leaves and nuts and carried them into the hollow tree. In winter the nuts provided her with food, and when the snow and ice came, she crept among the leaves like a poor little animal to keep from freezing. It wasn't long before her clothes were in tatters and fell away from her piece by piece. As soon as the warm sun was shining again, she came out to sit under the tree, and her long hair covered her completely like a cloak. She sat like that year after year and felt the grief and misery of the world.

One time, when the trees were fresh and green again, the king of that country was hunting in the forest, chasing a roe. It fled into the thicket around the clearing, so he dismounted, tore aside the briars, and hacked a path for himself with his sword. When he finally got to the other side, he saw a wondrously beautiful girl sitting under a tree. There she sat, and her golden hair covered her

down to her toes. He stood still and gazed at her, struck with amazement. Then he spoke to her and said, "Who are you? Why are you sitting here in this wilderness?"

She did not answer because she could not open her mouth.

The king continued, "Would you like to go with me to my castle?"

Then she nodded her head slightly.

The king took her in his arms, placed her on his horse, and rode home with her; and when he came to his royal castle, he had her dressed in beautiful clothes and gave her everything in abundance. And even though she could not talk, she was so sweet and beautiful that he fell deeply in love with her, and it was not long before he married her.

When about a year had gone by, the queen gave birth to a son. The next night, as she was lying in her bed alone, the Virgin Mary appeared to her and said, "If you will tell the truth and confess that you opened the forbidden door, I will open your mouth and give back your speech, but if you continue to sin and to deny it stubbornly, I will take your newborn child away with me."

Then the queen was permitted to answer, but she remained obstinate and said, "No, I did not open the forbidden door," and the Virgin Mary took the newborn child out of her arms and disappeared with it.

The next morning, when the child was nowhere to be found, a rumor spread among the people that the queen ate human flesh and had killed her own child. She heard all and could say nothing to defend herself, but the king would not believe it because he loved her so much.

After a year the queen gave birth to a second son. During the night the Virgin Mary appeared again and said, "If you will confess that you opened the forbidden door, I will return your child and set your tongue free, but if you continue to sin and to deny it, I will take this newborn child too."

Then the queen said again, "No, I did not open the forbidden door," and the Virgin took the child out of her arms and carried it away with her to heaven.

In the morning, when this child too had disappeared, the people said openly that the queen had devoured it, and the king's counselors demanded that she be brought to justice. But the king loved her so much that he would not believe it, and he commanded his counselors, as they valued their lives, not to speak of it again.

The next year the queen gave birth to a beautiful little daughter, and the Virgin Mary appeared for the third

time at night and said, "Follow me!" She took her by the
hand and led her to heaven, and there she showed her
the two older children, who were laughing and playing
with the globe of the world. When the queen rejoiced
at the sight, the Virgin Mary said, "Has your heart still
not softened? If you confess that you opened the forbidden door, I will give back your two little sons."

But the queen answered for the third time, "No, I did
not open the forbidden door." Then the Virgin let her
sink down to earth again, and she took the third child
away from her too.

The next morning, when the news spread, all the
people cried out, "The queen is an ogress. She must be
condemned," and the king could no longer overrule his
counselors. She was put on trial, and since she could not
answer to defend herself, she was sentenced to be burned
at the stake. The wood was piled up, and as she was
tied to the stake and the fire sprang up all around her, the
stubborn pride that had frozen her heart melted. She was
moved with remorse, and she thought, "If only I could
confess before I die that I opened the door."

Then she recovered her voice and cried out, "Yes,
Mary, I did do it!"

And immediately a rain fell from heaven and put out
the flames, and a light blazed out above her, and the
Virgin Mary came down with one little boy on each side
and the newborn daughter in her arms. She said to her
kindly, "Whoever is sorry for his sin and confesses it
shall be forgiven," and she returned the three children,
set free her tongue, and gave her happiness for the
rest of her life.

THE BREMEN
TOWN MUSICIANS

A certain man owned a donkey that for many long years had cheerfully borne sacks of grain to the mill, but now his strength was giving out so that he became less and less fit for work. His master decided to save the cost of his fodder, but the donkey suspected that the man was up to no good, ran away, and set out on the road to Bremen; he thought that there he could become a town musician.

After he had gone along for a little while, he found a hunting dog lying across the path, panting like an exhausted runner. "Well, what are you panting like that for, Hound Dog?" asked the donkey.

"Oh," sighed the dog, "because I'm old and get feebler day by day and can't keep up with the hunt anymore, my master wanted to get rid of me, so I took off. But how am I going to earn my bread now?"

"Do you know what?" said the donkey, "I'm on my way to Bremen to become a town musician. Come along, and you too can take up the music business. I'll play the guitar and you can beat the drums."

The dog liked the plan, and they went on together. It wasn't long before they met a cat sitting at the roadside making a face as gloomy as three rainy days. "Well, what's rubbed you the wrong way, Whiskers?" said the donkey.

"Who can be cheerful when he's about to get it in the neck?" answered the cat. "Because I'm getting along in years and my teeth are becoming blunt and I prefer sitting behind the stove and purring to chasing after mice, my mistress wanted to drown me. I managed to get away all right, but now I'm at a loss—where shall I go?"

"Come along with us to Bremen. You're a good serenader and you can become a town musician there." The cat thought this was a good idea and went along.

Next the three fugitives passed a farmyard where the cock was sitting on the gate and crowing with all his might. "You're crowing loud enough to split one's eardrums," said the donkey. "What are you up to?"

"I've just forecast fair weather," said the cock, "because it's the feast day of Our Lady, the day she washes the little shirts of the Christ Child and hangs them out to dry. But the mistress of the house has no mercy, and because guests are coming for Sunday dinner tomorrow, she told the cook that she wants to eat me in the stew. So tonight I'm supposed to get my head chopped off. Now I'm crowing with all my might while I still can."

"Nonsense, Redhead," said the donkey. "Better come along with us—we're going to Bremen. No matter where you go, you can find something better than getting yourself killed. You've got a good voice, and when we make music together, it's bound to have style." The cock took the advice, and all four set off together.

But they couldn't reach Bremen in one day, and in the evening they came to a forest, where they decided to spend the night. The donkey and the dog lay down under a big tree. The cat and the cock got up into the branches, but the cock flew to the very top, where he felt more at home. Before he went to sleep, he looked around once again in all four directions. It seemed to him that he saw a little spark of light in the distance, and he called down to his companions that there must be a house nearby because a light was shining.

The donkey said, "We'll have to get up again and go there—these are poor accommodations." The dog observed that a few bones with some meat on them would do him good. So they set out in the direction of the light and soon saw it gleaming brighter, and it got bigger and bigger, until they came up to a brightly lit house, which belonged to a gang of robbers.

The donkey, because he was the tallest, went up to the window and looked in. "What do you see, Old Gray Nag?" asked the cock.

"What do I see?" answered the donkey. "A table spread with good food and drink, and the robbers are sitting there having a good time."

"That would be something for us," said the cock.

"Yes, indeed, I wish we were inside," said the donkey. Then the animals held a council to see how they might chase out the robbers, and at last they found a way. The donkey put his two front hooves on the windowsill, the dog jumped onto the donkey's back, the cat climbed on top of the dog, and finally the cock flew up and sat on the head of the cat. When they had done this, at a signal they all began to make music together. The donkey brayed, the dog barked, the cat meowed, and the cock crowed. Then they plunged through the window into the room so that the panes rattled. The robbers jumped up at the ghastly noise. They were sure a ghost was coming in and fled into the forest in a panic. And now the companions sat down at the table, helped themselves with gusto to what was left, and ate as if they were going to starve for a month.

When the four performers had finished, they put out the light and looked for a place to sleep, each one where his kind would be most comfortable. The donkey stretched out on the manure pile, the dog behind the door, and the cat on the hearth beside the warm ashes, and the cock perched on the roofbeam. And being tired after their long journey, they soon went to sleep. After midnight the robbers saw from a distance that the light had gone out in the house and that everything seemed quiet. The captain said, "We were fools to let ourselves be frightened away by nothing," and he ordered one of his men to go and investigate the house.

The man he sent found that all was quiet. He went into the kitchen to get a light, and mistaking the glowing,

fiery eyes of the cat for live coals, he held a match to them. But the cat was not in a playful mood and sprang in his face, spitting and scratching. The man was terrified and ran to get out the back door, but the dog, who was lying there, jumped up and bit him on the leg, and as he ran through the yard past the manure pile, the donkey gave him a solid kick with his rear hoof, and the cock, who had been thoroughly aroused by the uproar, cried from the rafters: "Cock-a-doodle-doo."

The robber ran as fast as he could back to the captain and said, "Oh, there's a horrible witch in the house. She breathed in my face and scratched me with her long fingernails. There's a man with a knife standing by the door; he stabbed me in the leg. And there's a black monster lying in the yard; he started beating me with a club. And up on the roof, there sits the judge; he shouted, 'Bring the rascal to me!' So I got out of there."

From that time on, the robbers did not dare to enter the house, but the four Bremen town musicians liked it so much there that they decided never to leave.

And as for the person who just finished telling this story, his mouth is still watering.

Peter Christen Asbjörnsen and Jörgen Moe

‖‖‖

EAST OF THE SUN
AND
WEST OF THE MOON

‖‖‖

There was once a poor cotter who had a cottage full of children, but not much to give them either of food or of clothing. They were all fair, but the fairest of them all was the youngest daughter, who was so beautiful that the like of it had never been seen.

Now it was a Thursday evening late in autumn, the weather outside was bad, and it was as dark as pitch; it rained and blew so hard that the walls creaked. All of a sudden there were three raps on the pane. The man went out to see what was going on, and when he came outside, a great big white bear was standing there.

"Good evening to you!" said the white bear.

"Good evening!" said the man.

"If you will give me your youngest daughter, I will make you just as rich as you now are poor," said the white bear.

Well, the man thought it would be pretty fine to be so rich, but then he thought he had to talk with his daughter first. He went in and told her there was a big white bear outside who promised to make them very rich if only he could have her. She said "No," and wasn't any too willing, and so the man went out again and came to such terms with the white bear that he was to come back the next Thursday evening to get his answer. In the meantime, they gave her neither peace nor quiet; they talked and lectured to her about all the riches they would come into and how well off she herself would be, and at last she gave in. She washed and put her rags in order, and made herself as presentable as she could, and got ready to travel. Nor did she have much to take with her, either.

The next Thursday evening the white bear came to fetch her; she seated herself upon his back with her bundle, and then off they went.

When they had come a good bit on the way, the white bear said, "Are you afraid?"

No, that she wasn't, in any case.

"Well, just hold tight to my fur, then there's no danger either," he said.

She rode and she rode, and at long last they came to a big mountain. There the white bear knocked, and then a gate opened and they came into a castle; there were lights in every room, and it shone from both gold and silver, and then there was a great hall where a table stood decked, and it was so fine that you can't imagine how fine it was. Then the white bear gave her a silver bell; whenever there was anything she wanted, she should just ring it and she would get it. Well, after she had eaten and it was getting late, she became sleepy from the journey and thought she would like to go to bed; so she rang the bell, and scarcely had she touched it before she was in a chamber where a made-up bed was standing, as inviting as anyone could wish to lie in, with silken quilts and bed curtains and golden fringes; and everything there was of gold and silver. But when she had gone to bed and blown out the candle, a man came in and lay down beside her. It was the white bear, who threw off his skin at night; but she never saw him, for he always came after she had blown out the candle, and before it was light in the morning, he was gone again.

It went both fine and well for a while; but then she came to be so quiet and downcast because she went about there so alone the whole day and was homesick for her parents and her brothers and sisters. When the white bear asked what ailed her, she said it was so dull there, she was so lonesome and longed to go home to her parents and her brothers and sisters, and it was because she couldn't go to them that she was so sad. "That can easily be arranged," said the white bear, "but you shall promise me one thing: that you won't talk with your mother alone, but only when others are listening. For she'll take you by the hand," he said, "and will want to take you in a chamber and talk with you alone; but that you mustn't do by any means or else you will bring misfortune upon us both!"

One Sunday the white bear came and said that now they could journey to her parents. Well, they set out. She sat on his back, and they went both far and wide; at last they came to a big white manor. There her brothers and sisters were running in and out playing, and it was so lovely that it was a joy to behold. "There live your parents," said the white bear, "but don't forget what I've told you or else you'll make us both unhappy!" No, of course she wouldn't forget, and when she was there, the white bear turned around again and was gone.

There was no end to the rejoicing when she came in to her parents; they didn't think they could thank her enough for what she had done for them; now they were so well off, and then they all wanted to know how she was getting along where *she* was. She was very well off and had everything she could wish for, she said; what she answered to the rest, I'm not able to say, but I don't think they really got it straight.

But then in the evening, after they had eaten dinner, it happened just as the white bear had said: the mother wanted to talk with her alone in the chamber. But she remembered what the white bear had said, and wasn't at all willing. "Whatever we have to talk of," she said, "we can always say it here." But however it happened or didn't, the mother persuaded her at last, and then she had to tell how she was getting on.

She said that a man always came and lay down beside her after she had blown out the candle in the evening, but she never saw him, for he was always gone before it was light in the morning. She was so unhappy about that, for she thought she would like to see him, and during the day it was so dull there because she went about alone.

"*Huff!* It may very well be a troll you're sleeping with!" said the mother. "But now I'll teach you a remedy so you can catch a glimpse of him. I'll give you a candle stub, which you can hide in your bodice; then shine the light on him while he sleeps, but take good care not to drip tallow on him!"

Well, she took the candle and hid it in her bodice; and in the evening the white bear came and fetched her.

When they had come a bit on the way, the white bear asked if it hadn't gone as he had said.

Why yes, that she couldn't deny.

"If you have followed your mother's advice, you have brought misfortune upon us both, and then it's over between us," he said.

No, she hadn't done that at all.

Now when she had come home and gone to bed, it went the way it usually did: a man came in and lay down beside her. But later on in the night, when she heard that he was asleep, she got up and struck a light and lit the candle and shone it on him, and then she saw it was the handsomest prince anyone could wish to behold, and she fell so in love with him that she thought she would die if she didn't kiss him that very moment. She did it, too, but at the same moment she dripped three hot drops of tallow onto his shirt, so that he woke up.

"Oh, what have you done now?" he said. "Now you've brought misfortune upon us both. If only you had held out the year, I would have been freed, for I have a stepmother who has bewitched me so that I am a white bear by day and a man by night. But now it's over between us. Now I must leave you and go to her. She lives in a castle that lies east of the sun and west of the moon, and there's a princess there with a nose three ells long, and her I must have now!"

She cried and carried on, but there was nothing to be done about it; go he must. Then she asked if she couldn't go with him.

No, that could never be!

"Can't you tell me the way? Then I can search for you. Surely I could be allowed to do that?" she said.

Yes, that she could. But there were no roads there;

it lay east of the sun and west of the moon, it did, and she'd never find her way there.

In the morning, when she woke up, both the prince and the castle were gone; she was lying on a little green spot right in the midst of a deep, dark forest, and beside her was lying the same bundle of rags she had brought with her from home. Now, after she had rubbed the sleep from her eyes and cried until she was tired, she set out on the way; and then she walked for many, many days until she came to a big mountain.

Outside it was sitting an old hag who was playing with a golden apple. She asked her if she knew the way to the prince who lived with his stepmother in a castle that lay east of the sun and west of the moon and who was to have a princess with a nose three ells long.

"Where do you know him from?" asked the old hag. "Maybe you were to have had him?"

Yes, that she was.

"So it's you, is it?" said the hag. "Well, I don't know any more about him, I don't, except that he lives in that castle that is east of the sun and west of the moon, and you'll get there either late or never. But you can borrow my horse, and then you can ride on it to my neighbor; maybe she can tell you. And when you get there, you can just tap the horse under its left ear and tell it to go home again. And you can take this golden apple with you."

She seated herself on the horse and rode for a long, long time, and at last she came to a big mountain; there sat an old hag outside, winding yarn on a golden reel. She asked her if she knew the way to the castle that lay east of the sun and west of the moon. She said, like the other hag, that she didn't know anything about it, but it was east of the sun and west of the moon all right. "And you'll get there either late or never; but you can borrow my horse to ride to my closest neighbor; maybe she just might know it, and when you get there, you can just tap it under the left ear and tell it to go home again." And then she gave her the golden reel, for she'd probably have use for that, she said.

The girl seated herself on the horse and rode for ever

so long again, and at long last she came to a big mountain; there sat an old hag spinning on a golden spinning wheel. She asked her if she knew the way to the prince and where the castle was that lay east of the sun and west of the moon.

Then it went just as before: "Maybe you were to have had the prince there?" said the hag.

Yes, that she was.

But she didn't know the way any better than the other two; east of the sun and west of the moon it was, that she knew. "And you'll get there either late or never," she said, "but you can borrow my horse. Then I think you'd better ride to the East Wind and ask him; maybe he knows the way and can blow you there. When you get there, you can just tap the horse under the ear so it'll come home again," said the hag. And then she gave her the golden spinning wheel. "Maybe it will come in handy," said the hag.

She rode for ever so long before she was there, but at long last she arrived, and then she asked the East Wind if *he* could tell her the way to the prince who lived east of the sun and west of the moon.

Yes, he'd heard tell of that prince all right, said the East Wind, and of the castle too. But he didn't know the way, for he'd never blown so far. "But if you like, I'll take you to my brother the West Wind. Maybe he knows, for he's much stronger. You can sit on my back and I'll carry you there."

Well, this she did, and it went pretty briskly. When they got there, they went in, and the East Wind said he had with him the one who was to have had the prince in the castle that lay east of the sun and west of the moon; now she was searching for him, and so he had brought her here to find out if the West Wind knew where it was.

"No, so far have I never blown," said the West Wind, "but if you like, I'll take you to the South Wind, for he's much stronger than either of us, and he's blown both far and wide; maybe he can tell you. You can sit on my back and I'll carry you there."

Well, she did just so! They went to the South Wind, and didn't take long on the way, I daresay. When they got there, the West Wind asked if *he* could tell the girl the way to the castle that lay east of the sun and west of the moon; she was the one who was to have had the prince there.

"That so?" said the South Wind. "Is it she? Well, indeed, I've visited practically every place a bit in my time," he said, "but so far away I've never blown. But if you like, I'll take you to my brother the North Wind. He's the oldest and the strongest of us all, and if he doesn't know where it is, then you'll never in the world find out. You can sit on my back and I'll carry you there."

Well, she sat on his back, and he set out, and it didn't take long either.

When they came to where the North Wind lived, he was so wild and furious that cold gusts blew off him from afar.

"WHAT DO YOU WANT?" he shrieked from a long way off, chilling them to the bone.

"Oh, you needn't be so bleak now," said the South Wind, "for it's me and then I've brought the girl who was to have had the prince who lives in the castle east of the sun and west of the moon, and now she'd like to ask if you've been there and can tell her the way, for she'd so like to find him again."

"Yes, I know where it is, all right," said the North Wind. "I blew an aspen leaf there once, but then I was

so tired I wasn't able to blow for many days afterward.
But if it's true that you still want to go there and you're
not afraid to go with me, then I'll take you on my back
and try to blow you there."

Yes, she would and she must go there if there was
any possible way of getting there, and she wasn't frightened, no matter how wrong it might go.

"Very well, then you'll have to spend the night here,"
said the North Wind, "for we'll need the whole day and
then some if we're to get there."

Early the next morning the North Wind woke her, and
blowing himself up, he made himself so big and strong
that it was terrible; and then off they went, high up and
away through the air as if they were going to the world's
end that very moment. Down below there was such a
storm that both houses and whole forests were blown
down, and when they came out over the great sea, ships
went down by the hundreds. Thus they flew on, so far,
so far that no one can imagine how far they flew, and
always they headed out to sea; and the North Wind
grew wearier and wearier, and so worn out that he
could hardly blow any longer, and he sank lower and
lower, and at last he was so low that the tops of the
waves were beating about her heels.

"Are you afraid?" said the North Wind.

No, she said, that she wasn't.

But they weren't far from land either, and the North
Wind had so little strength left that he was barely able
to throw her onto the shore under the windows of the
castle that lay east of the sun and west of the moon.
But now he was so tired and worn out that he had to
rest for many days before he could come home again.

The next morning she sat down outside the windows of
the castle and started playing with the golden apple, and
the first thing she saw was that long-nose who was to
have the prince.

"You there! What'll you have for that golden apple of
yours?" she said, opening the window a crack.

"It's not for sale for either gold or money," said the
girl.

"If it's not for sale for gold or money, what do you

want for it? You can have anything you want," said the princess.

"Well, if I can come up to the prince who is here and spend the night with him, you can have it," said the girl who had come with the North Wind.

Yes, that she could do all right. That could be arranged.

The princess got the golden apple. But when the girl came up to the prince's room in the evening, he was fast asleep; she shouted at him and shook him, and in between she cried, but she wasn't able to wake him, for they had given him a sleeping potion in the evening. In the morning, at daybreak, the princess with the long nose came and chased her out again.

Later on in the day she seated herself outside the windows of the castle and started winding yarn on the golden reel, and it went just as before. The princess asked what she wanted for it, and she said that it was not for sale for either gold or money, but if she could be allowed to come up to the prince and spend the night with him, she could have it. But when she came up there, he was asleep again, and for all she shouted and shrieked and shook him, and for all she cried, he slept so hard that she couldn't for the life of her wake him up; and as day was breaking, the princess with the long nose came and chased her out the door again.

Later on in the day, the girl sat down outside the windows of the castle and started spinning on the golden spinning wheel, and the princess with the long nose wanted this too. She opened the window and asked what she wanted for it. The girl said, as she had the other two times, that it wasn't to be had for gold or money, but if she could just come up to the prince who was there and spend the night with him, she could have it. Yes, that she could do.

Now, there were some Christian folk who had been captured there, and they had been sitting in the room next to the prince's chamber. They had heard a woman in there crying and shouting at him for two nights in a row, and they told this to the prince. In the evening, when the princess came with the sleeping potion, he pretended to drink, but threw it behind him, for he now understood that it would make him sleep.

When the girl came in this time, the prince was awake, and she had to tell him how she had come there. "Well, now you've really arrived in the nick of time," said the prince, "for tomorrow I was to have been wed. But I don't want that long-nose, and you're the only one who can save me. I'll say that I want to see what my bride can do and ask her to wash the shirt with the three drops of tallow on it. This she'll agree to, for she doesn't know that you've made them, but it takes Christian folk to do that and not a pack of trolls like this. And then I'll say that I won't have anyone for my bride but the one who can do it. And you can do it, that I know."

Well, there was great joy and rapture that night. But the next day, when the wedding was to take place, the prince said, "I want to see what my bride can do first."

Yes, that could be, said the stepmother.

"I have a fine shirt that I'd like to wear for my wedding shirt, but I've gotten three drops of tallow on it, which I want washed out, and I've sworn that I will take only the one who is able to do it; if she can't do that, then she's not worth having!"

Well, that was an easy matter, they thought, and this they agreed to; and the princess with the long nose started washing as best she could. But the more she washed and rubbed, the bigger the spots grew.

"Oh, you don't know how to wash!" said the old troll hag, her mother. "Let me have it!" But scarcely had she taken hold of the shirt before it became even uglier; and the more she washed and rubbed it, the bigger and blacker the spots grew.

Then the other trolls were going to wash it, but the longer it went on, the dirtier and nastier it became, until at last the whole shirt looked as though it had been up the chimney.

"Oh you're no good, none of you!" said the prince. "There's a tramp of a girl sitting outside the windows here. I'm sure she's much better at washing than any of you. You there, come in!" he shouted.

Well, in she came.

"Can you wash this shirt clean?" he said.

"Oh, I don't know," she said. "I'll have to try."

And scarcely had she touched the shirt and dipped it

in the water before it was as white as the newly fallen snow, and even whiter.

"Well, you're the one I'll have!" said the prince.

Then the old troll hag became so angry that she burst, and the princess with the long nose and the other small trolls must have burst too, for I haven't heard any more about them since. The prince and his bride let out all the Christian folk who had been captured there, and then they took with them as much gold and silver as they could carry and moved far, far away from the castle that lay east of the sun and west of the moon.

Peter Christen Asbjörnsen

IIIIIIIIIIIIIIIIIIIIIIIIIIIIIIIIIIIIIIIIIIIIIIIIIIIIIIIIIIIIIIIIIII

THE COMPANION

IIIIIIIIIIIIIIIIIIIIIIIIIIIIIIIIIIIIIIIIIIIIIIIIIIIIIIIIIIIIIIIIIII

There was once a peasant boy who dreamed he was to wed a king's daughter in a far-off land; and she was as red and as white as milk and blood and so rich that there could never be an end to her riches. When he awoke, it seemed to him that she was still standing before him in the flesh, and he thought her so fine and pretty that he could not live if he did not marry her. So he sold all he owned and set out into the world to seek her.

He walked far, and farther than far, and in the winter he came to a land where all the highways lay end to end in a straight line and made no turning. When he had wandered straight ahead a three-months' time, he came to a city; and outside the church door stood a big block of ice with a body inside it, and the whole congregation spat on it as they went past.

The boy wondered about this, and when the parson came out of the church, he asked him what it was all about.

"That is a grievous evildoer," said the parson. "He has been put to death for the sake of his ungodliness and set up there to be scoffed and scorned."

"What did he do, then?" asked the boy.

"In this life he was a wine tapper," said the parson, "and he mixed the wine with water!"

That didn't seem to the boy to be such an evil deed, and as long as he had paid for it with his life, they might just as well let him have a Christian burial and rest in peace after death.

No, said the parson, that could never be, not in any shape or form; for folk were needed to break him out of the ice, money was needed to buy consecrated ground from the church, the gravedigger had to be paid for the grave, the sexton for the hymns, and the parson for the commitment.

"Do you think anyone would pay all that for an executed sinner?" he asked.

Yes, said the boy, once he got him into the ground, *he* certainly would pay for the burial out of the little he had.

So they broke the wine tapper out of the block of ice and laid him in consecrated ground; they rang and sang over him, and the parson scattered on the earth, and they caroused so at the burial feast that they laughed and cried by turns.

But when the boy had paid for the burial feast, he hadn't many shillings left in his pocket.

He set out on his way again, but he hadn't gone far before a man caught up with him and asked if he didn't think it was dreary to walk alone.

No, the boy didn't think so, for he always had something to think about, he said.

But maybe he might need a servant all the same, asked the man.

"No," said the boy. "I'm used to being my own servant, and even if I wanted to ever so much, I couldn't afford one, for I haven't money for board and wages."

"You need a servant; I know that better than you," said the man, "and you need a servant you can rely on in life and death. If you won't have me for a servant, you can take me as a companion. I promise that you will benefit by me, and it shan't cost you a shilling. I shall transport myself, and there won't be any need for food and clothing."

Well, on these conditions he'd be glad to have him as a companion.

From then on they traveled together, and most of the time the Companion went ahead and showed the way.

When they had traveled a long way through many a land, over hill and dale, they came to a mountain spur. Here the Companion knocked and bade whoever was inside to open up. An opening appeared in the rock, and when they had gone a long way inside the mountain, a Troll hag came forth with a chair and bade them, "Pray sit down. You must be tired," she said.

"Sit down yourself!" said the man.

So she had to sit down, and when she was seated, she remained sitting there, for the chair was such that it did not let go whatever came near it. In the meantime they walked about inside the mountain, and the Companion looked around until he caught sight of a sword hanging over the door. He insisted on having it, and in return he promised the Troll hag that he would let her out of the chair.

"Nay!" she shrieked. "Ask me for anything else! You can have anything else, but not that, for that's my three-sister sword!" There were three sisters who owned it together.

"Then you can sit there until the end of the world," said the man.

But when she heard that, she said he could have the sword if only he would let her go.

So he took the sword and left with it, but he left her sitting there just the same.

When they had gone a long way, over bare mountains and broad moors, they came to another mountain spur. There the Companion knocked and bade whoever was inside to open up. The same thing happened as before: an opening appeared, and when they had gone a long way inside the mountain, a Troll hag came forth with a chair and bade them sit down; they must be tired, she said.

"Sit down yourself," said the Companion, and then she fared just as her sister. She dared not do otherwise, and when she sat down in the chair, she remained sitting there.

In the meantime the boy and the Companion walked about inside the mountain, and the Companion opened all the cupboards and drawers until he found what he was looking for: a ball of golden yarn. He insisted on having it, and he promised the Troll hag that if she would give it to him, he would let her out of the chair. She said he could have anything else she owned, but *that* she didn't want to lose, for it was her three-sister ball. But when she heard she would be sitting there until Doomsday if he didn't get it, she said he'd better take it all the same if only he would let her go. The Companion took it, but he left her sitting where she was.

Then they walked for many days, over moors and through forests, until they came to another mountain spur. There the same thing happened as before: the Companion knocked, an opening appeared, and inside the mountain a Troll hag came up with a chair and bade them sit down. But the Companion said, "Sit down yourself," and there she sat. They hadn't gone through many of the rooms before he caught sight of an old hat hanging on a peg behind the door. The Companion wanted to have it, but the hag wouldn't part with it, for it was her three-sister hat, and if she gave *that* away she would be downright unhappy. But when she heard that she would have to remain sitting until the end of the world if he didn't get it, she said he could take it if only he would let her go. When the Companion had safely got hold of the hat, he left her sitting where she was, just like her sisters.

At long last they came to a fiord. There the Companion took the ball of golden yarn and threw it so hard against the cliff on the other side of the water that it came back again; and when he had thrown it a few times it became a bridge. They went over the fiord on it, and when they were on the other side, the man bade the boy wind up the yarn again as fast as he could. "For if we don't get it up quickly, the three Troll hags will come and tear us to bits!" he said. The boy started winding as fast as he could, and when no more than the last thread was left, the Troll hags came rushing up. They plunged down into the water so the spray rose before them, and made a grab at the end; but they couldn't get hold of it, and so they were drowned in the fiord.

When they had walked some days more, the Companion said, "Now we shall soon come to the castle where she lives—the king's daughter that you've dreamed of. And when we get there, you must go in and tell the king what you've dreamed and what you're searching for."

When they arrived, the boy did just as he had been told, and he was quite well received; he was given a room to himself and one for his servant, which they were to stay in, and when it was getting on toward dinnertime, he was invited to sit at the king's own table.

When he set eyes on the king's daughter, he recognized her right away and said that she was the one he had dreamed he was to marry. He told her his errand, and she replied that she liked him well and would as soon take him. But first, she said, he must undergo three trials. When they had eaten, she gave him a pair of golden scissors, and then she said, "The first trial is that you must take these scissors and hide them, and give them back to me again tomorrow at midday. That's not a difficult trial, I hardly think," she said, making a face. "But if you fail, you'll lose your life; that's the law. And then you'll be executed and broken on the wheel, and your head placed on a stake, just like those suitors whose skulls you see outside the windows!" Men's skulls were hanging around the king's manor like crows sitting on the fence pickets in the fall.

That was easy enough, thought the boy. But the king's daughter was so frolicsome and wild and rollicked with him so that he forgot both the scissors and himself; and while they were romping and disporting themselves, she stole the scissors from him when he wasn't looking.

When he came up to his chamber in the evening and related what had happened and what she had said about the scissors she had given him to hide, the Companion said, "You do have the scissors she gave you?"

He felt about in his pockets, but no scissors were there, and the boy was more than beside himself when he realized they were gone.

"Well, well, have patience. I'll have to try to get them

back for you again," said the Companion, and went down
to the stable. There stood a great big ram which belonged to the king's daughter, and it could fly many
times faster through the air than walk on the ground.
So he took the three-sister sword and struck it between
its horns and said, "When does the king's daughter
ride to her lover tonight?"

The ram bleated and said it dared not say, but when it
was struck one more blow, it said that the king's daughter
would come at eleven o'clock. The Companion put on the
three-sister hat, which made him invisible, and waited
until she came. She smeared the ram with a salve which
she had in a great horn, and then she said, "Aloft! Aloft!
Over rooftree and church spire, over land, over water,
over hill, over dale, to my lover, who waits for me in the
mountain tonight!"

At the same moment as the ram set off, the Companion flung himself onto its back, and off they went like the
wind through the air. They weren't long on the way. All at

once they came to a mountain spur. There she knocked, and they passed inside the mountain to the Troll who was her lover.

"Now a new suitor has come to woo me, my friend," said the king's daughter. "He's young and handsome, but I won't have anyone else but you," she said, making herself pleasing to the Mountain Troll. "So I put him to a test, and here are the scissors he was to hide and look after. You take care of them now," she said. Then they both laughed heartily, as though the boy were already being broken on the wheel.

"Yes, I'll hide them, and I'll take care of them! And I'll be sleeping in the arms of the bride when the raven pecks at the boy's insides!" said the Troll, and put the scissors in an iron casket which had three locks. But at the same moment as he dropped the scissors into the casket, the Companion took them. Neither of them could see him, for he was wearing the three-sister hat, and so the Troll locked the casket for nothing, and he hid the keys in the hollow tooth where he had a toothache. The boy would have a hard time finding it there, he thought.

When it was getting on past midnight, the princess went home again. The Companion sat on the ram behind her, and they weren't long on the homeward journey.

At dinnertime the boy was invited to dine at the king's table, but now the king's daughter made such bored grimaces and she sat so stiff and straight that she would hardly look in the direction where the boy was sitting.

When they had eaten, she put on her most angelic expression, made herself as sweet as butter, and said, "Perhaps you have the scissors I asked you to hide yesterday?"

"Yes, I have. There they are," said the boy, and he pulled them out and drove them into the table so that plates and dishes jumped. The king's daughter couldn't have been more uncomfortable if he'd hurled the scissors in her face. But she made herself nice and sweet all the same, and said, "Since you've taken such good care of the scissors, it won't be difficult for you to hide my ball of golden yarn and take care of it so that you can give it back to me by midday tomorrow. But if you haven't got it, then you'll lose your life and be put to death, for that's the law," she said.

That was an easy matter, thought the boy, and put the ball in his pocket. But she started joking and rollicking with him again, so he forgot both himself and the ball; and while they were romping and disporting themselves to their heart's content, she stole it from him and let him go.

When he came up to his chamber and told the Companion what they had said and done, he asked, "You do have the ball of golden yarn which she gave you?"

"Yes, I have it," said the boy and grabbed at the pocket where he had put it. But no, he hadn't any golden ball, and now he was so beside himself again that he didn't know what to do.

"All right, have patience," said the Companion. "I'll have to try to get hold of it," he said, and taking the sword and the hat, he strode off to a blacksmith and had twelve iron crowbars put on his sword.

When he came into the stall, he gave the ram a blow between the horns with the sword so that the sparks flew, and then he asked, "When does the king's daughter ride to her lover tonight?"

"Twelve o'clock," bleated the ram.

The Companion put on the three-sister hat again and waited until she came rushing in with the horn and smeared the ram. Then she said, like the first time, "Aloft! Aloft! Over rooftree and church spire, over land, over water, over hill, over dale, to my lover, who waits for me in the mountain tonight!"

Just as they set off, the Companion jumped up onto the ram's back, and they went like the wind through the air. All at once they came to the Troll mountain, and when she had knocked three times, they flew in to the Troll who was her lover.

"How did you hide the golden scissors I gave you yesterday, my friend?" asked the king's daughter. "My suitor had them and gave them back to me again," she said.

That was downright impossible, said the Troll, for he had locked them in a casket with three locks and hidden the keys in his hollow tooth. But when they opened it up to look for them, the Troll had no scissors in the casket. Then the king's daughter told him that she had given the suitor her ball of golden thread.

"Here it is," she said, "for I took it from him when he wasn't looking. But what shall we think of now, since he knows such tricks?"

Well, the Troll didn't quite know. But when they had thought about it a bit, they decided to make a big fire and burn the golden ball. Then they'd be certain that he couldn't get hold of it. But at the same moment as she threw the yarn onto the fire, the Companion was ready and grabbed it, and neither of them saw him take it, for he was wearing the three-sister hat!

When the king's daughter had been with the Troll awhile and it was getting on toward morning, she went home again. The Companion sat on the ram behind her, and they traveled both fast and well.

When the boy was invited to dinner, the Companion gave him the ball. The king's daughter was even more stiff and staid than the last time, and when they had eaten, she pursed her lips and said, "I don't suppose it's likely that I'll get back my ball of golden yarn which I gave you yesterday to hide?"

"Why, yes," said the boy. "You shall have it. Here it is!" And he threw it down on the table so that the table jumped and the king hopped high in the air.

The king's daughter turned as pale as a corpse. But she soon made herself cheerful again and said that it was well done. Now she had only one more little trial. "If you're clever enough to fetch me what I'm thinking about by midday tomorrow, then I'm yours to have and to hold," she said.

The boy felt as though he had been sentenced to death, for he thought there was no way of knowing what she was thinking about, let alone getting it for her; and when he went up to his chamber, it was almost impossible to calm him. But the Companion told him not to worry. *He* would take care of the matter just as he had done on the other two occasions. And at last the boy calmed down and went to sleep.

In the meantime, the Companion rushed off to the blacksmith and had twenty-four iron crowbars put on his sword. And when that was done, he went to the stall and gave the ram such a blow between the horns that the sound rang around the walls.

"When does the king's daughter go to her lover tonight?" he said.

"One o'clock," bleated the ram.

As the hour approached, the Companion waited in the stall with the three-sister hat on. And when the princess had smeared the ram and said what she usually said, that they were to fly through the air to her lover, who was waiting for her in the mountain, they were off through wind and weather again, with the Companion sitting behind. But this time he wasn't gentle, for all at once he gave the king's daughter a squeeze here and a squeeze there, so hard that he almost crippled her for life. When they came to the mountain spur, she knocked on the gate until it opened, and they flew in through the mountain to her lover.

When she got there, she wailed and carried on and said that she didn't know the weather could be so rough. But she thought there must have been someone along beating both her and the ram; and indeed she was both black and blue all over her body, so badly had she fared on the way. And then she said that the suitor had found the ball of golden yarn too; how that had happened neither she nor the Troll could understand.

"But do you know what I've hit upon now?" she said.

No, the Troll couldn't know that.

"Well," she replied, "I've told him to get me what I'm thinking about by midday tomorrow, and that was your head. Do you think he can get *that*, my friend?" she said and hugged the Troll.

"I hardly think so!" said the Troll, and he swore to that, and then he laughed and roared, worse than a spirit in torment. And both the king's daughter and the Troll thought that before the boy could get the Troll's head he would be broken on the wheel and the ravens would peck out his eyes.

As it was getting on toward morning, she had to go

home again. But she was afraid, she said, for she thought
there was someone behind her, and she dared not go
home alone. The Troll would have to see her home. Yes,
he'd go with her, and he got out his ram, for he had
one like the king's daughter's, and smeared it well between the horns too. When the Troll had seated himself,
the Companion mounted behind *him,* and off they went
through the air, back to the king's manor. But on the
way the Companion struck the Troll and the ram and
dealt them blow upon blow with his sword so that they
sank lower and lower, and at last they were almost on
the point of sinking in the sea they were flying over.
When the Troll realized he was so far out of the way, he
followed the king's daughter straight back to the king's
manor and waited outside to see that she got home safe
and sound. But at the very moment she closed the door
behind her, the Companion cut off the Troll's head and
strode up to the boy's chamber.

"This is what the king's daughter is thinking about!"
he said.

Now, that was both well and good, you might know,
and when the boy was invited down to dinner and had
eaten, the king's daughter was as happy as a lark.

"Perhaps you have what I was thinking about?" she
said.

"Indeed I have!" said the boy. He pulled it out from
under the flap of his robe and threw it on the table so
that the table and all the things on it were overturned.
The king's daughter was as pale as if she had lain in the
ground, but she couldn't deny that it was what she had
been thinking about, and now he was to have her, as she
had promised. So the wedding was celebrated, and there
was great joy throughout the whole kingdom.

But the Companion took the boy aside and told him
that he could close his eyes and pretend he was asleep
on the wedding night, but if he valued his life and
would listen to him, he mustn't sleep a wink before he
had rid her of the Trollhide which she was wearing. He
was to beat it off her with the twigs of nine new birch
brooms and then rub it off her in three tubs of milk:
first he was to scrub her in a tub of last year's whey,

and then he was to rub her in sour milk, and then he was to rinse her in a tub of sweet milk. The brooms lay under the bed, and he had put the tubs in the corner. It was all ready. Well, the boy promised he would heed him and do as he said.

When they went to the marriage bed in the evening, the boy pretended to go to sleep. The king's daughter raised herself on her elbows to see if he were asleep and tickled him under the nose. The boy went on sleeping just as soundly as before. Then she pulled his hair and beard, but he still slept like a log, she thought. Then she took out a big butcher's knife from under the pillow and was going to hack off his head, but the boy jumped up, knocked the knife out of her hand, and grabbed her by the hair. Then he beat her with the broom twigs and went on thrashing her until there wasn't a stick left. When *that* was done, he threw her in the tub of whey, and then he saw what kind of animal she was: she was as black as a raven all over her body. But when he'd scrubbed her in whey and rubbed her in sour milk and rinsed her in sweet milk, the Trollhide was gone and she was sweet and pretty as she had never been before.

Next day the Companion told him that they had to leave. Well, the boy was ready to travel, and the king's daughter too, for the dowry had long since been ready. During the night, the Companion had carried all the gold and silver and precious things the Troll had left in the mountain to the king's manor, and when they were about to leave in the morning, the yard was so full that they could hardly get out. The dowry was worth more than the king's land and kingdom itself, and they didn't know how they were to carry it with them. But the Companion knew a way out of all difficulty. There were six of the Troll's rams left, which could fly through the air. These they loaded with so much gold and silver that they had to walk on the ground and weren't able to raise themselves and fly with it. And what the rams couldn't carry had to remain at the king's court. So they journeyed far, and farther than far, but at last the rams became so tired that they weren't able to go another step. The boy and the king's daughter didn't know what to do, but when the Companion saw that they couldn't move, he put the whole load on his back, placed the rams on top, and carried it so far that there wasn't much more than half a mile left to where the boy had his home.

Then the Companion said, "Now I must leave you. I cannot stay with you any longer."

But the boy didn't want to be parted from him. He didn't want to lose him at any cost. So the Companion stayed with him half a mile more, but he wouldn't come any farther, and although the boy begged and pleaded with him to come home and stay with him, or at least come inside and celebrate the homecoming with his father, the Companion said "No," he couldn't do that.

Then the boy asked what he wanted for having helped him.

If it was to be anything, it must be half of what he bred in five years, said the Companion.

Yes, he would get that.

When he was gone, the boy left all his riches behind and went home empty handed. Then they celebrated the homecoming until it was both heard of and talked about in seven kingdoms; and when they had finished, it took them the whole winter, using the rams as well as the twelve horses which his father had, to cart all the gold and silver home.

At the end of five years, the Companion came back for his share. Then the boy had divided everything into two equal parts.

"But there's one thing you haven't divided," said the Companion.

"What's that?" said the boy. "I thought I had divided everything."

"You have bred a child," said the Companion. "You must also divide it into two parts."

Yes, that was so. The boy took the sword, but just as he raised it to cleave the child, the Companion grabbed hold of the sword so that he could not strike.

"Weren't you glad that you weren't allowed to strike?" he said.

"Yes, happier than I've ever been," said the boy.

"Well, *I* was just as happy when you released me

from that block of ice, for I am a wandering spirit," he said.

He was the wine tapper who had been frozen fast in the block of ice on which everyone spat outside the church door. And he had been the boy's Companion and helped him because he had spent all he had to give him peace and lay him in consecrated ground. He had received permission to serve the boy for a year, and his time had been up when they parted the last time. Then he had been allowed to see him again. But now they must part forever, for the heavenly chimes were calling for him.

Aleksandr Nikolaevich Afanasiev

VASILISA
THE BEAUTIFUL

In a certain kingdom there lived a merchant. Although
he had been married for twelve years, he had only
one daughter, called Vasilisa the Beautiful. When
the girl was eight years old, her mother died. On
her deathbed the merchant's wife called her daughter,
took a doll from under her coverlet, gave it to the girl,
and said: "Listen, Vasilisushka. Remember and heed my
last words. I am dying, and together with my maternal
blessing I leave you this doll. Always keep it with you
and do not show it to anyone; if you get into trouble,
give the doll food and ask its advice. When it has eaten,
it will tell you what to do in your trouble." Then the
mother kissed her child and died.

After his wife's death the merchant mourned as is
proper and then began to think of marrying again. He
was a handsome man and had no difficulty in finding a
bride, but he liked best a certain widow. Because she
was elderly and had two daughters of her own, of almost
the same age as Vasilisa, he thought that she was an experienced housewife and mother. So he married her, but
was deceived, for she did not turn out to be a good
mother for his Vasilisa. Vasilisa was the most beautiful
girl in the village; her stepmother and stepsisters were
jealous of her beauty and tormented her by giving her

all kinds of work to do, hoping that she would grow thin
from toil and tanned from exposure to the wind and sun;
in truth, she had a most miserable life. But Vasilisa bore
all this without complaint and became lovelier and more
buxom every day, while the stepmother and her daughters
grew thin and ugly from spite, although they always sat
with folded hands, like ladies.

How did all this come about? Vasilisa was helped by
her doll. Without its aid the girl could never have managed all that work. In return, Vasilisa sometimes did not
eat, but kept the choicest morsels for her doll. And at
night, when everyone was asleep, she would lock herself
in the little room in which she lived and would give the

doll a treat, saying: "Now, little doll, eat, and listen to
my troubles. I live in my father's house but am deprived
of all joy; a wicked stepmother is driving me from the
white world. Tell me how I should live and what I
should do." The doll would eat, then would give her advice and comfort her in her trouble, and in the morning

she would perform all the chores for Vasilisa, who rested in the shade and picked flowers while the flower beds were weeded, the cabbage sprayed, the water brought in, and the stove fired. The doll even showed Vasilisa an herb that would protect her from sunburn. She led an easy life, thanks to her doll.

Several years went by. Vasilisa grew up and reached the marriage age. She was wooed by all the young men in the village, but no one would even look at the step-mother's daughters. The stepmother was more spiteful than ever, and her answer to all the suitors was: "I will not give the youngest in marriage before the elder ones." And each time she sent a suitor away, she vented her anger on Vasilisa in cruel blows.

One day the merchant had to leave home for a long time in order to trade in distant lands. The stepmother moved to another house. Near that house was a thick forest, and in a glade of that forest there stood a hut, and in the hut lived Baba Yaga. She never allowed any-one to come near her and ate human beings as if they were chickens. Having moved into the new house, the merchant's wife, hating Vasilisa, repeatedly sent the girl to the woods for one thing or another; but each time Vasilisa returned home safe and sound: her doll had showed her the way and kept her far from Baba Yaga's hut.

Autumn came. The stepmother gave evening work to all three maidens: the oldest had to make lace, the sec-ond had to knit stockings, and Vasilisa had to spin; and each one had to finish her task. The stepmother put out the lights all over the house, leaving only one candle in the room where the girls worked, and went to bed. The girls worked. The candle began to smoke; one of the stepsisters took up a scissors to trim it, but instead, following her mother's order, she snuffed it out, as though inadvertently. "What shall we do now?" said the girls. "There is no light in the house and our tasks are not finished. Someone must run to Baba Yaga and get some light." "The pins on my lace give me light," said the one who was making lace. "I shall not go." "I shall not go either," said the one who was knitting stockings; "my knitting needles give me light." "Then you must go," both of them cried to their stepsister. "Go to Baba Yaga!" And they pushed Vasilisa out of the room. She went into her own little room, put the supper she had prepared before her doll, and said: "Now, dolly, eat and aid me in my need. They are sending me to Baba Yaga for a light, and she will eat me up." The doll ate the supper and its eyes gleamed like two candles. "Fear not, Vasilisushka," it said. "Go where you are sent, only keep me with you all the time. With me in your pocket you will suffer no harm from Baba Yaga." Vasilisa made ready, put her doll in her pocket, and having made the sign of the cross, went into the deep forest.

She walked in fear and trembling. Suddenly a horseman galloped past her; his face was white, he was dressed in white, his horse was white, and his horse's trappings were white—daybreak came to the woods.

She walked on farther, and a second horseman galloped past her; he was all red, he was dressed in red, and his horse was red—the sun began to rise.

Vasilisa walked the whole night and the whole day, and only on the following evening did she come to the glade where Baba Yaga's hut stood. The fence around the hut was made of human bones, and on the spikes were human skulls with staring eyes; the doors had human legs for doorposts, human hands for bolts, and a mouth with sharp teeth in place of a lock. Vasilisa was numb with horror and stood rooted to the spot. Suddenly another horseman rode by. He was all black, he was dressed in black, and his horse was black. He galloped up to Baba Yaga's door and vanished as though the earth had swallowed him up—night came. But the darkness did not last long. The eyes of all the skulls on the fence began to gleam and the glade was as bright as day. Vasilisa shuddered with fear, but not knowing where to run, remained on the spot.

Soon a terrible noise resounded through the woods; the trees crackled, the dry leaves rustled; from the woods Baba Yaga drove out in a mortar, prodding it on with a pestle and sweeping her traces with a broom. She rode up to the gate, stopped, and sniffing the air around her,

cried: "Fie, fie! I smell a Russian smell! Who is here?"
Vasilisa came up to the old witch, and trembling with

fear, bowed low to her and said: "It is I, grandmother.
My stepsisters sent me to get some light." "Very well,"
said Baba Yaga. "I know them; but before I give you
the light, you must live with me and work for me; if not,
I will eat you up." Then she turned to the gate and
cried: "Hey, my strong bolts, unlock! Open up, my wide
gate!" The gate opened, and Baba Yaga drove in whistling. Vasilisa followed her, and then everything closed
again.

Having entered the room, Baba Yaga stretched herself
out in her chair and said to Vasilisa: "Serve me what is
in the stove; I am hungry." Vasilisa lit a torch from
the skulls on the fence and began to serve Yaga the
food from the stove—and enough food had been prepared
for ten people. She brought kvass, mead, beer, and wine

from the cellar. The old witch ate and drank everything, leaving for Vasilisa only a little cabbage soup, a
crust of bread, and a piece of pork. Then Baba Yaga made
ready to go to bed and said: "Tomorrow, after I go,
see to it that you sweep the yard, clean the hut, cook
the dinner, wash the linen, and go to the cornbin and
sort out a bushel of wheat. And let everything be done,
or I will eat you up!" Having given these orders, Baba
Yaga began to snore. Vasilisa set the remnants of the
old witch's supper before her doll, wept bitter tears, and
said: "Here, dolly, eat and aid me in my need! Baba
Yaga has given me a hard task to do and threatens to
eat me up if I do not do it all. Help me!" The doll
answered: "Fear not, Vasilisa the Beautiful! Eat your supper, say your prayers, and go to sleep; the morning is
wiser than the evening."

Very early next morning Vasilisa awoke, after Baba
Yaga had arisen, and looked out of the window. The
eyes of the skulls were going out; then the white horseman flashed by, and it was daybreak. Baba Yaga went out
into the yard, whistled, and the mortar, pestle, and
broom appeared before her. The red horseman flashed
by, and the sun rose. Baba Yaga sat in the mortar,
prodded it on with the pestle, and swept her traces with
the broom. Vasilisa remained alone, looked about Baba
Yaga's hut, was amazed at the abundance of everything,
and stopped wondering which work she should do first.
For lo and behold, all the work was done; the doll was
picking the last shreds of chaff from the wheat. "Ah, my
savior," said Vasilisa to her doll, "you have delivered
me from death." "All you have to do," answered the
doll, creeping into Vasilisa's pocket, "is to cook the dinner; cook it with the help of God and then rest, for
your health's sake."

When evening came Vasilisa set the table and waited
for Baba Yaga. Dusk began to fall, the black horseman
flashed by the gate, and night came; only the skulls' eyes
were shining. The trees crackled, the leaves rustled;
Baba Yaga was coming. Vasilisa met her. "Is everything
done?" asked Yaga. "Please see for yourself, grandmother," said Vasilisa. Baba Yaga looked at everything,

was annoyed that there was nothing she could complain about, and said: "Very well, then." Then she cried: "My faithful servants, my dear friends, grind my wheat!" Three pairs of hands appeared, took the wheat, and carried it out of sight. Baba Yaga ate her fill, made ready to go to sleep, and again gave her orders to Vasilisa. "Tomorrow," she commanded, "do the same work you have done today, and in addition take the poppy seed from the bin and get rid of the dust, grain by grain; someone threw dust into the bins out of spite." Having said this, the old witch turned to the wall and began to snore, and Vasilisa set about feeding her doll. The doll ate and spoke as she had spoken the day before: "Pray to God and go to sleep; the morning is wiser than the evening. Everything will be done, Vasilisushka."

Next morning Baba Yaga again left the yard in her mortar, and Vasilisa and the doll soon had all the work done. The old witch came back, looked at everything, and cried: "My faithful servants, my dear friends, press the oil out of the poppy seed!" Three pairs of hands appeared, took the poppy seed, and carried it out of sight. Baba Yaga sat down to dine; she ate, and Vasilisa stood silent. "Why do you not speak to me?" said Baba Yaga. "You stand there as though you were dumb." "I did not dare to speak," said Vasilisa, "but if you'll give me leave, I'd like to ask you something." "Go ahead. But not every question has a good answer; if you know too much, you will soon grow old." "I want to ask you, grandmother, only about what I have seen. As I was on my way to you, a horseman on a white horse, all white himself and dressed in white, overtook me. Who is he?" "He is my bright day," said Baba Yaga. "Then another horseman overtook me; he had a red horse, was red himself, and was dressed in red. Who is he?" "He is my red sun." "And who is the black horseman whom I met at your very gate, grandmother?" "He is my dark night—and all of them are my faithful servants."

Vasilisa remembered the three pairs of hands, but kept silent. "Why don't you ask me more?" said Baba Yaga. "That will be enough," Vasilisa replied. "You said yourself, grandmother, that one who knows too much will grow old soon." "It is well," said Baba Yaga, "that you ask only about what you have seen outside my house, not inside my house; I do not like to have my dirty linen washed in public, and I eat the overcurious. Now I shall ask you something. How do you manage to do the work I set for you?" "I am helped by the blessing of my mother," said Vasilisa. "So that is what it is," shrieked Baba Yaga. "Get you gone, blessed daughter! I want no blessed ones in my house!" She dragged Vasilisa out of the room and pushed her outside the gate, took a skull with burning eyes from the fence, stuck it on a stick, and gave it to the girl, saying: "Here is your light for your stepsisters. Take it; that is what they sent you for."

Vasilisa ran homeward by the light of the skull, which went out only at daybreak, and by nightfall of the following day she reached the house. As she approached the gate, she was about to throw the skull away, thinking that surely they no longer needed a light in the house. But suddenly a dull voice came from the skull, saying: "Do not throw me away; take me to your stepmother." She looked at the stepmother's house, and seeing that there was no light in the windows, decided to enter with her skull. For the first time she was received kindly. Her stepmother and stepsisters told her that since she had left they had had no fire in the house; they were unable to strike a flame themselves, and whatever light was brought by the neighbors went out the moment it was brought into the house. "Perhaps your fire will last," said the stepmother. The skull was brought into the room, and its eyes kept staring at the stepmother and her daughters and burned them. They tried to hide, but wherever they went the eyes followed them. By morning they were all burned to ashes; only Vasilisa remained untouched by the fire.

In the morning Vasilisa buried the skull in the ground, locked up the house, and went to the town. A certain childless old woman gave her shelter, and there she lived, waiting for her father's return. One day she said to the woman: "I am weary of sitting without work, grandmother. Buy me some flax, the best you can get;

at least I shall be spinning." The old woman bought good flax and Vasilisa set to work. She spun as fast as lightning and her threads were even and thin as a hair. She spun a great deal of yarn; it was time to start weaving it, but no comb fine enough for Vasilisa's yarn could be found, and no one would undertake to make one. Vasilisa asked her doll for aid. The doll said: "Bring me an old comb, an old shuttle, and a horse's mane; I will make a loom for you." Vasilisa got everything that was required and went to sleep, and during the night the doll made a wonderful loom for her.

By the end of the winter the linen was woven, and it was so fine that it could be passed through a needle like a thread. In the spring the linen was bleached, and Vasilisa said to the old woman: "Grandmother, sell this linen and keep the money for yourself." The old woman looked at the linen and gasped: "No, my child! No one can wear such linen except the czar; I shall take it to the palace." The old woman went to the czar's palace and walked back and forth beneath the windows. The czar saw her and asked: "What do you want, old woman?" "Your Majesty," she answered, "I have brought rare merchandise; I do not want to show it to anyone but you." The czar ordered her to be brought before him, and when he saw the linen he was amazed. "What do you want for it?" asked the czar. "It has no price, little father czar! I have brought it as a gift to you." The czar thanked her and rewarded her with gifts.

The czar ordered shirts to be made of the linen. It was cut, but nowhere could they find a seamstress who was willing to sew them. For a long time they tried to find one, but in the end the czar summoned the old woman and said: "You have known how to spin and weave such linen, you must know how to sew shirts of it." "It was not I that spun and wove this linen, your Majesty," said the old woman. "This is the work of a maiden to whom I give shelter." "Then let her sew the shirts," ordered the czar.

The old woman returned home and told everything to Vasilisa. "I knew all the time," said Vasilisa to her, "that I would have to do this work." She locked herself in her room and set to work; she sewed without rest and soon a dozen shirts were ready. The old woman took them to the czar, and Vasilisa washed herself, combed her hair, dressed in her finest clothes, and sat at the window. She sat there waiting to see what would happen. She saw a servant of the czar entering the courtyard. The messenger came into the room and said: "The czar wishes to see the needle woman who made his shirts and wishes to reward her with his own hands." Vasilisa appeared before the czar. When the czar saw Vasilisa the Beautiful he fell madly in love with her. "No, my beauty," he said, "I will not separate from you; you shall be my wife." He took Vasilisa by her white hands, seated her by his side, and the wedding was celebrated at once. Soon Vasilisa's father returned, was overjoyed at her good fortune, and came to live in his daughter's house. Vasilisa took the old woman into her home too, and carried her doll in her pocket till the end of her life.

PRINCE IVAN,
THE FIREBIRD,
AND THE GRAY WOLF

IIIIIIIIIIIIIIIIIIIIIIIIIIIIIIIIIIIIIIIIIIIIIIIIIIIIIIIIIIIIIIIII

In a certain land in a certain kingdom there lived a king called Vyslav Andronovich. He had three sons: the first was Prince Dimitri, the second Prince Vasily, and the third Prince Ivan. King Vyslav Andronovich had a garden so rich that there was no finer one in any kingdom. In this garden there grew all kinds of precious trees, with and without fruit; one special apple tree was the king's favorite, for all the apples it bore were golden.

The firebird took to visiting King Vyslav's garden; her wings were golden and her eyes were like Oriental crystals. Every night she flew into the garden, perched on King Vyslav's favorite apple tree, picked several golden apples from it, and then flew away. King Vyslav Andronovich was greatly distressed that the firebird had taken so many apples from his golden apple tree. So he summoned his three sons to him and said: "My beloved children, which of you can catch the firebird in my garden? To him who captures her alive I will give half my kingdom during my life, and all of it upon my death!" His sons, the princes, answered in one voice: "Your Majesty, gracious sovereign, little father, with great joy will we try to take the firebird alive!"

The first night Prince Dimitri went to keep watch in

the garden. He sat under the apple tree from which the firebird had been picking apples, fell asleep, and did not hear her come, though she picked much golden fruit. Next morning King Vyslav Andronovich summoned his son Prince Dimitri to him and asked: "Well, my beloved son, did you see the firebird or not?" The prince answered: "No, gracious sovereign, little father! She did not come last night!"

The next night Prince Vasily went to keep watch in the garden. He sat under the same apple tree; he stayed one hour, then another hour, and finally fell so sound asleep that he did not hear the firebird come, though she picked many apples. In the morning King Vyslav summoned his son to him and asked: "Well, my beloved son, did you see the firebird or not?" "Gracious sovereign, little father, she did not come last night!"

The third night Prince Ivan went to keep watch in the garden and sat under the same apple tree; he sat one hour, a second hour, and a third—then suddenly the whole garden was illumined as if by many lights. The firebird had come; she perched on the apple tree and began to pick apples. Prince Ivan stole up to her so softly that he was able to seize her tail. But he could not hold the firebird herself; she tore herself from his grasp and flew away. In Prince Ivan's hand there re-

mained only one feather of her tail, to which he held very fast. In the morning, as soon as King Vyslav awoke

from his sleep, Prince Ivan went to him and gave him
the feather of the firebird. King Vyslav was greatly
pleased that his youngest son had succeeded in getting
at least one feather of the firebird. This feather was
so marvelously bright that when it was placed in a dark
room it made the whole room shine as if it were lit
up by many candles. King Vyslav put the feather in his
study as a keepsake, to be treasured forever. From that
moment the firebird stopped visiting the garden.

Once again King Vyslav summoned his sons and said:
"My beloved children, set out. I give you my blessing.
Find the firebird and bring her to me alive, and that
which I promised before will go to him who brings me
the firebird." At this time Princes Dimitri and Vasily
bore a grudge against their youngest brother, Ivan, because he had succeeded in tearing a feather from the
firebird's tail; they accepted their father's blessing and
together went forth to seek the firebird. But Prince Ivan
too began to beg for his father's blessing that he might
go forth. King Vyslav said to him: "My beloved son,
my dear child, you are still young and unused to such
long and hard journeys; why should you depart from
my house? Your brothers have gone; what if you too
leave me, and all three of you do not return for a long
time? I am old now and I walk in the shadow of the
Lord; if during your absence the Lord takes my life, who
will rule the kingdom in my place? A rebellion might
break out, or dissension among the people, and there
would be no one to pacify them; or an enemy might
approach our land, and there would be no one to command our troops." But no matter how King Vyslav tried
to hold Prince Ivan back, he finally had to yield to his
son's insistent prayer. Prince Ivan received his father's
blessing, chose a horse, and set out on his way; and he
rode on and on, himself not knowing whither.

He rode near and far, high and low, along bypaths
and byways—for speedily a tale is spun, but with less
speed a deed is done—until he came to a wide, open
field, a green meadow. And there in the field stood a
pillar, and on the pillar these words were written: "Whosoever goes from this pillar on the road straight be-

fore him will be cold and hungry. Whosoever goes to the right side will be safe and sound, but his horse will be killed. And whosoever goes to the left side will be killed himself, but his horse will be safe and sound." Prince Ivan read this inscription and went to the right, thinking that although his horse might be killed, he himself would remain alive and would in time get another horse.

He rode one day, then a second day, then a third. Suddenly an enormous gray wolf came toward him and said: "Ah, so it's you, young lad, Prince Ivan! You saw the inscription on the pillar that said that your horse would be killed if you came this way. Why, then, have you come hither?" When he had said these words, he tore Prince Ivan's horse in twain and ran off to one side.

Prince Ivan was sorely grieved for his horse; he shed bitter tears and then continued on foot. He walked a whole day and was utterly exhausted. He was about to sit down and rest for a while when all at once the gray wolf caught up with him and said: "I am sorry for you, Prince Ivan, because you are exhausted from walking; I am also sorry that I ate your good horse. Therefore mount me, the gray wolf, and tell me whither to carry you and for what purpose." Prince Ivan told the gray wolf what errand he had come on; and the gray wolf darted off with him more swiftly than a horse and after some time, just at nightfall, reached a low stone wall. There he stopped and said: "Now, Prince Ivan, climb down from me, the gray wolf, and climb over that stone wall; behind the wall you will find a garden, and in the garden the firebird is sitting in a golden cage. Take the firebird, but touch not the golden cage; if you take the cage, you will not escape, you will be caught at once!"

Prince Ivan climbed over the stone wall into the garden, saw the firebird in the golden cage, and was utterly charmed by the beauty of the cage. He took the bird out and started back across the garden, but on his way he changed his mind and said to himself: "Why have I taken the firebird without her cage—where will I put her?" He returned, and the moment he took down the golden cage a thunderous noise resounded through the whole garden, for there were strings tied to the cage. The guards woke up at once, rushed into the garden, caught Prince Ivan with the firebird, and led him before their king, whose name was Dolmat. King Dolmat was furious at Prince Ivan and cried in a loud and angry voice: "How now! Are you not ashamed to steal, young lad! Who are you, from what land do you come, what is your father's name, and what is your own name?"

Prince Ivan answered: "I am from Vyslav's kingdom. I am the son of king Vyslav Andronovich, and my name is Prince Ivan. Your firebird took to visiting our garden night after night; she plucked golden apples from my father's favorite apple tree and spoiled almost the whole tree. For that reason my father sent me to find the firebird and bring her to him."

"Oh, young lad, Prince Ivan," said King Dolmat, "is it fitting to do what you have done? If you had come to me, I would have given you the firebird with honor. But now, will you like it if I send to all the kingdoms to proclaim how dishonorably you have acted in my kingdom? However, listen, Prince Ivan! If you will do me a service, if you go beyond thirty lands, to the thirtieth kingdom, and get for me the horse with the golden mane from the realm of King Afron, I will forgive you your offense and hand the firebird over to you with great honor. But if you do not perform this service, I shall let it be known in all the kingdoms that you are a dishonorable thief." Prince Ivan left King Dolmat in great distress, promising to get for him the horse with the golden mane.

He came to the gray wolf and told him everything that King Dolmat had said. "Oh, young lad, Prince Ivan," said the gray wolf, "why did you not heed my words, why did you take the golden cage?" "It is true, I am guilty before you," answered Prince Ivan. "Well, let it be so," said the gray wolf. "Sit on me, the gray wolf; I will carry you where you have to go."

Prince Ivan mounted to the gray wolf's back, and the wolf ran fast as an arrow. He ran till nightfall, a short distance or a long one, until he came to King Afron's kingdom. And reaching the white-walled royal stables, the gray wolf said to Prince Ivan: "Go, Prince Ivan, into those white-walled stables—all the stableboys on guard are now sleeping soundly—and take the horse with the golden mane. However, on the wall there hangs a golden bridle; do not take it, otherwise there will be trouble!"

Prince Ivan entered the white-walled stables, took the steed, and began to retrace his steps; but he noticed the golden bridle on the wall, and was so charmed with it that he removed it from its nail. And he had no sooner removed it than a thunderous clatter and noise resounded through all the stables, for there were strings tied to that bridle. The stableboys on guard woke up at once, rushed in, caught Prince Ivan, and brought him before King Afron. King Afron began to question him. "Young lad," he said, "tell me from what kingdom you are come, whose son you are, and what your name may be." Prince Ivan answered: "I am from Vyslav's kingdom. I am King Vyslav Andronovich's son, and I am called Prince Ivan."

"Oh, young lad, Prince Ivan," said King Afron, "is the deed you have done befitting an honorable knight? If you had come to me I would have given you the horse with the golden mane in all honor. But now, will you like it if I send to all the kingdoms to proclaim how dishonorably you have behaved in my kingdom? However, listen, Prince Ivan! If you do me a service, if you go beyond the thrice ninth land, to the thrice tenth kingdom, and get for me Princess Elena the Fair, with whom I have been in love, heart and soul, for long years, but whom I cannot win for my bride, I will forgive you your offense and give you the horse with the golden mane in all honor. But if you do not perform this service for me, I shall let it be known in all the kingdoms that you are a dishonorable thief and will put down in writing how badly you have behaved in my kingdom." Then Prince Ivan promised King Afron to get Princess Elena the Fair for him and left the palace, weeping bitterly.

He came to the gray wolf and told him everything that had happened to him. "Oh, young lad, Prince Ivan," said the gray wolf, "why did you not heed my words, why did you take the golden bridle?" "It is true, I am guilty before you," answered Prince Ivan. "Well, let it be so," said the gray wolf. "Sit on me, the gray wolf; I will carry you where you have to go."

Prince Ivan mounted to the gray wolf's back, and the wolf ran fast as an arrow; he ran as beasts run in fairy tales so that in a very short time he arrived in the kingdom of Elena the Fair. And reaching the golden fence that surrounded the wonderful garden, the wolf said to Prince Ivan: "Now, Prince Ivan, climb down from me, the gray wolf, and go back along the same road that we took to come here, and wait for me in the open field under the green oak."

Prince Ivan went where he was bid. But the gray wolf sat near the golden fence and waited till Princess Elena the Fair should come to take her walk in the garden. Toward evening, when the sun began to set in the west and the air became cool, Princess Elena the Fair went to walk in the garden with her governesses and ladies-in-waiting. She entered the garden, and when she came near the place where the gray wolf was sitting behind the fence, he quickly jumped across the fence into the garden, caught the princess, jumped back again, and ran with all his strength and power. He came to the green oak in the open field where Prince Ivan was waiting for him and said: "Prince Ivan, quickly seat yourself on me, the gray wolf!" Prince Ivan seated himself and the gray wolf darted off with him and the princess toward King Afron's kingdom.

The nurses and governesses and ladies-in-waiting who had been walking in the garden with the beautiful Princess Elena ran at once to the palace and sent men-at-arms to pursue the gray wolf; but no matter how fast they ran, they could not overtake him, and so they turned back.

Sitting on the gray wolf with the beautiful Princess Elena, Prince Ivan came to love her with all his heart, and she to love Prince Ivan. And when the gray wolf came to King Afron's kingdom and Prince Ivan had to lead the beautiful princess to the palace and give her to King

Afron, he grew extremely sad and began to weep bitter
tears. The gray wolf asked him: "Why are you weeping,
Prince Ivan?" And Prince Ivan answered: "Gray wolf, my
friend, why should I not weep and grieve? I have come
to love the beautiful Princess Elena with all my heart,
and now I must give her to King Afron in return for
the horse with the golden mane; if I do not give her
to him, he will dishonor me in all the kingdoms."

"I have served you much, Prince Ivan," said the gray
wolf, "and I will do you this service too. Listen to me,
Prince Ivan! I will turn myself into the beautiful Princess Elena, and do you lead me to King Afron and take
from him the horse with the golden mane; he will think
me the real princess. And later, when you have mounted
the horse with the golden mane and gone far away, I

shall ask King Afron to let me walk in the open field. And when he lets me go with the nurses and governesses and ladies-in-waiting, and I am with them in the open field, remember me, and once again I shall be with you." The gray wolf said these words, struck himself against the damp earth, and turned into Princess Elena the Fair so that there was no way of knowing that he was not the princess. Prince Ivan took the gray wolf, went to King Afron's palace, and told the real Princess Elena to wait for him outside the town.

When Prince Ivan came to King Afron with the false Elena the Fair, the king was greatly rejoiced to receive the treasure that he had so long desired. He accepted the false princess and gave Prince Ivan the horse with the golden mane.

Prince Ivan mounted the horse and rode out of the town; he had seated Princess Elena the Fair behind him, and they set out in the direction of King Dolmat's kingdom. As for the gray wolf, he lived with King Afron one day, a second day, then a third, in the place of Elena the Fair; and on the fourth he went to King Afron and asked his permission to take a walk in the open field to dispel the cruel sadness and grief that lay on him. And King Afron said to him: "Ah, my beautiful Princess Elena! For you I will do anything; I will even let you go to walk in the open field!" And at once he commanded the governesses and nurses and all the ladies-in-waiting to walk with the beautiful princess in the open field.

Meanwhile Prince Ivan rode along byways and bypaths with Elena the Fair, conversed with her, and forgot about the gray wolf. But then he remembered. "Ah," he said, "where is my gray wolf?" Suddenly, as though he had come from nowhere, the gray wolf stood before Prince Ivan and said: "Prince Ivan, sit on me, the gray wolf, and let the beautiful princess ride on the horse with the golden mane."

Prince Ivan sat on the gray wolf and they set out for King Dolmat's kingdom. They traveled a long time or a short time, and having come to the kingdom, stopped three versts from the town. Prince Ivan began to implore the gray wolf, saying: "Listen to me, gray wolf, my dear friend! You have done many a service for me; do me this last one. Could you not turn yourself into a horse with a golden mane instead of this one? For I long to have myself a horse with a golden mane."

Suddenly the gray wolf struck himself against the damp earth and turned into a horse with a golden mane; Prince Ivan left Princess Elena the Fair in the green meadow, bestrode the gray wolf, and went to the palace of King Dolmat. And when King Dolmat saw Prince Ivan riding on the horse with the golden mane, he was overjoyed and at once came out of his apartment, met the prince in the great courtyard, kissed him on his sweet lips, took him by the right hand, and led him into the white-walled palace hall. In honor of this joyous occasion King Dolmat gave a great feast, and the guests sat at oaken tables with checked tablecloths; they ate, drank, laughed, and enjoyed themselves for exactly two days. And on the third day King Dolmat handed to Prince Ivan the firebird in the golden cage. The prince took the firebird, went outside the town, mounted the golden-maned horse together with Princess Elena the Fair, and set out for his native land, the kingdom of King Vyslav Andronovich.

As for King Dolmat, he decided on the next day to break in his golden-maned horse in the open field; he had the horse saddled, then mounted him and rode off; but as soon as he began to spur the beast, it threw him, and turning back into the gray wolf, darted off and overtook Prince Ivan. "Prince Ivan," said he, "mount me, the gray wolf, and let Princess Elena the Fair ride on the horse with the golden mane."

Prince Ivan sat on the gray wolf and they continued on their way. The moment the gray wolf brought Prince Ivan to the place where he had torn the horse asunder, he stopped and said: "Well, Prince Ivan, I have served you long enough in faith and in truth. Upon this spot I tore your horse in twain, and to this spot I have brought you back safe and sound. Climb down from me, the gray wolf; now you have a horse with a golden mane; mount him and go wherever you have to go; I am no longer your servant." After he had said these words the gray wolf ran off, and Prince Ivan wept bitterly and set out on his way with the beautiful princess.

He rode with Princess Elena for a long time or a short time; when they were still about twenty versts from his own land, he stopped, dismounted from his horse, and lay down with the beautiful princess to rest under a tree from the heat of the sun; he tied the horse with the golden mane to the same tree and put the cage with the firebird by his side. The two lovers lay on the soft grass, spoke amorous words to each other, and fell fast asleep.

At that very moment Prince Ivan's brothers, Prince Dimitri and Prince Vasily, having traveled through various kingdoms and having failed to find the firebird, were on their way back to their native land; they were returning empty handed. They chanced to come upon their brother, Prince Ivan, lying asleep beside Princess Elena the Fair. Seeing the golden-maned horse on the grass and the firebird in the golden cage, they were sorely tempted and decided to slay their brother. Prince Dimitri drew his sword from its scabbard, stabbed Prince Ivan, and cut him in little pieces; then he awakened Princess Elena the Fair and began to question her. "Lovely maiden," he said, "from what kingdom have you come, who is your father, and what is your name?"

The beautiful Princess Elena, seeing Prince Ivan dead, was terribly frightened and began to weep bitter tears, and amid her tears she said: "I am Princess Elena the Fair; I was carried off by Prince Ivan, whom you have brought to an evil end. If you were valiant knights you would have gone with him into the open field and conquered him in fair combat; but you slew him while he was asleep, and what praise will that get you? A sleeping man is the same as a dead man!"

Then Prince Dimitri put his sword to the heart of Princess Elena and said to her: "Listen to me, Elena the Fair! You are now in our hands; we shall take you to our father, King Vyslav Andronovich, and you must tell him that we captured you as well as the firebird and the horse with the golden mane. If you do not promise to say this, I shall put you to death at once!" The beautiful Princess Elena was frightened by the threat of death; she promised them and swore by everything sacred that she would speak as they commanded. Then Prince Dimitri and Prince Vasily cast lots to see who should get Princess Elena and who the horse with the golden mane. And it fell out that the beautiful princess went to Prince Vasily and the horse with the golden mane to Prince Dimitri. Then Prince Vasily took the beautiful Princess Elena and seated her on his good horse, and Prince Dimitri mounted the horse with the golden mane and took the firebird to give to his father, King Vyslav Andronovich, and they all set out on their way.

Prince Ivan lay dead on that spot exactly thirty days; then the gray wolf came upon him and knew him by his odor. He wanted to help the prince, to revive him, but he did not know how to do it. At that moment the gray wolf saw a raven with two young ravens flying above the body, making ready to swoop down and eat the flesh of Prince Ivan. The gray wolf hid behind a bush; and as soon as the young ravens lighted on the ground and began to eat the body of Prince Ivan, he leaped from behind the bush, caught one young raven, and prepared to tear him in twain. Then the raven flew to the ground, sat at some distance from the gray wolf, and said to him: "O gray wolf, do not touch my young child; he has done nothing to you."

"Listen to me, raven," said the gray wolf; "I shall not touch your child and will let him go safe and sound if you will do me a service. Fly beyond the thrice ninth land, to the thrice tenth kingdom, and bring me the water of death and the water of life." Thereupon the raven said to the gray wolf: "I will do this service for you, but touch not my son." Having said these words, the raven took wing and was soon out of sight. On the third day the raven came back carrying two vials, one containing the water of life, the other the water of death, and she gave these vials to the gray wolf.

The gray wolf took the vials, tore the young raven in twain, sprinkled him with the water of death, and the young raven's body grew together; he sprinkled him with the water of life, and the young raven shook his wings and flew away. Then the gray wolf sprinkled Prince Ivan with the water of death, and his body grew together; he sprinkled him with the water of life, and Prince Ivan stood up and said: "Ah, I have slept very long!"

The gray wolf answered him: "Yes, Prince Ivan, you would have slept forever had it not been for me; your brothers cut you in pieces and carried off the beautiful Princess Elena and the horse with the golden mane and the firebird. Now hasten as fast as you can to your native land; your brother Prince Vasily is this very day to marry your bride, Princess Elena the Fair. And in order to get there quickly, you had better sit on me, the gray wolf." Prince Ivan mounted the gray wolf; the wolf ran with him to King Vyslav Andronovich's kingdom and after a short time or a long time reached the town.

Prince Ivan dismounted from the gray wolf, walked into the town, and having arrived at the palace, found that his brother Prince Vasily was indeed wedding the beautiful Princess Elena that very day; he had returned with her from the ceremony and was already sitting at the feast. Prince Ivan entered the palace, and no sooner did Elena the Fair see him than she sprang up from the table, began to kiss his sweet lips, and cried out: "This is my beloved bridegroom, Prince Ivan—not the evildoer who sits here at the table!"

Then King Vyslav Andronovich rose from his place and began to question Princess Elena. "What is the meaning of the words you have spoken?" he demanded. Elena the Fair told him the whole truth about what had happened—how Prince Ivan had won her, the horse with the golden mane, and the firebird, how his older brothers had killed him in his sleep, and how they had forced her under threat of death to say that they had won all this. King Vyslav grew terribly angry at Prince Dimitri and Prince Vasily and threw them into a dungeon; but Prince Ivan married Princess Elena the Fair and began to live with her in such true friendship and love that neither of them could spend a single minute without the other's company.

Charles Perrault

IIIIIIIIIIIIIIIIIIIIIIIIIIIIIIIIIIIIIIIIIIIIIIIIIIIIIIIIIII

SLEEPING BEAUTY

IIIIIIIIIIIIIIIIIIIIIIIIIIIIIIIIIIIIIIIIIIIIIIIIIIIIIIIIIII

Once upon a time there were a king and a queen who were very unhappy that they did not have any children, so unhappy that it can hardly be expressed. They went to all the watering places in the world, tried vows, pilgrimages, and acts of devotion, but nothing would do. Finally, however, the queen did become pregnant and gave birth to a daughter. They had a fine christening, and for godmothers they gave the little princess all the fairies that could be found in the country (and seven of them were found) so that when each of them had given her a gift, as was the custom of fairies in those days, the princess would in this way have all the perfections imaginable.

After the christening ceremonies, the whole company returned to the palace of the king, where a great banquet was held for the fairies. A magnificent set of dinner things was placed before each one of them, with a case of heavy gold in which there were a spoon, a fork, and a knife of solid gold ornamented with diamonds and rubies. But as everyone was taking his place at the table, there appeared an old fairy who had not been invited because she had not left her tower for fifty years, and she was believed to be dead or enchanted.

The king ordered a place set for her, but he was unable to give her a solid gold case, as he had the others because he had had only seven made for the seven fairies. The old fairy thought she was being held in contempt and muttered several threats under her breath. One of the young fairies who was near her overheard her, and since she suspected that she might give some harmful gift to the little princess, she went and hid herself behind the tapestry as soon as they got up from the table in order to be the last to speak and to be able to undo as much as possible the evil that the old fairy might do.

Meanwhile the fairies began to present their gifts to the princess. The gift of the youngest was that she should be the most beautiful person in the world; of the next fairy, that she should have an angelic disposition; of the third, that she should do whatever she did with a wonderful grace; of the fourth, that she should dance perfectly; of the fifth, that she should sing like a nightingale; of the sixth, that she should play all sorts of musical instruments with absolute perfection. When the turn of the old fairy came, she said, shaking her head more from spite than from old age, that the princess should pierce her hand with a spindle and that she should die of it.

This dreadful gift made the whole company shudder, and there was not a single person who did not weep. At this moment, the young fairy stepped out from behind the tapestry and spoke these words in a loud voice: "Be assured, King and Queen, that your daughter shall not die. It is true that I have not enough power to undo completely what my elder has done. The princess will pierce her hand with a spindle, but instead of dying she will only fall into a deep sleep that will last one hundred years, at the end of which the son of a king will come to awaken her."

The king, to attempt to avoid the misfortune announced by the old fairy, had an edict published forbidding everyone to spin with spindles or to keep spindles in their homes, on the pain of death.

After some fifteen or sixteen years, while the king and queen were away at one of their country estates, it happened that the young princess was running about in the castle, and going from room to room, she went up to the top of a tower, and there in a little garret was an old woman who was sitting alone at her distaff, spinning. This good woman had never heard of the king's prohibition of spinning with a spindle. "What are you doing there, my good woman?" said the princess.

"I'm spinning, my pretty little one," said the old woman, who did not know who she was.

"Oh, isn't that fascinating!" said the princess. "How do you do that? Give it to me so that I may see if I can do

as well." No sooner had she taken the spindle than she pricked her hand—either because she was too hasty or too careless, or because the decree of the fairies had so ordained it—and she fell down in a swoon.

The old woman, in great confusion, called for help, and people rushed in from all sides. They threw water on the princess' face, unlaced her, chafed her hands, and rubbed her temples with Queen of Hungary water, but nothing could bring her to.

Then the king, who had come upstairs when he heard the noise, remembered the fairies' prediction, and deciding that this had had to happen because the fairies had said it would, had the princess placed in the most beautiful apartment in the palace on a bed with hangings embroidered in gold and silver. She was so beautiful she might have been thought an angel, for her swoon had not taken away the color of her complexion. Her cheeks were still rosy and her lips were like coral; her eyes were closed, but one could still hear her breathing softly, which made it clear that she was not dead.

The king ordered that she be allowed to sleep in peace until the hour of her awakening had come. The good fairy who had saved her life by condemning her to sleep a hundred years was off in the kingdom of Mataquin, a thousand miles away, when the accident happened to the princess, but she had been informed of it in an instant by a little dwarf who had seven-league boots (these are boots with which one can go seven leagues at one step). The fairy left immediately and appeared within an hour in a fiery chariot drawn by dragons. The king went to hand her from the chariot. She approved of everything he had done, but since she was extremely foresighted, she thought that when the princess came to awaken she would be quite distressed to find herself all alone in the old castle. Accordingly she did the following:

She touched with her wand everyone who was in the castle (except the king and queen)—governesses, ladies-in-waiting, chambermaids, gentlemen, officers, stewards, cooks, scullery boys, errand boys, guards, Swiss mercenaries, pages, and footmen; she also touched the horses in the stable and the grooms, the huge mastiffs in the stableyard, and little Puff, the princess' puppy, who was beside her on the bed. As soon as she touched them, they all fell asleep, and they would not wake up until their mistress did so that they would all be ready to serve her when she needed them—the very spits on the fire, all loaded with partridges and pheasants, went to sleep, and the fire also. All this was done in a moment—fairies do not take long at their work.

Then the king and queen, when they had kissed their darling child without awakening her, left the castle and had notices put up forbidding anyone to approach it. These notices were not necessary, for within a quarter of an hour there grew up around the park such a great number of trees, large and small, as well as brambles and thorns, all intertwined with one another, that neither man nor beast could have passed through. One could see only the tops of the towers of the castle, and that only from quite a distance. It can hardly be doubted that the fairy had exercised a bit of her skill in this so that the princess would not have to fear curious visitors while she was sleeping.

At the end of the hundred years, the son of the king who was then reigning, who was of a different family from that of the sleeping princess, was hunting in that vicinity and asked what were those towers that he could see beyond the large, dense forest. Everyone told him what he had heard said about it. Some said it was an old castle haunted by ghosts, others said that all the magicians in the country held their witches' sabbath there. The most common opinion was that an ogre lived there, that he carried off all the children he could seize in order to eat them at his leisure, and that no one could pursue him since he alone had the power to make his way through the woods.

The prince did not know what to think until an old peasant spoke up and said to him, "Prince, it was more than fifty years ago that I heard my father say that there was in this castle the most beautiful princess that anyone had ever seen and that she had to sleep a hundred years until she was awakened by the son of a king for whom she had been destined."

At this speech the young prince felt himself all on fire. Without worrying too much about it, he believed that he could bring about the conclusion of such a fine adventure, and spurred on by love and honor, he resolved on the spot to undertake it. Hardly had he advanced toward the woods when all those huge trees, brambles, and thorns opened of themselves to let him pass. He walked toward the castle that he saw at the end of a broad avenue into which he had entered, and what surprised him was that he saw that none of his servants could follow him because the branches came together again after he had passed. He did not turn back from his path—

a young Prince in love is always valiant. He went
into a great forecourt where everything he saw at first
might have frozen him with fear. The silence was horrible and the image of death appeared everywhere in the
bodies of men and animals stretched out on the ground,
apparently dead. He realized, however, from the pimpled
noses and crimson faces of the Swiss guards that they
were only asleep, and their cups, in which a few drops of
wine remained, showed clearly that they had fallen asleep
while drinking.

He passed through a great court paved with marble,
climbed the staircase, and entered the guardroom, where
the guards were lined up in a row, their muskets on their
shoulders, snoring away. He crossed several rooms full of
lords and ladies, all asleep, some standing and others
sitting, and went into a room all done in gold, in which
he saw the loveliest sight he had ever seen—a princess
who seemed to be about fifteen or sixteen years old, the
splendor of whose striking beauty seemed to have something divinely luminous about it. He approached her,
trembling with wonder, and knelt down beside her.

Then, since the end of the enchantment had come, the
princess woke up, and looking at him with eyes more
tender than a first glance would seem to permit, she said
to him, "Is it you, my prince? You have indeed waited a
long time!" The prince, charmed by these words, and
even more by the way in which she spoke them, did not
know how to express his joy and gratitude; he assured
her that he loved her more than himself. Their conversation was halting but it was the more pleasing because of
this—little eloquence, much love. He was more confused
than she, and one should not be surprised at this since
she had had the time to dream about what she should
say to him. It seems (although history does not say anything about it) that the good fairy had obtained for her
the enjoyment of pleasant dreams during that long sleep.
Even after they had spoken together for four hours, they
still had not said half the things they had to tell each
other.

However, all the palace had awakened with the princess and each person thought of carrying out his duty, but

since they were not in love, they were all dying of hunger. The chief lady-in-waiting, famished like the others, lost patience and told the princess firmly that dinner was served. The prince assisted the princess to arise; she was magnificently dressed, but he refrained from telling her that she was dressed like his grandmother and that she was wearing a high collar. She did not appear any the less beautiful because of this.

They went into a hall of mirrors, and there they dined, served by the princess' household. The violins and oboes played tunes that were old but still excellent, although they had not been played for nearly a hundred years. After dinner, without losing any time, the lord almoner married them in the palace chapel, and the chief lady-in-waiting drew the curtains. Actually they slept very little, since the princess hardly needed any sleep, and the prince left her as soon as it was morning to return to the city where his father had naturally been much worried about him. The prince told him that he had lost his way in the forest while hunting and that he had spent the night in the hut of a charcoal burner who had given him black bread and cheese to eat. The king, his father, who was a good soul, believed him, but his mother was not convinced, and seeing that he went hunting every day and that he always had a ready excuse when he had to spend two or three nights away from the castle, she suspected that he had a mistress. He lived this way with the princess for more than two years and had two children by her, of whom the first, who was a daughter, was named Dawn, and the second, a son, was called Day because he seemed even more beautiful than his sister.

The queen said several times to her son, in order to get him to explain himself, that he really ought to settle down, but he never dared to trust her with his secret. Although he loved her, he feared her because she was descended from the race of ogres, and the king had married her only because of her great wealth. It was even rumored at court that she had ogreish inclinations, and that when she saw little children she had all the trouble in the world to keep herself from pouncing upon them, and thus the prince did not want to tell her anything.

But when the king had died, which happened at the end of the two years, and the prince realized that he was his own master, he acknowledged his marriage publicly and went with great ceremony to fetch the queen, his wife, from her castle. She came to the capital city with her two children on each side of her, and she was given a magnificent reception.

Some time afterward, the king went to make war on the Emperor Cantalabutte, his neighbor. He left the regency of the kingdom to the queen, his mother, and commended his wife and children to her care. He had to be at war all summer, and as soon as he had gone, the queen mother sent her daughter-in-law to a country house in the woods in order to satisfy her horrible desire. She went there several days later and said to the steward one evening, "I want to eat little Dawn tomorrow for my dinner."

"Ah, Madame," said the steward.

"I want to," said the queen (and she said it in the tone of an ogress who longs to eat fresh meat). "And I want to eat her with a *sauce Robert*." The poor man, seeing clearly that it would not do to trifle with an ogress, took his large knife and went up to the room of little Dawn. She was then about four years old and came jumping and laughing and threw herself upon him, demanding some candy. He began to cry, and the knife fell from his hand. He then went to the stableyard and cut the throat of a young lamb and made a sauce for it that was so good that his mistress assured him that she had never eaten anything so delicious.

A week later the wicked queen said to her steward, "I want to eat little Day for my supper." He did not reply, but decided to deceive her as he had the other time. He went to look for little Day, whom he found with a little foil in his hand, with which he was fencing with a large monkey, although he was only three years old. The steward took him to his wife, who hid him with little Dawn, and substituted a very tender young kid for little Day, and the ogress found it admirably cooked.

Things had gone well up to this point, but one evening this wicked queen said to the steward, "I want to eat the queen with the same sauce in which I had her children." Then the poor steward really despaired of being able to deceive her. The young queen was past twenty, not counting the hundred years that she had slept, and her skin, although fair and lovely, was a little tough. The problem was to find an animal in the menagerie just that tough. He decided to cut the queen's throat in order to save his own life and went up to the queen's room with the intention of doing it at once. He roused himself to a fury and entered the queen's room with a dagger in his hand. He did not wish, however, to take her by surprise, and he told her, with great respect, the order he had received from the queen mother. "Do it, do it," she said, stretching out her neck toward him. "Carry out the order you have been given, and I shall see my children again—my poor children, whom I loved so much." She thought they were dead since they had been taken from her without any explanation.

"No, no, Madame," answered the poor steward, deeply moved. "You shall not die and you will not fail to see your dear children again, but it will be at my home where I have hidden them, and I shall deceive the queen again by having her eat a young roe in your place." He immediately took her to his room, where he left her embracing her children and crying with them while he went down to dress the roe, which the queen ate for her supper with as good an appetite as if it had been the young queen. She was quite pleased with her own cruelty and prepared to tell the king when he returned that wild wolves had eaten the queen, his wife, and his two children.

One evening as she was prowling through the courtyards and stableyards of the castle, as was her custom, to see if she could scent any fresh meat, she heard in one of the lower rooms the sound of little Day crying because the queen, his mother, wished to whip him for some naughtiness, and she also heard little Dawn, who was asking that her brother be forgiven. The ogress recognized the voices of the queen and her children, and furious at having been deceived, she gave orders in a frightful voice that the next day in the morning there be brought into the courtyard a huge vat, which she had filled with toads, vipers, snakes, and serpents in order to have the queen

thrown into it along with her children and the chief
steward and his wife and servant girl, and she gave orders
to have them brought forth with their hands tied behind
their backs.

They were already there, and the executioners were
preparing to throw them into the vat when the king, who
was not expected back so soon, rode into the court. He
had come back posthaste and asked in astonishment what
this horrible sight could mean. No one dared inform him,

and the ogress, unable to think what to say, threw herself headfirst into the vat and was devoured in an instant by the ugly beasts she had had put in it. The king could not help being distressed—after all, she was his mother—but he soon consoled himself with his wife and children.

MORAL

It is natural to wait a little while to get a rich, handsome, gallant, and gentle husband, but no woman today can sleep peacefully enough to wait a hundred years for a husband, sleeping all the while. This story thus seems to give us to understand that often the pleasant bonds of matrimony are no less happy for being put off and that one loses nothing by waiting. But the female sex yearns so ardently for the nuptial vows that I have neither the strength nor the heart to preach them this moral.

PUSS IN BOOTS

〰〰〰〰〰〰〰〰〰〰〰〰〰〰〰〰〰〰〰〰〰〰〰〰〰

A miller left no other possessions to his three children than his mill, his donkey, and his cat. The division was soon made, and neither the notary nor the attorney was consulted about it. They would have soon devoured all of the little patrimony. The eldest son received the mill, the second the donkey, and the youngest only the cat. This last-named young man was disconsolate at receiving such a poor share. "My brothers," he said to himself, "will be able to earn an honest living by joining forces. As for me, when I've eaten my cat and made myself a muff out of its fur, I shall just have to die of hunger."

The cat, who had heard this speech but pretended he hadn't, said to him with a sober and serious air, "Don't suffer on this account, Master. All you have to do is give me a sack and order me a pair of boots for going through thickets, and you will see that your lot is not so bad as you think." Although the cat's master did not put much stock in this, still he had seen the cat perform so many clever tricks in order to catch rats and mice—for instance, when he hung by his feet or hid himself in the flour and played dead—that he did not despair of being helped in his misery.

When the cat received what he had asked for, he

pulled on his fine boots, slung the sack over his shoulder, taking the cords between his two front paws, and went off to a warren where there were a great number of rabbits. He put some bran and some greens into the sack, and stretching himself out beside it as if he were dead, he waited for some young rabbit, as yet inexperienced in the snares of this world, to come and creep into his sack to eat what had been put there. Hardly had he lain down when he got what he wanted: a silly young rabbit went into the sack, and the master cat, pulling the strings, caught and killed it without mercy.

Feeling quite proud of his catch, the cat went to the king and asked to speak to him. He was shown up to his Majesty's apartment, and when he had gone in, he bowed deeply to the king and said, "Sire, here is a rabbit from the warren of my lord, the Marquis of Carabas (for such is the name he'd taken it into his head to give his master), which he has ordered me to present to you with his respects."

"Tell your master," replied the king, "that I thank him and that he has given me pleasure."

Another time the cat went and hid in a wheat field with the open sack beside him, and when two partridges had gone in, he pulled the strings and caught both of them. He then went to present them to the king, as he had done with the rabbit. The king was even more pleased with the partridges and had him suitably rewarded.

The cat continued for two or three months in the same way, from time to time bringing the king game from his master's preserves. One day when he knew the king was going for a drive along the river with his daughter, the most beautiful princess in the world, he said to his master, "If you follow my advice, your fortune is made. You have only to bathe in the river, at the place I shall show you, and then let me manage."

The Marquis of Carabas did what his cat had advised, without knowing what good it would do. While he was bathing, the king happened to pass by, and the cat began to shout as loudly as he could, "Help! Help! My lord, the Marquis of Carabas, is drowning!" At this cry, the king put his head out the coach window, and when he recognized the cat who had brought him game so many times, he gave orders to his guards that someone should go quickly to the rescue of the Marquis of Carabas.

While they were pulling the poor marquis from the river, the cat went up to the coach and told the king that while his master was bathing, some robbers had come and made off with his clothes, although he himself had shouted "Stop, thief!" as loudly as he could. The rascal had really hidden them under a large stone. The king immediately ordered the officers of his wardrobe to go fetch one of his handsomest suits for the Marquis of Carabas.

The king paid him a thousand attentions, and as the fine clothes that he had just been given set off his good looks (for he was handsome and well built), the daughter of the king found him much to her liking. The Marquis of Carabas had no sooner cast two or three highly respectful but rather tender glances in her direction than she fell madly in love with him.

The king asked him to enter the coach and to join them in the promenade. The cat, delighted to see his scheme beginning to succeed, went on ahead. When he met some peasants who were mowing a meadow, he said to them, "Good people, if you do not tell the king that the meadow you are mowing belongs to the Marquis of Carabas, you shall be chopped up in little pieces for mincemeat."

The king did not fail to ask the mowers whose meadow they were mowing. "It belongs to the Marquis of Carabas," they all said together because the cat's threat had frightened them.

"You have a nice property there," said the king to the marquis of Carabas.

"As you see, sire," replied the marquis. "It is a meadow that has never failed to produce abundantly every year."

The master cat, who had continued on ahead, met some reapers and said to them, "Good people, if you do not say that all this grain belongs to the Marquis

of Carabas, you shall all be chopped up in little pieces for mincemeat." The king, who came by the next moment, wished to know to whom all the grain he saw belonged. "It belongs to the Marquis of Carabas," replied the reapers, and the king again congratulated the marquis. The cat, who was continuing on ahead of the coach, said the same thing to everyone he met, and the king was astonished at the great possessions of the Marquis of Carabas.

The master cat arrived at last at a beautiful castle whose owner was an ogre, the richest that had ever been seen, because all the lands that the king had passed were in the domain of this castle. The cat, who had taken care to inform himself who this ogre was and what he could do, asked to speak to him, saying that he had not wished to pass by so close to his castle without having the honor of paying his respects to him.

The ogre received him as politely as an ogre can and had him sit down. "They tell me," said the cat, "that you have the gift of being able to change yourself into all sorts of animals—that you can, for example, transform yourself into a lion or an elephant."

"That is true," said the ogre brusquely, "and to prove it to you, you are going to see me become a lion." The cat was so terrified to see a lion in front of him that he jumped up to the roof, not without some trouble and danger on account of his boots, which were no good for walking on the tiles. A little while later, the cat, seeing that the ogre had returned to his own shape, came down and admitted that he had been really afraid. "They have further told me, but I cannot believe it," said the cat, "that you also have the power to take the form of the smallest animals—that you can, for instance, change yourself into a rat or a mouse. I assure you, I consider that to be completely impossible."

"Impossible?" answered the ogre. "You shall see," and at the same time he changed himself into a mouse, which began to run about on the floor. The cat had no sooner seen it than he pounced upon it and ate it.

The king, meanwhile, saw the beautiful castle of the ogre as they were passing by and expressed the desire to enter it. The cat, who heard the noise of the coach as it passed over the drawbridge, ran to meet them and said to the king, "Your Majesty is welcome to the castle of my lord, the Marquis of Carabas."

"What, my Lord Marquis," cried the king, "this castle is also yours! Nothing could be more beautiful than this courtyard and all these buildings that surround it. Let us go in, if you please."

The marquis gave his hand to the young princess, and following the king, who went up first, they entered a great hall, where they found a magnificent supper that the ogre had prepared for some friends of his who were to come that very day but who had not dared to enter, knowing that the king was there. The king was delighted with the marquis' good qualities, and the princess loved him madly. Since the king had seen the great property the marquis possessed, he said to him after drinking five or six glasses, "It is entirely up to you, my Lord Marquis, if you choose to be my son-in-law." The marquis, after bowing profoundly several times, accepted the honor that the king offered him and married the princess on the same day. The cat became a great lord and no longer chased mice except to amuse himself.

MORAL

However great may be the advantage of enjoying a rich patrimony, handed down to us from father to son, in general, industry and knowing how to get on in the world are worth more to young men than inherited property.

ANOTHER MORAL

If the son of a miller can so quickly win the heart of a princess and make her gaze at him with languishing eyes, it is only because clothes, a good appearance, and youth are not the least effective ways to inspire affection.

THE FAIRIES

|||||||||||||||||||||||||||||||||||||||||

Once upon a time there was a widow who had two daughters. The elder resembled her greatly in disposition so that whoever saw her saw the mother. They were both so disagreeable and so haughty that there was no living with them. The younger daughter, who was the very image of her father for sweetness and courtesy, was in addition one of the most beautiful girls imaginable. Since we naturally like those who resemble us, the mother was very fond of her older child and at the same time had an intense loathing for the younger. She made her eat in the kitchen and work all the time.

Among other duties, this poor child had to go twice a day to draw water from a spring a good half mile from the house, and she had to bring back a large pitcherful. One day when she was at the spring, there came a poor old woman who begged her to give her a drink. "Yes indeed, good mother," said this beautiful girl, and she immediately rinsed her pitcher and drew water from the clearest part of the spring and gave it to her, holding the pitcher all the time so that she might drink more easily. When the woman had drunk, she said, "You are so beautiful, so good, and so courteous that I cannot help giving you a gift." (It was really a fairy who had taken the form of a poor woman of the village to see just how courteous this girl would be.) "I shall give you as a gift," continued the fairy, "that at every word you speak there will fall from your mouth either a flower or a precious stone."

When the beautiful girl reached home, her mother scolded her for coming back from the fountain so late. "I beg your pardon, Mother," said the poor girl, "for having delayed so long." And as she said these words, two roses, two pearls, and two large diamonds fell from her mouth.

"What do I see?" said her mother in astonishment. "I do believe that pearls and diamonds are coming out of her mouth—how does this happen, my child?" (This was the first time that she had ever called her "my child.") The poor girl candidly told her everything that had happened, letting fall at the same time an infinite number of diamonds. "Really," said the mother, "I'll have to send my daughter. Look here, Fanny, do you see what is coming out of your sister's mouth when she speaks—wouldn't you be happy to have the same gift? All you have to do is draw water from the spring, and when a poor woman asks you for a drink, give it to her very courteously."

"I'll certainly be a lovely sight going to the spring," she replied sulkily.

"I want you to go—and right away," replied the mother.

She went, but grumbled the whole time. She took the handsomest silver flask in the house. She had no sooner arrived at the spring than she saw coming from the woods a magnificently dressed lady who asked her for a drink. It was the same fairy who had appeared to her sister but who had now taken the manner and dress of a princess to see just how discourteous this girl would be.

"Have I come here only to give you a drink?" she said sulkily and disdainfully. "Have I brought along a silver flask just to give your ladyship a drink? As far as I am concerned, you should help yourself if you want a drink."

"You are not at all courteous," replied the fairy without becoming angry. "Well, since you are so unobliging, I shall give you as a gift that with each word you speak there will fall from your mouth either a snake or a toad."

As soon as her mother saw her she said, "Well, daughter?" "Well, Mother," she answered sullenly, letting fall two vipers and two toads.

"Oh, heavens," cried the mother. "What do I see! It's your sister who's responsible for this—she'll pay for it!" And she rushed off to beat her. The poor girl fled and went to hide in the surrounding forest. The son of the king, who was coming back from the hunt, met her, and seeing how beautiful she was, asked what she was doing all alone and why she was crying. "Alas, sir, my mother has put me out of the house."

The king's son, who saw five or six pearls and as many diamonds fall from her mouth, begged her to tell him how this had happened to her. She told him the whole story. The king's son fell in love with her, and considering that such a gift would be more valuable than all the dowry that could be given with anyone else he might marry, took her to the palace of the king, his father, and there he married her.

As for her sister, she made herself so hated that her own mother put her out of the house, and the unfortunate girl, after having gone far and wide without finding anyone who would welcome her, went off to a corner of the forest to die.

MORAL

Diamonds and doubloons make a powerful impression, but sweet words have even more force and are of greater worth.

ANOTHER MORAL

Courtesy is worth the effort it takes and requires a little good nature, but sooner or later it has its reward, and often when one least expects it.

CINDERELLA

iiiiiiiiiiiiiiiiiiiiiiiiiiiiiiiiiiiiiiiii

Once upon a time there was a gentleman who
married as his second wife the proudest and
haughtiest woman who had ever been seen. She
had two daughters with a disposition like her own, who
resembled her in everything. The husband had for his
part a young daughter who was of unparalleled sweetness
and goodness—she got this from her mother, who was
the best person in the world.

The marriage ceremony was no sooner over than the
stepmother gave free rein to her bad disposition. She
could not endure the little girl's good qualities, which
made her own daughters seem even more hateful. She
made her do the most unpleasant household chores—
it was she who washed the dishes and the steps and who
scrubbed madame's bedroom and that of the young
ladies, her daughters. She slept at the top of the house
in a garret on an ugly straw mattress, while her sisters
were in bedrooms that had parquet floors and furnish-
ings in the latest style and mirrors in which they could
see themselves from head to toe.

The poor girl bore everything patiently and did not
dare complain to her father, who would have scolded
her because his wife dominated him completely. When

she had finished her work, she would go to the chimney
corner and sit in the ashes, which made everyone
in the house call her Cinderslut. The younger sister,
who was not so disagreeable as the older, called her
Cinderella. Cinderella, however, with her poor clothes,
could not help being a hundred times more beautiful
than her sisters, even though they were dressed magnificently.

It happened that the king's son gave a ball, and he
invited all the people of quality. Our two young ladies
were also invited, for they cut a fine figure in that
country. They were quite pleased and busied themselves
choosing the clothes and the headdresses that would be
most becoming to them. This was a new trouble for
Cinderella, for it was she who ironed the sisters' linen
and pleated their frills. They did nothing but talk
about how they would dress.

"I shall wear my red velvet gown with the English
trimmings," said the elder.

"As for me," said the younger, "I haven't anything
but my everyday petticoat, but to make up for it, I
shall wear my manteau with the gold flowers and my
diamond stomacher, which is not of the most ordinary
kind."

They sent for the best coiffeuse to adjust their caps
with the double rows of ruffles, and they bought beauty
patches at the best shop. They summoned Cinderella
to ask her opinion, for she had excellent taste. Cinderella
advised them with the best will in the world and even
offered to arrange their hair, which they were willing
to have her do. As she was arranging their hair, they
said to her, "Cinderella, would it make you very happy
to go to the ball?"

"Oh dear, young ladies, you are making fun of me.
That would be no place for me."

"You are right—they would certainly laugh to see a
cinderslut at a ball." Any other person but Cinderella
would have done their hair badly, but she had a good
heart and she did their hair beautifully. They went for
almost two days without eating because they were in
such transports of joy. They broke more than a dozen

laces trying to squeeze their waists smaller, and they were constantly in front of the mirror.

At last the happy day arrived. They left, and Cinderella followed them with her eyes as long as she could. When she could see them no longer, she began to cry. Her godmother, who saw her in tears, asked what was the matter.

"I would like—I would like—" She was crying so hard she could not finish. Her godmother, who was a fairy, said, "You would like to go to the ball, wouldn't you?"

"Oh dear, yes," said Cinderella, sighing.

"All right, will you be a good girl?" said her godmother. "I'll see to it that you go." She led her to her room and said, "Go into the garden and bring me back a pumpkin." Cinderella immediately went and cut the

best one she could find and took it to her godmother,
although she could not guess how that pumpkin could
make her go to the ball. Her godmother hollowed it
out so that only the shell was left and struck it with her
wand, and the pumpkin was changed into a beautiful
gold coach.

Then she went to look in the mousetrap, and she
found six mice still alive. She told Cinderella to open
the door of the trap slightly, and as each mouse left,
she struck it with her wand and the mouse was changed
at once into a handsome horse, which made a handsome
equipage of six horses of a fine dappled mouse gray.
Since she was in some difficulty as to what she should
turn into the coachman, Cinderella said, "I'll go see if
there isn't a rat in the rat trap that we could make the
coachman."

"You're right," said her godmother. "Go and look."

Cinderella brought the rat trap, in which there were
three large rats. The fairy took one of the three because of his splendid whiskers, and when she touched
him, he was changed into a fat coachman who had the
handsomest mustaches ever seen. Then she said, "Go
into the garden and you will find six lizards behind the
watering can—bring them to me."

Cinderella had no sooner brought them than her godmother changed them into six footmen who got up immediately behind the coach in their lace-trimmed liveries
and clung there as if they had never done anything else
all their lives. Then the fairy said to Cinderella, "Well,
here is what you need for going to the ball—aren't you
pleased?"

"Yes, but am I to go like this, in these ugly clothes?"
Her godmother just touched her with her wand, and at
once her clothes were changed into clothes of gold and
silver brocade, all studded with precious stones. Next
she gave her a pair of the prettiest glass slippers in the
world. When she was thus arrayed, she got into the
coach, but her godmother charged her above all not to
stay beyond midnight, warning her that if she remained
at the ball a moment longer, her coach would become a
pumpkin again, her horses mice, her footmen lizards,

and all her beautiful clothes would turn back into rags. She promised her godmother that she would not fail to leave the ball before midnight, and she left, beside herself with happiness.

The king's son, who had been told that a beautiful princess whom no one knew had just arrived, hastened to receive her. He gave her his hand as she descended from the coach and led her into the hall where the company were. A great silence fell; people stopped dancing and the violins ceased to play, so eager was everyone to gaze upon the great beauty of this unknown princess. All that could be heard was a confused murmur of "Oh, isn't she beautiful!" Even the king, old as he was, could not take his eyes off her and whispered to the queen that it had been a long time since he had seen such a lovely person. All the ladies were eager to examine her headdress and her clothes in order to have similar ones ordered for the next day, provided they could find material beautiful enough and seamstresses skillful enough.

The king's son set her in the place of honor and then begged her to let him lead her out to dance. She danced so gracefully that they admired her even more. A fine supper was brought but the young prince did not eat any of it, he was so occupied with gazing upon her. She went to sit next to her sisters and did them a thousand kindnesses, and she shared with them the oranges and lemons the prince had given her, all of which greatly astonished them because they did not know her at all. As they were conversing thus, Cinderella heard it strike a quarter to twelve. She made a deep curtsy to the company and went away as fast as she could.

As soon as she got home she went to find her godmother in order to thank her, and she told her that she wished she could go to the ball again the next night because the king's son had begged her to come. As she was busy telling her godmother all that had happened at the ball, the two sisters knocked at the door and Cinderella went to let them in. "What a long time you've been coming back!" she said, yawning and rubbing her eyes and stretching as if she had just awakened. How-

ever, she had felt no desire to sleep ever since they
left her.

"If you had come to the ball," one of her sisters said,
"you wouldn't have been bored. The most beautiful princess came, the most beautiful ever seen. She did us a
thousand courtesies, and she gave us oranges and lemons." Cinderella could not hide her joy. She asked them
the name of that princess, but they replied that they
did not know it and that the king's son was greatly dis-
turbed by this and would give anything in the world
to know who she was. Cinderella smiled and said, "Was
she really so beautiful? My goodness, how lucky you are!
Oh dear, Mademoiselle Javotte, won't you lend me the
yellow dress you wear for every day?"

"Well, really," said Mademoiselle Javotte, "that's a
fine idea! To just go and lend my dress to an ugly
cinderslut, I'd have to be out of my mind." Cinderella
had expected this refusal, and she was quite pleased by
it, for she would not have known what to do if her
sister had wanted to lend her the dress.

The next day the two sisters were at the ball, and
Cinderella also, but even more richly clothed than the
first time. The king's son was constantly at her side and
kept on whispering sweet nothings to her. The young
lady was not at all bored and forgot her godmother's
command so that while she was thinking it was only
eleven o'clock, she heard the first stroke of midnight.
She got up and fled as swiftly as a fawn. The prince
followed her but could not catch up with her. She
dropped one of her glass slippers and the prince picked
it up carefully.

Cinderella reached home out of breath, without her
coach, without her footmen, and in her poor clothes.
Nothing was left of all her magnificence but one of her
little slippers, the mate of that which she had dropped.
The guards at the palace gates were asked if they had
not seen a princess leave. They said that they had seen
no one leave but a young girl who was very badly
dressed and who looked more like a peasant than a
young lady.

When her two sisters came back from the ball, Cin-

derella asked them if they had had a good time again
and if the beautiful lady had been there. They told her
that she had but that she had rushed away when midnight struck, and so quickly that she had dropped
one of her little glass slippers, the prettiest in the
world, and that the king's son had picked it up and
had done nothing but look at it all during the rest of
the ball, and that undoubtedly he was in love with the
beautiful person to whom the little slipper belonged.

They spoke the truth, for a few days later the king's
son had his herald proclaim that he would marry the
girl whose foot fitted exactly into the slipper. They began
trying it on the princesses, next the duchesses, and then
all the court, but in vain. They brought it to the two
sisters, who did all they could to get their foot into the
slipper, but they were unsuccessful.

Cinderella, who was watching them and who recognized her slipper, said laughingly, "Let me see if it
won't fit me!" Her sisters began to laugh and make fun
of her. The gentleman who was trying on the slipper
looked at Cinderella attentively, and finding her very
beautiful, said that that was only fair and that he had
orders to try it on all the girls. He made Cinderella sit
down, and when he had placed the slipper on her little
foot, he saw that it went on without difficulty and that it
fit as if it had been of wax.

The astonishment of the two sisters was great, and
it became even greater when Cinderella took the other
little slipper from her pocket and put it on. At that moment her godmother arrived, and having touched Cinderella's clothes with her wand, she made them even
more magnificent than all the others. Then the two
sisters recognized her for the beauty they had seen
at the ball. They threw themselves at her feet to ask
her forgiveness for all the harsh treatment they had
made her suffer. Cinderella raised them up, kissed them,
told them she forgave them with all her heart, and begged
them to love her forever.

Dressed as she was, she was led to the palace of the
young prince. He found her more beautiful than ever,
and a few days later he married her. Cinderella, who

was as good as she was beautiful, had her two sisters come live at the palace and married them the same day to two great lords of the court.

MORAL

Beauty is a rare treasure in women and one should never tire of admiring it, but that which is called graciousness is without price and is even more valuable. That is what Cinderella's godmother gave her by training her and teaching her so much and so well that she made her a queen (for that is the moral of this tale). Lovely ladies, this gift is worth more than having a fine headdress. In order to succeed in capturing a heart, graciousness is the true gift of fairies. Without it one can do nothing; with it, one can do everything.

ANOTHER MORAL

It is undoubtedly a great advantage to have wit, courage, birth, good sense, and other similar talents of which one receives one's share from heaven; but you will have them in vain—they will not get you advancement if you lack a godfather or a godmother to make them effective.

Madame Leprince de Beaumont

BEAUTY AND THE BEAST

Once upon a time there was a merchant who was extremely rich. He had six children, three sons and three daughters, and since this merchant was an intelligent man, he did not stint on anything in educating his children and gave them all sorts of teachers.

His daughters were very beautiful, but the youngest was especially admired and was never called anything but Beautiful Child, with the result that the name became attached to her, which made her sisters very jealous. This youngest girl, who was more beautiful than her sisters, was also better than they. The two older ones were very proud because they were rich; they played the great lady and did not wish to receive visits from other merchants' daughters, and they had to have people of quality as companions. They went to balls, to the theater, and out promenading every day, and they made fun of their younger sister, who spent most of her time reading good books.

Since everyone knew that these girls were very rich, several well-to-do merchants asked for them in marriage, but the two older ones replied that they would never marry, not unless they could find a duke or, at the very least, a count. Beauty (for, as I have told you, that was the name of the youngest) sincerely thanked those who wished to marry her, but told them that she was too young and that she hoped to be a companion to her father for a few years.

All at once the merchant lost all that he had, and nothing was left to him but a little house in the country, far away from the city. Weeping, he told his children that they must go to this house and that by working like peasants they might be able to make a living. His two older daughters replied that they did not want to leave the city and that they had several suitors who would be only too happy to marry them even though they no longer had a fortune. But the young ladies were mistaken and their suitors did not want even to look at them when they were poor. Since no one liked them because of their arrogance, everyone said, "They don't deserve pity. We are quite pleased to see their pride humbled; let them play the great lady while they watch their sheep. As for Beauty, we are really sorry about her misfortune; she is such a good girl! She used to talk to the poor people with such kindness, she was so sweet, so sincere!" There were even several gentlemen who would have liked to marry her, even though she did not have a cent, but she told them that she could not bring herself to abandon her poor father in his misfortune and that she would follow him into the country to comfort him and to help him work. Poor Beauty suffered a great deal at first over losing her fortune, but she said to herself, "Crying will not bring back my possessions; I must try to be happy without a fortune."

When they had arrived at their house in the country, the merchant and his three sons busied themselves in working the land. Beauty would get up at four o'clock in the morning and hasten to clean the house and get dinner ready for the family. At first it was a great hardship for her because she had not been used to working like a servant girl, but by the end of two months she became stronger, and hard work gave her perfect health. When she had finished her housework, she would read or play the harpsichord or even sing while weaving. Her two sisters, on the other hand, were bored to death. They got up at ten in the morning, went out for walks all day long, and amused themselves by regretting their pretty clothes and their parties. "Look at our younger sister," they said to each other; "she is so common and stupid that she is contented with her unhappy situation."

The good merchant did not agree with his daughters. He knew that Beauty would outshine them in any company, and he admired the virtue of this younger girl, and especially her patience, for her sisters, not content with leaving all the housework to her, insulted her at every opportunity.

This family had lived in solitude for a year when the merchant received a letter by which he was advised that a ship, on which he had some goods, had just arrived safely. This news all but turned the heads of his two older daughters, who thought that at last they would be able to leave the country where they were so bored; and when they saw that their father was ready to depart, they begged him to bring them dresses, fur tippets, and all sorts of trifles. Beauty did not ask him for anything, for she thought that all the money the goods were worth would not be enough to buy what her sisters were wishing for.

"Aren't you going to ask me to buy you something?" her father asked her.

"Since you are so good as to think of me," she said, "I ask you to bring me a rose because there are none blooming here." It is not that Beauty really wanted a rose, but she did not want to criticize her sisters' behavior by her example because they would have believed that it was to set herself apart from them that she did not ask for anything.

The good merchant departed, but when he had arrived, he was sued for his goods so that after having had much trouble, he went back as poor as he had been before. He had not more than thirty leagues to go to his house, and he was rejoicing already at the pleasure of seeing his children. Since, however, it was necessary for him to pass through a large forest before reaching his house, he lost his way. It was snowing dreadfully and the wind was so strong that twice it knocked him off his horse. When night came he thought that he would die of hunger or cold or that he would be eaten by the wolves he heard howling around him.

Suddenly, as he was looking down a long alley of trees, he saw a great light, which seemed, however, quite far away. He walked in that direction and saw that this light came from a great palace, which was all illuminated. The merchant thanked God for the help that had been sent him and hastened to make his way to this castle. He was quite surprised not to find anyone in the courtyards. His horse, which was following him, saw an open stable, went into it, and found hay and oats there. The poor animal, which was dying of hunger, fell eagerly upon this fodder. The merchant shut him into the stable and walked toward the house, but he found no one. When he had entered, however, he did find a good fire and a table laden with food at which a place was set for only one person.

Since the rain and the snow had soaked him to the skin, he drew close to the fire to dry himself, and he said to himself, "The master of the house or the servants will excuse the liberty I have taken and will undoubtedly come soon." He waited for quite a while, but when eleven o'clock struck without his having seen anyone, he could not restrain his hunger and took a chicken, which he ate in two mouthfuls, trembling the while. He also drank a few swallows of wine, and then, becoming bolder, left the room and went across several large apartments, magnificently furnished. At the end he found a bedroom in which there was a good bed, and since it was past midnight and he was tired, he decided to shut the door and go to bed.

It was ten o'clock in the morning when he woke up the next day, and he was quite surprised to find a new suit of clothes to replace his own, which had been completely spoiled.

"Assuredly," he said to himself, "this palace belongs to some good fairy who has taken pity on my situation." He looked out the window and saw not snow but arbors of flowers that delighted the eye. He went back to the great hall in which he had had supper the night before and saw a little table on which there was a cup of chocolate. "I'm very grateful to you, Madame Fairy," he said aloud, "for your kindness in thinking of my breakfast." The good merchant, after drinking his chocolate, left to look for his horse, and as he was passing beneath an arbor of roses, he remembered that Beauty had asked for one, and he plucked a branch on which there were several blossoms.

At the same instant he heard a loud noise, and he saw coming toward him a beast so horrible that he nearly fainted. "You are truly ungrateful," said the beast in a terrible voice. "I saved your life by receiving you in my castle, and for my trouble you are stealing my roses, which I love better than anything in the world. You must die to atone for this fault. I shall give you no more than a quarter of an hour to ask forgiveness of God." The merchant threw himself on his knees, and clasping his hands, said to the beast, "My lord, forgive me; I did not believe I should offend you by picking a rose for one of my daughters, who had asked me for one."

"I am not called 'My lord,' but 'Beast,'" responded the monster. "I do not like compliments; instead, I want people to say what they think, so do not believe that you can move me by your flattery. You have told me you have daughters. I will forgive you on the condition that one of your daughters comes of her own free will to die in your place. Do not argue with me—leave, and if your daughters refuse to die for you, swear that you will return in three months."

The good merchant did not intend to sacrifice one of his daughters to this ugly monster, but he said to himself, "At least I shall have the pleasure of embracing them one more time." He accordingly swore to return, and the beast told him he could leave when he wished. "But," he added, "I do not want you to go away empty handed. Go back to the room in which you slept; you will find a large empty chest there and you can put in it whatever pleases you, and I shall have it taken to your house." At this the beast went away, and the poor man said to himself, "If I have to die, I shall have the consolation of leaving something to my poor children."

He went back to the room where he had slept, and

when he had found a large quantity of gold pieces, he filled the chest that the beast had mentioned and closed it up. After he had retrieved his horse, which he found in the stable, he set out from this palace as sad as he had been happy when he had entered it.

His horse of its own accord took one of the roads through the forest, and in a few hours the good merchant arrived at his little house. His children gathered around him, but instead of responding to their affectionate greetings, the merchant looked at them and began to cry. He held in his hand the branch of roses that he had brought to Beauty, and he gave it to her and said, "Take these roses, Beauty; they will be dearly paid for by your unhappy father." And he immediately told his family about the disaster that had befallen him.

At this account, the two older girls shrieked and spoke harshly to Beauty, who did not cry at all. "See what the arrogance of this little thing has brought about," they said. "Why didn't she ask for clothes, as we did? But no, because the young lady wished to set herself apart from us, she is going to cause the death of our father, and she isn't even crying."

"It would be quite useless," replied Beauty. "Why should I cry over the death of my father? He shall not perish. Since the monster really wishes to accept one of the daughters, I shall give myself up to all his fury, and I consider myself quite fortunate since by dying I shall have the joy of saving my father and of proving my affection for him."

"No, sister," her three brothers said to her, "you shall not die. We will go find this monster, and we shall perish beneath his blows if we cannot kill him."

"You cannot hope to do that, my children," said the merchant. "The power of that beast is so great that I have no hope of destroying him. I am delighted at Beauty's goodness of heart, but I do not wish to expose her to death. I am old and I have only a short time to live so that I shall be losing only a few years of life, which I do not regret except on your account, my dear children."

"I tell you, Father," Beauty said, "that you shall not go to this palace without me. You cannot prevent me from

following you. Although I am young, I have no strong
attachment to life, and I should prefer being devoured
by this monster to dying of the grief that your death
would cause me."

It was useless to say anything. Beauty had resolved
absolutely to leave for the beautiful palace, and her sisters were delighted because the virtues of this youngest
daughter had inspired them with extreme jealousy.

The merchant had been so taken up by his grief at
losing his daughter that he had not thought of the chest
that he had filled with gold. But as soon as he had entered his bedroom to go to sleep, he was astonished to
find it between the bed and the wall. He decided not to
tell his children that he had become so rich because his
daughters would have wished to return to the city, and
he had decided to die in the country. However, he did
entrust the secret to Beauty because she had informed
him that several gentlemen had come during his absence
and that there were two who loved her sisters. She begged
her father to let them be married because she loved them
and forgave them with all her heart the evil they had
done her.

These two wicked sisters rubbed their eyes with an
onion in order to cry when Beauty left with her father,
but her brothers cried in earnest, and so did the merchant. Only Beauty did not cry at all because she did not
want to increase their sorrow.

The horse took the way to the palace, and at evening
they saw it, illuminated as on the first occasion. The
horse went to the stable still saddled, and the good
merchant with his daughter entered the great hall, where
they found a table magnificently laid for two people.
The merchant had not the heart to eat, but Beauty, forcing herself to appear calm, took her place at the table
and served him. Then she said to herself, "The beast
must want to fatten me up before eating me since he
gives me such a good supper."

When they had eaten, they heard a loud noise, and the
merchant bade his daughter a tearful farewell, for he
thought it was the beast. Beauty could not prevent herself from shuddering when she saw that horrible figure,
but she reassured herself as best she could. When the

monster asked her if she had come willingly, she trembled but said that she had.

"You are very good," the beast said, "and I am much obliged to you. My good man, leave tomorrow morning, and do not count on ever coming back here. Farewell, Beauty."

"Farewell, Beast," she replied. And the monster went away at once.

"Ah, daughter," said the merchant, embracing Beauty, "I am half dead with fright. Trust me; leave me here."

"No, Father," said Beauty firmly. "You will leave tomorrow morning, and you will entrust me to the care of heaven; perhaps heaven will pity me." They went to bed and did not believe they could sleep at all that night, but hardly were they in their beds when their eyes closed.

During her sleep, Beauty saw a lady who said to her, "I am happy at your goodness of heart, Beauty. The good deed that you have done in giving your life to save that of your father will not pass without being rewarded." When she awoke, Beauty told this dream to her father, and although it consoled him a bit, it did not prevent him from uttering loud cries of grief when he had to be separated from his daughter.

When he had left, Beauty sat down in the great hall and began to cry also; then, since she had a great deal of courage, she commended herself to God and resolved to grieve no longer in the short time she had to live, for she firmly believed that the beast would eat her that evening. She decided to go for a walk while waiting and to look over this lovely castle. She could not help admiring its beauty. But she was surprised to find an apartment on whose door was written "Beauty's Apartment." She opened the door quickly and was overwhelmed by its magnificence, but what struck her most was the sight of a large bookcase, a harpsichord, and several books of music. "They don't want me to be bored," she said under her breath. And she thought next, "If I were to live here only a day, they would not have provided these things." This thought revived her courage.

She opened the bookcase and saw a book on which was written in gold letters: "Wish, command—you are the queen and mistress here." "Alas," she sighed, "I do not wish for anything except to see my poor father and to know what he is doing now." She had said this to herself, but what was her surprise, in casting her eyes upon a large mirror, to see in it her home as her father was arriving there with an extremely sad face. Her sisters came to him, and in spite of the grimaces they made in order to appear to be suffering, the joy that they felt at the loss of their sister appeared on their faces. A moment later all this had disappeared, and Beauty could not avoid thinking that the beast was very kind and that she had nothing to fear from him.

At noon she found the table set, and during her dinner, she heard an excellent concert, although she saw no one. In the evening as she was about to sit down at the table, she heard the noise that the beast made and could not help shuddering.

"Beauty," the monster said, "would you object if I were to watch you have supper?"

"You are the master," Beauty answered, trembling.

"No," replied the beast, "there is no mistress here but you. You have only to tell me to go away if I annoy you and I shall leave immediately. Tell me—you find me very ugly, do you not?"

"That is true," said Beauty, "for I cannot lie—but I believe that you are very good."

"You are right," said the monster. "However, in addition to being ugly, I lack wit and intelligence. I know very well that I am only a stupid beast."

"One is not stupid," replied Beauty, "if one thinks that one has no intelligence. A fool would never realize that."

"Eat your supper, then, Beauty, and try not to be unhappy in your home, for everything here is yours, and I shall be grieved if you are not happy."

"You are good indeed," said Beauty. "I assure you that I am pleased with your heart, and when I think of it, you do not seem so ugly to me."

"Oh, as for that, yes," replied the beast. "I have a good heart, but I am still a monster."

"There are men who are greater monsters than you," said Beauty, "and I prefer you and your appearance to those who under the appearance of men hide hearts that are false, corrupt, and ungrateful."

"If I had wit and intelligence," replied the beast, "I should make you a grand compliment in order to thank you; but I am a dolt, and all that I can say to you is that I am much obliged to you."

Beauty ate her supper with a good appetite. She had hardly any more fear of the monster, but she almost died of fright when he said, "Beauty, will you be my wife?" She remained some time without replying, for she was afraid of arousing the anger of the monster by refusing; nevertheless, she replied trembling, "No, beast." At that the poor monster tried to sigh and made a hissing noise so horrible that it could be heard all over the palace, but Beauty was much reassured because the beast, saying sadly, "Farewell, then, Beauty," left the room, turning back from time to time to look at her again. Beauty, when she realized that she was alone, felt a great compassion for this poor beast. "Alas," she said, "it is really a pity that he is ugly, because he is so kind."

Beauty spent three months in this palace in comparative peace and quiet. Every evening the beast would pay her a visit, conversing with her during supper with much good sense but never with what is called "wit" in the world. Every day Beauty discovered new kindnesses in this monster. The habit of seeing him had accustomed her to his ugliness, and far from fearing the moment of his visit, she often looked at her watch to see if it were nine o'clock yet, for the beast never failed to come at that hour. There was only one thing that troubled Beauty, and this was that the monster, before retiring, always asked her if she would be his wife and seemed overcome by sorrow when she refused him. She said to him one day, "You grieve me, beast. I should like to be able to marry you, but I am too truthful to make you believe that that could ever happen. I shall always be your friend; try to content yourself with that."

"I shall have to," replied the beast. "I do myself justice—I know very well that I am horrible, but I love you very much. However, I am only too happy that you really want to stay here; promise me that you will never leave me." Beauty blushed at these words. She had seen in her mirror that her father had become ill from his sorrow at losing her, and she wished to see him again.

"I really should be able to promise never to leave you, but I have such a yearning to see my father again that I shall die of grief if you refuse me this pleasure."

"I should prefer to die myself," said the monster, "rather than give you pain. I shall send you to your father and you will stay there, and your poor beast will die of grief."

"No," said Beauty tearfully, "I love you too much to wish to cause your death. I promise you to come back within a week. You have let me see that my sisters have married and that my brothers have left for the army. My father is all alone; allow me to stay with him for one week."

"You shall be there tomorrow in the morning," said the beast, "but remember your promise. You have only to place your ring upon the table as you go to bed when you wish to come back. Farewell, Beauty." Saying these words, the beast sighed as he usually did, and Beauty went to bed saddened at having caused him to suffer.

When she woke up in the morning, she found herself in her father's house, and when she had rung the bell beside the bed, she saw the maidservant come in. The latter gave a loud cry on seeing her, and the good merchant came running at the commotion. He almost died of joy at seeing his dear daughter again, and they remained embracing one another for more than a quarter of an hour. Beauty, after the first emotion had passed, remembered that she had no clothes to put on in order to get up, but the maid told her that she had just found in the next room an enormous chest full of golden gowns ornamented with diamonds. Beauty thanked the good beast for his thoughtfulness. She took the least elaborate of the gowns and told the servant to lock up the others because she wished to give them to her sisters as presents. But she had hardly spoken these words when the chest disappeared. Her father told her that the beast wanted her to keep all those things for herself, and at once the gowns and the chest came back to the same place.

Beauty got dressed, and while she was doing so, someone went to tell her sisters, who came running in with their husbands. Both of them were very unhappy. The oldest had married a gentleman as handsome as the god of love, but he was so enamored of his own face that he was concerned with nothing else from morning till night, and he was jealous of the beauty of his wife. The second had married a man who had great wit, but he used it only to irritate the whole world, beginning with his wife.

Beauty's sisters nearly died of grief when they saw her dressed like a princess and more beautiful than the day. It was useless for her to embrace them; nothing could stifle their jealousy, which increased when she told them how happy she was. These two jealous young women went down into the garden to weep there without interruption, and they said to each other, "Why is this little creature happier than we are? Are we not more lovely than she?"

"Sister," said the older, "an idea has just come to me. Let's try to make her stay here more than a week. Her foolish beast will become angry because she will have broken her word, and perhaps he will devour her."

"You are right, sister," replied the other. "To do this it will be necessary to be very affectionate toward her." And having made this resolution, the two went back up and were so loving to their sister that Beauty cried for joy. When the week had passed, the two sisters tore their hair and pretended to be suffering so much because of her departure that she promised to remain another week. Beauty reproached herself, however, for the grief that she was going to cause her poor beast, whom she loved with all her heart, and she was troubled at no longer seeing him. On the tenth night that she spent at her father's, she dreamed that she was in the garden of the palace and that she saw the beast lying on the grass about to die, reproaching her for her ingratitude. Beauty woke up with a start and burst into tears. "Am I not wicked," she said to herself, "to grieve a beast who has had so much kindness for me? Is it his fault that he is so ugly and that he has so little wit? He is good, and that is worth more than all the rest. Why have I not wanted to marry him? I should be happier with him than my sisters are with their husbands. It is neither the handsomeness nor the wit of a husband that makes a wife contented; it is goodness of character, virtue, kindness, and the beast has all these good qualities. I feel no love for him, but I feel admiration, friendship, and gratitude. Come now, I mustn't make him unhappy—I should reproach myself all the rest of my life for my ingratitude."

With these words, Beauty got up, placed her ring on the table, and went back to bed. Hardly was she there when she fell asleep; and when she awoke next morning, she saw with joy that she was in the beast's palace. She dressed herself magnificently in order to please him, and she was bored to death the whole day waiting until nine o'clock in the evening. But the clock struck in vain—the beast did not appear. Beauty feared then that she had caused his death. She ran all through the palace uttering loud cries of despair. When she had looked everywhere, she remembered her dream and ran into the garden toward the stream where she had seen him in her sleep. She found the poor beast stretched out unconscious, and she believed him dead. She threw herself upon his body

without experiencing any horror at his appearance, and when she felt that his heart was still beating, she took some water from the stream and sprinkled it on his forehead.

The beast opened his eyes and said to Beauty, "You have forgotten your promise. The grief of losing you made me decide to let myself die of hunger, but I shall die content because I have had the pleasure of seeing you again."

"No, dear beast, you shall not die," said Beauty. "You will live in order to become my husband. From this moment on, I give you my hand and I swear that I shall be yours alone. Alas! I thought that I felt only friendship for you, but the sorrow that I feel now makes me see that I cannot live without you."

Hardly had Beauty spoken these words when she saw the castle blazing with lights—there were fireworks and music and everything to indicate a celebration. None of these wonders held her attention, however; she turned her eyes back toward her dear beast, whose danger had made her tremble. But to her surprise, the beast had disappeared and at her feet she saw instead a prince handsomer than the god of love, who thanked her for having ended his enchantment. Although this prince deserved all her attention, she could not help asking where the beast was.

"You see him at your feet," the prince told her. "A wicked fairy had condemned me to remain in that shape until a beautiful girl should agree to marry me, and she had forbidden me to reveal my wit and intelligence. You were the only person in the world good enough to let yourself be moved by the goodness of my character, and in offering you my crown, I am only freeing myself of my obligations to you."

Beauty, pleasantly surprised, gave her hand to this handsome prince to help him to rise. They went together to the castle, and Beauty almost died of joy to find in the great hall her father and all her family, transported to the castle by the beautiful lady who had appeared to her in her dream.

"Beauty," said the lady, who was a powerful fairy,

"come and receive the reward of your good choice. You have preferred virtue to handsomeness and wit, and you deserve to find all these qualities united in one single person. You are going to become a great queen; I hope the throne will not spoil your virtues. As for you, ladies," said the fairy to Beauty's two sisters, "I know your hearts and all the malice they contain. Become two statues, but keep your ability to feel and think beneath the stone that will enclose you. You will stand at the door of your sister's palace, and I do not impose upon you any other punishment except that of being witnesses to her good fortune. You will be able to resume your original shapes only when you recognize your faults, but I am very much afraid that you will remain statues forever. One can overcome pride, anger, gluttony, and laziness in oneself, but the reform of a wicked and envious heart is a miracle."

Saying this, the fairy waved her wand, and everyone who was in the hall was transported to the prince's kingdom. His subjects received him with joy, and he married Beauty, who lived with him for a long time in a state of happiness that was perfect because it was based upon virtue.

Hans Jacob Christoffel von Grimmelshausen

THE FIRST OF THE BEARSKINS

The Derivation of the Name "Bearskin"

Those who have attempted to trace *per etymologiam* the name "Bearskin," which the Germans employ as a term of abuse,* have supposed that in the old days, when the ancient Germans slept on all sorts of skins, the name was used to jeer at those who would remain lying slothfully upon their bearskins, never showing any desire to do brave deeds. Perhaps—it happened too long ago to recall exactly—I could shed light upon the subject. In any case, a very ancient portrait was discovered at Castle Hohenrot together with the following account of how the name originated.

In the year 1396, when the Turkish Emperor Celapino defeated Sigismund, who was king of Hungary in those days, a German mercenary fled from the battle into a forest and lost his way. Furthermore, since he didn't know of any master, any war, any money, or even any trade or other means by which he might earn his living, he had many gloomy thoughts. Suddenly he was taken unawares by the apparition of a horrible ghost or spirit —whether or not it was the evil one himself, I cannot tell—who told the soldier that if he would enter his service, he would give him plenty of money and even make a gentleman out of him at the end.

* In German "Bearskin" is a colloquial expression for an idle fellow, a good-for-nothing.

"Oh yes!" answered the soldier. "But only on the condition that serving you won't endanger my salvation."

"Well, but first I'll have to see what you can do," said the spirit, "and test your mettle so that I won't throw my money away." As he was saying this, a huge, enormous bear came loping along. "Shoot him in the head," said the spirit.

The soldier, who wasn't clumsy, hit the bear squarely on the nose so that it rolled over and over.

When he had done this, the ghost or spirit began to bargain and said, "If you want to serve me, you must promise to serve me for seven years and for this period to stand one hour of guard duty every night at midnight; *item*, not to comb your hair and your beard nor to cut the aforesaid or your nails; *item*, not to blow your nose nor to wash your hands or your face nor to wipe your bottom; *item*, to wear this bearskin instead of your coat and to sleep on it instead of on a bed; and never to say the Lord's Prayer. In return, I'll provide you with rations, beer, tobacco, and brandy, and you'll lack for nothing. And when the seven years are over, I'll make such a fellow out of you that you'll be amazed at yourself."

The soldier agreed to everything and said to the spirit, "All those things you've forbidden me, it's always gone against my nature to do. I don't like to wash, I don't like to pray, etc."

When they had reached an agreement, the spirit asked the soldier his name in order to enter it in the record book that he carried with him. But when the soldier pronounced the name of one of the saints, the spirit said, "That one won't do. You'll be called Bearskin because of the bearskin that has been presented to you today."

Then he skinned the bear and made a coat out of the hide for his new servant. And he transported him, along with the hide and all the rest of his baggage, through the clouds to his country place, a dismal castle that is said to owe its name to this marvelous journey.

There the soldier served out his seven years, and during this time his skin, hair, beard, and nails became so horribly filthy that he looked more like the spirit himself than like a rational creature created in the glorious image of God, especially when he was wearing his lovely bearskin instead of a respectable coat. For his hair grew into elflocks that wound around his shoulders looking like the thick tails of Asiatic sheep. His beard was all matted together like a coarse felt hat with (no offense to the reader) snot, spittle, and other slime. His nails were shaped like eagles' talons, and his face was so covered with filthy scum that one could have planted turnip seed there, as the saying goes.

When the seven years were almost up, the spirit came of his own accord and pointed out to him that it was time to settle accounts and pay the wages he had coming. However, to start with he filled his pockets with ducats and doubloons and told him to have a good time, not to skimp, but to empty his pockets doing or not doing whatever his heart desired. But because the seven years of the contract were not completely up, he was under no circumstances to break the terms of their agreement or to give up his old habits.

The soldier obeyed. However, since no one wanted to take him in because he was such a gruesome and horrible sight, he became downhearted. When even an innkeeper, whose profession it is to give food and lodging to strangers for a price, turned him away, the soldier showed him a handful of ducats out of one pocket and a handful of doubloons out of the other, and right away he became a welcome guest. The innkeeper put him up in a separate room and also gave him special room service so that the other guests would not be revolted by his ugly appearance and so that the inn would not get a bad name.

In this room Bearskin stuffed himself at the expense of the spirit, until one day the spirit found out that a gentleman, one of the landed nobility, was making a journey and intended to take lodging at this very inn. At this, the spirit came to the room during the night and painted portraits of all the most famous people who have existed since the Creation, just the way they looked when they were alive, such as Cain, Lamech, Nimrod, Ninus, Zoroaster, Helen, the Greek and Trojan princes, Sosostris, Nebuchadnezzar, Cyrus, Alexander the Great, Julius Caesar, Nero, Caligula, Muhammad, etc. He even painted the portraits of those still to come into the world, such as the anti-Christ and others. The innkeeper was no little amazed at this, especially when Bearskin passed off these pictures as his own work.

When the aforesaid gentleman took lodging there in the evening and asked the innkeeper, who was an acquaintance of his, for the news, the latter told him all that he knew and all that he didn't know about his strange guest, such as his singular appearance, his great skill as a painter, and the fact that he had plenty of money.

The gentleman replied, "I'll have to see this wonder of wonders tomorrow or I won't be able to believe what you've told me." When early the next morning he saw for himself that what he had heard was true, he agreed absolutely with the innkeeper's opinion that this man understood the art of painting better than anyone. Moreover, he marveled for more than one reason, both at the artist's skill and at the works themselves. They were perfect beyond compare, and noticing the similarity between these portraits and ancient works of art that he recalled seeing in other places, he believed that the rest must also look like the men they represented, whose portraits he had never seen before.

He asked Bearskin whether he had done the work. The latter replied with the question "Who else?"

The gentleman answered, "Then you must know a lot since you know how to draw the appearance of the men of the future."

"Yes, indeed!" answered Bearskin. "I know more than people give me credit for."

"Who are you?" asked the gentleman.

"I am Colonel Bearskin," replied the other, "a soldier of fortune, and I recently served in the Turkish wars."

Since this was still a new name and not yet a badge of shame, the gentleman didn't pursue the matter but said instead: "I have three daughters, all so much alike in beauty that even their mother often cannot tell them apart. I am going to show them to you. If you can tell me which is the oldest, which the middle one, and which the youngest, I'll give you whichever one you choose as a wife. If not, then you and all your possessions shall be forfeited to me."

Since Bearskin was satisfied with the proposal, the nobleman took him along home in order to show him his daughters. But the spirit appeared to Bearskin again and said, "You ought to know that on such an occasion this gentleman always puts the youngest in the middle, the oldest on the left, and the middle one on the right." Thus instructed, the soldier was able to tell which was the first, which the second, and which the third, and at the same time he asked to marry the youngest.

The gentleman swore on the spot that he would keep his word as was proper for an honest cavalier. Heaven knows what the mother might say or how the child might take it. Moreover, he wanted to celebrate the wedding right away, before there were any other complications, but Bearskin didn't want to, pleading other business as an excuse, but he promised to come back soon. He took apart a precious ring, made with special screws for this purpose, gave one part to his bride, and then went on his way.

The young bride wore black in mourning, and she wished in vain that she might remain single rather than marry the horrible Bearskin. But what was the use? That was the way her father was determined to have it.

Her sisters didn't envy her the match and teased her every day about her handsome bridegroom. Every hour and every day they made her sore heart bleed afresh; yet she bore it all patiently.

However, the spirit came back and took Bearskin to the Rhine, where he gave him a bath. He put his hair in order and cut it and also trimmed the horrid beard according to the latest fashion, and he beautified him to the point that he looked like the handsomest cavalier. "Now go to X," he said to him, "and make a figure in the world like a bona fide colonel, and live like a gentleman. I'll dig up my treasures that are buried around here and I'll give you money enough." Bearskin, who desired nothing more than this, was all the more eager to obey. He set himself up like a grand vizier with fine horses, splendid carriages, rich clothes, and many servants in livery.

When the time seemed ripe to the spirit, he appeared again and said, "Now go back and get married." And in order to make him appear even wealthier, he filled his carriages and trunks full of money, which he gave him both for a reward and for a marriage portion.

He set out on his journey and sent his herald ahead to give respectful greetings to his future father-in-law and to inform him that an honorable cavalier was en route to pay suit to him and to wait upon his wife and daughters—in a word, to ask for the hand of one of his daughters if it might be permitted and would cause no inconvenience.

When he received the courteous answer that he would be most welcome, he made a splendid entry with his suite and was well received. Moreover, to give him all the more polite encouragement, he was put at the head of the table between the two older daughters, who had adorned themselves magnificently on his account because each hoped to get him for herself. The youngest, however, had to make do at the foot of the table, like a turtledove that has lost its mate, because she was engaged and could not hope to get this fine-looking gentleman. Her sisters gave her many a mocking look and cut her to the heart with many a sharp and scornful word.

After the parents had been shown all the gold and had given Bearskin their consent to choose between their daughters, and while each of the older ones was still desperately hoping to get him, he revealed himself to the youngest by means of his part of the ring, the other piece of which he had given to her before. She was overjoyed, and the other two were just as greatly dismayed to see themselves suddenly robbed of their hopes. They were so confounded that they no longer knew what they were doing, and their parents were so delighted at the luck of the one daughter that they paid no attention to the chagrin of the other two. The daughters were so overwhelmed with shame and with envy of their sister, that one hanged herself and the other jumped into a well.

"There," said the spirit, who seemed extremely cheerful to Bearskin, "now we're all square. You've got one, and I've got two of the daughters, whom their father has refused to give to many an honorable cavalier."

My very dear, most respected, and therefore most indulgent reader, for the time being you must rest content with this tale and make of it what you will. Eventually I hope to elucidate it with a commentary.

Wilhelm Hauff

IIIIIIIIIIIIIIIIIIIIIIIIIIIIIIIIIIIIIIIII

DWARF LONGNOSE

IIIIIIIIIIIIIIIIIIIIIIIIIIIIIIIIIIIIIIIIIIIIIIIIIIIIIIIIIIIIII

Many years ago in a busy town in Germany, a cobbler and his wife were leading a simple and honest life. He spent his days sitting on the street corner repairing shoes and slippers, and sometimes he made new ones when someone ordered a pair. But in that case he had to buy the leather first because he was poor and had no material in stock. His wife sold fruit and vegetables that she grew in a little garden before the city gate, and most people were glad to buy from her because she was neatly and cleanly dressed and knew how to spread out and display her vegetables in an appetizing way.

The couple had a handsome boy, who had pleasant features and was well built and already quite big for his age of eight years. He usually sat with his mother at the vegetable market, and he generally helped the housekeepers and cooks, who bought a lot from the cobbler's wife, to carry home their purchases. He rarely returned from such an errand without a beautiful flower, a bit of change, or a piece of cake because the ladies and gentlemen were pleased when their cooks came back home with the fine-looking boy, and they always tipped him generously.

One day the cobbler's wife was sitting in the marketplace as usual. In front of her she had several baskets of cabbages and other vegetables and a variety of herbs and seeds, and also, in a smaller basket, the first pears, apples, and apricots of the season. Little Jacob, for that was the boy's name, sat beside her calling out in a clear voice: "See here, masters, fine cabbages, savory herbs; new pears, mistresses, new apples and apricots; who'll buy? My mother has them for sale." As the boy was calling out like this, an old woman came across the marketplace. She looked somewhat tattered and ragged, and she had a small, sharp face all wrinkled with age, red eyes, and a pointed hook nose that curved down toward her chin. She walked with a long stick, yet it would have been impossible to say how she walked, for she hobbled and slid and reeled so that it seemed as if she had wheels in her legs and might topple over at any moment and fall down on the pavement on her pointed nose.

The cobbler's wife looked at the woman carefully, for she had been sitting in the marketplace every day for sixteen years and had never noticed this strange figure. But she couldn't help starting when the old woman limped toward her and stopped before her baskets.

"Are you Hannah, the vegetable woman?" asked the old hag in an unpleasant, croaking voice, all the while wagging her head back and forth.

"Yes, that's me," answered the cobbler's wife. "May I help you with something?"

"We'll see, we'll see! Let's take a look at the little vegetables, take a look at the little vegetables, and let's see if you have what I need," answered the old woman, and she bent down over the baskets and thrust a pair of dark-brown, ugly hands into the vegetable basket. With her long, spidery fingers she grasped the vegetables, which had been so nicely and daintily spread out, lifted one after another up to her long nose and sniffed them all over. It wrung the heart of the cobbler's wife to see the way the old hag laid hands on her rare vegetables, but she didn't dare protest, for it was the buyer's right to inspect the wares, and besides, she felt a strange horror of the woman. When she had examined the whole basket, she murmured, "Wretched stuff, wretched vegetables, not one thing that I want, much better things fifty years ago. Wretched stuff, wretched stuff!"

Such talk exasperated little Jacob. "Listen, you are an impudent old woman," he cried angrily. "First you grab the fine vegetables with your horrible brown fingers and squeeze them, and then you hold them up to your long nose so that no one looking on would buy them, and now, on top of all this, you abuse our wares and call them wretched stuff when even the duke's cook himself buys everything from us!"

The old hag squinted at the plucky boy, gave a repulsive laugh, and said in a hoarse voice, "Little boy, little boy! So you like my nose, my nice long nose? You'll have one, too, right in the middle of your face, all the way down below your chin." As she was saying this, she slithered over to the other basket, where the cabbages were displayed. She picked up the most magnificent of the white heads of cabbage in her hands, squeezed them so that they moaned, then threw them back in the basket in disorder, saying again, "Wretched stuff, wretched cabbage!"

"Don't waggle your head so horribly," the child cried anxiously. "Your neck is as thin as a cabbage stem. It could break off easily and then your head would fall into the basket. Then who would buy?"

"Don't you like thin necks?" murmured the old woman, laughing. "You won't have one at all. Your head will be stuck between your shoulders so it won't fall off your little trunk!"

"Don't talk such nonsense to the child," the cobbler's wife said at last, angry at all the testing, inspecting, and smelling. "If you want to buy something, then hurry up— you're driving away my other customers."

"Good, it shall be as you say," cried the old woman with a furious look. "I'll buy these six heads of cabbage. But see here, I have to lean on my stick and can't carry anything. Let your little boy bring the things home for me. I'll pay him for it."

The child didn't want to go with her and cried, for he was afraid of the ugly woman, but the mother solemnly ordered him to go because she considered that it would be sinful to make the feeble old woman carry the burden all by herself. Almost weeping, he did as she ordered, wrapped the heads of cabbage in a cloth, and followed the old hag across the marketplace.

She didn't go very fast, and it took her almost three quarters of an hour to get to a very remote part of the town, where she finally stopped before a dilapidated little house. She pulled out a rusty old hook and stuck it adroitly into a little hole in the door, which sprang open with a crash. But what a surprise for little Jacob when he entered! The interior of the house was splendidly furnished. The ceilings and walls were of marble and the woodwork of the finest ebony inlaid with gold and polished stones, but the floors were of glass and so smooth that the child slipped and fell several times. The old woman took a silver whistle out of her pocket and blew it so that it echoed shrilly through the house. Immediately several guinea pigs came down the stairs, but it seemed very strange to Jacob that they walked upright on two legs, had nutshells instead of shoes on their paws, and wore human clothes. On their heads they were even wearing hats of the latest style. "Where have you put my slippers, you miserable riffraff?" cried the old woman and flailed at them with her stick so that they jumped about whimpering. "How much longer do you expect me to wait here like this?"

They scrambled up the stairs and returned with a pair of leather-lined coconut shells, which they nimbly put on the old woman's feet.

Now there was no more hobbling and slipping. She threw the stick away and glided very rapidly across the glass floor, pulling little Jacob along by the hand. Finally she came to a stop in a room provided with all sorts of utensils, almost like a kitchen, although the mahogany tables and the sofas draped with thick rugs would have been more appropriate for a chamber of state. "Sit down, little boy," said the old woman rather kindly, crowding him into a sofa corner and placing a table in front of him so that he couldn't get out again. "Sit down, you've had a heavy load to carry; human heads weigh quite a bit, quite a bit."

"But, mistress, what strange things are you saying?" cried the child. "I'm tired all right, but those were heads of cabbage I carried. You bought them from my mother."

"Well, you're wrong about that," laughed the woman, and she raised the lid of the basket and lifted out a human head by the hair. The child was beside himself with terror; he couldn't understand how all these things came about, but he thought of his mother. If someone found out anything about these heads, he thought, they would certainly accuse his mother of it.

"We must get something for you now as a reward for being such a good boy," murmured the old woman. "Just be patient for a little while—we'll prepare you a bit of soup that you'll remember for the rest of your life." Having said this, she whistled again. First came a great many guinea pigs in human dress with aprons tied around their waists and stirring ladles and carving knives in their belts. Next a troop of squirrels came skipping into the room; they had on wide pantaloons, walked on their hind legs, and wore green velvet caps on their heads. These seemed to be the scullery boys, for they ran up the walls at great speed and fetched down pots and pans, butter and eggs, herbs and flour, and carried everything to the stove. The old woman scurried about continually in her coconut slippers, and the child saw that she was really anxious to prepare something good for him. Now the fire blazed up and crackled, now the pan began to fume and simmer, and a pleasing aroma filled the room. The old woman ran up and down with the squirrels and guinea pigs at her heels, and every time she passed in front of the stove she poked her long nose into the pot. Finally it started to hiss and bubble, the steam came out of the pot, and the froth ran down into the fire. Then she lifted the pot off, poured some of the contents into a silver bowl, and served it to little Jacob.

"There you are, little boy, there you are," she said; "eat your little bowl of soup and then you'll get all the things you liked so well about me. You're going to become a skillful cook, too, so you'll amount to something, but not the little herb, no, you'll never find the little herb—why didn't your mother have it in her basket?"

The child didn't understand very well what she was saying, but he concentrated his attention on the soup, which tasted simply delicious to him. His mother had prepared many a tasty dish for him, but he had never enjoyed anything as much as this. An aroma of fine herbs and spices rose from the bowl. The soup was sweet, and yet at the same time sour, and very strong. As he was draining the last few drops of the exquisite dish, the guinea pigs ignited some Arabian incense, which drifted through the room in bluish clouds. The clouds grew thicker and thicker and floated downward. The smell of the incense had a narcotic effect on the child; no matter how often he reminded himself that he must go back to his mother, he repeatedly sank back into a drowsiness and finally fell into a deep sleep on the sofa of the old hag.

He had strange dreams. It seemed to him that the old

woman was taking off his clothes and dressing him in a
squirrel skin. Now he could jump and climb like a squirrel. He joined the company of squirrels and guinea pigs,
who were extremely polite and well behaved folk, and
had to help them do household chores for the old hag. At
first he served only as shoeshine boy—that is, he had to
smear the coconut shells, which the old woman wore instead of slippers, with oil and to polish them till they
gleamed. Since he had often been asked to perform similar chores at home, the work came easy to him. He
kept on dreaming that after a year he was employed at a
more elegant task: along with a number of squirrels,
he had to catch the motes in sunbeams, and when they
had enough, to strain them through the finest of sieves.
The woman could not chew very well because she had
lost all her teeth, and since she regarded the motes in a
sunbeam as the finest of all substances, she had her bread
made out of them.

After another year had gone by, he was promoted to
the job of collecting the old woman's drinking water.
You mustn't think that she had had a cistern dug for this
purpose or that she put a barrel in the courtyard to
catch the rain. It involved something much more special.
The squirrels, and Jacob with them, had to dip dew out of
the roses with hazelnut shells—that was the old woman's
drinking water; and since she drank a good deal, the
water carriers had to work hard. After a year he was
put to work inside: he was given the job of cleaning the
floors. Since these were made of glass on which the
faintest breath would show up, this was no small task.
They had to brush them and fasten old rags to their
feet on which they skated gracefully through the room.
In the fourth year he was finally promoted to the kitchen.
This was the post of honor that one could attain only
after a long period of trial. Here Jacob rose from scullery
boy to first pastry cook and arrived at such an extraordinary degree of skill and experience about everything
that concerns a kitchen that he often had to wonder
at himself. The most difficult things—pastries with two
hundred ingredients, herb soups concocted out of all the
herbs in the world—he learned it all and knew how to

prepare everything quickly and to season it well. Thus he spent about seven years in the old woman's service. One day as she was taking off her coconut shoes and picking up her market basket and her stick, preparing to go out, she ordered him to pluck a young chicken, stuff it with herbs, and have it roasted a nice golden brown by the time she got back. He did everything according to the rules of the art. He twisted the neck of the chicken, scalded it in hot water, neatly plucked the feathers, scraped the skin to make it smooth and tender, and removed the entrails. Next he collected the herbs with which he was supposed to stuff the chicken. In the pantry where the herbs were kept, however, he observed this time that there was a little cabinet on the wall standing half open. He had never noticed it before. He approached full of curiosity to find out what could be inside and, see, there were many little baskets that gave out a strong and pleasing aroma. He opened one of the baskets and found it full of herbs of a very strange shape and color. The stems and leaves were a blue-green and bore a little flower at the top, red as fire with a yellow edge. He studied this flower thoughtfully and smelled it, and it gave off the same strong odor as the soup that the old woman had prepared for him long ago. The odor was so strong that he began to sneeze and had to sneeze harder and harder and—at last woke up sneezing.

He was lying on the old woman's sofa and looked around in astonishment. "How is it possible to have such vivid dreams!" he said to himself. "I could have sworn that I turned into a lowly squirrel, the comrade of guinea pigs and other vermin, and that at the same time I got to be a great cook. How Mother is going to laugh when I tell her all that! But won't she scold me for falling asleep in a strange house instead of helping her at the market?" At this thought he started to pull himself together in order to leave. His limbs were still stiff from sleeping, especially his neck, because he couldn't quite move his head from side to side. He also had to smile at himself for being so drowsy because he was every second bumping his nose against a cupboard or wall, or when he turned quickly around, he hit it against a doorpost. The squirrels and guinea pigs ran all around him whimpering as if they wanted to go with him, and on the threshold, he actually invited them to come along, for they were graceful little creatures, but they scurried quickly back into the house on their nutshells, and finally he could hear only their squealing in the distance.

The old woman had led him into a fairly remote part of town, and he had a hard time finding his way through the narrow alleys. Besides, there was a terrible crowd just then because, so it seemed to him, a dwarf must have been exhibiting himself in the neighborhood. Everywhere people were shouting: "Oh, come look at the ugly dwarf! Where does the dwarf come from? Oh, what a long nose, and see the way his head is stuck down between his shoulders, and what ugly brown hands he has!" At any other time he probably would have run after them because he was tremendously fond of looking at giants or dwarfs or foreigners in funny clothes, but right now he had to hurry to get back to his mother.

He was very uneasy when he reached the market. His mother was still sitting there, and a lot of fruit was still left in the basket, so he couldn't have slept for very long. Even from a distance, though, he thought he could see that she was very sad because she didn't call out to the passers-by and invite them to buy. Instead, she was leaning her head on her hand, and as he approached, it seemed to him that she was paler than usual. He hesitated over what he should do. At last he took heart, crept up behind her, trustingly put his hand on her arm, and said, "Mother, dear, what's the matter? Are you angry with me?"

The woman turned around, but recoiled with an exclamation of horror. "What do you want from me, you ugly dwarf!" she cried. "Get away from here! I can't bear pranks like that."

"But, Mother, what ails you?" Jacob asked, greatly upset. "You must be ill—what makes you want to chase away your son?"

"I've already told you, go about your business!" replied Mistress Hannah angrily. "You won't get any money out of me with your foolish tricks, ugly monster."

"It must be true, God has taken away the light of her reason," the little fellow said to himself sorrowfully. "What can I do to get her home? Dear Mother, please be reasonable. Just look me in the face. I'm your son, your Jacob."

"Oh, this is carrying the joke too far," Hannah called out to her neighbor. "Just look at the ugly dwarf. There he stands driving my customers away, and he even has the nerve to mock at my misfortune, telling me, 'I'm your son, your Jacob,' the brazen creature!"

At this her neighbors started scolding as hard as they could, and market women, as you well know, are expert at it. They chided him for making fun of poor Hannah's misfortune, who had had her adorable boy stolen from her seven years ago, and they threatened to fall on him in a body and to scratch him to death if he didn't get away from there immediately.

Poor Jacob didn't know what to think. Hadn't he come to the market with his mother as usual early this morning? Hadn't he helped her set out her fruit? And afterward hadn't he gone to the old hag's house, eaten a little bowl of soup, and taken a little nap? Now he was back, and yet his mother and her neighbors were talking about seven years. And they were calling him a horrible dwarf! What in the world had happened to him? When he saw that his mother would no longer listen to a word he said, the tears came into his eyes, and he went mournfully down the street to the stall where his father repaired shoes all day long. "Let's see," he thought, "whether he, too, will refuse to recognize me. I'll stand in the doorway and I'll speak to him." When he got to the cobbler's stall, he stood in the doorway and looked in. The cobbler was working away so busily that he didn't even see him, but when he happened to glance at the door, thread, awl, and shoes fell from his hand and he exclaimed, horrified: "For God's sake, what is it, what is it!"

"Good evening, master!" said the little fellow, stepping all the way into the shop. "How are you?"

"Poorly, poorly, little gentleman!" his father answered to Jacob's great astonishment, because he too didn't

seem to recognize him. "The work isn't so easy for me.
I'm all alone and getting old, but still I can't afford a
helper."

"But don't you have a little son who could give you a
hand with the work?" the little fellow persisted.

"I had one called Jacob, who must be a slender and
lively young man of twenty by now and who could be
a great help to me. Ah, what a life that would be. When
he was only eight he was already handy and dexterous
and knew quite a few tricks of the trade. He was a nice-
looking boy, and well mannered too. He would have
brought in the business so that I wouldn't have been
mending old shoes for long and would be turning out
nothing but new goods now. But that's how the world
goes!"

"But where is your son?" Jacob asked his father in a
trembling voice.

"God only knows," he answered. "Seven years ago,
yes, that's how long it's been, he was stolen from us in
the marketplace."

"SEVEN YEARS AGO!" Jacob exclaimed, horrified.

"Yes, little gentleman. I can still remember as though
it were today how my wife came home weeping and crying because the child had been gone all day. She had
asked and searched everywhere, but she couldn't find
him. I always knew it would happen like that and said
so. Jacob was a handsome lad, if I do say it, and my
wife was proud of him. She liked to hear the people
singing his praises. She often let him deliver vegetables
and the like to the better class of homes. There was
nothing wrong with that—he always got plenty of presents. But look out, said I! It's a big town and a lot of
bad elements live here. Look out well for Jacob! And so
it came about, just like I said. An ugly old crone comes
to the market, haggles over fruit and vegetables, and
finally buys more than she can carry. My wife, the com-
passionate soul, let her take the boy and—hasn't laid eyes
on him since."

"And you say it's been seven years?"

"It will be seven years come spring. We had him
cried for in the streets, and we asked from house to

house. A lot of people knew the pretty boy and were
fond of him, and now they helped us search, but all in
vain. What's more, no one had ever heard of the woman
who bought the vegetables, but one ancient woman, who
was ninety years old, said it might have been the
wicked fairy Herblore who comes to town once every
fifty years to make all sorts of purchases."

That was the story Jacob's father told, all the while
hammering away vigorously at his shoes and pulling the
thread a long way out with both fists. It gradually dawned
on the little fellow what had happened to him: he hadn't
been dreaming at all but had really been serving a
wicked fairy as a squirrel for seven years. His heart
almost broke with rage and grief. The old hag had robbed
him of seven years of his youth, and what did he have
in return? Knowing how to shine coconut slippers and
how to clean rooms with glass floors? Or learning all
the secrets of cookery from guinea pigs? He remained
standing there for quite a while contemplating his fate,
till his father asked him at last: "Is there some work I
could do for you, young gentleman? Perhaps a new pair
of slippers or," he added, smiling, "a case for your
nose?"

"Why does my nose concern you?" said Jacob. "Why
should I need a case for it?"

"Well," replied the cobbler, "everyone to his own taste.
But, let me tell you frankly, if I had such a terrible nose,
I'd have someone make me a case of shiny pink patent
leather to fit over it. Look, I just happen to have a fine
piece in stock. Of course it would take at least a yard.
But how useful you'd find it, little gentleman. As things are,
I'm sure that you must be running into every doorpost and
every cart when you try to get out of people's way."

The little fellow was struck speechless with fear. He
ran his hand over his nose. It was thick and about two
feet long! So the old hag had changed his appearance,
too, and that was why his mother couldn't recognize
him and why people were calling him an ugly dwarf!
"Master!" he said, almost weeping, to the cobbler. "Have
you a mirror in your shop in which I could take a look
at myself?"

"Young gentleman," answered his father gravely, "nature has hardly endowed you with a shape that could make you vain, and you have no cause to look in a mirror all the time. You should get out of the habit because, especially for you, it's a ridiculous affectation."

"Oh, please, let me look in a mirror," the little fellow exclaimed. "I assure you it's not out of vanity!"

"Leave me in peace; I haven't got one to lend you. My wife has a little mirror, but I don't know where she keeps it. If you absolutely must look in a mirror, Urban the Barber lives across the way. He's got a mirror twice the size of your head. Look in that, and meanwhile, good day!"

With these words his father shoved him very gently outside, shut the door behind him, and sat down at his work again. The little fellow, utterly dejected, crossed the street to the shop of Urban the Barber, whom he remembered well from former times. "Good morning, Urban," he said to him; "I've come to beg a favor of you. Would you be so kind as to let me look in your mirror for a bit?"

"With pleasure—there it is," the barber cried, laughing, and his customers, who had come to have their beards trimmed, also laughed heartily. "You're a pretty little fellow, slender and graceful, a neck like a swan's, little hands like a princess', and a tiny turned-up nose —you can't imagine a lovelier one. You're somewhat vain, it's true, but look as long as you like. I don't want anyone to reproach me for not letting you use my mirror because I was jealous."

Thus said the barber, and the shop was filled with hoots of laughter. Meanwhile, the little fellow had stepped in front of the mirror and had seen himself. His eyes filled with tears. "No wonder you couldn't recognize your Jacob, dear Mother," he said to himself. "That is not what he looked like in those happy days when you were fond of showing him off!" His eyes had become small, like pigs' eyes. His nose was enormous and hung down below his mouth and his chin. His neck seemed to have disappeared completely, for his head was set deep down between his shoulders and only at the cost of great pain could he move it to the left or the right. He was just as tall as he had been when he was twelve, but whereas others grow taller between twelve and twenty, he had grown broader. His back and his chest were distended and looked like a little sack, very thick and very full. This thick trunk sat on top of two weak little legs, which seemed incapable of supporting such a weight. But to make up for it, the arms dangling from his body were that much larger; they were as big as those of a full-grown man. His hands were coarse and a dirty yellow, his fingers long and spidery, and if he stretched them out all the way, he could touch the ground without stooping. That's how he looked, little Jacob: he had become a misshapen dwarf.

Now he remembered the morning when the old hag had come up to his mother's stand. She'd seen to it that he had got all the things he once had found so objectionable in her—the long nose, the ugly fingers, everything except the long, wobbly neck, which she had left out altogether.

"Well, have you admired yourself long enough, my prince?" said the barber, who had walked up to him and was looking him over, laughing. "Really, one couldn't dream of anything so comical, even if one wanted to. But I'm going to make you a proposition, little man. My barbershop is very popular, but recently not as much as I could wish. That's because my neighbor, Barber Foam, has managed to find a giant somewhere to lure the trade to his shop. Well, it doesn't require much talent to become a giant, but a mannikin like you, why that's something altogether different. Come to work for me, little man. I'll give you room and board and clothing—you'll have everything. In return, you stand in the doorway in the morning and invite the people in; you whip up the lather, hand the customers a towel, and you can be sure that it will work out to our mutual advantage. I'll get more clientele than that other chap with his giant, and everyone will be glad to give you a tip."

The little fellow was indignant at the thought of serving as a side-show attraction for a barbershop. But what could he do but put up with the insult patiently? Therefore, he told the barber very calmly that he didn't have time for this sort of work and went his way.

Although the evil woman had distorted his body, she had had no power over his mind. That much he knew, for his thoughts and feelings were not what they had been seven years ago. No, he believed that during that time he had become wiser and more mature. He did not regret his lost beauty or his ugly shape, but only that he had been driven like a dog from his father's door. Therefore, he resolved to make one last effort with his mother. He went up to her in the marketplace and begged her to hear him out calmly. He reminded her of the day when he had gone off with the old woman; he reminded her of all the particulars of his childhood; then he told her how he had served the fairy for seven years as a squirrel and how she had transformed him because he had rebuked her. The cobbler's wife didn't know what to think. Everything that he told her about his childhood was true, but when he talked of having been a squirrel for seven long years, she said: "It's impossible, and fairies don't exist." And when she looked at him she was repelled by the ugly dwarf and didn't believe that this could be her son. Finally she thought it best to talk it over with her husband. She gathered up her baskets and told him to come along. Thus they came to the cobbler's stall.

"Listen to me," she said to him, "that creature says he is our lost Jacob. He told me all about how he had been stolen seven years ago and how he has been bewitched by a fairy."

"Is that so?" the cobbler interrupted angrily. "Is that what he told you? Just wait, you rascal! I told him everything less than an hour ago, and off he goes to make a fool of you! You've been bewitched have you, sonny? Just wait and I'll unwitch you." He took a bundle of leather straps he had just finished cutting out, sprang after the little fellow, and struck him on his humped back and on his long arms so that he screamed and ran away weeping.

In this town, no more than anywhere else, there are few people with enough compassion to help out an unfortunate wretch, who also happens to be, in some way, ridiculous. That is why the miserable dwarf went the whole day without anything to eat or drink and in the evening was forced to make his bed on the steps of a church, which were very hard and very cold.

When the first rays of the sun awakened him the next morning, he seriously considered how he might put an end to himself since his mother and father had rejected him. He was too proud to serve as signpost for a barbershop, and he didn't want to hire himself out as a jester or to exhibit himself for money. What could he do? Suddenly it occurred to him that as a squirrel he had made great progress in the art of cooking. He thought that he would be justified in the hope of matching many a cook at this trade. He resolved to make use of his skill.

As soon as the streets became active and it was fully morning, he went first of all inside the church to say his prayers. Then he set off. The duke, the lord of that province, was famous as a gourmet and glutton who loved a good table and recruited his cooks from all parts of the world. The little fellow went to his palace. When he arrived at the outermost gate, the sentries asked him what he wanted and had their fun with him, but he asked for the commandant of the kitchen. They laughed and led him through the outlying courtyards. Wherever he passed the lackeys stood and stared after him, laughed heartily, and joined the procession so that by and by a huge train of servants of every sort wound its way up the palace steps. The grooms cast away their currying combs, the runners ran as fast as they could, the carpet beaters left off beating their carpets, everybody pushed and shoved, there was a tumult as though the enemy were at the gates, and a clamor—"A dwarf, a dwarf! Have you seen the dwarf?"—filled the air.

The majordomo appeared in the doorway, looking furious and clutching an enormous whip. "In heaven's name, you dogs, what is the meaning of this uproar! Don't you know that the duke is still sleeping?" And he swung his whip, letting it fall, not too gently, upon the backs of several grooms and sentries. "Oh, sir," they exclaimed, "can't you see? We're bringing a dwarf, a dwarf such as you've never seen the equal of." The majordomo had difficulty forcing himself not to laugh out loud when he saw the little fellow, for he was afraid of compromising his dignity by laughing. And so he drove away the others with his whip, conducted the little fellow into the house, and asked what he wanted. When he was told that the dwarf wished to see the commandant of the kitchen, he answered: "You are mistaken, my little man. You wish to see me, the majordomo. You'd like to become the duke's official dwarf, isn't that right?"

"No, sir!" answered the dwarf. "I am a skillful cook and have experience in many rare dishes. If your worship would bring me to the commandant of the kitchen, he could perhaps make use of my art."

"Just as you please, little man. To tell the truth, you're not a very bright boy. You want to work in the kitchen? As official dwarf you wouldn't have had to work at all, you'd have had as much to eat and drink as your heart desired, and beautiful clothes besides. But we'll see. Your culinary skills will hardly stretch so far as would be necessary for one of his lordship's personal chefs, and you're too good for a scullery boy." With these words, the majordomo took him by the hand and led him to the apartment of the commandant of the kitchen.

"Gracious sir," said the dwarf and bowed down so low that his nose touched the carpet, "can you use a skillful cook?"

The commandant looked him over from head to toe and broke into loud laughter. "What?" he cried. "You, a cook? Do you think our stoves are so low that you could see the top of one even by standing tiptoe and really stretching your neck? Oh, my dear little fellow! Whoever sent you to me for a position as cook was pulling your leg." So said the commandant of the kitchen, laughing heartily, and all the lackeys in the room laughed with him.

But the dwarf didn't let this disturb his composure. "You can spare an egg or two, a bit of syrup and wine, some flour and herbs, in a household where there is an

abundance of such things," he said. "Order me to prepare some delicacy, give me the ingredients I need, and
it shall be prepared quickly before your own eyes, and
you will have to admit: he cooks according to rule
and regulation."

"Very well!" cried the commandant of the kitchen
and put his arm around the majordomo. "Very well,
anything for the sake of a joke—let's go to the kitchen."
They went through numerous halls and corridors and
finally arrived in the kitchen. This was a great, sprawling
structure, magnificently equipped. The fire was kept
going all the time in twenty stoves. A clear stream of
water, serving also as a tank for fresh fish, flowed
right through the middle. The staples were kept ready
at hand in cabinets made of marble and precious kinds
of wood. And to the right and left there were ten chambers containing everything that has ever been found
dainty and delicious to the palate—from Europe all the
way to the Orient. Kitchen help of every sort ran around
handling and rattling the pots and pans, forks, and
ladles, but when the commandant entered the kitchen,
they all froze in their tracks and one could hear only
the crackling of the flames and the rippling of the little
brook.

"What has the duke ordered for breakfast this morning?" the commandant asked the officer-in-charge-of-
breakfast, an old cook.

"Sir! He was pleased to order Danish soup and red
Hamburg dumplings."

"Good," said the commandant. "Have you heard what
the duke wants for breakfast? Do you trust yourself to
prepare these difficult dishes? You'll certainly never manage the Hamburg dumplings, for the recipe is a secret."

"Nothing is easier," the dwarf replied to universal astonishment, for as a squirrel he had often prepared these
dishes. "Nothing is easier. For the soup let me have such
and such herbs, this and that seasoning, the fat of a wild
boar, roots, and eggs. But for the dumplings," he said
speaking more softly so that only the commandant and
the officer-of-the-breakfast could hear him, "for the
Hamburg dumplings I need four kinds of meat, some

wine, duck grease, ginger, and a certain little herb that
is called stomachsease."

"Blessed Saint Benedict! What sorcerer taught you
that?" exclaimed the cook in amazement. "You've told
us everything down to the least particle, and we hadn't
even thought of the herb stomachsease. Yes, that would
make it taste even better. Oh, you wonder of a cook!"

"I'd never have believed it," said the commandant,
"but let's put him to the test. Give him what he asked
for, dishes and all the rest, and let him prepare the
breakfast."

It was done as he ordered, and everything was laid
out in readiness on the stove. But now it turned out
that the dwarf could hardly reach the top of the stove
with his nose. A couple of stools were pushed together
and covered with a marble slab, and the little magician
was invited to begin his act. The cooks, the scullions,
the lackeys, and a variety of other help stood around
in a circle to watch, and they were amazed at how
everything was managed with such speed and assurance
and how all was prepared so neatly and daintily. When
he had finished the preparations, he ordered both pots
to be placed on the fire and to let them cook until he
gave the signal. Then he started to count one, two,
three, etc., and just when he had counted five hundred,
he called out: "Stop!" The pots were removed, and
the little fellow invited the commandant to taste.

The officer-of-the-breakfast had a scullion hand him
a golden spoon, which he rinsed in the brook and passed
to the commandant. The latter stepped up to the stove
with a ceremonial air, took a spoonful, tasted, and
closed his eyes and smacked his lips with pleasure.
Finally he said: "Delicious! By the soul of the duke,
delicious! Wouldn't you like to try a little spoonful,
majordomo?"

The majordomo bowed, took the spoon, tasted, and
was beside himself with enjoyment and delight. "With
all due respect to your talents, my dear officer-of-the-
breakfast, you are an experienced cook, but you've never
been able to make soup or Hamburg dumplings as
heavenly as this!" Now the cook also took a taste. Then

he respectfully shook the dwarf by the hand and said:
"Little man! You are a master of the art. Yes, the little
herb stomachsease gives everything a unique flavor."

At this moment the duke's valet appeared in the
kitchen and reported that the duke wanted his breakfast. The dishes were placed on a silver platter and
sent to the duke. The commandant of the kitchen, however, took the little fellow to his room and conversed
with him. They had hardly been there long enough to re-
peat the Lord's Prayer halfway through when a messenger arrived summoning the commandant to the duke.
He quickly threw on his finest uniform and followed
the messenger.

The duke was looking very pleased. He had cleaned
off the silver platter and was just wiping his beard as
the commandant of the kitchen entered. "Listen, Commandant," he said, "I've always been very well satisfied
with your staff, but tell me, who prepared my breakfast
this morning? It hasn't been this delicious since I
ascended the throne of my ancestors. Tell me the name
of the cook so that we may send him a few ducats as
a present."

"My lord! It is a strange story," answered the commandant, and he told how early that morning a dwarf
had been brought to him who insisted on being hired
as a cook, and how everything had happened. The duke
was greatly astonished, had the dwarf summoned, and
asked him who he was and where he came from. Naturally poor Jacob could not tell him that he had been
bewitched and that he had formerly done service as a
squirrel. Nevertheless, he told the truth in saying that
he had lost his father and mother and had learned to
cook from an old woman. The duke didn't ask him anything else, but instead made merry over the peculiar shape
of his new cook.

"If you will stay with me," he said, "you shall receive an annual salary of fifty ducats, a complete holiday outfit, and two pairs of breeches in addition. In
return, you will personally prepare my breakfast each
day, supervise the preparation of dinner, and in general occupy yourself with my cuisine. Since I give every-

one in this palace a name, you shall be called Longnose and shall receive the rank of assistant-commandant-
of-the-kitchen."

The dwarf prostrated himself before the mighty Duke
of Frankistan, kissed his feet, and promised to serve him
faithfully.

Thus the little fellow was well taken care of for the
time being, and he did honor to his office. For it may be
said that the duke was a changed man as long as Dwarf
Longnose remained in his household. Formerly it had
often been his habit to fling the dishes and plates that
were served to him at the heads of the cooks. Yes, in one
of his rages he had even thrown a baked calf's foot, which
had not been cooked tender enough, at the commandant
of the kitchen and hit him so hard on the forehead
that he was knocked down and had to spend three days
in bed. Although the duke later made up for his acts of
violence with a handful of ducats, no cook had ever
served his meals without fear and trembling. After the
dwarf entered his service, everything seemed changed as
if by magic. The duke now ate five meals a day instead of
three in order to take full advantage of the artistry of
the smallest of his servants. All the same, he never
showed the slightest trace of ill humor. No, he found
everything novel and excellent, he was pleasant and so-
ciable, and he got fatter every day.

Often he had the commandant of the kitchen and
Dwarf Longnose summoned right in the middle of dinner,
placed one to his left, the other to his right, and with his
own fingers fed them tidbits of the most delicious of
the dishes, a special favor they were both wise enough
to appreciate.

The dwarf was the talk of the town. The commandant
was implored on all sides for permission to watch the
dwarf cooking, and a few of the most distinguished citi-
zens managed to persuade the duke to allow their servants to take lessons from the dwarf in the kitchen. This
proved a very profitable enterprise because they were
charged half a ducat a day. In order to keep up the
morale of the other cooks and to prevent them from
getting jealous, Longnose let them have the money that

the gentlemen paid to have their cooks instructed.

And so Longnose lived for almost two years in apparent luxury and honor, and only the thought of his parents saddened him. He lived thus, experiencing nothing unusual, until the following incident took place. Dwarf Longnose was especially clever and successful at purchasing supplies, and so he personally went to market, whenever he could afford the time, in order to buy fowl and fruit. One morning he went to the goose market in search of heavy, fat geese, the kind that the duke loved. He had already wandered up and down several times, making a tour of inspection. His figure, far from exciting laughter and ridicule, commanded the greatest respect. For he was recognized as the duke's famous personal chef, and every market woman who sold geese was in ecstasies when he turned his nose in her direction.

At last he noticed a woman sitting in a corner at the very end of a row, who also had geese for sale, but unlike the others, she was not extolling the quality of her wares or crying out for buyers. He went over to her and measured and weighed her geese. They were exactly what he was looking for, so he bought three, together with the cage, loaded them on his broad back, and started on the way home. It seemed strange to him that only two of the geese squawked and cackled like real geese. The third sat there very quiet and pensive and sighed and groaned like a human being. "That one is about to get sick," he told himself. "Better hurry so that I can slaughter and roast her." But the goose answered very loud and clear:

> "Run me through,
> And I'll bite you.
> Have my neck wrung,
> And you'll die young."

The dwarf set the cage down, terribly frightened, and the goose looked at him with beautiful and intelligent eyes and sighed. "By thunder!" exclaimed Longnose. "Can you talk, young Mistress Goose? I never would have believed it. Come now, don't be afraid! Live and let live—

one isn't going to harm such a rare bird as you. But
I'll wager you haven't always worn these feathers. I myself was a despised squirrel once upon a time."

"You're right," answered the goose, "when you say
that I was not born in this ignominious form. Alas, no one
prophesied to me in my cradle that Mimi, the daughter of
mighty Buckweather, was fated to be slaughtered in the
kitchen of a duke!"

"Please be calm, dear Mistress Mimi," the dwarf
consoled her. "As sure as I am an honest fellow and as-
sistant-commandant of His Highness' kitchen, no one
shall lay a hand on you. I'll give you a cage in my private
apartment. You shall have plenty of feed, and I shall
devote my spare time to keeping you company. I'll tell
the rest of the kitchen staff that I am fattening a goose
for the duke on special herbs, and as soon as I find an
opportunity, I will set you free."

The goose thanked him with tears in her eyes, and
the dwarf did as he had promised. He slaughtered the two
geese, but for Mimi he built a private cage under the pre-
text of preparing her as an extra-special treat for the
duke. He didn't give her ordinary feed either, but provided her with pastries and sweets. As often as he had
the leisure, he went to converse with her and to console
her. They told each other their histories, and in this way
Longnose learned that the goose was a daughter of
the magician Buckweather, who lived on the island of
Gotland. He had quarreled with an old fairy, who conquered him through deceit and treachery and in revenge
had changed his daughter into a goose and carried her
far away to this country. When Dwarf Longnose had, in
turn, told her his story, she said: "I don't lack experience in such matters. My father had initiated my sisters
and me in herb lore—as far as he dared reveal its secrets. Your story of the quarrel at the vegetable stand,
your sudden transformation when you were smelling the
little herb, and also a few of the old woman's words
that you repeated to me are proof that you are under
an herb spell, and that means that if you can find the
herb of which the fairy was thinking when she bewitched you, the spell can be broken." This was not much

consolation to the little fellow, for where should he find this herb? Nevertheless, he thanked her and felt a ray of hope.

At this time, the duke was receiving the visit of a neighboring prince who was a friend of his. For this reason he had Dwarf Longnose summoned and told him: "The time has come for you to show me that you are my faithful servant and a master of your art. The prince who is visiting me is well known to set the best table after my own; he is a great connoisseur of fine cooking and an intelligent man. See to it that my table is provided each day in such a fashion as to keep him in continually growing astonishment. At the risk of my displeasure, you must never serve the same menu twice as long as he is here. You may ask the treasurer for whatever you require. And if you have to fry gold and diamonds in lard, do it. I would rather grow poor than to have to blush before him." So said the duke, and the dwarf said, making a respectful bow: "It shall be as you desire, my lord! Please God, I shall prepare everything in such a way as to please this prince of epicures."

The little cook now called upon all the resources of his art. He did not spare the treasure of his lord, but he spared himself even less. All day long he was surrounded by a cloud of smoke and fire, and his voice was constantly heard echoing through the vaults of the kitchen, giving orders to the scullions and all the lower ranks of cooks. To tell of all the dishes that were served would make your mouth water, but it would take too long.

The visiting prince had already stayed two weeks with the duke, living in the utmost delight and pleasure. They ate no less than five times a day, and the duke was contented with the artistry of his dwarf, for he saw his guest beaming with satisfaction. On the fifteenth day, however, the duke happened to summon the dwarf to the table in order to present him to the prince, and he asked the latter whether he was well satisfied with the dwarf.

"You are a wonderful cook," answered the visitor, "and you know what it means to set a good table. As long as I've been here, you haven't repeated a single dish, and you've prepared everything excellently. But please tell me why you are waiting so long to serve the queen of recipes, a soufflé suzerain?"

The dwarf was thunderstruck, for he had never heard of this queen of soufflés. However, he collected himself and said, "Oh, sir, I hoped that your countenance might yet illuminate our court for many days, and therefore I have postponed this dish. For how else might the cook salute you on the day of your departure if not with the queen of soufflés?"

"Indeed," the duke replied, laughing. "And I suppose with me you were waiting for the day of my death in order to salute me? You have never served me this soufflé. But think of something else for the farewell dinner, for tomorrow the soufflé must appear at the table."

"It shall be as you wish, sir," answered the dwarf and left the room. But he didn't leave in high spirits. The day of his shame and undoing had come. He had no idea how to make the soufflé. Therefore, he returned to his room and wept over his fate.

The goose Mimi, who had the run of his chambers, went to him and asked the reason for his sorrow. "Dry your tears," she said when he told her about the soufflé suzerain. "This dish was often served at my father's table, and I know the recipe fairly well. You take this and that, so and so much, and even if it doesn't contain absolutely all the necessary ingredients, their lordships won't have such fine palates so as to tell the difference." So said Mimi. But the dwarf jumped up with joy and blessed the day on which he had purchased the goose, and he set to work preparing the queen of soufflés. He first made a trial batch, and, sure enough, it was superb, and the commandant of the kitchen, whom he permitted to taste it, renewed the praises of the dwarf's immense knowledge of his art.

The next day he made a bigger batch and sent the soufflé to the table, hot from the oven and decorated with garlands of flowers. He put on his finest holiday costume and went to the banquet hall. At the very moment he entered, the officer-in-charge-of-slicing was dividing the soufflé and serving the pieces to the duke and his guest with a silver cake knife. The duke took a large mouthful, swallowed, and rolled his eyes up to the ceiling. "Ah! Ah! Ah! This deserves to be called the queen of soufflés, but my dwarf, good friend, deserves to be called the king of all cooks, is it not so?"

His guest took a small bite and savored it slowly with a supercilious and mysterious smile. "It's not badly prepared," he answered, pushing away his plate, "but it isn't quite what I would call suzerain. Just as I expected."

The duke's brow contracted with displeasure and reddened with shame. "Dog of a dwarf!" he cried. "How dare you do this thing to your master? Do you want to have your big head chopped off because of your wretched cooking?"

"Oh, sir! By merciful heaven, I prepared the dish according to the rules of the art. There cannot be anything missing!" So said the dwarf, quaking.

"You lie, you knave!" replied the duke, kicking him away from the table. "My guest would not say something is missing if it were not true. I am going to have *you* cut up and baked in a soufflé!"

"Be merciful!" the little fellow cried, and on his knees he crawled over to the prince and embraced his feet. "Say what this dish is lacking to cause displeasure to your palate. Do not let me die for want of a scrap of meat or a handful of flour."

"That won't be much help to you, my dear Longnose," the visitor answered, laughing. "I was already convinced yesterday that you would not be able to make this dish as my own cook makes it. I'll tell you that a little herb is missing, which doesn't even grow in this region—the herb sneezewell. Without this, the soufflé lacks flavor, and your master will never eat it the way I do."

At this, the Duke of Frankistan grew furious. "By heaven, I *will* eat it that way," he cried with flashing eyes. "For I swear on my honor as a duke, tomorrow I will either show you the soufflé as you wish it—or else this fellow's head spiked on the palace gate. Go, you dog, you have another twenty-four hours."

So shouted the duke. The dwarf once more returned to his room weeping and lamented his fate to the goose—that he would have to die. For he knew nothing of this herb. "Is that all?" she said. "In that case I can surely help you, for my father taught me all the herbs. At any other time you would have been doomed, but fortunately there is a new moon, and that is when this herb blooms. But, tell me, are there any chestnut trees near the palace?"

"Oh yes!" answered Longnose, greatly relieved. "There's a grove of them beside the lake, two hundred yards from the palace. But why chestnut trees?"

"The herb grows only at the foot of the chestnut," said Mimi. "Therefore, let us lose no time and search for what you need. Take me in your arms and set me free outside. I will search for you."

He did as she said and went to the palace gate. But there the sentry extended his rifle and said: "My poor Longnose, you're done for. I've got strict orders not to let you out."

"But can't I go into the garden?" answered the dwarf. "Be so kind as to send one of your comrades to the majordomo to ask whether I may not go into the garden to look for herbs?" The sentry did it, and permission was granted because the garden was surrounded by a high wall and escape would have been impossible. When Longnose and Mimi got outside, he put her down carefully and she waddled quickly ahead of him down to the lake where the chestnut trees stood. He followed her with an anxious heart, for this was his last and only hope. Should they fail to find the herb, he was firmly resolved to drown himself in the lake rather than to be beheaded. The goose searched in vain. She waddled under every chestnut tree and turned over every blade of grass with her beak, but nothing could be found. She began to cry from pity and fear, for the evening was already getting darker and all objects were becoming harder to identify.

The dwarf looked across the lake, and suddenly he called out: "Look, look, there across the lake is another big old tree. Let us go and look. Perhaps my good luck will be blooming there." The goose hopped and flew on ahead, and he ran after her as fast as his little legs would carry him. The chestnut tree cast a great shadow, and it was dark underneath. It had become almost impossible to recognize anything. But suddenly the goose stopped and beat her wings for joy. She quickly thrust her head down into the tall grass and plucked something that she daintily presented in her beak to the astonished dwarf. "This is the herb," she said, "and there is a lot of it growing here so that you will never run short."

The dwarf examined the herb thoughtfully. A sweet aroma spread from it that involuntarily brought to his mind the scene of his transformation. The stem and the leaves were a bluish-green and they bore a fire-red flower with a yellow border.

"God be praised!" he cried out at last. "What a miracle! I believe this is the very same herb that changed me from a squirrel into this infamous shape. Shall I make the experiment?"

"Not yet," advised the goose. "Take a handful of the herb with you, and let us go to your room and gather up your money and your other possessions, and then let us try the power of the herb."

They did so and returned to the room, the dwarf's

heart beating audibly with excitement. He tied fifty or sixty ducats he had saved and a few articles of clothing and shoes together in a bundle. Then he said, "May it please God to release me from this burden," and he put his nose deeply into the herbs and breathed in the aroma.

Suddenly there was a pulling and snapping in his joints, and he felt his head rising from between his shoulders. He squinted down at his nose and saw that it was shrinking smaller and smaller. His back and his chest started to level out, and his legs were growing longer.

The goose looked on in astonishment. "Oh, how tall and handsome you are!" she cried. "God be thanked, there is nothing left of your former features!" Jacob was overjoyed, and he clasped his hands in prayer. But his happiness did not make him forget the debt of gratitude he owed the goose Mimi. His heart was on fire to go to his parents, but his gratitude conquered his desire. "Who but you," he said, "deserves the thanks for my restoration? Without you I would never have found the herb and would have remained forever in that shape or might even have died under the executioner's ax. Well, then, I shall repay you. I shall take you to your father. He, who is experienced in all the magic arts, will easily break your spell." The goose shed tears of joy and accepted his offer. Jacob, without being recognized, escaped from the palace with the goose and set out for the seashore on his way to Mimi's native country.

Why tell the rest, how they successfully completed the journey and how Buckweather freed his daughter and sent Jacob home loaded with presents; how he returned to his native city and how his parents recognized their long-lost son; how with Buckweather's presents he purchased a shop and became rich and happy?

Only this much remains to be said. After the escape from the duke's palace, there was a great commotion. On the following day, when the duke wanted to carry out his oath and have the dwarf beheaded if he had failed to find the herb, there was not a trace of him. The prince insisted that the duke had let him escape secretly in order not to lose his best cook, and that he had not kept his word. A great war resulted between these two lords, which is famous in the history books as The War of the Herbs. Many battles were fought, but at last peace was made, and the peace treaty is called The Peace of Soufflé because for the peace banquet the cook of the prince made a soufflé suzerain, the queen of soufflés, which the duke enjoyed immensely.

Thus great oaks from little acorns grow, and that is the history of Dwarf Longnose.

Hans Christian Andersen

THE TINDERBOX

A soldier came marching along the highway: One, two! One, two! He had his knapsack on his back and a sword at his side, for he had been to war and now he was on his way home. Then he met an old witch on the highway. She was so hideous that her lower lip hung right down to her chest.

She said, "Good evening, soldier! My, what a pretty sword and a big knapsack you have! You're a real soldier! Now you shall have as much money as you'd like to have!"

"Thanks, old witch!" said the soldier.

"Do you see that big tree?" said the witch and pointed to a tree beside them. "It's quite hollow inside. You're to climb up to the top. Then you'll see a hole you can slide through, and you'll come way down inside the tree! I'll tie a rope around your waist so I can pull you up again when you call me."

"What'll I do down in the tree, then?" asked the soldier.

"Fetch money!" said the witch. "Now I'll tell you: when you're down at the bottom of the tree, you'll find yourself in a great hall. It's quite light, for over a hundred lamps are burning there. Then you'll see three doors. You can open them, the keys are in them. If you go into the first chamber, you'll see a big chest in the middle of the floor. On top of it sits a dog with a pair of eyes as big as teacups. But you needn't pay any attention to that. I'll give you my blue-checked apron, which you can spread out on the floor. Then go over quickly and get the dog, put him on my apron, open the chest, and take as many shillings as you like! They're all of copper. But if you'd rather have silver, then go into the next room. There sits a dog with a pair of eyes as big as mill wheels! But you needn't pay any attention to that. Put him on my apron and take the money. On the other hand, if you'd rather have gold, you can also have that, and as much as you can carry, if you just go into the third chamber. But the dog on the money chest there has a pair of eyes, each one as big as the Round Tower! That's a real dog, I'll have you know! But you needn't pay any attention to that. Just put him on my apron so he won't do you any harm and take as much gold as you like from the chest."

"There's nothing wrong with that!" said the soldier. "But what'll I get for you, old witch? For I daresay you want something too!"

"No," said the witch, "not a single shilling will I have! You can just bring me an old tinderbox, which my grandmother forgot the last time she was down there."

"Well, put the rope around my waist," said the soldier.

"Here it is," said the witch, "and here's my blue-checked apron."

Then the soldier climbed up into the tree, let himself drop down through the hole, and stood now, as the old witch had said, down in the great hall where the many hundreds of lamps were burning.

Now he unlocked the first door. Ugh! There sat the dog with eyes as big as teacups, and it glowered at him.

"You're a pretty fellow!" said the soldier, put it on the witch's apron, and took as many copper shillings as he could get in his pocket. Then he closed the chest, put the dog up on it again, and went into the second chamber. Yeow! There sat the dog with eyes as big as mill wheels.

"You shouldn't look at me so hard," said the soldier; "it might strain your eyes!" Then he put the dog on the witch's apron, but when he saw all the silver coins in the chest, he got rid of all the copper money he had and filled his pocket and his knapsack with only silver. Now he went into the third chamber! My, how hideous it was! The dog in there really did have two eyes as big as the Round Tower, and they rolled around in his head like wheels!

"Good evening," said the soldier and touched his cap, for he had never seen a dog like that before. But after he had looked at it for a while, he thought, "Now that's enough," and lifted it down to the floor and opened the chest. Well, heaven be praised! What a lot of gold there was! He could buy all of Copenhagen with it, and all the gingerbread pigs sold by the cake women, and all the tin soldiers and whips and rocking horses in the world! Yes, that was really a lot of money! Now the soldier threw away all the silver shillings in his pocket and knapsack and took gold instead. Yes, all his pockets, and his knapsack, and his cap and boots were so full that he could hardly walk! Now he had money! He put the dog up on the chest, shut the door, and then shouted up through the tree:

"Pull me up now, old witch!"

"Do you have the tinderbox with you?" asked the witch.

"That's right," said the soldier, "I'd clean forgotten it." And then he went and got it. The witch pulled him up, and now he was standing on the highway again with his pockets, boots, knapsack, and cap full of money.

"What do you want that tinderbox for?" asked the soldier.

"That's none of your business!" said the witch. "Why, you've gotten the money now. Just give me the tinderbox!"

"Fiddlesticks!" said the soldier. "Tell me at once what you want it for, or I'll draw my sword and chop off your head!"

"No!" said the witch.

Then the soldier chopped off her head. There she lay! But he tied all his money in her apron, carried it like a pack on his back, put the tinderbox in his pocket, and went straight to the town.

It was a lovely town, and he put up at the finest inn and demanded the very best rooms and all the food he liked, for he was rich, now that he had so much money.

The servant who was to polish his boots thought, of course, that they were queer old boots for such a rich gentleman to have, for he hadn't bought any new ones yet. The next day he got boots to walk in and pretty clothes. Now the soldier had become a fine gentleman, and they told him about all the things to do in their town, and about their king, and what a lovely princess his daughter was.

"Where can she be seen?" asked the soldier.

"She can't be seen at all," they said. "She lives in a big copper castle with many walls and towers around it. No one but the king dares go in and out, for it has

been prophesied that she will be married to a common
soldier, and the king can't stand that one bit!"

"I'd like to see her, all right," thought the soldier,
but this he wasn't allowed to do at all.

Now he lived merrily and well, went to the theater,
drove in the royal park, and gave lots of money away to
the poor; and that was well done! He remembered very
well from the old days how bad it is to be penni-
less! Now he was rich and had fine clothes and many
friends who all said what a nice fellow he was, a real
cavalier; and the soldier certainly didn't mind hearing
that. But as he spent money every day and didn't get any
back at all, it happened at last that he had no more than
two shillings left and had to move from the nice rooms
where he had lived to a tiny little room way up under
the roof, and he had to brush his boots himself and mend
them with a needle; and none of his friends came to see
him, for there were so many stairs to climb.

One evening it was quite dark and he couldn't even buy
a candle, but then he remembered there was a little stub
in the tinderbox he had taken out of the hollow tree
where the witch had helped him. He took out the tinderbox and the candle stub, but just as he struck a light and
the sparks flew from the flint, the door flew open and
the dog with eyes as big as teacups, which he'd seen
down under the tree, stood before him and said, "What
does my master command?"

"What's that?" said the soldier. "Why, this is a funny
tinderbox if I can get whatever I like! Get me some
money," he said to the dog. And whoops! It was gone!
Whoops! It was back again, holding a bag full of coins in
its mouth.

Now the soldier understood what a marvelous tinderbox it was. If he struck it once, the dog that sat on the
chest full of copper money came; if he struck it twice,
the one with the silver money came; and if he struck it
three times, the one with the gold came. Now the soldier
moved back down to the lovely rooms again, put on
the fine clothing, and then all his friends knew him again
right away, and they were so fond of him.

Then one day he thought: "Now it's really quite odd

that no one is allowed to see the princess. Everyone says she's supposed to be so lovely. But what's the good of it when she always has to sit inside that big copper castle with all the towers. Can't I even get to see her at all? Now where's my tinderbox?" And then he struck a light, and whoops! There stood the dog with eyes as big as teacups.

"I know it's the middle of the night," said the soldier, "but I'd so like to see the princess, just for a tiny moment."

The dog was out of the door at once, and before the soldier had given it a thought, it was back again with the princess. She sat on the dog's back and was asleep, and she was so lovely that anyone could see that she was a real princess. The soldier couldn't resist; he had to kiss her, for he was a real soldier.

Then the dog ran back again with the princess. But in the morning, when the king and queen were having their tea, the princess said that she had dreamed such a remarkable dream last night about a dog and a soldier. She had ridden on the dog, and the soldier had kissed her.

"That was a pretty story, indeed!" said the queen.

Now one of the old ladies-in-waiting was to keep watch by the princess' bed the next night to see if it really were a dream, or what it could be.

The soldier wanted very much to see the lovely princess again, and so the dog came during the night, took her, and ran as fast as it could, but the old lady-in-waiting pulled on a pair of rubber boots and ran after it just as fast. When she saw that they disappeared inside a big house, she drew a big cross on the door with a piece of chalk. Then she went home and went to bed, and the dog came back with the princess. But when it saw that a cross had been made on the door, it also took a piece of chalk and made crosses on all the doors in the city, and that was wisely done, for now, of course, the lady-in-waiting couldn't find the right door when there was a cross on every single one.

Early the next morning the king and the queen, the old lady-in-waiting, and all the officers came to see where the princess had been.

"There it is!" said the king when he saw the first door with a cross on it.

"No, *there* it is, my dear husband," said the queen, who saw the second door with a cross on it.

"But there's one and there's one!" they all said. No matter where they looked, there was a cross on the door. So then they could see that there was no use searching one bit.

But the queen was a very wise woman, who knew about more than just riding in the royal coach. She took her big golden scissors, cut up a large piece of silk, and sewed a lovely little bag. This she filled with small, fine grains of buckwheat, tied it to the princess' back, and when that was done, clipped a tiny hole in the bag so the grain could dribble out all along the way, wherever the princess went.

That night the dog came again, took the princess on his back, and carried her straight to the soldier, who had fallen in love with her and would have gladly been a prince so he could make her his wife.

The dog didn't notice at all how the grains dribbled out all the way from the castle to the soldier's window, where it ran up the wall with the princess. In the morning the king and queen saw where their daughter had been, all right, and so they took the soldier and put him in jail. There he sat! Ugh! How dark and dreary it was! And then they said to him, "Tomorrow you're to be hanged!" That wasn't a nice thing to hear, and he had forgotten his tinderbox back at the inn. In the morning he could see the people through the bars in the tiny window, hurrying out of the city to see him hanged. He heard drums and saw the soldiers marching. Everybody was rushing out, including a shoemaker's apprentice in his leather apron and slippers, who was in such a hurry that one of his slippers flew off and landed right over by the wall where the soldier sat peering out through the iron bars.

"Hey there, shoemaker's boy, you needn't be in such a hurry," said the soldier. "Nothing will happen until I get there. But if you'll run to my lodgings and fetch my tinderbox, you'll get four shillings. But then you must really run." The shoemaker's boy was only too glad to have four shillings and scurried away after the tinderbox, gave it to the soldier, and—yes, now we shall hear:

Outside the city a big gallows had been built; around it stood the soldiers and many hundreds of thousands of people. The king and the queen sat on a lovely throne right above the judge and the whole court. The soldier was already up on the ladder, but as they were going to put the noose around his neck, he said, oh yes, a sinner is always granted one little innocent wish before he receives his punishment. He would so like to smoke a pipeful of tobacco. After all, it was the last pipe he'd have in this world.

The king didn't want to say no to that, and so the soldier took out his tinderbox and struck a light: One! Two! Three! And there stood all the dogs: the first with eyes as big as teacups, the second with eyes as big as mill wheels, and the third with eyes as big as the Round Tower.

"Help me now so I won't be hanged!" said the soldier. And then the dogs flew right at the judge and the whole court, took one by the legs and one by the nose, and tossed them many miles up in the air so they fell down and broke into pieces.

"I won't!" said the king, but the biggest dog took both him and the queen and threw them after all the others. Then the soldiers were frightened, and all the people shouted: "Little soldier, you shall be our king and have the lovely princess!"

Then they put the soldier in the king's coach, and all three dogs danced in front and shouted "Hurrah!" And all the boys whistled through their fingers, and the soldiers presented arms. The princess came out of the copper castle and was made queen, and that she liked very well. The wedding lasted eight days, and the dogs sat at the table and made eyes at everybody.

THE SWINEHERD

‖‖‖

There was once a poor prince. He had a kingdom that was quite small, but then it was always big enough to get married on, and marry he would.

Now it was, of course, a bit presumptuous of him to dare to say to the emperor's daughter: "Will you have me?" But that he dared, all right, for his name was known far and wide, and there were hundreds of princesses who would have been only too glad to have him. But see if she was!

Now we shall hear:

On the grave of the prince's father there grew a rose tree. Oh such a lovely rose tree! It bore flowers every fifth year, and then only a single rose. But it was a rose that smelled so sweet that by smelling it one forgot all one's cares and woes. And then he had a nightingale that could sing as though all the lovely melodies in the world were in its little throat. That rose and that nightingale the princess was to have, and so they were put into two big silver cases and sent to her.

The emperor had them brought in before him to the great hall, where the princess was playing "Visitors" with her ladies-in-waiting—they had nothing else to do

—and when she saw the big cases with the presents inside, she clapped her hands for joy.

"If only it were a little pussycat!" she said—but then out came the lovely rose.

"My, how nicely it has been made!" said all the ladies-in-waiting.

"It is more than nice," said the emperor, "it is beautiful!"

But the princess touched it, and then she was on the verge of tears.

"Fie, Papa!" she said. "It's not artificial! It's real!"

"Fie!" said all the ladies-in-waiting. "It's real!"

"Now let us first see what is in the other case before we lose our tempers," thought the emperor, and then the nightingale came out. It sang so sweetly that to begin with no one could find fault with it.

"Superbe! Charmante!" said the ladies-in-waiting, for they all spoke French, each one worse than the other.

"How that bird reminds me of the late lamented empress' music box," said one old courtier. "Ahhh yes, it is quite the same tune, the same rendering."

"Yes," said the emperor, and then he cried like a little baby.

"I should hardly like to think that it's real," said the princess.

"Why yes, it is a real bird," said the people who had brought it.

"Well, then let that bird go!" said the princess, and she would in no way permit the prince to come.

But he didn't lose heart. He stained his face brown and black, and pulling his cap down over his eyes, he knocked at the door.

"Good morning, Emperor!" he said. "Can't you take me into your service here at the palace?"

"Well, there are so many who apply here," said the emperor, "but—let me see—I need someone to keep the pigs, for we have a lot of them."

And so the prince was hired as the imperial swineherd. He was given a wretched little room down by the pigsty, and there he had to stay. But the whole day he sat working, and when it was evening he had made a pretty little pot. Around it were bells, and as soon as the pot boiled they started ringing quite delightfully, and played the old tune:

> Ach, du lieber Augustin,
> Alles ist weg! Weg! Weg! *

But the most curious thing of all, however, was that anyone holding his finger in the steam from the pot could smell at once what food was cooking on every stove in the town, so that was certainly a far cry from a rose.

Now the princess came walking along with all her ladies-in-waiting, and when she heard the tune, she stood still and looked very pleased, for she could also play "Ach, du lieber Augustin." It was the only tune she knew, and she played it with one finger.

"Why, that's the tune I can play!" she said. "This must be a cultivated swineherd! Listen! Go in and ask him what that instrument costs."

And then one of the ladies-in-waiting had to run in, but she put on wooden shoes.

"What will you have for that pot?" said the lady-in-waiting.

"I want ten kisses from the princess," said the swineherd.

"Heaven help us!" said the lady-in-waiting.

"Well, it can't be less!" said the swineherd.

"Now! What does he say?" asked the princess.

"That I really can't tell you!" said the lady-in-waiting. "It is too horrible!"

"Then you can whisper!" And so she whispered.

"Why, how rude he is!" said the princess and left at once. But when she had gone a little way, the bells tinkled so prettily:

> Ach, du lieber Augustin,
> Alles ist weg! Weg! Weg!

---

* Ah, dear Augustine,
  All is over and done! Done! Done!

"Listen," said the princess. "Ask him if he will take ten kisses from my ladies-in-waiting."

"No thanks!" said the swineherd. "Ten kisses from the princess, or else I keep the pot."

"How really vexatious!" said the princess. "But then you must stand around me so that no one sees it."

And the ladies-in-waiting lined up in front of her and spread out their skirts, and then the swineherd got the ten kisses and she got the pot.

Oh, what fun they had! All that evening and the next day the pot had to boil. There wasn't a stove in the whole town that they didn't know what was cooking there, whether at the chamberlain's or at the shoemaker's. The ladies-in-waiting danced and clapped their hands.

"We know who's going to have fruit soup and pancakes! We know who's going to have porridge and meatballs! Oh, how interesting!"

"Extremely interesting," said the mistress of the robes.
"Yes, but keep it a secret, for I am the emperor's daughter!"

"Heaven help us!" they all said.

The swineherd—that is to say, the prince, but they didn't know, of course, that he was anything but a real swineherd—didn't let the next day pass before he had made something else, and this time he made a rattle. Whenever anyone swung it around, it played all the waltzes and quadrilles and polkas that were known since the creation of the world.

"But that is *superbe!*" said the princess as she went by. "I have never heard a lovelier composition! Listen, go in and ask what that instrument costs. But no kissing!"

"He wants a hundred kisses from the princess!" said the lady-in-waiting, who had been inside to ask.

"I do believe he's mad!" said the princess. And then she left. But after she had gone a little way, she stopped. "One should encourage the arts!" she said. "I *am* the emperor's daughter. Tell him he shall get ten kisses just like yesterday. The rest he can take from my ladies-in-waiting."

"Yes, but not unless we have to!" said the ladies-in-waiting.

"That's just talk!" said the princess. "If I can kiss him, then you can too! Remember, I give you board and wages!" And then the lady-in-waiting had to go in to him again.

"One hundred kisses from the princess," he said, "or else each keeps what he has!"

"Stand in front!" she said. So all the ladies-in-waiting lined up in front of her, and then he started kissing.

"What can all that commotion be down by the pigsty?" said the emperor, who had stepped out onto the balcony. He rubbed his eyes and put on his glasses. "Why, it's the ladies-in-waiting! They're up to something. I certainly must go down to them!" And then he pulled his slippers up in back, for they were shoes that he had worn down at the heel.

My, how he hurried!

As soon as he came down into the courtyard, he walked quite softly, and the ladies-in-waiting were so busy counting the kisses to make sure there was fair play—so he shouldn't get too many, but not too few either—that they didn't notice the emperor at all. He stood up on tiptoe.

"What on earth!" he said when he saw them kissing, and then he hit them on the head with his slipper just as the swineherd got the eighty-sixth kiss. "Get out!" said the emperor, for he was furious, and both the swineherd and the princess were put out of his empire.

There she stood now and cried, the swineherd swore, and the rain poured down.

"Ohhhh, what a miserable soul I am," said the princess. "If only I'd taken that lovely prince! Ohhhh, how unhappy I am!"

And the swineherd went behind a tree, wiped away the brown and black from his face, threw away the ugly clothes, and stepped forth in his prince's clothing, so lovely that the princess had to curtsy to him.

"I have come to despise you," he said. "You wouldn't have an honest prince! You didn't understand about the rose and the nightingale, but you could kiss the swineherd for a mechanical music box! Now it serves you right!"

And then he went into his kingdom and closed and bolted the door, so she really could stand outside and sing:

> "Ach, du lieber Augustin,
> Alles ist weg! Weg! Weg!"

THE PRINCESS ON THE PEA

IIIIIIIIIIIIIIIIIIIIIIIIIIIIIIIIIIIIIIIIIIIIIIIIIIIIIIIIIIIIIIIIII

There was once a prince. He wanted a princess, but it had to be a true princess! So he journeyed all around the world to find one, but no matter where he went, something was wrong. There were plenty of princesses, but whether or not they were true princesses he couldn't quite find out. There was always something that wasn't quite right. So he came home again and was very sad, for he wanted a true princess so very much.

One evening there was a terrible storm. The lightning flashed, the thunder boomed, and the rain poured down! It was really frightful. Then somebody knocked at the city gate, and the old king went out to open it.

A princess was standing outside, but heavens how she looked from the rain and the bad weather! Water poured off her hair and clothes and ran in at the toe of her shoe and out at the heel, but she said she was a true princess!

"Well, we'll soon find that out!" thought the old queen, but she didn't say anything. She went into the bedroom, took off all the bedding, and put a pea on the bottom of the bed. Then she took twenty mattresses and laid them on top of the pea, and then twenty eiderdown quilts on top of the mattresses. There the princess was to sleep that night.

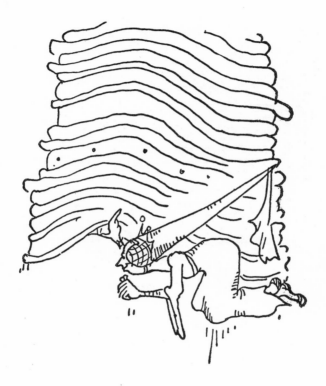

In the morning they asked her how she had slept.
"Oh, just miserably!" said the princess. "I've hardly
closed my eyes all night! Heaven knows what was in my
bed! I've been lying on something hard so that I'm black
and blue all over! It's simply dreadful!"

Then they could tell that this was a true princess because through the twenty mattresses and the twenty eiderdown quilts she had felt the pea. Only a true princess
could have such a delicate skin.

So the prince took her for his wife, for now he knew
that he had a true princess, and the pea was put into the
museum, where it can still be seen, if no one has taken
it!

See, this was a true story!

THE UGLY DUCKLING

It was so lovely out in the country—it was summer. The wheat stood golden, the oats green. The hay had been piled in stacks down in the green meadows, and there the stork went about on his long red legs and spoke Egyptian, for that is the language he had learned from his mother. Around the fields and meadows were great forests, and in the midst of the forests were deep lakes. Yes, it really was lovely out there in the country.

Squarely in the sunshine stood an old manor house with a deep moat all around it, and from the walls down to the water grew huge dock leaves that were so high that little children could stand upright under the biggest. It was as dense in there as in the deepest forest, and here sat a duck on her nest. She was about to hatch out her little ducklings, but now she had just about had enough of it because it was taking so long and she seldom had a visitor. The other ducks were fonder of swimming about in the moat than of running up and sitting under a dock leaf to chatter with her.

Finally one egg after the other started cracking: "Cheep! Cheep!" they said. All the egg yolks had come to life and stuck out their heads.

"Quack! Quack!" she said, and then they quacked as hard as they could and peered about on all sides under the green leaves. And their mother let them look about as much as they liked, for green is good for the eyes.

"My, how big the world is!" said all the youngsters, for now, of course, they had far more room than when they were inside the eggs.

"Do you think this is the whole world?" said the mother. "It stretches all the way to the other side of the garden, right into the parson's meadow. But I've never been there! Well, you're all here now, aren't you?" And then she got up. "No, I don't have them all! The biggest egg is still there. How long will it take? Now I'll soon get tired of it!" And then she settled down again.

"Well, how's it going?" said an old duck who had come to pay her a visit.

"One egg is taking so long!" said the duck who was hatching. "It won't crack! But now you shall see the others. They're the prettiest ducklings I've seen. They all look just like their father, the wretch! He doesn't even come to visit me!"

"Let me see that egg that won't crack!" said the old duck. "You can be certain it's a turkey egg! I was fooled like that myself once. And I had my sorrows and troubles with those youngsters, for they're afraid of the water, I can tell you! I couldn't get them out in it! I quacked and I snapped, but it didn't help! Let me have a look at that egg! Yes, it's a turkey egg, all right. You just let it lie there and teach the other children how to swim."

"Oh, I still want to sit on it a little longer," said the duck. "I've been sitting on it for so long that I can just as well wait a little longer!"

"Suit yourself!" said the old duck, and then she left.

Finally the big egg cracked. "Cheep! Cheep!" said the youngster and tumbled out. He was very big and ugly. The duck looked at him.

"Now that's a terribly big duckling!" she said. "None of the others looks like that! Could he be a turkey chick after all? Well, we'll soon find out. Into the water he'll go if I have to kick him out into it myself!"

The next day the weather was perfect. The sun shone

on all the green dock leaves. The mother duck came down to the moat with her whole family: Splash! She jumped into the water. "Quack! Quack!" she said, and one duckling after the other plumped in. The water washed over their heads, but they came up again at once and floated splendidly. Their feet moved of themselves, and they were all out in the water. Even the ugly gray youngster was swimming too.

"That's no turkey," she said. "See how splendidly he uses his legs, how straight he holds himself. That's my own child! As a matter of fact, he is quite handsome when one looks at him in the right way. Quack! Quack! Now come with me, and I'll take you out in the world and present you to the duck yard. But always keep close to me so that no one steps on you. And keep an eye out for the cat!"

And then they came to the duck yard. There was a terrible commotion, for two families were fighting over an eel's head, and then the cat got it of course.

"See, that's the way it goes in this world," said the mother duck and smacked her bill, for she would have liked to have had the eel's head herself. "Now use your legs," she said; "see if you can't step lively and bow your necks to that old duck over there. She's the most aristocratic of anyone here: she has Spanish blood in her veins. That's why she's so fat. And see? She has a red rag around her leg. That is something very special and the highest honor any duck can receive. It means that no one wants to get rid of her and that she is to be recognized by animals and men! Be quick! Out with your toes! A well brought up duck places his feet wide apart, just like his father and mother. Now then! Bow your necks and say 'Quack!' "

This they did, but the other ducks all around looked at them and said quite loudly, "Look there! Now we're to have one more batch, as if there weren't enough of us already! And fie, how that duckling looks! We won't put up with him!" And at once a duck flew over and bit him in the neck.

"Leave him alone!" said the mother. "He's not bothering anyone."

"Yes, but he's too big and queer!" said the duck who had bitten him. "So he has to be pushed around."

"Those are pretty children the mother has," said the old duck with the rag around her leg. "They're all pretty except that one; it didn't turn out right. I do wish she could make it over again."

"That can't be, your Grace," said the mother duck. "He's not pretty, but he has an exceedingly good disposition, and he swims as well as any of the others; yes, I might venture to say a bit better. I do believe he'll grow prettier, or in time a little smaller. He's lain in the egg too long, so he hasn't gotten the right shape!" And then she ruffled his feathers and smoothed them down. "Besides, he's a drake, so it doesn't matter very much. I think he'll grow much stronger. He'll get along all right."

"The other ducklings are lovely," said the old duck. "Just make yourselves at home, and if you can find an eel's head, you may bring it to me!"

And so they made themselves quite at home.

But the poor duckling, who had been the last one out of the egg and looked so ugly, was bitten and shoved and ridiculed by both the ducks and the hens. "He's too big!" they all said. And the turkey cock, who had been born with spurs on and so believed himself to be an emperor, puffed himself up like a ship in full sail, went right up to him, and gobbled until he got quite red in the face. The poor duckling didn't know where to stay or go. He was miserable because he was so ugly and the laughingstock of the whole duck yard.

So the first day passed, and afterward it grew worse and worse. The poor duckling was chased by everyone. Even his brothers and sisters were nasty to him and were always saying: "If only the cat would get you, you ugly wretch!" And his mother said, "If only you were far away!" And the ducks bit him, and the hens pecked him, and the girl who fed the poultry kicked at him.

Then he ran and flew over the hedge. The little birds in the bushes flew up in fright. "It's because I'm so ugly!" thought the duckling and shut his eyes, but he still kept on running. Then he came out into the big marsh where the wild ducks lived. He was so exhausted and unhappy that he lay there all night.

In the morning the wild ducks flew up and looked at their new comrade. "What kind of a duck are you?" they asked, and the duckling turned from one side to the other and greeted them as best he could.

"How ugly you are!" said the wild ducks. "But it makes no difference to us as long as you don't marry into our family!"

Poor thing! He certainly wasn't thinking about marriage. All he wanted was to be allowed to lie in the rushes and to drink a little water from the marsh.

There he lay for two whole days, and then there came two wild geese, or rather two wild ganders, for they were both males, not long out of the egg, and therefore they were quite saucy.

"Listen, comrade!" they said. "You're so ugly that you appeal to us. Want to come along and be a bird of passage? In another marsh close by are some sweet lovely wild geese, every single one unmarried, who can say 'Quack!' You're in a position to make your fortune, ugly as you are!"

Bang! Bang! Shots suddenly rang out above them, and both the wild geese fell down dead in the rushes, and the water was red with blood. Bang! Bang! It sounded again, and whole flocks of wild geese flew up out of the rushes, and the guns cracked again. A great hunt was on. The hunters lay around the marsh. Yes, some were even sitting up in the branches of the trees that hung over the water. The blue smoke drifted in among the dark trees and hovered over the water. Into the mud came the hunting dogs. Splash! Splash! Reeds and rushes swayed on all sides. The poor duckling was terrified. He turned his head to put it under his wing and at the same moment found himself standing face to face with a terribly big dog! Its tongue was hanging way out of its mouth, and its eyes gleamed horribly. It opened its jaws over the duckling, showed its sharp teeth and—splash!—went on without touching him.

"Oh, heaven be praised!" sighed the duckling. "I'm so ugly that even the dog doesn't care to bite me!"

And then he lay quite still while the buckshot whistled through the rushes and shot after shot resounded.

Not until late in the day did it become quiet, but even

then the poor duckling didn't dare get up. He waited several hours before he looked around, and then he hurried out of the marsh as fast as he could. He ran over field and meadow, and there was such a wind that the going was hard.

Toward evening he came to a wretched little house. It was so ramshackle that it didn't know which way to fall, and so it remained standing. The wind blew so hard around the duckling that he had to sit on his tail to keep from blowing away. Then he noticed that the door was off one of its hinges and hung so crookedly that he could slip into the house through the crack, and this he did.

Here lived an old woman with her cat and her hen. And the cat, which she called Sonny, could arch his back and purr, and he even gave off sparks, but only if one stroked him the wrong way. The hen had quite short, tiny legs, so she was called Chicky Low Legs. She laid good eggs, and the old woman was as fond of her as if she had been her own child.

In the morning the strange duckling was noticed at once, and the cat started to purr and the hen to cluck.

"What's that?" said the old woman and looked around, but she couldn't see very well, so she thought the duckling was a fat duck that had lost its way. "Why, that was a fine catch!" she said. "Now I can get duck eggs, if only it's not a drake. That we'll have to try!"

So the duckling was accepted on trial for three weeks, but no eggs came. And the cat was master of the house, and the hen madame. And they always said, "We and the world," for they believed that they were half of the world, and the very best half at that. The duckling thought there might be another opinion, but the hen wouldn't stand for that.

"Can you lay eggs?" she asked.

"No!"

"Then keep your mouth shut!"

And the cat said, "Can you arch your back, purr, and give off sparks?"

"No!"

"Well, then, keep your opinion to yourself when sensible folks are speaking."

And the duckling sat in the corner in low spirits. Then he started thinking of the fresh air and the sunshine. He had such a strange desire to float on the water. At last he couldn't help himself; he had to tell it to the hen.

"What's wrong with you?" she asked. "You have nothing to do. That's why you're putting on these airs! Lay eggs or purr, then it'll go over."

"But it's so lovely to float on the water!" said the duckling. "So lovely to get it over your head and duck down to the bottom."

"Yes, a great pleasure I daresay!" said the hen. "You've gone quite mad! Ask the cat, he's the wisest one I know, if *he* likes to float on the water or duck under it. Not to mention myself. Ask our mistress, the old woman; there is no one wiser than she in the whole world. Do you think she wants to float and get water over her head?"

"You don't understand me," said the duckling.

"Well, if we don't understand you, who would? Indeed, you'll never be wiser than the cat and the old woman, not to mention myself. Don't put on airs, my child! And thank your Creator for all the good that has been done for you. Haven't you come into a warm house, into a circle from which you can learn something? But you're a fool, and it's no fun associating with you! Believe you me! When I tell you harsh truths it's for your own good, and this way one can know one's true friends. See to it now that you start laying eggs or learn to purr and give off sparks."

"I think I'll go out into the wide world!" said the duckling.

"Yes, just do that!" said the hen.

So the duckling went out. He floated on the water and dived down to the bottom, but he was shunned by all the animals because of his ugliness.

Now it was autumn. The leaves in the forest turned golden and brown. The wind took hold of them and they danced about. The sky looked cold, and the clouds hung heavy with hail and snow. A raven stood on the fence and shrieked "Off! Off!" just from the cold. Merely thinking of it could make one freeze. The poor duckling was really in a bad way.

One evening as the sun was setting in all its splendor,

a great flock of beautiful large birds came out of the
bushes. The duckling had never seen anything so lovely.
They were shining white, with long supple necks. They
were swans, and uttering a strange cry, they spread their
splendid broad wings and flew away from the cold meadows to warmer lands and open seas. They rose so high,

so high, and the ugly little duckling had such a strange
feeling. He moved around and around in the water like
a wheel, stretching his neck high in the air after them
and uttering a cry so shrill and strange that he frightened

even himself. Oh, he couldn't forget those lovely birds, those happy birds; and when he could no longer see them, he dived right down to the bottom, and when he came up again he was quite beside himself. He didn't know what those birds were called or where they were flying, but he was fonder of them than he had ever been of anyone before. He didn't envy them in the least. How could it occur to him to wish for such loveliness for himself? He would have been glad if only the ducks had tolerated him in their midst—the poor ugly bird.

And the winter was so cold, so cold. The duckling had to swim about in the water to keep from freezing. But each night the hole in which he swam became smaller and smaller; it froze so the crust of the ice creaked. The duckling had to keep moving his legs so it wouldn't close, but at last he grew tired, lay quite still, and froze fast in the ice.

Early in the morning a farmer came along. He saw the duckling, went out and made a hole in the ice with his wooden shoe, and then carried him home to his wife. There he was brought back to life.

The children wanted to play with him, but the duckling thought they wanted to hurt him, and in his fright he flew into the milk dish so the milk splashed out in the room. The woman shrieked and waved her arms. Then he flew into the butter trough and down into the flour barrel and out again. My, how he looked now! The woman screamed and hit at him with the tongs, and the children knocked each other over trying to capture him, and they laughed and shrieked. It was a good thing the door was standing open. Out flew the duckling among the bushes, into the newly fallen snow, and he lay there as if stunned.

But it would be far too sad to tell of all the suffering and misery he had to go through during that hard winter. He was lying in the marsh among the rushes when the sun began to shine warmly again. The larks sang—it was a beautiful spring.

Then all at once he raised his wings. They beat more strongly than before and carried him powerfully away. And before he knew it, he was in a large garden where the apple trees were in bloom and the fragrance of lilacs filled the air, where they hung on the long green branches right down to the winding canal. Oh, it was so lovely here with the freshness of spring. And straight ahead, out of the thicket came three beautiful swans. They ruffled their feathers and floated so lightly on the water. The duckling recognized the magnificent birds and was filled with a strange melancholy.

"I will fly straight to them, those royal birds, and they will peck me to death because I am so ugly and yet dare approach them. But it doesn't matter. Better to be killed by them than to be bitten by the ducks, pecked by the hens, and kicked by the girl who takes care of the poultry yard, or suffer such hardships during the winter!" And he flew out into the water and swam over toward the magnificent swans. They saw him and hurried toward him with ruffled feathers.

"Just kill me," said the poor creature and bowed down his head toward the surface of the water and awaited his death. But what did he see in the clear water? Under him he saw his own reflection, but he was no longer a clumsy, grayish-black bird, ugly and disgusting. He was a swan himself!

It doesn't matter being born in a duck yard, if one has lain in a swan's egg!

He felt quite happy about all the hardships and suffering he had gone through. Now he could really appreciate his happiness and all the beauty that greeted him. And the big swans swam around him and stroked him with their bills.

Some little children came down to the garden and threw bread and seeds out into the water, and the smallest one cried, "There's a new one!" And the other children joined in shouting jubilantly, "Yes, a new one has come!" And they all clapped their hands and danced for joy and ran to get their father and mother. And bread and cake were thrown into the water, and they all said, "The new one is the prettiest! So young and lovely!" And the old swans bowed to him.

Then he felt very shy and put his head under his wing—he didn't know why. He was much too happy, but not proud at all, for a good heart is never proud.

He thought of how he had been persecuted and ridiculed, and now he heard everyone saying that he was the loveliest of all the lovely birds. And the lilacs bowed their branches right down to the water to him, and the sun shone so warm and bright. Then he ruffled his feathers, lifted his slender neck, and from the depths of his heart said joyously:

"I never dreamed of so much happiness when I was the ugly duckling."

THE NIGHTINGALE

᠊᠊᠊

In China, you know of course, the emperor is Chinese, and everyone he has around him is Chinese too. Now this happened many years ago, but that is just why the story is worth hearing, before it is forgotten. The emperor's palace was the most magnificent in the world. It was made entirely of fine porcelain, so precious but so fragile and delicate to touch that one really had to watch one's step. In the garden the most unusual flowers were to be seen, and the most beautiful had silver bells fastened to them that tinkled so that no one would go past without noticing them. Yes, everything had been very well thought out in the emperor's garden, and it stretched so far that even the gardener didn't know where it stopped. If one kept on walking, one came to the loveliest forest with great trees and deep lakes. The forest stretched all the way down to the sea, which was blue and so deep that great ships could sail right in under the branches. And in these branches lived a nightingale that sang so sweetly that even the poor fisherman, who had so many other things to keep him busy, lay still and listened when he was out at night pulling in his net.

"Good heavens! How beautiful!" he said. But then he had to look after his net and he forgot the bird, although the next night, when it sang again and the fisherman came out there, he said the same thing: "Good heavens! How beautiful!"

From every land in the world travelers came to the emperor's city. They admired the city, the palace, and the garden. But when they heard the nightingale, they all said: "But this is really the best thing of all!" And the travelers told about it when they got home, and scholars wrote many books about the city, the palace, and the garden. But they didn't forget the nightingale—it was given the highest place of all. And those who were poets wrote the loveliest poems, each one about the nightingale in the forest by the sea.

These books went around the world, and once some of them came to the emperor. He sat in his golden chair, reading and reading and nodding his head, for he was pleased by the lovely descriptions of the city, the palace, and the garden. "But the nightingale is really the best thing of all"—there it stood in print.

"What's that?" said the emperor. "The nightingale? Why, I don't know anything about it! Is there such a bird in my empire, in my very own garden? I have never heard of it before! Fancy having to find this out from a book!"

And then he summoned his chamberlain, who was so grand that if anyone of lower rank dared speak to him or ask about something, he would only say: "P!" And that doesn't mean anything at all.

"There is supposed to be a highly remarkable bird here called a nightingale!" said the emperor. "They say it's the very best thing of all in my great kingdom! Why hasn't anyone ever told me about it?"

"I have never heard it mentioned before!" said the chamberlain. "It has never been presented at court!"

"I want it to come here this evening and sing for me," said the emperor. "The whole world knows what I have, and I don't!"

"I have never heard it mentioned before!" said the chamberlain. "I shall look for it! I shall find it!"

But where was it to be found? The chamberlain ran up and down all the stairs, through great halls and corridors. But no one he met had ever heard of the night-

ingale, and the chamberlain ran back again to the emperor
and said it was probably a fable made up by the people
who write books. "Your Imperial Majesty shouldn't believe what is written in them. They are inventions and
belong to something called black magic!"

"But the book in which I read it was sent to me by
the mighty emperor of Japan, so it cannot be false. I
will hear the nightingale! It shall be here this evening! I
bestow my highest patronage upon it! And if it doesn't
come, I'll have the whole court thumped on their stomachs
after they have eaten supper!"

"Tsing-pe!" said the chamberlain and again ran up
and down all the stairs and through all the great halls
and corridors. And half the court ran with him, for they
weren't at all willing to be thumped on their stomachs.
They asked and asked about the remarkable nightingale
that was known to the whole world but not to the court!

Finally they met a little peasant girl in the kitchen.
She said, "The nightingale? Heavens! I know it well.
Yes, how it can sing! Every evening I'm permitted to
take a few scraps from the table home to my poor, sick
mother—she lives down by the shore. And on my way
back, when I'm tired and rest in the forest, I can hear
the nightingale sing. It brings tears to my eyes. It's just
as though my mother were kissing me."

"Little kitchen maid!" said the chamberlain. "You shall
have a permanent position in the kitchen and permission to stand and watch the emperor eating if you can
lead us to the nightingale. It has been summoned to appear at court this evening."

And so they all set out into the forest where the
nightingale usually sang. Half the court went with them.
As they were walking along at a fast pace, a cow started
mooing.

"Oh!" said a courtier. "There it is! Indeed, what remarkable force for so tiny an animal. I am certain I have
heard it before."

"No, that's the cow mooing," said the little kitchen
maid. "We're still quite a long way from the spot."

Now the frogs started croaking in the marsh.

"Lovely," said the Chinese imperial chaplain. "Now I can hear her. It's just like tiny church bells."

"No, that's the frogs!" said the little kitchen maid. "But now I think we'll soon hear it."

Then the nightingale started to sing.

"That's it!" said the little girl. "Listen! Listen! There it sits!" And then she pointed to a little gray bird up in the branches.

"Is it possible?" said the chamberlain. "I had never imagined it like this. How ordinary it looks! No doubt seeing so many fine people has made it lose its *couleur!*"

"Little nightingale," shouted the little kitchen maid quite loud, "our gracious emperor would so like you to sing for him!"

"With the greatest pleasure," said the nightingale and sang in a way to warm one's heart.

"It is just like glass bells!" said the chamberlain. "And look at that tiny throat. How it vibrates! It's remarkable that we have never heard it before. It will be a great success at court."

"Shall I sing for the emperor again?" said the nightingale, who thought the emperor was there.

"My enchanting little nightingale," said the chamberlain, "it gives me the greatest pleasure to command you to appear at a court celebration this evening, where you will delight his High Imperial Eminence with your *charmante* song!"

"It sounds best out of doors," said the nightingale, but it followed them gladly when it heard it was the emperor's wish.

The palace had been properly polished up. Walls and floors, which were of porcelain, glowed from the lights of thousands of golden lamps. The loveliest flowers, which really could tinkle, had been lined up in the halls. There was such a running back and forth that it caused a draft that made all the bells tinkle so one couldn't hear oneself think.

In the middle of the great hall, where the emperor sat, a golden perch had been placed for the nightingale to sit on. The whole court was there, and the little kitchen maid had been given permission to stand behind the door, for now she really did have the title of kitchen maid. Everyone was wearing his most splendid attire. They all looked at the little gray bird, to which the emperor was nodding.

And the nightingale sang so sweetly that tears came to the emperor's eyes and rolled down his cheeks. And then the nightingale sang even more sweetly. It went straight to one's heart. And the emperor was so pleased that he said the nightingale was to have his golden slipper to wear around its neck. But the nightingale said no thank you— it had been rewarded enough.

"I have seen tears in the emperor's eyes. To me, that is the richest treasure. An emperor's tears have a won-

drous power. Heaven knows I have been rewarded
enough!" And then it sang again with its sweet and
blessed voice.

"That is the most adorable *coquetterie* I know of,"
said the ladies standing around. And then they put water
in their mouths so they could gurgle whenever anyone
spoke to them, for now they thought that they were
nightingales too. Yes, even the lackeys and chambermaids let it be known that they were also satisfied, and
that was saying a lot, for they are the hardest to please.
Yes indeed, the nightingale had really been a success.

Now it was to remain at court and have its own cage
as well as freedom to take a walk outside twice during
the day and once at night. It was given twelve servants,
too, each one holding tightly to a silken ribbon fastened
to its leg. That kind of walk was no pleasure at all.

The whole city talked about the remarkable bird, and
whenever two people met, the first merely said, "Night!"
and the other said "Gale!" And then they sighed and understood one another! Yes, eleven shopkeepers' children
were named after it, but not one of them could ever sing
a note in his life!

One day a big package came for the emperor. On the
outside was written "Nightingale."

"Here's a new book about our famous bird," said the
emperor. But it was no book, it was a little work of art
in a case: an artificial nightingale made to resemble the
real one, except that it was encrusted with diamonds and
rubies and sapphires! As soon as the artificial bird was

wound up, it could sing one of the melodies the real one sang, and then its tail bobbed up and down, glittering with gold and silver. Around its neck hung a ribbon, and on it was written: "The emperor of Japan's nightingale is poor compared to the emperor of China's."

"How lovely!" said everyone. And the person who had brought the artificial nightingale immediately had the title of chief-imperial-nightingale-bringer bestowed upon him.

"Now they must sing together! What a duet that will be!"

And then they had to sing together, but it didn't really come off because the real nightingale sang in its own way and the artificial bird worked mechanically.

"It is not to blame," said the music master. "It keeps time perfectly and according to the rules of my own system!" Then the artificial bird had to sing alone. It was as much of a success as the real one, and besides, it was so much more beautiful to look at: it glittered like bracelets and brooches.

Thirty-three times it sang one and the same melody, and still it wasn't tired. People were only too willing to hear it from the beginning again, but the emperor thought that now the living nightingale should also sing a little. But where was it? No one had noticed it fly out the open window, away to its green forest.

"But what kind of behavior is that?" said the emperor. And all the courtiers berated it and said the nightingale was a most ungrateful bird.

"We still have the best bird," they said, and again the artificial bird had to sing. And it was the thirty-fourth time they had heard the same tune, but they didn't know it all the way through yet, for it was so hard. And the music master praised the bird very highly—yes, even assured them that it was better than the real nightingale, not only as far as its clothes and the many diamonds were concerned, but internally as well.

"You see, my lords and ladies, and your Imperial Majesty above all! You can never figure out what the real nightingale will sing, but with the artificial bird everything had already been decided. This is the way it will be, and not otherwise. It can be accounted for, it can be opened up to reveal the human logic that has gone into the arrangement of the works, how they operate and how they turn one after the other."

"Those are my thoughts precisely!" they all said. And on the following Sunday the music master was allowed to show the bird to the people. They were also going to hear it sing, said the emperor. And they heard it, and were as happy as if they had all drunk themselves merry on tea, for that is so very Chinese. And then they all said "Oh" and held their index fingers high in the air and nodded. But the poor fisherman, who had heard the real nightingale, said: "It sounds pretty enough, and it is similar too. But something is missing. I don't know what it is."

The real nightingale was banished from the land.

The artificial bird had its place on a silken pillow close to the emperor's bed. All the gifts it had received, gold and precious stones, lay around it, and its title had risen to high-imperial-bedside-table-singer. It ranked number one on the left, for the emperor considered the side where the heart lies to be the most important. And the heart of an emperor is on the left side too. The music master wrote a treatise in twenty-five volumes about the artificial bird. It was very learned and very long and contained the biggest Chinese words, and all the people said they had read and understood it, for otherwise they would have been regarded stupid and would have been thumped on their stomachs.

It went on like this for a whole year. The emperor, the court, and all the other Chinese knew every little "cluck" in the song of the artificial bird by heart. But this is why they prized it so highly now: they could sing along with it themselves, and this they did! The street boys sang "Zizizi! Cluck-cluck-cluck!" And the emperor sang it too. Yes, it was certainly lovely.

But one evening, as the artificial bird was singing away and the emperor was lying in bed listening to it, something went "Pop!" inside the bird. "Whirrrrrrrrrrrrr!" All the wheels went around, and then the music stopped.

The emperor sprang out of bed and had his personal

physician summoned. But what good was he? Then they summoned the watchmaker, and after much talk and many examinations of the bird he put it more or less in order again. But he said it must be used as sparingly as possible. The cogs were so worn down that it wasn't possible to put in new ones in a way that would be sure to make music. What a great affliction this was! Only once a year did they dare let the artificial bird sing, and even that was hard on it. But then the music master made a little speech, with big words, and said it was just as good as new, and then it *was* just as good as new.

Five years passed, and then a great sorrow fell upon the land. They were all fond of their emperor, but now he was sick and it was said he could not live. A new emperor had already been picked out, and people stood out in the street and asked the chamberlain how their emperor was.

"P!" he said and shook his head.

Cold and pale, the emperor lay in his great magnificent bed. The whole court thought he was dead, and they all ran off to greet the new emperor. The lackeys ran out to talk about it, and the chambermaids had a big tea party. Cloths had been put down in all the halls and corridors to deaden the sound of footsteps. And now it was so quiet, so quiet. But the emperor was not yet dead. Stiff and pale, he lay in the magnificent bed with the long velvet curtains and the heavy gold tassels. High above him a window stood open, and the moon shone in on the emperor and the artificial bird.

The poor emperor could hardly breathe. It was as though something heavy were sitting on his chest. He opened his eyes and then he saw that Death was sitting on his chest. He had put on his golden crown and was holding the emperor's golden sword in one hand and his magnificent banner in the other. All around from the folds of the velvet curtains strange faces were peering out. Some were quite hideous, others so kindly and mild. These were all the emperor's good and wicked deeds that were looking at him now that Death was sitting on his heart.

"Do you remember that?" whispered one after the other. "Do you remember that?" And then they told him so much that the sweat stood out on his forehead.

"I never knew that!" said the emperor. "Music! Music! The big Chinese drum!" he shouted. "So I don't have to hear all the things they're saying!"

But they kept it up, and Death nodded, just the way the Chinese do, at everything that was being said.

"Music! Music!" shrieked the emperor. "Blessed little golden bird, sing now! Sing! I've given you gold and costly presents. I myself hung my golden slipper around your neck. Sing now! Sing!"

But the bird kept silent. There was no one to wind it up, so it didn't sing. But Death kept on looking at the emperor out of his big, empty sockets, and it was so quiet, so terribly quiet.

Suddenly the loveliest song could be heard close to the window. It was the little real nightingale sitting on the branch outside. It had heard of the emperor's need and had come to sing him comfort and hope. And as it sang, the faces became paler and paler, and the blood started flowing faster and faster in the emperor's weak body, and Death himself listened and said, "Keep on, little nightingale, keep on!"

"If you will give me the magnificent golden sword! If you will give me the rich banner! If you will give me the emperor's crown!"

And Death gave each treasure for a song, and the nightingale kept on singing. And it sang about the quiet churchyard where the white roses grow and the scent of the elder tree perfumes the air, and where the fresh grass is watered by the tears of the bereaved. Then Death was filled with longing for his garden and drifted like a cold, white mist out of the window.

"Thank you, thank you!" said the emperor. "Heavenly little bird. I know you, all right. I have driven you out of my land and empire, and still you have sung the bad visions away from my bed and removed Death from my heart! How can I reward you?"

"You have already rewarded me!" said the nightingale. "You gave me the tears from your eyes the first time I sang. I will never forget that. Those are the jewels that do a singer's heart good. But sleep now, and get well and strong. I shall sing for you."

And it sang, and the emperor fell into a sweet sleep, which was calm and beneficial.

The sun was shining in on him through the windows when he awoke, refreshed and healthy. None of his servants had returned yet, for they thought he was dead, but the nightingale still sat there and sang.

"You must always stay with me," said the emperor. "You shall sing only when you yourself want to, and I shall break the artificial bird into a thousand bits!"

"Don't do that!" said the nightingale. "Why, it has done what good it could. Keep it as before. I cannot build my nest and live at the palace, but let me come whenever I want to. Then in the evening I will sit on the branch here by the window and sing for you. I shall sing about those who are happy and those who suffer. I shall sing of good and evil, which is kept hidden from you. The little songbird flies far, to the poor fisherman, to the farmer's roof, to everyone who is far from you and your court. I love your heart more than your crown, and yet your crown has an odor of sanctity about it. I will come. I will sing for you. But you must promise me one thing!"

"Everything!" said the emperor, standing there in his imperial robe, which he himself had put on, and holding the heavy golden sword up to his heart.

"One thing I beg of you. Tell no one that you have a little bird that tells you everything! Then things will go even better!"

And then the nightingale flew away.

The servants came in to have a look at their dead emperor. Yes, there they stood, and the emperor said, "Good morning!"

THE LITTLE MERMAID

‖‖

Far out to sea the water is as blue as the petals on the loveliest cornflower and as clear as the purest glass. But it is very deep, deeper than any anchor rope can reach. Many church steeples would have to be placed one on top of the other to reach from the bottom up to the surface of the water. Down there live the mermen.

Now it certainly shouldn't be thought that the bottom is only bare and sandy. No, down there grow the strangest trees and plants, which have such flexible stalks and leaves that the slightest movement of the water sets them in motion as if they were alive. All the fish, big and small, slip in and out among the branches just the way the birds do up here in the air. At the very deepest spot lies the castle of the king of the sea. The walls are of coral, and the long tapering windows are of the clearest amber. But the roof is of mussel shells, which open and close with the flow of the water. The effect is lovely, for in each one there are beautiful pearls, a single one of which would be highly prized in a queen's crown.

For many years the king of the sea had been a widower, but his old mother kept house for him. She was a wise woman, but proud of her royal birth, and so she wore twelve oysters on her tail; the others of noble birth had to content themselves with only six. Otherwise she deserved much praise, especially because she was so fond of the little princesses, her grandchildren. They were six lovely children, but the youngest was the fairest of them all. Her skin was as clear and opalescent as a rose petal. Her eyes were as blue as the deepest sea. But like all the others, she had no feet. Her body ended in a fish tail.

All day long they could play down in the castle in the great halls where living flowers grew out of the walls. The big amber windows were opened, and then the fish swam in to them just as with us the swallows fly in when we open our windows. But the fish swam right over to the little princesses, ate out of their hands, and allowed themselves to be petted.

Outside the castle was a large garden with trees as red as fire and as blue as night. The fruit shone like gold, and the flowers like a burning flame, for their stalks and leaves were always in motion. The ground itself was the finest sand, but blue like the flame of brimstone. A strange blue sheen lay over everything down there. It was more like standing high up in the air and seeing only sky above and below than like being at the bottom of the sea. In a dead calm, the sun could be glimpsed. It looked like a purple flower from whose chalice the light streamed out.

Each of the little princesses had her own tiny plot in the garden where she could dig and plant just as she wished. One made her flower bed in the shape of a whale. Another preferred hers to resemble a little mermaid. But the youngest made hers quite round like the sun and had only flowers that shone red the way it did. She was a strange child, quiet and pensive, and while the other sisters decorated their gardens with the strangest things they had found from wrecked ships, the only thing she wanted, besides the rosy-red flowers that resembled the sun high above, was a beautiful marble statue. It was a handsome boy carved out of clear white stone, and in the shipwreck it had come down to the bottom of the sea. By the pedestal she had planted a

rose-colored weeping willow. It grew magnificently, and its fresh branches hung out over the statue and down toward the blue, sandy bottom, where its shadow appeared violet and moved just like the branches. It looked as if the top and roots played at kissing each other.

Nothing pleased her more than to hear about the world of mortals up above. The old grandmother had to tell everything she knew about ships and cities, mortals and animals. To her it seemed especially wonderful and lovely that up on the earth the flowers gave off a fragrance, since they didn't at the bottom of the sea, and that the forests were green and those fish that were seen among the branches there could sing so loud and sweet that it was a pleasure. What the grandmother called fish were the little birds, for otherwise the princesses wouldn't have understood her, as they had never seen a bird.

"When you reach the age of fifteen," said the grandmother, "you shall be permitted to go to the surface of the water, sit in the moonlight on the rocks, and look at the great ships sailing by. You will see forests and cities too!"

The next year the first sister would be fifteen, but the others—yes, each one was a year younger than the other, so the youngest still had five years left before she might come up from the bottom of the sea and find out how it looked in our world. But each one promised to tell the others what she had seen and found to be the most wonderful on that first day; for their grandmother hadn't told them enough—there was so much they had to find out.

No one was as full of longing as the youngest, the very one who had to wait the longest and who was so quiet and pensive. Many a night she stood by the open window and looked up through the dark blue water where the fish flipped their fins and tails. She could see the moon and stars. To be sure they shone quite pale, but through the water they looked much bigger than to our eyes. If it seemed as though a black shadow glided slowly under them, then she knew it was either a whale that swam over her or else it was a ship with many mortals on board. It certainly never occurred to them that a lovely little mermaid was standing down below stretching her white hands up toward the keel.

Now the eldest princess was fifteen and was permitted to go up to the surface of the water.

When she came back, she had hundreds of things to tell about. But the most wonderful thing of all, she said, was to lie in the moonlight on a sandbank in the calm sea and to look at the big city close to the shore, where the lights twinkled like hundreds of stars, and to listen to the music and the noise and commotion of carriages and mortals, to see the many church steeples and spires, and to hear the chimes ring. And just because the youngest sister couldn't go up there, she longed after all this the most.

Oh, how the little mermaid listened. And later in the evening, when she was standing by the open window and looking up through the dark-blue water, she thought of the great city with all the noise and commotion, and then it seemed to her that she could hear the church bells ringing down to her.

The next year the second sister was allowed to rise up through the water and swim wherever she liked. She came up just as the sun was setting, and she found this sight the loveliest. The whole sky looked like gold, she said—and the clouds! Well, she couldn't describe their beauty enough. Crimson and violet they had sailed over her. But even faster than the clouds, like a long white veil, a flock of wild swans had flown over the water into the sun. She swam toward it, but it sank, and the rosy glow went out on the sea and on the clouds.

The next year, the third sister came up. She was the boldest of them all, and so she swam up a broad river that emptied into the sea. She saw lovely green hills covered with grapevines. Castles and farms peeped out among great forests. She heard how all the birds sang, and the sun shone so hot that she had to dive under the water to cool her burning face. In a little bay she came upon a whole flock of little children. Quite naked, they ran and splashed in the water. She wanted to play with them, but they ran away terrified. And then a little black animal came; it was a dog, but she had never seen a dog before. It barked at her so furiously that she grew frightened and made for the open sea. But never could she forget the great forests, the green hills, and the lovely children who could swim in the water despite the fact that they had no fish tails.

The fourth sister was not so bold. She stayed out in the middle of the rolling sea and said that this was the loveliest of all. She could see many miles all around her, and the sky was just like a big glass bell. She had seen ships, but far away. They looked like seagulls. The funny dolphins had turned somersaults, and the big whales had spouted water through their nostrils so it had looked like hundreds of fountains all around.

Now it was the turn of the fifth sister. Her birthday

was in winter, so she saw what the others hadn't seen. The sea looked quite green, and huge icebergs were swimming all around. Each one looked like a pearl, she said, although they were certainly much bigger than the church steeples built by mortals. They appeared in the strangest shapes and sparkled like diamonds. She had sat on one of the biggest, and all the ships sailed, terrified, around where she sat with her long hair flying in the breeze. But in the evening the sky was covered with clouds. The lightning flashed and the thunder boomed, while the black sea lifted the huge icebergs up high, where they glittered in the bright flashes of light. On all the ships they took in the sails, and they were anxious and afraid. But she sat calmly on her floating iceberg and watched the blue streaks of lightning zigzag into the sea.

Each time one of the sisters came to the surface of the water for the first time, she was always enchanted by the new and wonderful things she had seen. But now that, as grown girls, they were permitted to go up there whenever they liked, it no longer mattered to them. They longed again for home. And after a month, they said it was most beautiful down there where they lived and that home was the best of all.

Many an evening the five sisters rose arm in arm up to the surface of the water. They had beautiful voices, sweeter than those of any mortals, and whenever a storm was nigh and they thought a ship might be wrecked, they swam ahead of the ship and sang so sweetly about how beautiful it was at the bottom of the sea and bade the sailors not to be afraid of coming down there. But the sailors couldn't understand the words. They thought it was the storm. Nor were they able to see the wonders down there either, for when the ship sank, the mortals drowned and came only as corpses to the castle of the king of the sea.

Now in the evening, when the sisters rose arm in arm up through the sea, the little sister was left behind quite alone, looking after them, and it was as if she were going to cry. But a mermaid has no tears, and so she suffers even more.

"Oh, if only I were fifteen," she said. "I know that I will truly come to love that world and the mortals who build and dwell up there."

At last she too was fifteen.

"See, now it is your turn!" said her grandmother, the old dowager queen. "Come now, let me adorn you just like your other sisters." And she put a wreath of white lilies on her hair. But each petal in the flowers was half a pearl. And the old queen had eight oysters squeeze themselves tightly to the princess' tail to show her high rank.

"It hurts so much!" said the little mermaid.

"Yes, you must suffer a bit to look pretty!" said the old queen.

Oh, how happy she would have been to shake off all this magnificence, to take off the heavy wreath. Her red flowers in her garden were more becoming to her, but she dared not do otherwise now. "Farewell," she said and rose as easily and as light as a bubble up through the water.

The sun had just gone down as she raised her head out of the water, but all the clouds still shone like roses and gold, and in the middle of the pink sky shone the evening star clear and lovely. The air was mild and fresh, and the sea was as smooth as glass. There lay a big ship with three masts. Only a single sail was up, for not a breeze was blowing, and around in the ropes and masts sailors were sitting. There was music and song, and as the evening grew darker, hundreds of many-colored lanterns were lit. It looked as if the flags of all nations were waving in the air. The little mermaid swam right over to the cabin window, and every time the water lifted her high in the air, she could see in through the glass panes to where many finely dressed mortals were standing. But the handsomest by far was the young prince with the big dark eyes, who was certainly not more than sixteen. It was his birthday, and this was why all the festivities were taking place. The sailors danced on deck, and when the young prince came out, over a hundred rockets rose into the air. They shone as bright as day, so the little mermaid became quite frightened and ducked down under the

water. But she soon stuck her head out again, and then
it was as if all the stars in the sky were falling down to
her. Never before had she seen such fireworks. Huge suns
whirled around, magnificent flaming fish swung in the
blue air, and everything was reflected in the clear, calm
sea. The ship itself was so lighted up that every little
rope was visible, not to mention mortals. Oh how handsome the young prince was, and he shook everybody by
the hand and laughed and smiled while the wonderful night
was filled with music.

It grew late, but the little mermaid couldn't tear her
eyes away from the ship or the handsome prince. The
many-colored lanterns were put out. The rockets no longer
climbed into the air, nor were any more salutes fired
from the cannons either. But deep down in the sea it
rumbled and grumbled. All the while she sat bobbing up
and down on the water so she could see into the cabin.
But now the ship went faster, and one sail after the
other spread out. Now the waves were rougher, great
clouds rolled up, and in the distance there was lightning.
Oh, it was going to be a terrible storm, so the sailors
took in the sails. The ship rocked at top speed over
the raging sea. The water rose like huge black mountains
that wanted to pour over the mast, but the ship dived
down like a swan among the high billows and let itself be
lifted high again on the towering water. The little mermaid
thought this speed was pleasant, but the sailors didn't
think so. The ship creaked and cracked and the thick
planks buckled under the heavy blows. Waves poured in
over the ship, the mast snapped in the middle just like a
reed, and the ship rolled over on its side while the water
poured into the hold. Now the little mermaid saw
they were in danger. She herself had to beware of planks
and bits of wreckage floating on the water. For a moment
it was so pitch black that she could not see a thing, but
when the lightning flashed, it was again so bright that she
could make out everyone on the ship. They were all
floundering for their lives. She looked especially for the
young prince, and as the ship broke apart, she saw him
sink down into the depths. At first she was quite
pleased, for now he would come down to her. But then

she remembered that mortals could not live in the water
and that only as a corpse could he come down to her
father's castle. No, die he mustn't! And so she swam
among beams and planks that floated on the sea, quite
forgetting that they could have crushed her. She dived
deep down in the water and rose up high again among
the waves, and thus she came at last to the young
prince, who could hardly swim any longer in the stormy
sea. His arms and legs were growing weak; his beautiful
eyes were closed. He would have died had not the little
mermaid arrived. She held his head up above the water

and thus let the waves carry them wherever they liked.
   In the morning the storm was over. Of the ship there
wasn't a chip to be seen. The sun climbed, red and shining,
out of the water; it was as if it brought life into the
prince's cheeks, but his eyes remained closed. The mermaid kissed his high, handsome forehead and stroked
back his wet hair. She thought he resembled the marble
statue down in her little garden. She kissed him again
and wished for him to live.
   Now she saw the mainland ahead of her, high blue
mountains on whose peaks the white snow shone as if
swans were lying there. Down by the coast were lovely
green forests, and ahead lay a church or a convent. Which,
she didn't rightly know, but it was a building. Lemon
and orange trees were growing there in the garden, and

in front of the gate stood high palm trees. The sea had made a little bay here, which was calm but very deep all the way over to the rock where the fine white sand had been washed ashore. Here she swam with the handsome prince, put him on the sand, but especially saw to it that his head was raised in the sunshine.

Now the bells rang in the big white building, and many young girls came out through the gate to the garden. Then the little mermaid swam farther out behind some big rocks that jutted up out of the water, covered her hair and breast with sea foam so no one could see her little face, and then kept watch to see who came out to the unfortunate prince.

It wasn't long before a young girl came over to where he lay. She seemed to be quite frightened, but only for a moment. Then she fetched several mortals, and the mermaid saw that the prince revived and that he smiled at everyone around him. But he didn't smile out to her, for he didn't know at all that she had saved him. She was so unhappy. And when he was carried into the big building, she dived sorrowfully down in the water and found her way home to her father's castle.

She had always been silent and pensive, but now she was more so than ever. Her sisters asked what she had seen the first time she was up there, but she told them nothing.

Many an evening and morning she climbed up to where she had left the prince. She saw that the fruits in the garden ripened and were picked. She saw that the snow melted on the high mountains, but she didn't see the prince, and so she returned home even sadder than before. Her only comfort was to sit in the little garden and throw her arms around the pretty marble statue that resembled the prince. But she didn't take care of her flowers. As in a jungle, they grew out over the paths, with their long stalks and leaves intertwined with the branches of the trees, until it was quite dark.

At last she couldn't hold out any longer, but told one of her sisters. And then all the others found out at once, but no more than they, and a couple of other mermaids, who didn't tell anyone except their closest friends. One of them knew who the prince was. She had also seen the festivities on the ship and knew where he was from and where his kingdom lay.

"Come, little sister," said the other princesses, and with their arms around each other's shoulders they came up to the surface of the water in a long row in front of the spot where they knew the prince's castle stood.

It was made of a pale-yellow, shiny kind of stone, with great stairways—one went right down to the water. Magnificent gilded domes soared above the roof, and among the pillars that went around the whole building stood marble statues that looked as if they were alive. Through the clear glass in the high windows one could see into the most magnificent halls, where costly silken curtains and tapestries were hanging, and all the walls were adorned with large paintings that were a joy to behold. In the middle of the biggest hall splashed a great fountain. Streams of water shot up high toward the glass dome in the roof, through which the sun shone on the water and all the lovely plants growing in the big pool.

Now she knew where he lived, and many an evening and night she came there over the water. She swam much closer to land than any of the others had dared. Yes, she went all the way up the little canal, under the magnificent marble balcony that cast a long shadow on the water. Here she sat and looked at the young prince, who thought he was quite alone in the clear moonlight.

Many an evening she saw him sail to the sound of music in the splendid boat on which the flags were waving. She peeped out from among the green rushes and caught the wind in her long silvery white veil, and if anyone saw it, he thought it was a swan spreading its wings.

Many a night, when the fishermen were at sea fishing by torchlight, she heard them tell so many good things about the young prince that she was glad she had saved his life when he drifted about half dead on the waves. And she thought of how firmly his head had lain upon her breast and how fervently she had kissed him then. He knew nothing about it at all, couldn't even dream of her once.

She grew fonder and fonder of mortals, wished more

and more that she could rise up among them. She thought their world was far bigger than hers. Why, they could fly over the sea in ships and climb the high mountains way above the clouds, and their lands with forests and fields stretched farther than she could see. There was so much she wanted to find out, but her sisters didn't know the answers to everything, and so she asked her old grandmother, and *she* knew the upper world well, which she quite rightly called The Lands Above the Sea.

"If mortals don't drown," the little mermaid asked, "do they live forever? Don't they die the way we do down here in the sea?"

"Why yes," said the old Queen, "they must also die, and their lifetime is much shorter than ours. We can live to be three hundred years old, but when we stop existing here, we only turn into foam upon the water. We don't even have a grave down here among our loved ones. We have no immortal soul; we never have life again. We are like the green rushes: once they are cut they can never be green again. Mortals, on the other hand, have a soul, which lives forever after the body has turned to dust. It mounts up through the clear air to all the shining stars. Just as we come to the surface of the water and see the land of the mortals, so do they come up to lovely unknown places that we will never see."

"Why didn't we get an immortal soul?" asked the little mermaid sadly. "I'd gladly give all my hundreds of years just to be a mortal for one day and afterwards to be able to share in the heavenly world."

"You mustn't go and think about that," said the old queen. "We are much better off than the mortals up there."

"I too shall die and float as foam upon the sea, not hear the music of the waves or see the lovely flowers and the red sun. Isn't there anything at all I can do to win an immortal soul?"

"No," said the old queen. "Only if a mortal fell so in love with you that you were dearer to him than a father and mother; only if you remained in all his thoughts and he was so deeply attached to you that he let the priest place his right hand in yours with a vow of faithful-

ness now and forever; only then would his soul float over
into your body, and you would also share in the happiness of mortals. He would give you a soul and still keep
his own. But that can never happen. The very thing that
is so lovely here in the sea, your fish tail, they find so
disgusting up there on the earth. They don't know any
better. Up there one has to have two clumsy stumps,
which they call legs, to be beautiful!"

Then the little mermaid sighed and looked sadly at her
fish tail.

"Let us be satisfied," said the old queen. "We will
frisk and frolic in the three hundred years we have to
live in. That's plenty of time indeed. Afterwards, one can
rest in one's grave all the more happily. This evening we
are going to have a court ball!"

Now this was a splendor not to be seen on earth.
Walls and ceiling in the great ballroom were of thick but
clear glass. Several hundred gigantic mussel shells, rosy
red and green as grass, stood in rows on each side with
a blue burning flame, which lit up the whole ballroom
and shone out through the walls so the sea too was
brightly illuminated. One could see the countless fish
that swam over to the glass wall. On some the scales
shone purple; on others they seemed to be silver and gold.
Through the middle of the ballroom flowed a broad
stream, and on this the mermen and mermaids danced
to the music of their own lovely song. No mortals on earth
have such beautiful voices. The little mermaid had the
loveliest voice of all, and they clapped their hands for
her. And for a moment her heart was filled with joy,
for she knew that she had the most beautiful voice of
all on this earth and in the sea. But soon she started
thinking again of the world above her. She couldn't
forget the handsome prince and her sorrow at not pos-
sessing, like him, an immortal soul. And so she slipped
out of her father's castle unnoticed, and while everything
inside was merriment and song, she sat sadly in her little
garden. Then she heard a horn ring down through the
water, and she thought: "Now he is sailing up there, the
one I love more than a father or a mother, the one who
remains in all my thoughts and in whose hand I would

place all my life's happiness. I would risk everything to win him and an immortal soul. While my sisters are dancing there in my father's castle, I will go to the sea witch. I have always been so afraid of her, but maybe she can advise and help me."

Now the little mermaid went out of her garden toward the roaring maelstroms behind which the sea witch lived. She had never gone that way before. Here no flowers grew, no sea grass. Only the bare, gray, sandy bottom stretched on toward the maelstroms, which like roaring mill wheels whirled around and tore everything that came their way down with them into the depths. In between these crushing whirlpools she had to go to enter the realm of the sea witch, and for a long way there was no other road than over hot bubbling mire that the sea witch called her peat bog. In back of it lay her house, right in the midst of an eerie forest. All the trees and bushes were polyps—half animal, half plant. They looked like hundred-headed serpents growing out of the earth. All the branches were long, slimy arms with fingers like sinuous worms, and joint by joint they moved from the roots to the outermost tips. Whatever they could grab in the sea, they wound their arms around it and never let it go. Terrified, the little mermaid remained standing outside the forest. Her heart was pounding with fright. She almost turned back, but then she thought of the prince and of an immortal soul, and it gave her courage. She bound her long, flowing hair around her head so the polyps could not grab her by it. She crossed both hands upon her breast and then off she flew, the way the fish can fly through the water, in among the loathsome polyps that reached out their supple arms and fingers after her. She saw where each of them had something it had seized; hundreds of small arms held onto it like strong iron bands. Rows of white bones of mortals who had drowned at sea and sunk all the way down there peered forth from the polyps' arms. Ships' wheels and chests they held tightly, skeletons of land animals, and—most terrifying of all—a little mermaid that they had captured and strangled.

Now she came to a large slimy opening in the forest

where big fat water snakes gamboled, revealing their ugly, yellowish-white bellies. In the middle of the opening had been erected a house made of the bones of shipwrecked mortals. There sat the sea witch letting a toad eat from her mouth, just the way mortals permit a little canary bird to eat sugar. She called the fat, hideous water snakes her little chickens and let them tumble on her big, spongy breasts.

"I know what you want all right!" said the sea witch. "It's stupid of you to do it. Nonetheless, you shall have your way, for it will bring you misfortune, my lovely princess! You want to get rid of your fish tail and have two stumps to walk on instead, just like mortals, so the young prince can fall in love with you, and you can win him and an immortal soul." Just then the sea witch let out such a loud and hideous laugh that the toad and the water snakes fell down to the ground and writhed there. "You've come just in the nick of time," said the witch. "Tomorrow, after the sun rises, I couldn't help you until another year was over. I shall make you a potion, and before the sun rises you shall take it and swim to land, seat yourself on the shore there, and drink it. Then your tail will split and shrink into what mortals call lovely legs. But it hurts. It is like being pierced through by a sharp sword. Everyone who sees you will say you are the loveliest mortal child he has ever seen. You will keep your grace of movement. No dancer will ever float the way you do, but each step you take will be like treading on a sharp knife so your blood will flow! If you want to suffer all this, then I will help you."

"Yes," said the little mermaid in a trembling voice and thought of the prince and of winning an immortal soul.

"But remember," said the witch, "once you have been given a mortal shape, you can never become a mermaid again. You can never sink down through the water to your sisters and to your father's castle. And if you do not win the love of the prince so that for your sake he forgets his father and mother and never puts you out of his thoughts and lets the priest place your hand in his so you become man and wife, you will not win an immortal soul. The first morning after he is married to another, your heart will break and you will turn into foam upon the water."

"This I want!" said the little mermaid and turned deathly pale.

"But you must also pay me," said the witch, "and what I demand is no small thing. You have the loveliest voice of all down here at the bottom of the sea, and you probably think you're going to enchant him with it. But that voice you shall give to me! I want the best thing you have for my precious drink. Why, I must put my very own blood in it so it will be as sharp as a two-edged sword."

"But if you take my voice," said the little mermaid, "what will I have left?"

"Your lovely figure," said the witch, "your grace of movement, and your speaking eyes. With them you can enchant a mortal heart, all right! Stick out your little tongue so I can cut it off in payment, and you shall have the potent drink!"

"So be it!" said the little mermaid, and the witch put her kettle on to brew the magic potion. "Cleanliness is a good thing," she said, and scoured her kettle with her water snakes, which she knotted together. Now she cut her breast and let the black blood drip down into the kettle. The steam made the strangest shapes that were terrifying and dreadful to see. Every moment the witch put something new into the kettle, and when it had cooked properly, it was like crocodile tears. At last the drink was ready, and it was as clear as water.

"There it is," said the witch and cut out the little mermaid's tongue. Now she was mute and could neither speak nor sing.

"If any of the polyps should grab you when you go back through my forest," said the witch, "just throw one drop of this drink on them and their arms and fingers will burst into a thousand pieces." But the little mermaid didn't have to do that. The polyps drew back in terror when they saw the shining drink that glowed in her hand like a glittering star. And she soon came through the forest, the bog, and the roaring maelstroms.

She could see her father's castle. The torches had been

extinguished in the great ballroom. They were probably
all asleep inside there, but she dared not look for them
now that she was mute and was going to leave them forever. It was as though her heart would break with grief.
She stole into the garden, took a flower from each of her
sisters' flower beds, threw hundreds of kisses toward the
castle, and rose up through the dark-blue sea.

The sun had not yet risen when she saw the prince's
castle and went up the magnificent marble stairway. The
moon shone bright and clear. The little mermaid drank the
strong, burning drink, and it was as if a two-edged sword
was going through her delicate body. At that she fainted
and lay as if dead. When the sun was shining high on the
sea, she awoke and felt a piercing pain, but right in
front of her stood the handsome prince. He fixed his
coal-black eyes upon her so that she had to cast down
her own, and then she saw that her fish tail was gone,
and she had the prettiest little white legs that any young
girl could have, but she was quite naked. And so she en-
veloped herself in her thick, long hair. The prince asked
who she was and how she had come there, and she looked
at him softly yet sadly with her dark-blue eyes, for
of course she could not speak. Each step she took was, as
the witch had said, like stepping on pointed awls and
sharp knives. But she endured this willingly. At the
prince's side she rose as easily as a bubble, and he and
everyone else marveled at her graceful, flowing move-
ments.

She was given costly gowns of silk and muslin to wear.
In the castle she was the fairest of all. But she was mute;
she could neither sing nor speak. Lovely slave girls,
dressed in silk and gold, came forth and sang for the
prince and his royal parents. One of them sang more
sweetly than all the others, and the prince clapped his
hands and smiled at her. Then the little mermaid was
sad. She knew that she herself had sung far more beautifully, and she thought, "Oh, if only he knew that to be
with him I have given away my voice for all eternity."

Now the slave girls danced in graceful, floating move-
ments to the accompaniment of the loveliest music. Then
the little mermaid raised her beautiful white arms, stood

up on her toes, and glided across the floor. She danced as no one had ever danced before. With each movement, her beauty became even more apparent, and her eyes spoke more deeply to the heart than the slave girl's song.

Everyone was enchanted by her, especially the prince, who called her his little foundling, and she danced on and on despite the fact that each time her feet touched the ground it was like treading on sharp knives. The prince said she was to stay with him forever, and she was allowed to sleep outside his door on a velvet cushion.

He had boys' clothes made for her so she could accompany him on horseback. They rode through the fragrant forests, where the green branches brushed her shoulders and the little birds sang within the fresh leaves. With the prince she climbed up the high mountains, and despite the fact that her delicate feet bled so the others could see it, she laughed at this and followed him until they could see the clouds sailing far below them like a flock of birds on their way to distant lands.

Back at the prince's castle, at night while the others slept, she went down the marble stairway and cooled her burning feet by standing in the cold sea water. And then she thought of those down there in the depths.

One night her sisters came arm in arm. They sang so mournfully as they swam over the water, and she waved to them. They recognized her and told her how unhappy she had made them all. After this they visited her every night, and one night far out she saw her old grandmother, who had not been to the surface of the water for many years, and the king of the sea with his crown upon his head. They stretched out their arms to her but dared not come as close to land as her sisters.

Day by day the prince grew fonder of her. He loved her the way one loves a dear, good child, but to make her his queen did not occur to him at all. And she would have to become his wife if she were to live, or else she would have no immortal soul and would turn into foam upon the sea on the morning after his wedding.

"Don't you love me most of all?" the eyes of the little mermaid seemed to say when he took her in his arms and kissed her beautiful forehead.

"Of course I love you best," said the prince, "for you
have the kindest heart of all. You are devoted to me,
and you resemble a young girl I once saw but will certainly never find again. I was on a ship that was wrecked.
The waves carried me ashore near a holy temple to which
several young maidens had been consecrated. The youngest of them found me on the shore and saved my life. I
only saw her twice. She was the only one I could love in
this world. But you look like her and you have almost
replaced her image in my soul. She belongs to the holy
temple, and so good fortune has sent you to me. We shall
never be parted!"

"Alas! He doesn't know that I saved his life!" thought
the little mermaid. "I carried him over the sea to the
forest where the temple stands. I hid under the foam and
waited to see if any mortals would come. I saw that
beautiful girl, whom he loves more than me." And the
mermaid sighed deeply, for she couldn't cry. "The girl
is consecrated to the holy temple, he said. She will
never come out into the world. They will never meet
again, but I am with him and see him every day. I will
take care of him, love him, lay down my life for him!"

But now people were saying that the prince is going
to be married to the lovely daughter of the neighboring
king. That is why he is equipping so magnificent a
ship. It is given out that the prince is traveling to see the
country of the neighboring king, but actually it is to see
his daughter. He is to have a great retinue with him.

But the little mermaid shook her head and laughed.
She knew the prince's thoughts far better than all the rest.
"I have to go," he had told her. "I have to look at the
lovely princess. My parents insist upon it. But they won't
be able to force me to bring her home as my bride. I
cannot love her. She doesn't look like the beautiful girl
in the temple, whom you resemble. If I should ever choose
a bride, you would be the more likely one, my mute little foundling with the speaking eyes!" And he kissed her
rosy mouth, played with her long hair, and rested his
head upon her heart, which dreamed of mortal happiness and an immortal soul.

"You're not afraid of the sea, are you, my mute
little child!" he said as they stood on the deck of the

magnificent ship that was taking him to the country of the neighboring king. And he told her of storms and calms and of strange fish in the depths and what the divers had seen down there. And she smiled at his story, for of course she knew about the bottom of the sea far better than anyone else.

In the moonlit night, when everyone was asleep—even the sailor at the wheel—she sat by the railing of the ship and stared down through the clear water, and it seemed to her that she could see her father's castle. At the very top stood her old grandmother, with her silver crown on her head, staring up through the strong currents at the keel of the ship. Then her sisters came up to the surface of the water. They gazed at her sadly and wrung their white hands. She waved to them and smiled and was going to tell them that all was well with her and that she was happy, but the ship's boy approached and her sisters dived down, so he thought the white he had seen was foam upon the sea.

The next morning the ship sailed into the harbor of the neighboring king's capital. All the church bells were ringing, and from the high towers trumpets were blowing, while the soldiers stood with waving banners and glittering bayonets. Every day there was a feast. Balls and parties followed one after the other, but the princess had not yet come. She was being educated far away in a holy temple, they said; there she was learning all the royal virtues. At last she arrived.

The little mermaid was waiting eagerly to see how beautiful she was, and she had to confess that she had never seen a lovelier creature. Her skin was delicate and soft, and from under her long, dark eyelashes smiled a pair of dark-blue, faithful eyes.

"It is you!" said the prince. "You, who saved me when I lay as if dead on the shore!" And he took his blushing bride into his arms. "Oh, I am far too happy," he said to the little mermaid. "The best I could ever dare hope for has at last come true! You will be overjoyed at my good fortune, for you love me best of all." And the little mermaid kissed his hand, but already she seemed to feel her heart breaking. His wedding morning would indeed bring her death and change her into foam upon the sea.

All the church bells were ringing. The heralds rode through the streets and proclaimed the betrothal. On all the altars fragrant oils burned in costly silver lamps. The priests swung censers, and the bride and bridegroom gave each other their hands and received the blessing of the bishop. The little mermaid, dressed in silk and gold, stood holding the bride's train, but her ears did not hear the festive music nor did her eyes see the sacred ceremony. She thought of the morning of her death, of everything she had lost in this world.

The very same evening the bride and bridegroom went on board the ship. Cannons fired their salutes, all the flags were waving, and in the middle of the deck a majestic purple and gold pavilion with the softest cushions had been erected. Here the bridal pair was to sleep in the still, cool night. The breeze filled the sails, and the ship glided easily and gently over the clear sea.

When it started to get dark, many-colored lanterns were lighted and the sailors danced merrily on deck. It made the little mermaid think of the first time she had come to the surface of the water and seen the same splendor and festivity. And she whirled along in the dance, floating as the swallow soars when it is being pursued, and everyone applauded her and cried out in admiration. Never had she danced so magnificently. It was as though sharp knives were cutting her delicate feet, but she didn't feel it. The pain in her heart was even greater. She knew this was the last evening she would see the one for whom she had left her family and her home, sacrificed her beautiful voice, and daily suffered endless agony without his ever realizing it. It was the last night she would breathe the same air as he, see the deep sea and the starry sky. An endless night without thoughts or dreams awaited her—she who neither had a soul nor could ever win one. And there was gaiety and merriment on the ship until long past midnight. She laughed and danced with the thought of death in her heart. The prince kissed his lovely bride and she played with his dark hair, and arm in arm they went to bed in the magnificent pavilion.

It grew silent and still on the ship. Only the helmsman stood at the wheel. The little mermaid leaned her white arms on the railing and looked toward the east for the dawn, for the first rays of the sun, which she knew would kill her. Then she saw her sisters come to the surface of the water. They were as pale as she was. Their long, beautiful hair no longer floated in the breeze. It had been cut off.

"We have given it to the witch so she could help you, so you needn't die tonight. She has given us a knife, here it is. See how sharp it is? Before the sun rises, you

must plunge it into the prince's heart! And when his warm blood spatters your feet, they will grow together into a fish tail, and you will become a mermaid again and can sink down into the water to us, and live your three hundred years before you turn into the lifeless salty sea foam. Hurry! Either you or he must die before the sun rises! Our old grandmother has grieved so much that her hair has fallen out, as ours has fallen under the witch's scissors. Kill the prince and return to us! Hurry! Do you see that red streak on the horizon? In a few moments the sun will rise, and then you must die!" And they uttered a strange, deep sigh and sank beneath the waves.

The little mermaid drew the purple curtain back from the pavilion and looked at the lovely bride asleep with her head on the prince's chest. She bent down and kissed his handsome forehead; looked at the sky, which grew rosier and rosier; looked at the sharp knife; and again fastened her eyes on the prince, who murmured the name of his bride in his dreams. She alone was in his thoughts, and the knife glittered in the mermaid's hand. But then she threw it far out into the waves. They shone red where it fell, as if drops of blood were bubbling up through the water. Once more she gazed at the prince with dimming eyes, then plunged from the ship down into the sea. And she felt her body dissolving into foam.

Now the sun rose out of the sea. The rays fell so mild and warm on the deathly cold sea-foam, and the little mermaid did not feel death. She saw the clear sun, and up above her floated hundreds of lovely transparent creatures. Through them she could see the white sails of the ship and the rosy clouds in the sky. Their voices were melodious but so ethereal that no mortal ear could hear them, just as no mortal eye could perceive them. Without wings, they floated through the air by their own lightness. The little mermaid saw that she had a body like theirs. It rose higher and higher out of the foam.

"To whom do I come?" she said, and her voice, like that of the others, rang so ethereally that no earthly music can reproduce it.

"To the daughters of the air," replied the others. "A mermaid has no immortal soul and can never have one unless she wins the love of a mortal. Her immortality depends on an unknown power. The daughters of the air have no immortal souls, either, but by good deeds they can create one for themselves. We fly to the hot countries where the humid pestilential air kills mortals. There we waft cooling breezes. We spread the fragrance of flowers through the air and send refreshment and healing. After striving for three hundred years to do what good we can, we then receive an immortal soul and share in the eternal happiness of mortals. Poor little mermaid, with all your heart you have striven for the same goal. You have suffered and endured and have risen to the world of the spirits of the air. Now by good deeds you can create an immortal soul for yourself after three hundred years."

And the little mermaid raised her transparent arms up toward God's sun, and for the first time she felt tears. On the ship there was again life and movement. She saw the prince with his lovely bride searching for her. Sorrowfully they stared at the bubbling foam, as if they knew she had thrown herself into the sea. Invisible, she kissed the bride's forehead, smiled at the prince, and with the other children of the air rose up onto the pink cloud that sailed through the air.

"In three hundred years we will float like this into the kingdom of God!"

"We can come there earlier," whispered one. "Unseen we float into the houses of mortals where there are children, and for every day that we find a good child who makes his parents happy and deserves their love, God shortens our period of trial. The child does not know when we fly through the room, and when we smile over it with joy a year is taken from the three hundred. But if we see a naughty and wicked child, we must weep tears of sorrow, and each tear adds a day to our period of trial!"

John Ruskin

||||||||||||||||||||||||||||||||||||||||||||||||||||||||||||

THE KING OF THE
GOLDEN RIVER
OR
THE BLACK BROTHERS

||||||||||||||||||||||||||||||||||||||||||||||||||||||||||||

*How the Agricultural System of the Black
Brothers Was Interfered With by Southwest Wind, Esquire*

In a secluded and mountainous part of Styria there
was, in old time, a valley of the most surprising
and luxuriant fertility. It was surrounded on all sides
by steep and rocky mountains, rising into peaks, which
were always covered with snow and from which a
number of torrents descended in constant cataracts. One
of these fell westward, over the face of a crag so high
that when the sun had set to everything else and all below was darkness, his beams still shone full upon this
waterfall so that it looked like a shower of gold. It was
therefore called by the people of the neighborhood the
Golden River. It was strange that none of these streams
fell into the valley itself. They all descended on the other
side of the mountains and wound away through broad
plains and by populous cities. But the clouds were drawn
so constantly to the snowy hills and rested so softly in
the circular hollow that in time of drought and heat,
when all the country round was burnt up, there
still rain in the little valley; and its crops were so heavy,
and its hay so high, and its apples so red, and its

grapes so blue, and its wine so rich, and its honey so sweet that it was a marvel to everyone who beheld it, and was commonly called the Treasure Valley.

The whole of this little valley belonged to three brothers, called Schwartz, Hans, and Gluck. Schwartz and Hans, the two elder brothers, were very ugly men, with overhanging eyebrows and small, dull eyes which were always half shut so that you couldn't see into *them* and always fancied they saw very far into *you*. They lived by farming the Treasure Valley, and very good farmers they were. They killed everything that did not pay for its eating. They shot the blackbirds because they pecked the fruit; and killed the hedgehogs lest they should suck the cows; they poisoned the crickets for eating the crumbs in the kitchen; and smothered the cicadas, which used to sing all summer in the lime trees. They worked their servants without any wages till they would not work any more, and then quarreled with them and turned them out of doors without paying them. It would have been very odd if with such a farm and such a system of farming they hadn't got very rich; and very rich they *did* get. They generally contrived to keep their corn by them till it was very dear and then sell it for twice its value; they had heaps of gold lying about on their floors, yet it was never known that they had given so much as a penny or a crust in charity; they never went to Mass, grumbled perpetually at paying tithes, and were, in a word, of so cruel and grinding a temper as to receive from all those with whom they had any dealings the nickname of the "Black Brothers."

The youngest brother, Gluck, was as completely opposed, in both appearance and character, to his seniors as could possibly be imagined or desired. He was not above twelve years old, fair, blue-eyed, and kind in temper to every living thing. He did not, of course, agree particularly well with his brothers, or rather, they did not agree with *him*. He was usually appointed to the honorable office of turnspit when there was anything to roast, which was not often, for, to do the brothers justice, they were hardly less sparing upon themselves than upon other people. At other times he used to clean the shoes, floors, and sometimes the plates, occasionally getting what was left on them, by way of encouragement, and a wholesome quantity of dry blows, by way of education.

Things went on in this manner for a long time. At last came a very wet summer and everything went wrong in the country around. The hay had hardly been got in when the haystacks were floated bodily down to the sea by an inundation; the vines were cut to pieces with the hail; the corn was all killed by a black blight; only in the Treasure Valley, as usual, all was safe. As it had rain when there was rain nowhere else, so it had sun when there was sun nowhere else. Everybody came to buy corn at the farm and went away pouring maledictions on the Black Brothers. They asked what they liked, and got it, except from the poor people, who could only beg, and several of whom were starved at their very door, without the slightest regard or notice.

It was drawing toward winter, and very cold weather, when one day the two elder brothers had gone out with their usual warning to little Gluck, who was left to mind the roast, that he was to let nobody in and give nothing out. Gluck sat down quite close to the fire, for it was raining very hard, and the kitchen walls were by no means dry or comfortable looking. He turned and turned, and the roast got nice and brown. "What a pity," thought Gluck, "my brothers never ask anybody to dinner. I'm sure, when they've got such a nice piece of mutton as this and nobody else has got so much as a piece of dry bread, it would do their hearts good to have somebody to eat it with them."

Just as he spoke, there came a double knock at the house door, yet heavy and dull as though the knocker had been tied up—more like a puff than a knock.

"It must be the wind," said Gluck; "nobody else would venture to knock double knocks at our door."

No; it wasn't the wind. There it came again, very hard; and what was particularly astounding, the knocker seemed to be in a hurry and not to be in the least afraid of the consequences. Gluck went to the window, opened it, and put his head out to see who it was.

It was the most extraordinary looking little gentleman he had ever seen in his life. He had a very large nose, slightly brass colored; his cheeks were very round and

very red and might have warranted a supposition that he had been blowing a refractory fire for the last eight-and-forty hours; his eyes twinkled merrily through long silky eyelashes, his mustaches curled twice around like a corkscrew on each side of his mouth, and his hair, of a curious mixed pepper-and-salt color, descended far over his shoulders. He was about four feet six in height and wore a conical pointed cap of nearly the same altitude, decorated with a black feather some three feet long. His doublet was prolonged behind into something resembling a violent exaggeration of what is now termed a swallowtail but was much obscured by the swelling folds of an enormous black, glossy-looking cloak, which must have been very much too long in calm weather, as the wind, whistling round the old house, carried it clear out from the wearer's shoulders to about four times his own length.

Gluck was so perfectly paralyzed by the singular appearance of his visitor that he remained fixed without uttering a word until the old gentleman, having performed another and a more energetic concerto on the knocker, turned around to look after his flyaway cloak. In so doing he caught sight of Gluck's little yellow head jammed in the window, with its mouth and eyes very wide open indeed.

"Hollo!" said the little gentleman, "that's not the way to answer the door. I'm wet; let me in."

To do the little gentleman justice, he *was* wet. His feather hung down between his legs like a beaten puppy's tail, dripping like an umbrella; and from the ends of his mustaches the water was running into his waistcoat pockets, and out again like a millstream.

"I beg pardon, sir," said Gluck, "I'm very sorry, but I really can't."

"Can't what?" said the old gentleman.

"I can't let you in, sir; I can't indeed; my brothers would beat me to death, sir, if I thought of such a thing. What do you want, sir?"

"Want?" said the old gentleman petulantly. "I want fire and shelter; and there's your great fire there blazing, crackling, and dancing on the walls, with nobody to feel it. Let me in, I say; I only want to warm myself."

Gluck had had his head, by this time, so long out of the window that he began to feel it was really unpleasantly cold, and when he turned and saw the beautiful fire rustling and roaring and throwing long bright tongues up the chimney, as if it were licking its chops at the savory smell of the leg of mutton, his heart melted within him that it should be burning away for nothing. "He does look *very* wet," said little Gluck; "I'll just let him in for a quarter of an hour." Around he went to the door and opened it; and as the little gentleman walked in, there came a gust of wind through the house that made the old chimneys totter.

"That's a good boy," said the little gentleman. "Never mind your brothers. I'll talk to them."

"Pray, sir, don't do any such thing," said Gluck. "I can't let you stay till they come; they'd be the death of me."

"Dear me," said the old gentleman, "I'm very sorry to hear that. How long may I stay?"

"Only till the mutton's done, sir," replied Gluck, "and it's very brown."

Then the old gentleman walked into the kitchen and sat himself down on the hob, with the top of his cap accommodated up the chimney, for it was a great deal too high for the roof.

"You'll soon dry there, sir," said Gluck, and sat down again to turn the mutton. But the old gentleman did *not* dry there, but went on drip, drip, dripping among the cinders, and the fire fizzed and sputtered and began to look very black and uncomfortable: never was such a cloak; every fold in it ran like a gutter.

"I beg pardon, sir," said Gluck at length after watching the water spreading in long, quicksilverlike streams over the floor for a quarter of an hour; "mayn't I take your cloak?"

"No, thank you," said the old gentleman.

"Your cap, sir?"

"I am all right, thank you," said the old gentleman rather gruffly.

"But—sir—I'm very sorry," said Gluck, hesitatingly; "but—really, sir—you're—putting the fire out."

"It'll take longer to do the mutton, then," replied his visitor drily.

Gluck was very much puzzled by the behavior of his guest; it was such a strange mixture of coolness and humility. He turned away at the string meditatively for another five minutes.

"That mutton looks very nice," said the old gentleman at length. "Can't you give me a little bit?"

"Impossible, sir," said Gluck.

"I'm very hungry," continued the old gentleman: "I've had nothing to eat yesterday, nor today. They surely couldn't miss a bit from the knuckle!"

He spoke in so very melancholy a tone that it quite melted Gluck's heart. "They promised me one slice today, sir," said he; "I can give you that, but not a bit more."

"That's a good boy," said the old gentleman again.

Then Gluck warmed a plate and sharpened a knife. "I don't care if I do get beaten for it," thought he. Just as he had cut a large slice out of the mutton, there came a tremendous rap at the door. The old gentleman jumped off the hob as if it had suddenly become inconveniently warm. Gluck fitted the slice into the mutton again, with desperate efforts at exactitude, and ran to open the door.

"What did you keep us waiting in the rain for?" said Schwartz as he walked in, throwing his umbrella in Gluck's face. "Aye! What for, indeed, you little vegabond?" said Hans, administering an educational box on the ear as he followed his brother into the kitchen.

"Bless my soul!" said Schwartz when he opened the door.

"Amen," said the little gentleman, who had taken his cap off and was standing in the middle of the kitchen, bowing with the utmost possible velocity.

"Who's that?" said Schwartz, catching up a rolling pin and turning to Gluck with a fierce frown.

"I don't know, indeed, brother," said Gluck in great terror.

"How did he get in?" roared Schwartz.

"My dear brother," said Gluck, deprecatingly, "he was so *very* wet!"

The rolling pin was descending on Gluck's head; but at the instant the old gentleman interposed his conical cap, on which it crashed with a shock that shook the water out of it all over the room. What was very odd, the rolling pin no sooner touched the cap than it flew out of Schwartz's hand, spinning like a straw in a high wind, and fell into the corner at the further end of the room.

"Who are you, sir?" demanded Schwartz, turning upon him.

"What's your business?" snarled .Hans.

"I'm a poor old man, sir," the little gentleman began very modestly, "and I saw your fire through the window and begged shelter for a quarter of an hour."

"Have the goodness to walk out again, then," said Schwartz. "We've quite enough water in our kitchen without making it a drying house."

"It is a cold day to turn an old man out in, sir; look at my gray hairs." They hung down to his shoulders, as I told you before.

"Ay!" said Hans. "There are enough of them to keep you warm. Walk!"

"I'm very, very hungry, sir; couldn't you spare me a bit of bread before I go?"

"Bread, indeed!" said Schwartz. "Do you suppose we've nothing to do with our bread but to give it to such red-nosed fellows as you?"

"Why don't you sell your feather?" said Hans sneeringly. "Out with you!"

"A little bit," said the old gentleman.

"Be off!" said Schwartz.

"Pray, gentlemen——"

"Off, and be hanged!" cried Hans, seizing him by the collar. But he had no sooner touched the old gentleman's collar than away he went after the rolling pin, spinning around and around till he fell into the corner on the top of it. Then Schwartz was very angry and ran at the old gentleman to turn him out; but he also had hardly touched him when away he went after Hans and the rolling pin, and hit his head against the wall as he tumbled into the corner. And so there they lay, all three.

Then the old gentleman spun himself around with velocity in the opposite direction, continued to spin until his long cloak was all wound neatly about him, clapped his cap on his head, very much on one side (for it could not stand upright without going through the ceiling), gave an additional twist to his corkscrew mustaches, and replied with perfect coolness: "Gentlemen, I wish you a

very good morning. At twelve o'clock tonight I'll call
again; after such a refusal of hospitality as I have just
experienced, you will not be surprised if that visit is the
last I ever pay you."

"If ever I catch you here again," muttered Schwartz,
coming, half frightened, out of the corner. But before he
could finish his sentence, the old gentleman had shut the
house door behind him with a great bang; and there drove
past the window at the same instant a wreath of ragged
cloud that whirled and rolled away down the valley in
all manner of shapes, turning over and over in the air
and melting away at last in a gush of rain.

"A very pretty business, indeed, Mr. Gluck!" said
Schwartz. "Dish the mutton, sir. If ever I catch you at
such a trick again—bless me, why, the mutton's been
cut!"

"You promised me one slice, brother, you know," said Gluck.

"Oh! And you were cutting it hot, I suppose, and going to catch all the gravy. It'll be long before I promise you such a thing again. Leave the room, sir; and have the kindness to wait in the coal cellar till I call you."

Gluck left the room melancholy enough. The brothers ate as much mutton as they could, locked the rest in the cupboard, and proceeded to get very drunk after dinner.

Such a night as it was! Howling wind and rushing rain without intermission. The brothers had just sense enough left to put up all the shutters and double bar the door before they went to bed. They usually slept in the same room. As the clock struck twelve, they were both awakened by a tremendous crash. Their door burst open with a violence that shook the house from top to bottom.

"What's that?" cried Schwartz, starting up in his bed.

"Only I," said the little gentleman.

The two brothers sat up on their bolster and stared into the darkness. The room was full of water, and by a misty moonbeam, which found its way through a hole in the shutter, they could see in the midst of it an enormous foam globe spinning around and bobbing up and down like a cork, on which, as on a most luxurious cushion, reclined the little old gentleman, cap and all. There was plenty of room for it now, for the roof was off.

"Sorry to incommode you," said their visitor ironically. "I'm afraid your beds are dampish; perhaps you had better go to your brother's room; I've left the ceiling on, there."

They required no second admonition, but rushed into Gluck's room, wet through, and in an agony of terror.

"You'll find my card on the kitchen table," the old gentleman called after them. "Remember, the *last* visit."

"Pray heaven it may!" said Schwartz, shuddering. And the foam globe disappeared.

Dawn came at last, and the two brothers looked out of Gluck's little window in the morning. The Treasure Valley was one mass of ruin and desolation. The inundation had swept away trees, crops, and cattle and left in their stead a waste of red sand and grey mud. The two brothers crept shivering and horror-struck into the kitchen. The water had gutted the whole first floor; corn, money, almost every movable thing had been swept away, and there was left only a small white card on the kitchen table. On it, in large, breezy, long-legged letters, were engraved the words:

Of the Proceedings of the Three Brothers After the Visit of Southwest Wind, Esquire; and How Little Gluck Had an Interview with the King of the Golden River

Southwest Wind, Esquire, was as good as his word. After the momentous visit above related, he entered the Treasure Valley no more; and what was worse, he had so much influence with his relations, the wet winds in general, and used it so effectually that they all adopted a similar line of conduct. So no rain fell in the valley from one year's end to another. Though everything remained green and flourishing in the plains below, the inheritance of the three brothers was a desert. What had once been the richest soil in the kingdom became a shifting heap of red sand; and the brothers, unable longer to contend with the adverse skies, abandoned their

valueless patrimony in despair to seek some means of
gaining a livelihood among the cities and people of
the plains. All their money was gone, and they had
nothing left but some curious old-fashioned pieces of
gold plate, the last remnants of their ill-gotten wealth.

"Suppose we turn goldsmiths?" said Schwartz to Hans
as they entered the large city. "It is a good knave's trade;
we can put a great deal of copper into the gold without
any one's finding it out."

The thought was agreed to be a very good one; they
hired a furnace and turned goldsmiths. But two slight
circumstances affected their trade: the first, that people
did not approve of the coppered gold; the second, that
the two elder brothers, whenever they had sold anything,
used to leave little Gluck to mind the furnace and go
and drink out the money in the alehouse next door. So
they melted all their gold without making money enough
to buy more and were at last reduced to one large drinking mug, which an uncle of his had given to little Gluck
and which he was very fond of and would not have parted with for the world, though he never drank anything out
of it but milk and water. The mug was a very odd mug
to look at. The handle was formed of two wreaths of
flowing golden hair, so finely spun that it looked more
like silk than metal, and these wreaths descended into,
and mixed with, a beard and whiskers of the same exquisite workmanship, which surrounded and decorated a
very fierce little face of the reddest gold imaginable right
in the front of the mug, with a pair of eyes in it which
seemed to command its whole circumference. It was im-

possible to drink out of the mug without being subjected to an intense gaze out of the side of these eyes; and Schwartz positively averred that once after emptying it, full of Rhenish, seventeen times, he had seen them wink! When it came to the mug's turn to be made into spoons, it half broke poor little Gluck's heart; but the brothers only laughed at him, tossed the mug into the melting pot, and staggered out to the alehouse, leaving him, as usual, to pour the gold into bars when it was all ready.

When they were gone, Gluck took a farewell look at his old friend in the melting pot. The flowing hair was all gone; nothing remained but the red nose and the sparkling eyes, which looked more malicious than ever. "And no wonder," thought Gluck, "after being treated in that way." He sauntered disconsolately to the window and sat himself down to catch the fresh evening air and escape the hot breath of the furnace. Now this window commanded a direct view of the range of mountains, which, as I told you before, overhung the Treasure Valley, and more especially of the peak from which fell the Golden River. It was just at the close of the day, and when Gluck sat down at the window, he saw the rocks of the mountaintops, all crimson and purple with the sunset; and there were bright tongues of fiery cloud burning and quivering about them; and the river, brighter than all, fell in a waving column of pure gold from precipice to precipice, with the double arch of a broad purple rainbow stretched across it, flushing and fading alternately in the wreaths of spray.

"Ah!" said Gluck aloud after he had looked at it for a little while. "If that river were really all gold, what a nice thing it would be."

"No it wouldn't, Gluck," said a clear, metallic voice close at his ear.

"Bless me! What's that?" exclaimed Gluck, jumping up. There was nobody there. He looked round the room, and under the table, and a great many times behind him, but there was certainly nobody there, and he sat down again at the window. This time he didn't speak, but he couldn't help thinking again that it would be very convenient if the river were really all gold.

"Not at all, my boy," said the same voice, louder than before.

"Bless me!" said Gluck again. "What *is* that?" He looked again into all the corners and cupboards, and then began turning round and round as fast as he could in the middle of the room, thinking there was somebody behind him, when the same voice struck again on his ear. It was singing now very merrily, "Lala-lira-la"; no words, only a soft, running, effervescent melody, something like that of a kettle on the boil. Gluck looked out of the window. No, it was certainly in the house. Upstairs and downstairs. No, it was certainly in that very room, coming in quicker time and clearer notes every moment. "Lala-lira-la." All at once it struck Gluck that it sounded louder near the furnace. He ran to the opening and looked in. Yes, he saw right. It seemed to be coming not only out of the furnace, but out of the pot. He uncovered it and ran back in a great fright, for the pot was certainly singing! He stood in the farthest corner of the room with his hands up and his mouth open for a minute or two, when the singing stopped, and the voice became clear and pronunciative.

"Hollo!" said the voice.

Gluck made no answer.

"Hollo! Gluck, my boy," said the pot again.

Gluck summoned all his energies, walked straight up to the crucible, drew it out of the furnace, and looked in. The gold was all melted, and its surface as smooth and polished as a river; but instead of reflecting little Gluck's head, as he looked in, he saw meeting his glance from beneath the gold the red nose and sharp eyes of his old friend of the mug, a thousand times redder and sharper than ever he had seen them in his life.

"Come, Gluck, my boy," said the voice out of the pot again, "I'm all right; pour me out."

But Gluck was too much astonished to do anything of the kind.

"Pour me out, I say," said the voice rather gruffly.

Still Gluck couldn't move.

"*Will* you pour me out?" said the voice passionately; "I'm too hot."

By a violent effort, Gluck recovered the use of his limbs, took hold of the crucible, and sloped it so as to pour out the gold. But instead of a liquid stream, there came out, first, a pair of pretty little yellow legs, then some coattails, then a pair of arms stuck akimbo, and finally the well-known head of his friend the mug; all which articles, uniting as they rolled out, stood up energetically on the floor in the shape of a little golden dwarf about a foot and a half high.

"That's right!" said the dwarf, stretching out first his legs and then his arms, and then shaking his head up and down, and as far round as it would go, for five minutes without stopping, apparently with the view of ascertaining if he were quite correctly put together, while Gluck stood contemplating him in speechless amazement. He was dressed in a slashed doublet of spun gold, so fine in its texture that the prismatic colors gleamed over it as if on a surface of mother-of-pearl; and over this brilliant doublet, his hair and beard fell full halfway to the ground in waving curls, so exquisitely delicate that Gluck could hardly tell where they ended; they seemed to melt into air. The features of the face, however, were by no means finished with the same delicacy; they were rather coarse, slightly inclining to coppery in complexion, and indicative in expression of a very pertinacious and intractable disposition in their small proprietor. When the dwarf had finished his self-examination, he turned his small sharp eyes full on Gluck and stared at him deliberately for a minute or two. "No, it wouldn't, Gluck, my boy," said the little man.

This was certainly rather an abrupt and unconnected mode of commencing conversation. It might indeed be supposed to refer to the course of Gluck's thoughts, which had first produced the dwarf's observations out of the pot; but whatever it referred to, Gluck had no inclination to dispute the dictum.

"Wouldn't it, sir?" said Gluck very mildly and submissively indeed.

"No," said the dwarf conclusively. "No, it wouldn't." And with that, the dwarf pulled his cap hard over his brows and took two turns of three feet long up and down the room, lifting his legs up very high and setting them down very hard. This pause gave time for Gluck to collect his thoughts a little, and seeing no great reason to view his diminutive visitor with dread, and feeling his curiosity overcome his amazement, he ventured on a question of peculiar delicacy.

"Pray, sir," said Gluck rather hesitatingly, "were you my mug?"

On which the little man turned sharp around, walked straight up to Gluck, and drew himself up to his full height. "I," said the little man, "am the king of the Golden River." Whereupon he turned about again and took two more turns, some six feet long, in order to allow time for the consternation which this announcement produced in his auditor to evaporate. After which he again walked up to Gluck and stood still, as if expecting some comment on his communication.

Gluck determined to say something at all events. "I hope your Majesty is very well," said Gluck.

"Listen!" said the little man, deigning no reply to this polite inquiry. "I am the king of what you mortals call the Golden River. The shape you saw me in was owing to the malice of a stronger king, from whose enchantments you have this instant freed me. What I have seen of you and your conduct to your wicked brothers renders me willing to serve you; therefore, attend to what I tell you. Whoever shall climb to the top of that mountain from which you see the Golden River issue and shall cast into the stream at its source three drops of holy water, for him, and for him only, the river shall turn to gold. But no one failing in his first can succeed in a second attempt; and if anyone shall cast unholy water into the river, it will overwhelm him, and he will become a black stone." So saying, the king of the Golden River turned away and deliberately walked into the center of the hottest flame of the furnace. His figure became red, white, transparent, dazzling—a blaze of intense light—rose, trembled, and disappeared. The king of the Golden River had evaporated.

"Oh!" cried poor Gluck, running to look up the chimney after him. "Oh dear, dear, dear me! My mug! My mug! My mug!"

How Mr. Hans Set Off on an Expedition to the Golden River, and How He Prospered Therein

The king of the Golden River had hardly made the extraordinary exit related in the last chapter before Hans and Schwartz came roaring into the house, very savagely drunk. The discovery of the total loss of their last piece of plate had the effect of sobering them just enough to enable them to stand over Gluck, beating him very steadily for a quarter of an hour, at the expiration of which period they dropped into a couple of chairs and requested to know what he had got to say for himself. Gluck told them his story, of which, of course, they did not believe a word. They beat him again, till their arms were tired, and staggered to bed. In the morning, however, the steadiness with which he adhered to his story obtained him some degree of credence, the immediate consequence of which was that the two brothers, after wrangling a long time on the knotty question which of them should try his fortune first, drew their swords and began fighting. The noise of the fray alarmed the neighbors, who, finding they could not pacify the combatants, sent for the constable.

Hans, on hearing this, contrived to escape and hid himself; but Schwartz was taken before the magistrate, fined for breaking the peace, and having drunk out his last penny the evening before, was thrown into prison till he should pay.

When Hans heard this, he was much delighted and determined to set out immediately for the Golden River. How to get the holy water was the question. He went to the priest, but the priest could not give any holy water to so abandoned a character. So Hans went to vespers in the evening for the first time in his life, and under pretence of crossing himself, stole a cupful and returned home in triumph.

Next morning he got up before the sun rose, put the

holy water into a strong flask, and two bottles of wine and
some meat in a basket, slung them over his back, took his
alpine staff in his hand, and set off for the mountains.

On his way out of the town he had to pass the prison,
and as he looked in at the windows, whom should he
see but Schwartz himself peeping out of the bars and
looking very disconsolate.

"Good morning, brother," said Hans; "have you any
message for the king of the Golden River?"

Schwartz gnashed his teeth with rage and shook the
bars with all his strength; but Hans only laughed at him,
and advising him to make himself comfortable till he
came back again, shouldered his basket, shook the
bottle of holy water in Schwartz's face till it frothed
again, and marched off in the highest spirits in the world.

It was, indeed, a morning that might have made anyone
happy, even with no Golden River to seek for. Level
lines of dewy mist lay stretched along the valley, out of
which rose the massy mountains, their lower cliffs in pale-
gray shadow, hardly distinguishable from the floating
vapor, but gradually ascending till they caught the sun-
light, which ran in sharp touches of ruddy color along
the angular crags and pierced, in long level rays,
through their fringes of spearlike pine. Far above shot
up red splintered masses of castellated rock, jagged and
shivered into myriads of fantastic forms, with here and
there a streak of sunlit snow traced down their chasms
like a line of forked lightning; and far beyond, and far
above all these, fainter than the morning cloud but purer
and changeless, slept, in the blue sky, the utmost peaks of
the eternal snow.

The Golden River, which sprang from one of the
lower and snowless elevations, was now nearly in shadow,
all but the uppermost jets of spray, which rose like slow
smoke above the undulating line of the cataract and floated away in feeble wreaths upon the morning wind.

On this object, and on this alone, Hans's eyes and
thoughts were fixed; forgetting the distance he had to
traverse, he set off at an imprudent rate of walking,
which greatly exhausted him before he had scaled the
first range of the green and low hills. He was, moreover,

surprised, on surmounting them, to find that a large glacier, of whose existence, notwithstanding his previous knowledge of the mountains, he had been absolutely ignorant, lay between him and the source of the Golden River. He entered on it with the boldness of a practiced mountaineer, yet he thought he had never traversed so strange or so dangerous a glacier in his life. The ice was excessively slippery, and out of all its chasms came wild sounds of gushing water; not monotonous or low, but changeful and loud, rising occasionally into drifting passages of wild melody, then breaking off into short melancholy tones or sudden shrieks resembling those of human voices in distress or pain. The ice was broken into thousands of confused shapes, but none, Hans thought, like the ordinary forms of splintered ice. There seemed a curious *expression* about all their outlines—a perpetual resemblance to living features, distorted and scornful. Myriads of deceitful shadows and lurid lights played and floated about and through the pale-blue pinnacles, dazzling and confusing the sight of the traveler while his ears grew dull and his head giddy with the constant gush and roar of the concealed waters. These painful circumstances increased upon him as he advanced; the ice crashed and yawned into fresh chasms at his feet, tottering spires nodded around him and fell thundering across his path; and though he had repeatedly faced these dangers on the most terrific glaciers, and in the wildest weather, it was with a new and oppressive feeling of panic terror that he leaped the last chasm and flung himself, exhausted and shuddering, on the firm turf of the mountain.

He had been compelled to abandon his basket of food, which became a perilous incumbrance on the glacier, and had now no means of refreshing himself but by breaking off and eating some of the pieces of ice. This, however, relieved his thirst; an hour's repose recruited his hardy frame, and with the indomitable spirit of avarice, he resumed his laborious journey.

His way now lay straight up a ridge of bare red rocks without a blade of grass to ease the foot or a projecting angle to afford an inch of shade from the south sun. It was past noon, and the rays beat intensely upon the steep path, while the whole atmosphere was motionless and penetrated with heat. Intense thirst was soon added to the bodily fatigue with which Hans was now afflicted; glance after glance he cast on the flask of water which hung at his belt. "Three drops are enough," at last thought he; "I may at least cool my lips with it."

He opened the flask and was raising it to his lips when his eye fell on an object lying on the rock beside him; he thought it moved. It was a small dog, apparently in the last agony of death from thirst. Its tongue was out, its jaws dry, its limbs extended lifelessly, and a swarm of black ants were crawling about its lips and throat. Its eye moved to the bottle which Hans held in his hand. He raised it, drank, spurned the animal with his foot, and passed on. And he did not know how it was, but he thought that a strange shadow had suddenly come across the blue sky.

The path became steeper and more rugged every moment; and the high hill air, instead of refreshing him, seemed to throw his blood into a fever. The noise of the hill cataracts sounded like mockery in his ears; they were all distant, and his thirst increased every moment. Another hour passed, and he again looked down to the flask at his side; it was half empty, but there was much more than three drops in it. He stopped to open it, and again, as he did so, something moved in the path above him. It was a fair child, stretched nearly lifeless on the rock, its breast heaving with thirst, its eyes closed, and its lips parched and burning. Hans eyed it deliberately, drank, and passed on. And a dark-gray cloud came over the sun, and long, snakelike shadows crept up along the mountainsides. Hans struggled on. The sun was sinking, but its descent seemed to bring no coolness; the leaden weight of the dead air pressed upon his brow and heart, but the goal was near. He saw the cataract of the Golden River springing from the hillside scarcely five hundred feet above him. He paused for a moment to breathe and sprang on to complete his task.

At this instant a faint cry fell on his ear. He turned and saw a gray-haired old man extended on the rocks.

His eyes were sunk, his features deadly pale and gathered into an expression of despair. "Water!" He stretched his arms to Hans and cried feebly, "Water! I am dying."

"I have none," replied Hans; "thou hast had thy share of life." He strode over the prostrate body and darted on. And a flash of blue lightning rose out of the east, shaped like a sword; it shook thrice over the whole heaven and left it dark with one heavy, impenetrable shade. The sun was setting; it plunged toward the horizon like a red-hot ball.

The roar of the Golden River rose on Hans's ear. He stood at the brink of the chasm through which it ran. Its waves were filled with the red glory of the sunset; they shook their crests like tongues of fire, and flashes of bloody light gleamed along their foam. Their sound came mightier and mightier on his senses; his brain grew giddy with the prolonged thunder. Shuddering, he drew the flask from his girdle and hurled it into the center of the torrent. As he did so, an icy chill shot through his limbs; he staggered, shrieked, and fell. The waters closed over his cry. And the moaning of the river rose wildly into the night as it gushed over the black stone.

How Mr. Schwartz Set Off on an Expedition to the Golden River, and How He Prospered Therein

Poor little Gluck waited very anxiously alone in the house for Hans's return. Finding he did not come back, he was terribly frightened and went and told Schwartz in the prison all that had happened. Then Schwartz was very much pleased and said that Hans must certainly have been turned into a black stone, and he should have all the gold to himself. But Gluck was very sorry and cried all night. When he got up in the morning there was no bread in the house nor any money; so Gluck went and hired himself to another goldsmith, and he worked so hard and so neatly and so long every day that he soon got money enough together to pay his brother's fine, and

he went and gave it all to Schwartz, and Schwartz got out
of prison. Then Schwartz was quite pleased and said he
should have some of the gold of the river. But Gluck only
begged he would go and see what had become of Hans.

Now when Schwartz had heard that Hans had stolen the
holy water, he thought to himself that such a proceeding
might not be considered altogether correct by the king
of the Golden River and determined to manage matters
better. So he took some more of Gluck's money and
went to a bad priest, who gave him some holy water
very readily for it. Then Schwartz was sure it was all
quite right. So Schwartz got up early in the morning
before the sun rose, and took some bread and wine in a
basket, and put his holy water in a flask, and set off for
the mountains. Like his brother, he was much surprised
at the sight of the glacier and had great difficulty in crossing it, even after leaving his basket behind him. The day
was cloudless, but not bright; there was a heavy purple
haze hanging over the sky, and the hills looked lowering
and gloomy. And as Schwartz climbed the steep rock
path, the thirst came upon him, as it had upon his
brother, until he lifted his flask to his lips to drink. Then
he saw the fair child lying near him on the rocks, and it
cried to him and moaned for water.

"Water, indeed," said Schwartz; "I haven't half enough
for myself," and passed on. And as he went he thought
the sunbeams grew more dim, and he saw a low bank of
black cloud rising out of the west, and when he had
climbed for another hour, the thirst overcame him again
and he would have drunk. Then he saw the old man
lying before him on the path and heard him cry out for
water. "Water, indeed," said Schwartz; "I haven't half
enough for myself," and on he went.

Then again the light seemed to fade from before his
eyes, and he looked up, and, behold, a mist of the color
of blood had come over the sun; and the bank of black
cloud had risen very high, and its edges were tossing and
tumbling like the waves of the angry sea. And they cast
long shadows, which flickered over Schwartz's path.

Then Schwartz climbed for another hour, and again
his thirst returned; and as he lifted his flask to his lips, he

thought he saw his brother Hans lying exhausted on the
path before him, and as he gazed, the figure stretched its
arms to him and cried for water. "Ha, ha," laughed
Schwartz, "are you there? Remember the prison bars,
my boy. Water, indeed! Do you suppose I carried it all
the way up here for *you!*" And he strode over the figure;
yet, as he passed, he thought he saw a strange expression of mockery about its lips. And when he had gone
a few yards farther, he looked back; but the figure was
not there.

And a sudden horror came over Schwartz, he knew not
why; but the thirst for gold prevailed over his fear, and
he rushed on. And the bank of black cloud rose to the
zenith, and out of it came bursts of spiry lightning, and
waves of darkness seemed to heave and float between
their flashes over the whole heavens. And the sky where
the sun was setting was all level and like a lake of blood;
and a strong wind came out of that sky, tearing its

crimson clouds into fragments and scattering them far into the darkness. And when Schwartz stood by the brink of the Golden River, its waves were black like thunder clouds, but their foam was like fire; and the roar of the waters below and the thunder above met as he cast the flask into the stream. And as he did so, the lightning glared into his eyes, and the earth gave way beneath him, and the waters closed over his cry. And the moaning of the river rose wildly into the night, as it gushed over the two black stones.

How Little Gluck Set Off on an Expedition to the Golden River, and How He Prospered Therein; With Other Matters of Interest

When Gluck found that Schwartz did not come back, he was very sorry and did not know what to do. He had no money and was obliged to go and hire himself again to the goldsmith, who worked him very hard and gave him very little money. So after a month or two, Gluck grew tired and made up his mind to go and try his fortune with the Golden River. "The little king looked very kind," thought he. "I don't think he will turn me into a black stone." So he went to the priest, and the priest gave him some holy water as soon as he asked for it. Then Gluck took some bread in his basket and the bottle of water and set off very early for the mountains.

If the glacier had occasioned a great deal of fatigue to his brothers, it was twenty times worse for him, who was neither so strong nor so practiced on the mountains. He had several very bad falls, lost his basket and bread, and was very much frightened at the strange noises under the ice. He lay a long time to rest on the grass after he had got over and began to climb the hill just in the hottest part of the day. When he had climbed for an hour, he got dreadfully thirsty and was going to drink like his brothers when he saw an old man coming down the path above him, looking very feeble and leaning on a staff. "My son," said the old man, "I am faint with

thirst; give me some of that water." Then Gluck looked
at him, and when he saw that he was pale and weary, he
gave him the water. "Only pray don't drink it all," said
Gluck. But the old man drank a great deal and gave him
back the bottle two thirds empty. Then he bade him good
speed, and Gluck went on again merrily. And the path
became easier to his feet, and two or three blades of
grass appeared upon it, and some grasshoppers began
singing on the bank beside it; and Gluck thought he had
never heard such merry singing.

Then he went on for another hour, and the thirst increased on him so that he thought he should be forced
to drink. But as he raised the flask, he saw a little child
lying panting by the roadside, and it cried out piteously
for water. Then Gluck struggled with himself and determined to bear the thirst a little longer; and he put the
bottle to the child's lips, and it drank it all but a few
drops. Then it smiled on him and got up and ran down
the hill; and Gluck looked after it till it became as small
as a little star, and then turned and began climbing again.
And then there were all kinds of sweet flowers growing
on the rocks: bright green moss, with pale-pink, starry
flowers and soft, belled gentians more blue than the sky
at its deepest, and pure-white, transparent lilies. And
crimson and purple butterflies darted hither and thither,
and the sky sent down such pure light that Gluck had
never felt so happy in his life.

Yet, when he had climbed for another hour, his
thirst became intolerable again; and when he looked at
his bottle, he saw that there were only five or six drops
left in it, and he could not venture to drink. And as he
was hanging the flask to his belt again, he saw a little
dog lying on the rocks, gasping for breath—just as Hans
had seen it on the day of his ascent. And Gluck stopped
and looked at it and then at the Golden River, not five
hundred yards above him; and he thought of the dwarf's
words, that no one could succeed, except in his first attempt; and he tried to pass the dog, but it whined piteously and Gluck stopped again. "Poor beastie," said
Gluck, "it'll be dead when I come down again if I don't
help it." Then he looked closer and closer at it, and its

eye turned on him so mournfully that he could not stand it. "Confound the king and his gold too," said Gluck; and he opened the flask and poured all the water into the dog's mouth.

The dog sprang up and stood on its hind legs. Its tail disappeared, its ears became long, longer, silky, golden; its nose became very red, its eyes became very twinkling; in three seconds the dog was gone, and before Gluck stood his old acquaintance the king of the Golden River.

"Thank you," said the monarch; "but don't be frightened, it's all right," for Gluck showed manifest symptoms of consternation at this unlooked-for reply to his last observation. "Why didn't you come before," continued the dwarf, "instead of sending me those rascally brothers of yours for me to have the trouble of turning into stones? Very hard stones they make too."

"Oh dear me!" said Gluck. "Have you really been so cruel?"

"Cruel!" said the dwarf. "They poured unholy water into my stream; do you suppose I'm going to allow that?"

"Why," said Gluck, "I am sure, sir—your Majesty, I mean—they got the water out of the church font."

"Very probably," replied the dwarf; "but," and his countenance grew stern as he spoke, "the water which has been refused to the cry of the weary and dying is unholy though it had been blessed by every saint in heaven; and the water which is found in the vessel of mercy is holy though it had been defiled with corpses."

So saying, the dwarf stooped and plucked a lily that grew at his feet. On its white leaves there hung three drops of clear dew. And the dwarf shook them into the flask which Gluck held in his hand. "Cast these into the river," he said, "and descend on the other side of the mountains into the Treasure Valley. And so good speed."

As he spoke, the figure of the dwarf became indistinct. The playing colors of his robe formed themselves into a prismatic mist of dewy light; he stood for an instant veiled with them as with the belt of a broad rainbow. The colors grew faint, the mist rose into the air; the monarch had evaporated.

And Gluck climbed to the brink of the Golden River,

and its waves were as clear as crystal and as brilliant as the sun. And when he cast the three drops of dew into the stream, there opened where they fell a small circular whirlpool into which the waters descended with a musical noise.

Gluck stood watching it for some time, very much disappointed, because not only the river was not turned into gold, but its waters seemed much diminished in quantity. Yet he obeyed his friend the dwarf and descended the other side of the mountains toward the Treasure Valley; and as he went, he thought he heard the noise of water working its way under the ground. And when he came in sight of the Treasure Valley, behold, a river, like the Golden River, was springing from a new cleft of the rocks above it and was flowing in innumerable streams among the dry heaps of red sand.

And as Gluck gazed, fresh grass sprang beside the new streams, and creeping plants grew and climbed among the moistening soil. Young flowers opened suddenly along the river sides, as stars leap out when twilight is deepening; and thickets of myrtle and tendrils of vine cast lengthening shadows over the valley as they grew. And thus the Treasure Valley became a garden again, and the inheritance which had been lost by cruelty was regained by love.

And Gluck went and dwelt in the valley, and the poor were never driven from his door: so that his barns became full of corn, and his house of treasure. And for him the river had, according to the dwarf's promise, become a River of Gold.

And to this day the inhabitants of the valley point out the place where the three drops of holy dew were cast into the stream and trace the course of the Golden River under the ground until it emerges in the Treasure Valley. And at the top of the cataract of the Golden River are still to be seen two BLACK STONES, around which the waters howl mournfully every day at sunset; and these stones are still called by the people of the valley

THE BLACK BROTHERS.

Oscar Wilde

THE SELFISH GIANT

Every afternoon, as they were coming from school, the children used to go and play in the giant's garden.

It was a large, lovely garden with soft green grass. Here and there over the grass stood beautiful flowers like stars, and there were twelve peach trees that in the springtime broke out into delicate blossoms of pink and pearl and in the autumn bore rich fruit. The birds sat on the trees and sang so sweetly that the children used to stop their games in order to listen to them. "How happy we are here!" they cried to each other.

One day the giant came back. He had been to visit his friend the Cornish ogre and had stayed with him for seven years. After the seven years were over he had said all that he had to say, for his conversation was limited, and he determined to return to his own castle. When he arrived he saw the children playing in the garden.

"What are you doing here?" he cried in a very gruff voice, and the children ran away.

"My own garden is my own garden," said the giant; "anyone can understand that, and I will allow nobody to play in it but myself." So he built a high wall all round it, and put up a notice board:

```
┌─────────────────────────────────────┐
│                                      │
│            TRESPASSERS               │
│                                      │
│            WILL   BE                 │
│                                      │
│            PROSECUTED.               │
│                                      │
└─────────────────────────────────────┘
```

He was a very selfish giant.

The poor children had now nowhere to play. They tried to play on the road, but the road was very dusty and full of hard stones, and they did not like it. They used to wander around the high wall when their lessons were over and talk about the beautiful garden inside. "How happy we were there!" they said to each other.

Then the spring came, and all over the country there were little blossoms and little birds. Only in the garden of the selfish giant it was still winter. The birds did not care to sing in it as there were no children, and the trees forgot to blossom. Once a beautiful flower put its head out from the grass, but when it saw the notice board it was so sorry for the children that it slipped back into the ground again and went off to sleep. The only people who were pleased were the snow and the frost. "Spring has forgotten this garden," they cried, "so we will live here all the year around." The snow covered up the grass with her great white cloak, and the frost painted all the trees silver. Then they invited the north wind to stay with them, and he came. He was wrapped in furs, and he roared all day about the garden and blew the chimney pots down. "This is a delightful spot," he said; "we must ask the hail on a visit." So the hail came. Every day for three hours he rattled on the roof of the castle till he broke most of the slates, and then he ran around and around the garden as fast as he could go. He was dressed in gray, and his breath was like ice.

"I cannot understand why the spring is so late in coming," said the selfish giant as he sat at the window and looked out at his cold, white garden; "I hope there will be a change in the weather."

But the spring never came, nor the summer. The autumn gave golden fruit to every garden, but to the giant's garden she gave none. "He is too selfish," she said. So it was always winter there, and the north wind, and the hail, and the frost, and the snow danced about through the trees.

One morning the giant was lying awake in bed when he heard some lovely music. It sounded so sweet to his ears that he thought it must be the king's musicians passing by. It was really only a little linnet singing outside his window, but it was so long since he had heard a bird sing in his garden that it seemed to him to be the most beautiful music in the world. Then the hail stopped dancing over his head, and the north wind ceased roaring, and a delicious perfume came to him through the open casement. "I believe the spring has come at last," said the giant; and he jumped out of bed and looked out.

What did he see?

He saw a most wonderful sight. Through a little hole in the wall the children had crept in, and they were sitting in the branches of the trees. In every tree that he could see there was a little child. And the trees were so glad to have the children back again that they had covered themselves with blossoms and were waving their arms gently above the children's heads. The birds were flying about and twittering with delight, and the flowers were looking up through the green grass and laughing. It was a lovely scene, only in one corner it was still winter. It was the farthest corner of the garden, and in it was standing a little boy. He was so small that he could not reach up to the branches of the tree, and he was wandering all around it, crying bitterly. The poor tree was still quite covered with frost and snow, and the north wind was blowing and roaring above it. "Climb up, little boy," said the tree, and it bent its branches down as low as it could; but the boy was too tiny.

And the giant's heart melted as he looked out. "How selfish I have been!" he said. "Now I know why the spring would not come here. I will put that poor little boy on the top of the tree, and then I will knock down the wall, and my garden shall be the children's playground forever and ever." He was really very sorry for what he had done.

So he crept downstairs and opened the front door quite softly and went out into the garden. But when the children saw him they were so frightened that they all ran away, and the garden became winter again. Only the little boy did not run, for his eyes were so full of tears that he did not see the giant coming. And the giant stole up behind him and took him gently in his hand and put him up into the tree. And the tree broke at once into blossom, and the birds came and sang on it, and the little boy stretched out his two arms and flung them around the giant's neck and kissed him. And the other children, when they saw that the giant was not wicked any longer, came running back, and with them came the spring. "It is your garden now, little children," said the giant, and he took a great ax and knocked down the wall. And when the people were going to market at twelve o'clock they found the giant playing with the children in the most beautiful garden they had ever seen.

All day long they played, and in the evening they came to the giant to bid him good-bye.

"But where is your little companion?" he said: "the boy I put into the tree." The giant loved him the best because he had kissed him.

"We don't know," answered the children; "he has gone away."

"You must tell him to be sure and come here tomorrow," said the giant. But the children said that they did not know where he lived and had never seen him before; and the giant felt very sad.

Every afternoon, when school was over, the children came and played with the giant. But the little boy whom the giant loved was never seen again. The giant was very kind to all the children, yet he longed for his first little friend and often spoke of him. "How I would like to see him!" he used to say.

Years went over, and the giant grew very old and feeble. He could not play about any more, so he sat in a huge

armchair and watched the children at their games and admired his garden. "I have many beautiful flowers," he said,
"but the children are the most beautiful flowers of all."

One winter morning he looked out of his window as he
was dressing. He did not hate the winter now, for he knew

that it was merely the spring asleep and that the flowers were resting.

Suddenly he rubbed his eyes in wonder and looked and looked. It certainly was a marvelous sight. In the farthest corner of the garden was a tree quite covered with lovely white blossoms. Its branches were all golden, and silver fruit hung down from them, and underneath it stood the little boy he had loved.

Downstairs ran the giant in great joy, and out into the garden. He hastened across the grass and came near to the child. And when he came quite close his face grew red with anger, and he said, "Who hath dared to wound thee?" For on the palms of the child's hands were the prints of two nails, and the prints of two nails were on the little feet.

"Who hath dared to wound thee?" cried the giant; "tell me, that I might take my big sword and slay him."

"Nay!" answered the child. "But these are the wounds of love."

"Who art thou?" said the giant, and a strange awe fell on him, and he knelt before the little child.

And the child smiled on the giant and said to him, "You let me play once in your garden; today you shall come with me to my garden, which is Paradise."

And when the children ran in that afternoon, they found the giant lying dead under the tree all covered with white blossoms.

James Thurber

||||||||||||||||||||||||||||||||||||||||||||||||||||||||||||||||||||

MANY MOONS

||||||||||||||||||||||||||||||||||||||||||||||||||||||||||||||||||||

Once upon a time, in a kingdom by the sea, there lived a little Princess named Lenore. She was ten years old, going on eleven. One day Lenore fell ill of a surfeit of raspberry tarts and took to her bed.

The Royal Physician came to see her and took her temperature and felt her pulse and made her stick out her tongue. The Royal Physician was worried. He sent for the King, Lenore's father, and the King came to see her.

"I will get you anything your heart desires," the King said. "Is there anything your heart desires?"

"Yes," said the Princess. "I want the moon. If I can have the moon, I will be well again."

Now the King had a great many wise men who always got for him anything he wanted, so he told his daughter that she could have the moon. Then he went to the throne room and pulled a bell cord, three long pulls and a short pull, and presently the Lord High Chamberlain came into the room.

The Lord High Chamberlain was a large, fat man who wore thick glasses which made his eyes seem twice as big as they really were. This made the Lord High Chamberlain seem twice as wise as he really was.

"I want you to get the moon," said the King. "The

Princess Lenore wants the moon. If she can have the moon, she will get well again."

"The moon?" exclaimed the Lord High Chamberlain, his eyes widening. This made him look four times as wise as he really was.

"Yes, the moon," said the King. "M-o-o-n, moon. Get it tonight, tomorrow at the latest."

The Lord High Chamberlain wiped his forehead with a handkerchief and then blew his nose loudly. "I have got a great many things for you in my time, your Majesty," he said. "It just happens that I have with me a list of the things I have got for you in my time." He pulled a long scroll of parchment out of his pocket. "Let me see, now." He glanced at the list, frowning. "I have got ivory, apes, and peacocks, rubies, opals, and emeralds, black orchids, pink elephants, and blue poodles, gold bugs, scarabs, and flies in amber, hummingbirds' tongues, angels' feathers, and unicorns' horns, giants, midgets, and mermaids, frankincense, ambergris, and myrrh, troubadours, minstrels, and dancing women, a pound of butter, two dozen eggs, and a sack of sugar—sorry, my wife wrote that in there."

"I don't remember any blue poodles," said the King.

"It says blue poodles right here on the list, and they are checked off with a little check mark," said the Lord High Chamberlain. "So there must have been blue poodles. You just forget."

"Never mind the blue poodles," said the King. "What I want now is the moon."

"I have sent as far as Samarkand and Araby and Zanzibar to get things for you, your Majesty," said the Lord High Chamberlain. "But the moon is out of the question. It is thirty-five thousand miles away and it is bigger than the room the Princess lies in. Furthermore, it is made of molten copper. I cannot get the moon for you. Blue poodles, yes; the moon, no."

The King flew into a rage and told the Lord High Chamberlain to leave the room and to send the Royal Wizard to the throne room.

The Royal Wizard was a little, thin man with a long face. He wore a high red peaked hat covered with silver stars, and a long blue robe covered with golden owls. His face grew very pale when the King told him that he wanted the moon for his little daughter and that he expected the Royal Wizard to get it.

"I have worked a great deal of magic for you in my time, your Majesty," said the Royal Wizard. "As a matter of fact, I just happen to have in my pocket a list of the wizardries I have performed for you." He drew a paper from a deep pocket of his robe. "It begins: 'Dear Royal Wizard: I am returning herewith the so-called philosopher's stone which you claimed'—no, that isn't it." The Royal Wizard brought a long scroll of parchment from another pocket of his robe. "Here it is," he said. "Now, let's see. I have squeezed blood out of turnips for you, and turnips out of blood. I have produced rabbits out of silk hats, and silk hats out of rabbits. I have conjured up flowers, tambourines, and doves out of nowhere, and nowhere out of flowers, tambourines, and doves. I have brought you divining rods, magic wands, and crystal spheres in which to behold the future. I have compounded philters, unguents, and potions to cure heartbreak, surfeit, and ringing in the ears. I have made you my own special mixture of wolfbane, nightshade, and eagles' tears to ward off witches, demons, and things that go bump in the night. I have given you seven-league boots, the golden touch, and a cloak of invisibility—"

"It didn't work," said the King. "The cloak of invisibility didn't work."

"Yes, it did," said the Royal Wizard.

"No, it didn't," said the King. "I kept bumping into things, the same as ever."

"The cloak is supposed to make you invisible," said the Royal Wizard. "It is not supposed to keep you from bumping into things."

"All I know is, I kept bumping into things," said the King.

The Royal Wizard looked at his list again. "I got you," he said, "horns from Elfland, sand from the Sandman, and gold from the rainbow. Also a spool of thread, a paper of needles, and a lump of beeswax—sorry, those are things my wife wrote down for me to get her."

"What I want you to do now," said the King, "is to get me the moon. The Princess Lenore wants the moon, and when she gets it, she will be well again."

"Nobody can get the moon," said the Royal Wizard. "It is a hundred and fifty thousand miles away, and it is made of green cheese, and it is twice as big as this palace."

The King flew into another rage and sent the Royal Wizard back to his cave. Then he rang a gong and summoned the Royal Mathematician.

The Royal Mathematician was a bald-headed, nearsighted man with a skullcap on his head and a pencil behind each ear. He wore a black suit with white numbers on it.

"I don't want to hear a long list of all the things you have figured out for me since 1907," the King said to him. "I want you to figure out right now how to get the moon for the Princess Lenore. When she gets the moon, she will be well again."

"I am glad you mentioned all the things I have figured out for you since 1907," said the Royal Mathematician. "It so happens that I have a list of them with me."

He pulled a long scroll of parchment out of a pocket and looked at it. "Now let me see. I have figured out for you the distance between the horns of a dilemma, night and day, and A and Z. I have computed how far is Up, how long it takes to get to Away, and what becomes of Gone. I have discovered the length of the sea serpent, the price of the priceless, and the square of the hippopotamus. I know where you are when you are at Sixes and Sevens, how much Is you have to have to make an Are, and how many birds you can catch with the salt in the ocean—187,796,132, if it would interest you to know."

"There aren't that many birds," said the King.

"I didn't say there were," said the Royal Mathematician. "I said if there were."

"I don't want to hear about seven hundred million imaginary birds," said the King. "I want you to get the moon for the Princess Lenore."

"The moon is three hundred thousand miles away," said the Royal Mathematician. "It is round and flat like a coin, only it is made of asbestos, and it is half the size of this kingdom. Furthermore, it is pasted on the sky. Nobody can get the moon."

The King flew into still another rage and sent the Royal Mathematician away. Then he rang for the Court Jester. The Jester came bounding into the throne room in his motley and his cap and bells, and sat at the foot of the throne.

"What can I do for you, your Majesty?" asked the Court Jester.

"Nobody can do anything for me," said the King mournfully. "The Princess Lenore wants the moon, and she cannot be well till she gets it, but nobody can get it for her. Every time I ask anybody for the moon, it gets larger and farther away. There is nothing you can do for me except play on your lute. Something sad."

"How big do they say the moon is," asked the Court Jester, "and how far away?"

"The Lord High Chamberlain says it is thirty-five thousand miles away and bigger than the Princess Lenore's room," said the King. "The Royal Wizard says it is a hundred and fifty thousand miles away and twice as big as this palace. The Royal Mathematician says it is three hundred thousand miles away and half the size of this kingdom."

The Court Jester strummed on his lute for a little while. "They are all wise men," he said, "and so they must all be right. If they are all right, then the moon must be just as large and as far away as each person thinks it is. The thing to do is find out how big the Princess Lenore thinks it is, and how far away."

"I never thought of that," said the King.

"I will go and ask her, your Majesty," said the Court Jester. And he crept softly into the little girl's room.

The Princess Lenore was awake, and she was glad to see the Court Jester, but her face was very pale and her voice very weak.

"Have you brought the moon to me?" she asked.

"Not yet," said the Court Jester, "but I will get it for you right away. How big do you think it is?"

"It is just a little smaller than my thumbnail," she

said, "for when I hold my thumbnail up at the moon, it just covers it."

"And how far away is it?" asked the Court Jester.

"It is not as high as the big tree outside my window," said the Princess, "for sometimes it gets caught in the top branches."

"It will be very easy to get the moon for you," said the Court Jester. "I will climb the tree tonight when it gets caught in the top branches and bring it to you."

Then he thought of something else. "What is the moon made of, Princess?" he asked.

"Oh," she said, "it's made of gold, of course, silly."

The Court Jester left the Princess Lenore's room and went to see the Royal Goldsmith. He had the Royal Goldsmith make a tiny round golden moon just a little smaller than the thumbnail of the Princess Lenore. Then he had him string it on a golden chain so the Princess could wear it around her neck.

"What is this thing I have made?" asked the Royal Goldsmith when he had finished it.

"You have made the moon," said the Court Jester. "That is the moon."

"But the moon," said the Royal Goldsmith, "is five hundred thousand miles away and is made of bronze and is round like a marble."

"That's what you think," said the Court Jester as he went away with the moon.

The Court Jester took the moon to the Princess Lenore, and she was overjoyed. The next day she was well again and could get up and go out in the gardens to play.

But the King's worries were not yet over. He knew that the moon would shine in the sky again that night, and he did not want the Princess Lenore to see it. If she did, she would know that the moon she wore on a chain around her neck was not the real moon.

So the King sent for the Lord High Chamberlain and said: "We must keep the Princess Lenore from seeing the moon when it shines in the sky tonight. Think of something."

The Lord High Chamberlain tapped his forehead with his fingers thoughtfully and said: "I know just the thing.

We can make some dark glasses for the Princess Lenore. We can make them so dark that she will not be able to see anything at all through them. Then she will not be able to see the moon when it shines in the sky."

This made the King very angry, and he shook his head from side to side. "If she wore dark glasses, she would bump into things," he said, "and then she would be ill again." So he sent the Lord High Chamberlain away and called the Royal Wizard.

"We must hide the moon," said the King, "so that the Princess Lenore will not see it when it shines in the sky tonight. How are we going to do that?"

The Royal Wizard stood on his hands and then he stood on his head and then he stood on his feet again. "I know what we can do," he said. "We can stretch some black velvet curtains on poles. The curtains will cover all the palace gardens like a circus tent, and the Princess Lenore will not be able to see through them, so she will not see the moon in the sky."

The King was so angry at this that he waved his arms around. "Black velvet curtains would keep out the air," he said. "The Princess Lenore would not be able to breathe, and she would be ill again." So he sent the Royal Wizard away and summoned the Royal Mathematician.

"We must do something," said the King, "so that the Princess Lenore will not see the moon when it shines in the sky tonight. If you know so much, figure out a way to do that."

The Royal Mathematician walked around in a circle, and then he walked around in a square, and then he stood still. "I have it!" he said. "We can set off fireworks in the gardens every night. We will make a lot of silver fountains and golden cascades, and when they go off they will fill the sky with so many sparks that it will be as light as day and the Princess Lenore will not be able to see the moon."

The King flew into such a rage that he began jumping up and down. "Fireworks would keep the Princess Lenore awake," he said. "She would not get any sleep at all and she would be ill again." So the King sent the Royal Mathematician away.

When he looked up again, it was dark outside and he saw the bright rim of the moon just peeping over the horizon. He jumped up in a great fright and rang for the Court Jester. The Court Jester came bounding into the room and sat down at the foot of the throne.

"What can I do for you, your Majesty?" he asked.

"Nobody can do anything for me," said the King mournfully. "The moon is coming up again. It will shine into the Princess Lenore's bedroom, and she will know it is still in the sky and that she does not wear it on a golden chain around her neck. Play me something on your lute, something very sad, for when the Princess sees the moon, she will be ill again."

The Court Jester strummed on his lute. "What do your wise men say?" he asked.

"They can think of no way to hide the moon that will not make the Princess Lenore ill," said the King.

The Court Jester played another song, very softly. The wise men know everything," he said, "and if they cannot hide the moon, then it cannot be hidden."

The King put his head in his hands again and sighed. Suddenly he jumped up from his throne and pointed to the windows. "Look!" he cried. "The moon is already shining into the Princess Lenore's bedroom. Who can explain how the moon can be shining in the sky when it is hanging on a golden chain around her neck?"

The Court Jester stopped playing on his lute. "Who could explain how to get the moon when your wise men said it was too large and too far away? It was the Princess Lenore. Therefore, the Princess Lenore is wiser than your wise men and knows more about the moon than they do. So I will ask *her*." And before the King could stop him, the Court Jester slipped quietly out of the throne room and up the wide marble staircase to the Princess Lenore's bedroom.

The Princess was lying in the bed but she was wide awake and she was looking out the window at the moon shining in the sky. Shining in her hand was the moon the Court Jester had got for her. He looked very sad, and there seemed to be tears in his eyes.

"Tell me, Princess Lenore," he said mournfully, "how

can the moon be shining in the sky when it is hanging on a golden chain around your neck?"

The Princess looked at him and laughed. "That is easy, silly," she said. "When I lose a tooth, a new one grows in its place, doesn't it?"

"Of course," said the Court Jester. "And when the unicorn loses his horn in the forest, a new one grows in the middle of his forehead."

"That is right," said the Princess. "And when the Royal Gardner cuts the flowers in the garden, other flowers come to take their place."

"I should have thought of that," said the Court Jester, "for it is the same way with the daylight."

"And it is the same way with the moon," said the Princess Lenore. "I guess it is the same way with everything." Her voice became very low and faded away, and the Court Jester saw that she was asleep. Gently he tucked the covers in around the sleeping Princess.

But before he left the room, he went over to the window and winked at the moon, for it seemed to the Court Jester that the moon had winked at him.